The Raven and The Crow:

Dark Storm Rising

By: Michael K Falciani

The Raven and The Crow: Dark Storm Rising By Michael K. Falciani

Published by Three Ravens Publishing

threeravenspublishing@gmail.com

P.O. Box 851. Chickamauga, Ga 30707

https://www.threeravenspublishing.com

Copyright © 2021 by Three Ravens Publishing

Publishers Note: This is a work of fiction. Names, characters, places, and incidents are a product of the author's imagination. Locales and public names are sometimes used for atmospheric purposes. Any resemblance to actual people, living or dead, or to businesses, companies, events, institutions, or locales is completely coincidental.

Credits:

The Raven and The Crow: Dark Storm Rising was written by Michael K. Falciani

Cover art by Damien King

The Raven And The Crow Series Logo art by: Jaden Anderson

The Raven and The Crow: Dark Storm Rising by: Michael K. Falciani /Three Ravens Publishing – 2nd edition, 2021

Trade Paperback ISBN: 978-1-951768-24-9

Hardback ISBN: 978-1-951768-25-6

For information about the story, contact;

michaelkfalciani@yahoo.com

@MichaelKFalcia1 on Twitter

https://www.facebook.com/Michaelkfalciani

Dedication

This book is dedicated to the memory of my father, who set my feet upon this path many years ago. I hope this story makes him smile.

It is also dedicated to my mother, who taught me the value of hard work. May she find solace inside these pages.

Acknowledgements

My thanks to my editor Kaylie and my test readers Andy, who gave good advice through the years, and Amy, who humored me when there was no need. Finally, thanks to my wife, who is far better at writing than I.

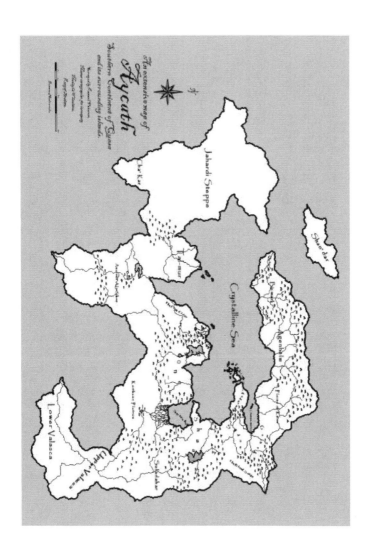

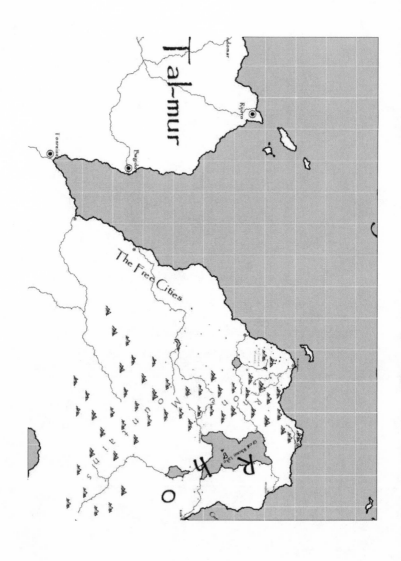

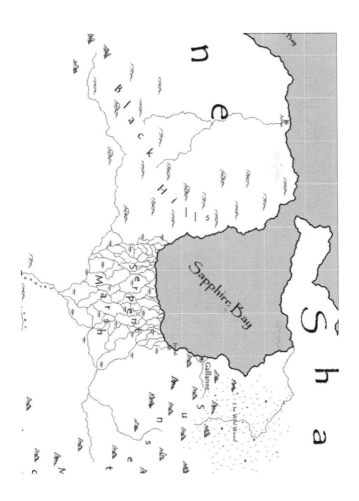

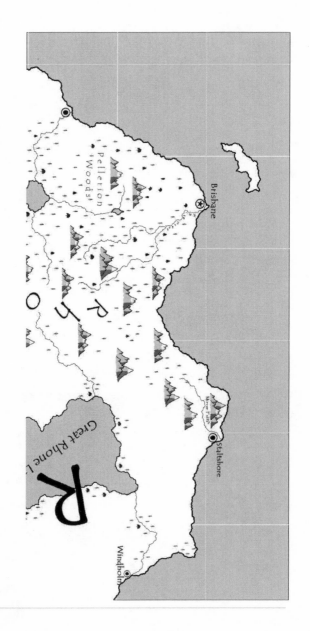

Chapter 1

They are late, Blade thought, suppressing the urge to sigh. *If they even bother to show.*

Absently, the sage rubbed her temple, trying to knead away the tension she felt building at the top of her skull. Standing near Dusk Gate on the westernmost edge of Staltshore, she waited inside a secluded alcove at the base of the city's fortifications. She could hear the staccato of boots striking granite overhead as a lone sentry walked along the frost-covered battlements, oblivious to Blade's presence below. Coming to the end of the wall, the guard performed an about-face and began retracing his steps. The sage listened as the march of his steady footfalls faded into the night.

Shivering, Blade wrapped her wool cloak more tightly around her shoulders in an effort to ward off the chill of new spring. Thankfully, there was no wind this night; else she may have succumbed to the siren's song of warmth crooning from her own bedchamber across town. Well past midnight, Blade stood determined to wait, with only the guard's hollow footsteps atop the battlements above marking the passage of time.

A quarter hour passed until Blade's perseverance was rewarded. Two figures slipped from behind the clump of buildings to the northeast, their flashing silhouettes illuminated for the briefest of moments by the glow of the crescent moon above.

With scarcely a whisper, the pair made their way to her, their faces concealed in the hoods of their cloaks. Even hidden in the darkness, she could sense irritation, especially in the first.

"What the *hell*, Blade," a voice spat, bubbling with anger. "We just got back into town a few hours ago. You said we were done for the week! We haven't even been paid yet, and now you're sending us back out? This was not our agreement."

"Easy, Kil," said the second, his voice more neutral. "Let her speak. It's not like she'd call us out here on a lark."

Blade hesitated, knowing those words were closer to the truth than he realized. This was no lark. For a moment, she questioned the wisdom of sending these men on this mission. Inwardly, she shook her head. It didn't matter what she thought; it was these two or no one.

"Still your tongue, Kildare," Blade responded coolly to the first. "You'd do well to listen to your brother," she continued, nodding to the taller of the two. "Had you bothered to ask, you'd know fifty drachmas had been credited to your account at Dobson's an hour ago, with a like sum in Zedaine's name as well."

"What about dragging us from our beds at this hour?" the elder of the two retorted, unwilling to release his irritation so easily. "With no warning, no idea of what we're doing? And what kind of meeting place is this? Skulking off to the outskirts of the city in the dead of night? Why couldn't we convene at Mason's in the morning?"

"I would not..." she began, but stopped as Zedaine raised his hand in warning. Overhead, the sentry strode into sight. As before, the guard stopped at the gate, turned, and headed back along the battlements, unaware of the trio below.

"I would not ask unless the need was great," Blade stated quietly. "To answer your question, we meet here and now because time is against us. I know you've just returned from the last assignment and wish to leave for Adian. I ask only that you delay that trip for a few days; a week at most."

"I have an appointment there that I cannot miss," Kildare argued.

"We have until the end of spring," chided Zedaine.

"I want it over and done," Kildare shot back. "That gluttonous pig is going to get what's coming to him."

"It won't hurt to wait the week," his brother replied with a wave of his hand. "It's not like Judoh's going anywhere."

Turning, Zedaine spoke directly to their employer. "However, as much as it bothers me to admit this," he said, jerking his thumb in his brother's direction, "Kildare has a point. Why call on us at this godforsaken hour? We just returned from that fiasco in Airspur, saving the Baroness from being deposed. That was headache enough. I've little desire to sign on for another of your missions of state."

"It is not politics this time," the sage responded.

"It's *always* some political shit with you," Kildare said with disgust. "Save your lies for someone else. Now that you've managed to ruin a perfectly good evening, why don't you tell us what's so important that it couldn't wait till tomorrow?"

"I need you to go into the Rhone Mountains," she answered.

Blade did not need the light of the moon to know their mouths hung open in surprise.

"The Rhone Mountains?" Zedaine asked, recovering first. "Why? The mountains aren't a particularly inviting place."

"I know," she responded simply. "I'm trying to save someone's life."

"By risking ours?" Kildare asked pointedly.

"I don't know anyone who's worth saving that badly," Zedaine mumbled skeptically.

"This is of the utmost importance," she continued, "or I would not ask."

"In what part of the mountains?" Kildare questioned. "If it's the foothills west of here, we could manage that for the right price. But if it's anything beyond the canyon…"

"It's miles past the canyon," she interrupted, having no patience to deal with the elder of the two.

Zedaine swore under his breath, "You don't believe in sugarcoating things, do you? Where *exactly* beyond the canyon do you need us to go?"

The tension in her head increased and she sighed, already knowing what their reaction would be. "It's near the Mirrored Falls."

Their shocked silence spoke volumes.

"You've got to be *shitting* me," Zedaine snarled when he found his voice. "The Mirrored Falls? No one's been there since Estan's idiotic incursion! That's right in the middle of magada country. He and his army were torn to pieces. For Dourn's sake, why don't we just fall on our swords now and save you the trouble?"

"Lower your voice," Blade warned, with a quick look around the surrounding darkness.

"I'm in complete agreement with Zedaine," Kildare said, his voice more hushed. "The Mirrored Falls lie on ground sacred to the magada, as the aforementioned Estan found out. We'd be killed upon discovery. Thanks for the offer, Blade, but you are wasting your time… and ours."

"I know how dangerous it is," she replied, steeling her resolve. "That's why I need the two of you. Unfortunately, that's not all. You need to locate a plant that grows in that area; it is called *Viasha*."

"Redcup?" Zedaine asked, calling it by its common name. "Why do we need to traipse into magada country to get that? It grows all over the valley, not half a league from here."

"I need a rare variant," Blade explained. "It blooms for only a few hours in early spring. Most of the time, the *Viasha* plant, or Redcup if you prefer, will flower red. However, there is a hybrid that blooms a pale violet, almost white. I have seen it a handful of times through the years and always near the Mirrored Falls. You must harvest it and bring it to me."

"When did you go to the Mirrored Falls?" Zedaine scoffed. "Was there some history convention among the tribes you forgot to mention?"

"Let me get this straight," Kildare interrupted. "You want us to risk our necks to find some rare plant in the middle of the deadliest stretch of mountains in the Rhone?"

"You're the only people who know the way," Blade said trying to explain.

"No doubt to save some lowlife politician who wouldn't give a rat's ass about us," Kildare continued, angry enough now that he wasn't even listening to Blade.

"I know it's dangerous," Blade responded.

"It's suicide!" Kildare hissed, close to losing his temper. "Send the Falcon, or... or the Owl, or better yet, drag your own ass into the mountains. There's no way in hell I'm going."

"I've considered my other resources," she said, unfazed by his outrage. "You two are the best at tracking, the best at wilderness survival. Both my buyer and I…" she bit her tongue, cursing inwardly at her slip.

"There it is," Zedaine said, acid dripping from his tongue. "Now we're getting to the heart of the matter. One of your infamous and unknown buyers. By the gods, you make me sick, Blade. Money and politics, that's all you give a damn about!"

"Of course not," she shot back. "As I told you, this is about saving a life. Also, I don't hear either of you complaining when you get paid."

"How come every time one of your buyers needs something out of the ordinary, we get dragged into it?" Zedaine continued. "This is such horseshit. Who *is* this buyer of yours, anyway?"

For the first time that night, Blade's stomach tightened. If they found out who had made the request, no power on the face of the earth could make them go. "The money is good," she answered, ignoring the question, "That's all you need kn…"

"Quiet, both of you," Kildare said, cutting them off, his eyes searching the top of the battlements.

Instantly, Zedaine was on guard, assuming a low crouch, hand on the hilt of his sword. "What is it?" he whispered.

"What happened to the sentry?" Kildare asked in a hushed tone. "He should have returned by now."

The battlements were shrouded in darkness, with only the faintest moonlight illuminating the causeway above. There was no sound of approaching footsteps, only the stillness of night.

"Maybe the rotation is changing?" Zedaine murmured as the moments dragged by.

"No," Kildare replied, eyes still searching. "There's no movement at all. Something is wrong."

A whirring from above was their only warning.

"Down," hissed Kildare, grabbing Blade by the collar and dragging her to the ground. Zedaine dropped instantly at his brother's words, rolling quickly to his left. Sparks flew where metal struck granite in the space in which Kildare had been standing a moment ago. Three more whirring sounds followed. Two objects *shuuucked* into the ground in rapid succession, narrowly missing Zedaine's rolling form. The last slammed into the wooden frame of the alcove, a hairsbreadth above where Kildare lay.

Cursing, Zedaine rose to one knee, sword in hand. The big hunter saw a dark blur detach itself from the shadows and flee atop the battlements.

"Hunt his ass down, Zee!" Kildare hissed, leaping to his feet, sword in hand.

Zedaine didn't need prompting. He set off at a dead sprint, bounding up the rampart, racing after the attacker.

"What the hell is going on?" Kildare demanded for the second time that night. "Who was that? Dammit, sage, talk to me! Are you alive or not?"

"I'm fine," she answered, rising to her feet. The sage took a moment to brush off the front of her tunic and leggings, her mind whirling. She'd told no one of this rendezvous. The message to meet at Dusk Gate had been delivered by her hand, dropped in a secret place only known to the two brothers and herself. There was no reason to suspect anyone would know of their whereabouts this night. Despite those precautions, someone had discovered them. Tensing, the sage cast her gaze toward Kildare, never truly knowing where his loyalties lie.

"Whom did you tell about this meeting?" she asked evenly, slipping a hand under her cloak.

His eyes never leaving the surrounding darkness, Kildare snorted in disgust. "You have the audacity to accuse me?" he breathed. "You should know better than that, sage. If I wanted you dead, you would be."

"Then how did you know there was an assassin in the shadows?" she challenged, fingering the knife at her belt.

"I didn't *know,* Blade, but something wasn't right," he answered evenly. "The post from Dusk Gate to section one is sixty-three paces," he explained. "The guard takes roughly two and a half minutes per rotation. It had been almost three since he last came this way, and he was nowhere in sight. Soldiers tend to follow a routine. The pattern changed; that's what drew my suspicion."

"You… timed how long he took on his rounds?" she asked.

"Yes, as we waited in the shadows," he answered. "Zedaine and I wanted to see if you were truly alone." He laughed harshly. "It seems trust is in short supply these days. Now kindly remove your hand from the knife under your cloak and explain what just happened."

Her misgivings subsided at his reasoning. For all the headaches he caused her, Kildare was pragmatic to a fault. The mercenary brothers were not cold-blooded killers; they'd not dispose of her on a whim. Despite their prickly demeanor, they had been loyal—if not to her, then to her coin. She let go of the knife and released a pent-up breath, "I should not have doubted you."

He turned to her grimly, "If you're done thinking the worst of me, we can get back to the question I asked. Who wants you dead?"

"Let's see what we can discover," she said in answer, peering down at the bottom portion of the doorway. In the light of the moon, she could make out a metal object with four razor sharp triangular points, one of which was embedded deep in the wooden frame of the door.

Glancing back, Kildare whispered, "What is that, a knife?"

"A shuriken," Blade answered in stunned amazement.

"A weapon of the *Hashin*," Kildare muttered under his breath, surprising the sage with his knowledge. Turning around, he took a step toward the alcove. "I've not seen one in some time," he continued, reaching for the weapon.

"Have a care," Blade warned. "It's likely coated with poison."

His hand froze halfway there. He let it drop to his side and stood up, looking at the sage. "The Lands of the Seven Provinces are thousands of miles away, Blade, across the Ariath Ocean. What do they want with you?"

Leaving his question unanswered, Blade bent and searched the ground, finding two more of the weapons half buried in the earth. Leaning close, she examined them for a few moments before climbing to her feet and stepping toward the wall where the initial throw had struck.

"Are you going to…" Kildare began, before he dropped into a fighting stance and spun around with blazing speed.

A figure emerged from the darkness on the wall.
Zedaine.

"Escaped," the big hunter grated between clenched teeth. "Son-of-a-bitch is well trained, I'll give him that. He didn't make a sound when he made off. No scraping of feet, no creaking boards, no slip in the mud, nothing. I kept waiting for a dog's bark to give him away, but he didn't disturb a one, and I can't track by moonlight, not someone that good."

Looking at Blade, Zedaine continued, "I checked the sentry on my way back. Kildare was right. Whoever it was took out the guard. He's alive, though he received a nasty blow to the head. Should be up and about in a few days. I suppose he's lucky to be breathing, considering the skill of our attacker. Now, will someone explain to me what that was all about?"

"That's what I've been trying to find out," Kildare replied in frustration. "She did something to piss off the Seven Provinces."

"No," Blade said quietly. She gestured to the spot where the first shuriken had struck. "It was not I who was standing there," she said, quietly letting her words sink in. "You were, Kildare."

"Don't talk nonsense," he scoffed. "We were right next to each other! That throw could have been meant for either one of us."

"The next two throws struck to Zedaine's left as he rolled away," she continued, pointing to the ground where the pair of shuriken were buried. "The last," she said, pointing back at the door frame, "struck inches above where *you* took cover."

"*We* were the targets?" Zedaine asked in disbelief. "But… what for? What have you dragged us into? Why would this assassin target *us*?"

She let out a long sigh. "It's possible that someone discovered who you…"

"No," Kildare spat, his words cutting through the darkness like a knife. "That's not possible."

"How can you be certain?" Blade asked. "Sooner or later, someone is going to recognize one of you."

"We're done talking about it," Zedaine said flatly.

The throbbing in her head increased. The sage knew she could not question them further without risking their service. Her task of convincing them to go into the mountains was difficult before the attack. Now it would be nearly impossible. "If we could get back to the task at hand," she began.

"You still want us to go into the mountains?" Zedaine questioned, incredulous. "Screw your buyer, Blade!" he seethed. "I've got a new task in mind. I'm all for hunting down that bastard who just tried to murder us in cold blood!"

"You'll not find him," Blade explained, trying to remain calm. "If it was one of the *Hashin*, he would leave no trace."

"I don't give a goddamn who he is," he raged. "I'll find him by tomorrow night and rip his bloody head off!"

"What will you be looking for?" she challenged. "I didn't see the assassin clearly—did you? All we saw was a blur in the night. For all we know, it could have been a woman! You wouldn't even know who you were hunting."

"I can track anyone," Zedaine countered, unrelenting. "Come dawn, I'll find the trail and hunt that bastard down."

"You're not listening," she replied, struggling to maintain her composure. "I know how skilled you are. You're one of the finest trackers in The Rhone, but the *Hashin* are trained from birth. You'll not find him."

"I don't care what skills he possesses," Zedaine said harshly. "No one tries to kill me and gets away with it! I'm going after that assassin at first light!"

"You won't be alone," Kildare grunted, turning to leave. "I'm done with this, Blade. Best of luck to you."

Near panic set in as the pair started off. If they walked away now, the fate of the entire Crystalline

Sea was sealed. "You cannot go!" she called in desperation, her voice shriller than she'd intended.

The brothers turned, blinking in surprise. After months of working with the sage, they had never seen her lose her cool.

"We work *for* you," the elder brother said, his voice dangerously quiet. "More accurately, we work for your gold. You don't own us. You don't tell us what to do—no one does. We left that life behind years ago. We're here as a courtesy, because we respect you, Blade. Once that respect goes, we go. You'd do well to remember that."

"I know," she said, her voice suddenly weary. "Please, forgive my words, they were spoken in haste. I just… please don't leave."

The brothers exchanged looks.

"*You* are offering *us* an apology?" Kildare said, surprise in his voice. "I've never heard you like this."

"Who's important enough for us to risk going into the Rhone Mountains?" Zedaine asked. "No games, sage."

"I don't have any answers you'd want to hear," she explained, deflecting his question. "I'd much rather send you into Shaara. That's where the real problems are."

"Then send us there," Kildare said. "I prefer civilization to running around the Rhone Mountains."

"Every fiber of me wants to do that very thing," the sage answered. "The greatest threat to the lands of the Crystalline Sea is Shaara. The country is in turmoil; it teeters on the brink of civil war. If the wrong person takes control of Gallanse, no one will be safe."

"How can that be?" Kildare asked skeptically. "Surely things haven't deteriorated so…"

"You know nothing of the world, son of Brisbane," Blade interrupted, shocking him into silence. "The politics of the Crystalline Sea have changed these past months. The power in Shaara is like a dark storm rising, ready to unleash its fury on every surrounding nation. It will take but a single spark to ignite the fires of war. I have seen it before. In your twenty-three summers you've seen battle, yes, but never war. Entire cities put to the torch, armies ravaging the countryside. Through my efforts and those of the Knights of Steel, the Crystalline Sea has remained in relative peace for years. This power in Shaara is something no one has seen in generations."

She paused, letting her words sink in.

"Despite the issue in Shaara, you *must* go into the mountains. That is the request I received, and

I will see it through. The plant I seek, the *Viasha*, is a medicine powerful enough to hold even death at bay. That's what my…buyer has requested. That's why you must go. I know how dangerous the journey is. I doubt any of my Knights could survive it. Without this medicine, a good man will die, and the Crystalline Sea will plunge into chaos. I have already delivered the last of the *Viasha* I had in storage. That is why I need you two. The fate of the entire region may well depend upon your success."

The two brothers looked at one another for a long moment. "All right, sage," Kildare said with a sigh. "We'll go. Though in all probability, we're going to die in those mountains."

"Fah! Maybe you will, brother," Zedaine snickered. "The magada won't even know I'm there. I'm *sneakier* than you."

"You couldn't sneak up on a three-day corpse," Kildare retorted.

"So, you'll go?" Blade asked, stunned at their sudden change of heart.

"That's what I just said, isn't it?" Kildare answered sarcastically.

"We'll go," Zedaine interjected, turning to Blade. "But I value my hide a lot more than fifty drachs."

"How much will it take?" she asked.

"Ten times that amount," Kildare answered. "Five hundred drachmas… each, with all expenses of this little outing paid for by your buyer, whoever it is. Saving a life doesn't come cheaply. They want to live? Then they can pay… and after this is over, we're taking a break—a month at least."

"Anything else?" she asked.

"Yes," Zedaine answered, his anger flashing again. "You find that assassin. I don't care what it takes, you find him!"

"I will do what I can," she said simply.

"Just like that, huh?" Kildare shook his head. "You'd drop a thousand silver for us to run into the Rhone Mountains? This person you want us to save had better be some kind of savior to mankind."

He leaned in close, his voice like ice. "If I find out you're using us for some other purpose, sage, you'll have more than Shaara to worry about."

"I've been as forthright as I can," Blade responded. "You are being paid a small fortune for your services."

"I suppose you want us to leave now?" grumbled Zedaine.

"Time is of the essence," she replied.

Both men reached down and grabbed their packs. She could make out longbows and sheaves of arrows strapped tightly in place, along with bedrolls and canteens of water.

"A day or two to find the falls and three to find this *Viasha*," Kildare said, tightening a cinch on his pack. "Five days in the mountains, not a second more. Have our payment ready whether we find your medicine or not. For your sake, I hope you're right about this."

"You'll have to harvest the entire plant," Blade said. "The petals, roots, leaves…"

"We know how to harvest a plant," Zedaine irritably. "Just don't forget about that assassin. You can bet your ass I won't."

They moved toward the ramp, but Kildare hesitated, turning back to her. She could feel his angry eyes on her skin. "One last thing, *sage*," he snarled. "Don't *ever* refer to me as a son of Brisbane again. That part of my life is long dead. Your politicians made damn sure of that."

"Shall I have the guard open the gate?" she asked, ignoring his threat.

Zedaine snorted over his shoulder, "Don't do us any favors."

Without another word, the two men climbed the ramparts and vanished over the wall.

Blade stood a moment longer, the lone witness to their departure. Of all her Knights, none had the skill to survive this trip. Neither the Owl nor the

Condor could track well enough. Even her best warrior, the Hawk, did not have the fighting skills necessary. Only these two men had a chance, and they were wild cards, both of them.

She sighed, thinking of the code names bestowed upon them by the other Knights in her network. "You have been aptly titled," she whispered.

Turning back to the alcove, Blade carefully gathered the shuriken for further study. She needed to send a chirurgeon to check on the sentry above. No doubt the poor man would be unsuitable for duty over the next few days.

"I hope you're right about this."

Kildare's words came back to her, and she shivered. This time, the cold had nothing to do with the chill she felt running down her spine.

"No," she whispered. "I pray I am wrong."

Chapter 2

The Prince of Dagor stood in a private wing of The Gray Stone Palace, honored guest of his family's greatest enemy. The walls inside his chambers hung with tapestries illustrating the history of his ancestors through the ages. Portraits of the Romano family lined the walls, some dulled with the age of centuries, while others looked as though they'd come from the easel that day. Sculptures and vases, rugs and furniture, all the comforts of home had been provided for the prince and his retinue.

Standing in the middle of the room, Dragomir saw none of it. Instead, he stared with a furrowed brow, reading the parchment his adviser had handed to him moments ago.

"What does he expect?" the fair-skinned prince muttered, turning to his councilor upon completion.

"Your father?" asked Anir knowingly. A balding man of advancing years, the elder statesman was absently rubbing the gold ring of First Councilor on his finger.

"Who else would it be?" Dragomir answered sharply, handing him the parchment. "He believes the succession goes too slowly, as if I could speed up Conidon's death simply by wishing for it."

"'Careful, highness," warned Cobal softly, his hand resting upon the hilt of his sword. "'Tis said these walls have ears."

Dragomir's lips curled in dark humor as he turned to the grizzled general. "They're welcome to listen. It's hardly a secret that he and my father despise one another. Short of breaking the peace accord, we simply have to wait for the old man to die."

Dragomir slumped into the chair at the end of the polished dining table and poured himself a cup of wine, drinking its contents anxiously. It was bad enough that the succession had dragged on days longer than anyone believed possible. Conidon, the High Lord of Gallanse, looked like death warmed over, yet somehow he'd defied all odds and retained a tenuous hold on life. This presented a multitude of problems for the prince of Dagor.

When Dragomir had arrived weeks ago, he was the obvious choice to become the new High Lord of Gallanse. As the days passed, however, his momentum waned. At least two others of royal blood had bent Conidon's ear toward their claims to the throne, though they lacked the political backing to achieve success in the Council of Barons.

He drew a deep breath, calming himself. A few more days would not matter one way or another, he reasoned. Everything was going according to plan, albeit more slowly than he would have liked. His anxiety drained away and Dragomir allowed himself a brief smile.

Looking up from the letter, Cobal frowned at the prince. "This is a serious matter, highness," he said, eyes narrowed in disapproval.

Dragomir's smile vanished. "I understand the matter perfectly well, general," he answered, rubbing the rim of his cup absently.

Cobal glanced to Anir. The heavyset councilor raised his eyebrows toward the general but said nothing.

"I don't think you fully comprehend your father's message," the rugged Cobal said, looking back to the prince.

Dragomir waved at him dismissively and poured himself more wine. "I'm the son of the most powerful ruler in all of Shaara. I hold the support of the majority of the barons at court, and I'm surrounded by the Blood Watch," he boasted arrogantly. "What matter is a few days more? Conidon must marry his bitch off to someone; I am the logical choice. Gallanse *will* be mine."

"Conidon may be old, highness," Anir interjected, "but he's no fool. Much can happen in the next few days. Lord Dillion of Janril still commands his attention, and just yesterday we received word from our source here in the palace that his son is but a day from joining his father at court."

"Bay is coming?" Dragomir asked, his tone becoming serious. The elder son of Lord Dillion was no friend to Dragomir.

"Not Bay, highness," Cobal said, shaking his head with disapproval. "If you'd read the report I'd given you yesterday, you would know Dillion's eldest son remains in Janril."

"Alexander, then," Dragomir scoffed, a smile working its way back onto his face. "His second son is but eleven years old. Conidon could not think of turning the city over to that welp."

"Use your head," Cobal stated bluntly.

"Have a care how you speak to me, *commander*," Dragomir answered, leaning forward in his chair coolly. "You may be First General of the Blood Watch, but you are still *just* a commoner. I am of the blood; you are not."

"I have served your family for years, boy," Cobal continued, unfazed. "Long before you were born. I was appointed this command by your father himself. Until he revokes my position as both general and advisor, I'll speak my mind."

Dragomir stared hard at the man for a long moment before easing back in his chair. "So, you think Alexander will be placed on the Gray Throne?" Dragomir questioned, with a grunt. "All the better. The boy won't survive a week. Can you imagine a child trying to navigate the politics of Shaara?"

Cobal shook his head in disgust and set the letter on the table. "Explain it to him," he said to Anir. Carefully he slid into the chair next to Dragomir, pouring wine into his own cup.

"Explain what?" Dragomir snapped in annoyance.

Anir pulled a chair out from under the table and wriggled his considerable paunch into it, clasping his hands in front of him. Anir was the fourth man in as many months to hold the coveted position of First Councilor to the prince. While Dragomir was not stupid, he was young, and his temper often got the better of him. Anir's predecessors had all been dismissed for dispensing advice the prince did not wish to hear. Anir had no desire to follow in their footsteps.

"Alexander would be a figurehead only, highness," Anir explained patiently. "You're correct in assuming he isn't ready to rule. The boy is years away from his majority. However, he would be a puppet for others to manipulate from behind the throne."

"And whom, pray tell, would be pulling the strings?" Dragomir responded, unimpressed with Anir's warning. "With Conidon dead there *is* no one else."

The balding councilor glanced at Cobal who shook his head in frustration.

"There is another with Gaida blood in Gallanse," Anir said carefully.

Dragomir's face flushed red and he stood up in outrage. "You cannot mean the princess?" he spat, angrily pointing at Anir. "That bitch cannot rule! It flies in the face of tradition. It…it's against the law! Surely that's not what you're suggesting?"

"Anir speaks the truth, highness," Cobal interjected firmly, his steely eyes locked on Dragomir's. "If Alexander marries the princess, he will become the new High Lord. Alexander would command publicly, but it is the princess who would run the city. She is surrounded by aids loyal to her family, and her understanding of politics is nearly as astute as her father's. She lacks only his experience. Conidon has foreseen this possibility and has trained the princess ever since her brother's passing. She would be ruling through Alexander until the boy was ready to take command."

"That's... it's outrageous," Dragomir stammered in shock. "The High Council would never allow it!"

"It takes but three votes, highness," Cobal said icily. "Conidon already commands his own. Coupled with the High Lord of Janril, he needs only to sway Lord Fallon or Lord Waymon to have his majority."

"You don't think they will see through this charade?" Dragomir argued.

"It's not a charade," Anir said wryly. "It has been done in the past. The precedent has been set, though not under these circumstances. Technically, no law would be broken. There is little you—or your father—could do to stop it."

Dragomir was speechless. He picked up the letter from where Cobal had placed it on the table. His eyes were immediately drawn to the last line.

"*Serve some purpose.*"

They were the same words his father had uttered over a month ago when Dragomir departed his home.

Nostrils flaring angrily, he crumpled the paper and hurled it to the floor in frustration. *Bastard*, he thought, *I serve a purpose. Am I not here fighting for the throne of Gallanse?* Despite his anger, Dragomir felt a tightening in his chest. His father was not known for his patience, nor his forgiveness. Failure was not tolerated.

"You two are supposed to be my advisors," Dragomir said in a choked voice. "Advise something!"

"Calm yourself, highness," Anir answered coolly. "You are still in position to win the throne."

"How?" Dragomir questioned, slumping back into his chair.

"Conidon does not yet have the support of Lord Fallon," he explained calmly. "Until he convinces the ruler of Northpass and his barons that the princess is fit to rule, he cannot claim victory."

"What are we doing to assure this doesn't happen?" Dragomir asked, struggling to regain his composure.

Anir smiled faintly. "Yesterday, I dispatched a message to Lord Fallon, inviting him to join you today to discuss the matter. He is very much entrenched in the traditions of Shaara. Convincing him to take our side should not be difficult, especially if we can come to an…understanding."

"How much will that understanding cost?" muttered Dragomir, leaning forward in his seat.

Anir smiled darkly and caressed his ring again. "The same as it cost to purchase Lord Waymon's vote: ten thousand gold minas. That should be enough to buy you the throne."

"It is too late for that," came a voice from behind them.

Instantly, Cobal was out of his chair, hand on the hilt of his sword and drawn out of its scabbard, ready to defend his prince.

"One move and you are dead," growled the massive general.

Standing next to the table stood a man dressed in white robes, trimmed in emerald and black. In his right hand he held a pale green staff of ivory.

"Be at ease, commander," the stranger continued from the depths of his hood. "Had I wished you harm, I wouldn't have announced my presence."

"How did you get in here?" demanded Cobal, his eyes searching behind the stranger.

The man drew back his hood, revealing a face of perhaps fifty winters. His thin lips parted in the faintest of smiles. "No sanctum is safe from one who practices the mystic arts," he answered.

"You are a magus?" Anir questioned skeptically.

"I am your replacement," the man said evenly. "And to answer your question, yes, I am magi."

Anir's mouth opened momentarily in surprise before he shook his head with annoyance. "It will take more than skulking about in the shadows to convince me of your so-called mystic arts, whoever you are," Anir said with irritation. "No one can remove me other than High Lord Rexor. Guards!" he yelled, turning his head toward the main entrance of the room.

Several moments went by without movement from the other side of the door.

"Where are your men?" Anir demanded, looking at Cobal.

"They cannot hear you," the magus said with amusement. "I have placed a spell of silence upon this room. Only those inside it can hear our discussion."

"I don't believe you," Anir replied.

"It would be… unwise to question me further, counselor," the magus said, tilting his head in warning. "I am not known to lie. Pack your things," he said with a contemptuous wave of his hand, "You are dismissed."

"I'm not going anywhere," Anir snapped angrily.

"Counselor," Dragomir said, standing slowly. "Look," he continued, pointing at the man's head.

The magus was completely bald. That however, was not what had caught the eye of the prince. Covering the entirety of his scalp were the green and black markings of a scaled claw, its talons draped over the man's forehead like some macabre crown.

"You are one of the *Moldronni Sor*," Dragomir uttered in surprise.

"That's highly unlikely," Anir said, narrowing his eyes. "That order ceased to exist years ago. Any common magicker can mark his head," he continued. "It does not make him a demon mage."

"Doubt me at your peril," Eliphas said, his eyes hardening. "I am not a forgiving man."

"Enough," rumbled Cobal, whose sword remained in his hand. "What are you doing here, magus?" he asked bluntly.

Eliphas reached under his robes and produced a tightly rolled parchment bound in gold thread. Turning his gaze toward Cobal, he handed it to the taciturn general. "The High Lord Rexor has entered into an agreement with the leader of my order," he said, his dark eyes turning to Dragomir. "Your father believes things have progressed too slowly here in Gallanse. I have been appointed your new First Counselor." He looked back toward Anir. "It's all there in the letter."

"Give me that," Anir hissed, snatching the parchment from Cobal.

"That is Rexor's seal," Cobal said, turning his eyes to the magus, "and his signature."

Anir's eyes widened as he scanned the parchment, his face flushed with anger. "This is preposterous!" he yelled, looking first at Cobal and then Dragomir.

"You've failed here, Anir," Eliphas said again, contempt in his voice. "Leave."

Anir's face reddened further. "I refuse," he barked. "This isn't over. I will write to Rexor immediately."

"You will leave," Eliphas insisted, "now!"

"I don't take orders from you!" Anir shouted. "You know nothing of the politics in Shaara. You have no authority…"

"*Mors ignis!*" hissed Eliphas, raising his staff and pointing it at Anir.

"No!" barked Cobal, taking a step toward the magus.

It was too late.

Green flames shot from Eliphas's staff, blasting Anir, throwing him across the room. The counselor crashed to the stone floor near the exit, writhing in pain as his clothing and skin burned in the mystical fire. The lead councilor rolled frantically on the ground, trying to smother the flames, but to no avail. His screams, filled with agony, echoed throughout the room over the span of a few seconds until his charred remains came to a complete and final halt.

"What have you done?" Dragomir gasped, looking to the magus, his eyes wide with horror. He raised a sleeve to his face and gagged as the smell of burnt flesh struck him.

Without answering, the magus stepped to what was left of the now-deceased councilor and snapped his fingers. The smoking remains turned instantly to dust.

"I warned him," Eliphas said evenly, bending over the charred ash. He reached down, picked up the gold ring of the First Councilor, and slipped it on his finger.

"You are insane," Cobal said, tearing his eyes from the pile of dust that was Anir.

"No, general," the magus answered. "I simply do not tolerate those who question my authority."

"I answer only to High Lord Rexor," Cobal growled. "You do not command me, magus."

"I do now," Eliphas said, walking past the general without a glance. The magus whispered something under his breath and the parchment Anir had dropped floated off the floor and came to rest in front of Cobal. "It is all in the letter."

Cobal took the parchment in his hands, but did not look at it. Instead, he narrowed his eyes angrily at the magus. He placed the parchment on the table and his hand tightened on the pommel of his blade.

"Was one lesson not enough?" the magus queried, his eyes never leaving the general. "I prefer to keep you on, general; however," he raised his staff again and it glowed green with magic, "the choice is yours."

Several heartbeats passed until Cobal loosened the grip on the hilt of his sword.

"Good," Eliphas said with a brief smile. "Be so kind as to have your men clean that up," he continued, gesturing toward Anir's remains, "after I'm done speaking with the prince."

Cobal's eyes narrowed dangerously. He flicked a quick glance toward the wild-eyed Dragomir, who was still stunned at the turn of events. The shoulders of the prince drooped and he gave a slow nod to the general.

"Your will...highness," Cobal said, defiantly slamming his fist to his heart. The rugged man strode toward the doorway and sheathed his sword without looking back.

Eliphas slid into the chair previously occupied by Anir. "Sit down, highness," Eliphas said, leaning his staff against the side of the table. The mage drew the cowl of his robe back up over his head. Dragomir could see his emerald green eyes glittering like agates within the depths of his hood.

The pale-skinned prince slowly sat opposite the magus and did not move.

"I fear the general has not yet learned his place," Eliphas mused absently, "but I will attend to that as needed."

"Why did you kill him?" Dragomir asked softly.

"Anir? He questioned my authority. As for his plan to bribe the lord of Northpass, it was doomed to fail," Eliphas continued, pouring himself a drink of wine. "Lord Waymon could be bought. Lord Fallon is another matter."

Dragomir's mouth went dry. He reached forward and sipped absently at his cup.

"Serve some purpose."

The memory of his father's words shook him anew after the shock of Anir's death.

"Tell me, magus," he said, choosing his words carefully. "My father doesn't easily enter into an alliance."

"No, he does not," Eliphas agreed.

Dragomir's lips pressed together tightly. "No one does something for nothing," he said plainly.

"I don't take your meaning," Eliphas said with a faint smile.

"You've said you will help me gain the Gray Throne of Gallanse."

"Indeed, I will."

"What is it you require from me?" he asked warily.

The smile on the mage's face broadened, but it was bereft of humor. "Right to the point, just like your father."

"Do you have an answer to my question?" Dragomir asked.

In response, the magus pulled a second parchment from inside his robes. Carefully, he untied the gold ribbon and unrolled the parchment. Drawn on the inside of the scroll was a picture of a man wearing blue robes, the mark of an ambassador of the realm.

"Who is he?" Dragomir asked in confusion.

"Ambassador Macklore of Brisbane," Eliphas answered flatly. "You and your Blood Watch are going to help me kill him," the magus said. "That is the price of the Gray Throne."

"That's it?" Dragomir asked, surprised. "A single death is all you require?"

"Believe me, highness," Eliphas said dryly, "he is no easy meat."

Chapter 3

It had taken the brothers until dusk of the first day to reach the Mirrored Falls. They'd run over thirty miles and climbed nearly six thousand feet in elevation since leaving Staltshore. Twice on the journey they'd encountered magada hunting parties, putting Blade's faith in them to the test. That trust had not been misplaced, as their wits and quick-thinking kept them from detection on both occasions. Using a blend of speed and stealth, Kildare and Zedaine arrived at their destination unscathed.

The falls themselves cascaded from a rocky outcropping some seventy feet above a wide plateau. Even someone standing a quarter of a mile away could hear the rush of water as it roared down the mountainside. The white froth of churning rapids morphed quickly into a bubbling stream, its swirling eddies running parallel to the surrounding foliage. As the stream widened, the once-raging water of the falls transformed into a pond of reverent serenity, its dark surface reflecting the surrounding trees and blue sky to perfection.

The brothers had found shelter on a ledge that ran along the northeastern side of the plateau, some fifty feet above ground. While the ascent of the rock face had proven difficult, it provided the pair with a wide view of the falls and surrounding area. Hanging over the ledge, a secondary formation of stone served as both cover and protection from the elements. It was a perfect vantage point, masking their presence both from above the plateau and below.

It was now the evening of the fourth day. Kildare's eyes searched the landscape for any glimpse of movement that might signal something out of the ordinary. He saw only the picturesque scene of the falls below. Turning with a scowl, he cursed under his breath.

"*What* is bothering you?" Zedaine asked, rather pointedly. The younger of the two was sitting comfortably on a bed of leaves and branches he'd woven together into a rudimentary cot. "You've been stomping around this ledge since we got here. If you're so restless, go scout the plateau again; see if you can find the *Viasha*."

"I don't need to scout the plateau again," Kildare responded irritably. "We were just down there. I doubt the *Viasha* popped up in the last ten minutes." He slid his sword halfway out of its sheath and slammed it back again, his frustration evident. "Blade is out of her mind thinking some magical flower is going to grow way up here in the mountains. There is still snow on the ground!"

"You've said as much a dozen times already," Zedaine answered with a wave of his hand. "And just so you know, big brother, *plenty* of Redcup's have sprouted near the falls, just as Blade said they would, despite the snow and altitude. The *Viasha* simply hasn't blossomed yet."

Kildare just shook his head and frowned. "We should have left at sunrise."

"I don't see what your problem is," Zedaine countered, leaning back in his cot. "There's been no sign of magada, we get to relax in the peace of the outdoors, *and* we're getting paid...handsomely, I might add. This is the sweetest job we've ever had!"

Kildare disagreed.

Nothing about this seemed right. Frustrated, the elder brother sat down on his own woven mat, absently scratching his elbow. Two things had been nagging at him since they'd left Staltshore. How had the assassin known where they were going to be, and were he and Zedaine truly the targets? His initial thought was that they'd been betrayed by Blade, but he'd dismissed that idea almost immediately. He suspected there was more to the sage than she had revealed, but Blade had proven to be a trustworthy employer. The message they'd received that night *had* been delivered by her own hand; he'd seen her drop it off himself.

There was no chance anyone might have gotten to it before they had.

Don't play the fool, he thought to himself. *That wasn't the proof that convinced you. It wasn't until she dropped her hand onto her own knife hilt. She thought* you *had betrayed* her. *That's when you knew she was innocent.*

No, it wasn't the sage. There was no reason for her to sell them out. They were far too valuable to her network of spies and informants. Besides, his instincts told him it was something else altogether. Some unseen force was at work here, and it was unsettling.

"I figured the magada would be camped all over the place up here," Zedaine broke the silence. "I thought you said the falls were holy to them?"

"They are," Kildare answered, absently interlacing his fingers atop his head.

"Well that begs the question," Zedaine continued, "if it's so important to them, where are they?"

Kildare sighed in irritation, his train of thought broken. "Did you ever learn anything from Thorn's lessons?"

"When they were interesting, I did," Zedaine answered honestly. "Besides, I knew you were taking notes and you'd tell me whatever I missed."

Kildare snorted, "You never bothered to listen, did you?"

"I'm listening now," Zedaine grinned.

Kildare shook his head in resignation, letting his hands fall back to his sides. "You're like a child, Zedaine, a big, lumbering, pain-in-the-ass child. Why do I even bother with you?"

"It's out of love," Zedaine replied impishly.

Kildare rolled his eyes and fought to suppress a smile. His brother was an irascible character, and he knew it. "Magada rituals take place late in the spring," he answered, managing to keep a frown on his face.

"Ah, yes," Zedaine said, thoughtfully scratching his chin, "now that you mention it, that does ring a bell."

"Spring is only a few days old," Kildare continued. "As you know, there's still snow this high in the mountains. You come back in a fortnight when it's completely melted, and I'd wager the place will be crawling with magada."

Kildare's sour mood returned. He rose, kicking at his cot. "I'm *sick* of sitting on this rock," he muttered. "We should have left at sunrise."

"So you've said," Zedaine replied, swatting absently at an insect. "But then we'd be breaking our word to Blade. Speaking of the sage, did you know all that stuff about the magada not yet arriving at the falls when you were negotiating with her?"

Kildare hmmphed but said nothing.

Zedaine laughed, "I should have known. We're out here, safe on our rocky perch, waiting for a magic flower to bloom." He sat back with his hands clasped behind his head and crossed his legs in front of him. "Sometimes, big brother, you amaze even me…"

His voice trailed off and the smile faded from his face. Slowly he drew himself to an upright position.

"What is it?" Kildare asked, eyes immediately searching the ground below.

"I thought I…" Zedaine whispered, his brow furrowed in concentration. The moments stretched by as he sat unmoving. "There," he said, quietly looking in the direction of the waterfall. "Do you hear it?"

"I don't hear anything," Kildare said, cocking his head sideways.

"Something on the wind…give it a second," Zedaine was on his feet, staring at the Mirrored Falls.

The seconds dragged by until they both heard it; a faint howling, still some distance away.

"Dire wolf?" Kildare questioned, knowing it was unlikely.

"Caniadon," Zedaine replied flatly. "More than one."

"Could be a pack out hunting deer or mountain goats," Kildare suggested.

"This high in the mountains, half an hour before nightfall?" asked Zedaine, skeptically. Grimly, he began gathering his pack and weapons. "Big game is scarce at this altitude and Caniadon are nocturnal." He frowned at this brother. "Surely you remember Thorn's lesson on that?"

Instead of answering, Kildare scratched at his chin. "They ride with their masters." It was not a question. "Climb up and take a look, and by the gods, don't let yourself be seen," Kildare ordered. "We should be safe enough here if you don't give away our position."

Zedaine was already moving. The big hunter clamored nimbly up the rock face and peered over the ledge, scanning the horizon.

"Well, what do you see?" Kildare asked impatiently.

"Nothing yet," Zedaine answered. "Don't worry professor, if I see something, I won't keep it to myself."

The moments stretched by until the howling returned, closer than before.

"I see them," Zedaine reported, "just beyond the tree line. Looks like three…no, four magada riders on the other side of the stream. No sign of what they're after, but they're running along the edge of the...what the hell?" he said suddenly.

"What?" Kildare demanded.

"Someone just jumped in the water," Zedaine answered in disbelief.

"What?" Kildare said in surprise. "A person this deep in the mountains? That can't be right."

"I know what I saw Kil," Zedaine said, eyes still fixed ahead. "Someone jumped into the water to escape the Caniadon."

Zedaine leapt down from his perch, landing lightly next to his brother. "Whoever it is won't survive without help."

"I agree," Kildare said, purposely leaning against the rock face.

Zedaine raised an eyebrow at his brother, saying nothing.

Kildare put his hands up. "No. Absolutely not, Zedaine. Don't give me that look. This isn't why we're here. This isn't our problem."

Zedaine shrugged and started gathering his gear. "Fine, if you want to let that innocent person die, I won't try to convince you otherwise."

Kildare rolled his eyes skyward. "You know nothing about that person, Zee. It could be a baby-killer for all we know. We are here for the money, not to play hero. We tried that once, remember?"

"Hey, you can stay right here on this safe ledge. I'm not asking you to help," Zedaine said.

Kildare stood, shaking his head for a moment, and then angrily snapped up his weapons belt. "You and your damn conscience. I hate you sometimes."

Zedaine chuckled and started his descent to the plateau floor. "At least this gives you something to do."

"Goddamn it!" Kildare swore bitterly. "Who in the hell is stupid enough to travel into the middle of magada lands?"

"We were," Zedaine said, raising his eyebrows.

"Shut up, Zee," Kildare snarled, "just shut your stupid face." Cursing under his breath, the elder brother grabbed the coiled rope he would need for his descent to the plateau below. "I knew we should have left at sunrise."

Pausing momentarily, Chameleon leaned against a lichen-covered boulder to wipe sweat from her brow. After miles of hard running through the rough mountain terrain, the Drannock's energy was nearly gone. Her legs ached and she knew without rest she would soon collapse. It was only fear that gave her body the strength to run on.

As she drew several labored breaths leaning against the boulder, Chameleon listened for the pursuit that had dogged her all afternoon.

She'd paused two hours past midday to fill her water skin at a small stream that was trickling down the embankment she was leaving behind. After drinking her fill, she'd chanced a look below. To her complete surprise, she saw four Caniadon, giant, wolf-like beasts that ran on six legs instead of four, spilling onto the trail. Mounted on each beast were magada, the none-too-friendly tribal creatures who called these mountains home.

Knowing all too well the danger that the hunting party presented, Chameleon crouched low to the ground and stole away as quietly as she could. Unfortunately, in her haste a stone had slipped under her foot and rolled noisily down the embankment.

She had been on the run ever since.

Chameleon blinked as her thoughts returned to the present. There had been no sound of pursuit for some time. Perhaps she had outrun the Caniadon and their masters after all.

A nearby howl dashed her hope as quickly as it had arisen. A raw burst of fear flooded through

Chameleon's veins, lending her new strength. She staggered away from the boulder, torn hide boots pounding heavily on the rugged stone beneath her feet.

Chameleon abandoned the thought of escape. Her pursuers were too close and much swifter than she. Her only chance now was to find a cave or ledge where she could keep their superior numbers at bay. She scanned the nearby terrain, searching, craving solace.

Her eyes were met only with an endless expanse of worn rocks and tiny shrubs as the howling grew near.

Chameleon ran on, her feet growing heavier with each step. She fumbled at her belt for the stone knife dangling there, knowing it was a painfully inadequate weapon.

She burst into a second clearing that housed only a few low-lying shrubs. Chameleon wanted to scream in frustration. As panic threatened to set in, she realized there was nowhere to hide, nowhere to stand her ground.

At that moment, she heard it; over the sound of her ragged breath and the approaching Caniadon, she heard something that gave her hope.

Somewhere close by was the sound of running water.

Frantically her eyes scanned the clearing until...there! Fifty paces distant, at the southeastern edge of the clearing, she saw a thick growth of green foliage, the kind that could exist only with a constant supply of water. Between the narrow trunks of trees and leaf-covered shrubs, she could make out the white rush of surging rapids.

Chameleon lurched forward, covering the distance in a handful of heartbeats before crashing headlong through the undergrowth. The jagged branch of an evergreen clawed against her head, leaving wet blood upon her brow. She came to a halt standing at the edge of a broad stream, spanning nearly forty feet across. Interspersed among the rapids were boulders slicing out of the crisply moving water. The air was much cooler here, and Chameleon, despite her labors, shivered with cold. It would be a difficult crossing under the best of circumstances, and nearly impossible with a pack of Caniadon at her heels.

She crouched low, turning back to the clearing she'd just crossed. Chameleon scarcely dared to breathe. She felt warm blood from the cut on her scalp dribble into her eye, but did not move for fear of being seen.

Four Caniadon entered the clearing and slowed to a walk, giving the Drannock her first real look at the creatures. They were large, standing as high as the top of Chameleon's head. Covered with coarse black fur from the bottom of their six-clawed feet to the tip of their keen noses, they bristled with savagery. Foot-long snouts housed teeth capable of ripping out her throat with ease. Their heads were canine in appearance, with a pair of saber-like fangs jutting downward, extending well beyond the creatures' lower jaws. In the light of the setting sun, four pairs of gleaming yellow eyes burned brightly as they searched the landscape for their prey.

Riding upon the backs of the beasts were the magada. Long-legged humanoids standing almost a hand taller than Chameleon, their arms and shoulders were heavy with corded muscle. Under the animal skins they wore, she could see mottled gray flesh. Each held a stone-tipped spear in fingers that ended with long, black nails. One might take them for primitive humans until you looked at their faces.

It was not the filthy mane of black hair that hung down past the creatures' shoulders in an unkempt mass that frightened the Drannock. Nor was it the broad noses protruding over thick, bestial lips. Not even the over-wide mouths housing needle-sharp teeth gave her pause.

The eyes, however, terrified her.

Sunken beneath a protruding brow, their eyes were deep amber, flecked with gold. They held no trace of humanity; only the promise of a savage and painful death.

Chameleon watched from her seclusion among the trees, dreading what she knew would happen. As though reading her thoughts, one of the Caniadon bared its teeth and stared straight at Chameleon's place of concealment. It let loose a blood-curdling howl, instantly getting the attention of the other three beasts. With guttural cries from their masters, the Caniadon surged forward.

Chameleon turned back to the churning waters, drawing a deep breath as her pursuers crashed through the underbrush. With the greatest effort she could muster, Chameleon threw herself into the stream.

The shock of cold *whooshed* the air from her lungs. This was snowmelt from the high mountains, near freezing in temperature. Even a short exposure to such extreme cold could prove fatal.

Chameleon immediately gave up trying to make the opposite shore. The current was too strong, throwing her slender form from one rock to another.

A huge boulder loomed directly in front of her. Bracing herself, the Drannock slammed into it, its jagged edge clawing at the flesh of her shoulder. Somehow, she managed to secure a handhold, despite the current that threatened to shake her loose.

Hastily, Chameleon scanned the area in search of a route to safety. She noted the stream had tapered somewhat, noting the far bank was closer than before. Ignoring the icy burn in her shoulder, Chameleon used her feet to thrust herself off the rock in a frantic attempt to gain the shore.

With the narrowing of the stream, however, came an increase in velocity of the water rushing past. Her feeble push off the rock was nothing compared to the rapid's onslaught.

Chameleon knew she was in trouble. In her efforts to escape the magada, she may well have exchanged one painful death for another.

That's when she saw it.

A tree, its trunk broken in half, had fallen across the stream. Moss-infested and rotten, it was lodged between two boulders a few feet above the rapids. Snaking downward, a thin branch was suspended just above the water's surface.

With only seconds to react, Chameleon reached out, willing her numbed fingers to close.

The limb was slick with condensation and the Drannock nearly lost her grip. Desperately, she fought against the pull of the current and managed to slide her left hand higher up the branch. Hanging precariously, the Drannock glanced downstream.

No more than two feet from where her legs lay in the water, the stream ended abruptly. The current had carried her to the brink of a waterfall. She'd been so focused on grabbing the branch, Chameleon had not seen how close she had come to plunging over the falls.

Turning her attention back to her grip, Chameleon reached out with her right hand, hoping to secure her hold and pull herself from the raging waters.

At that moment, the branch snapped.

She only had time to scream a single word, "No!" before plummeting over the falls.

Both men halted in astonishment as they watched the figure drop from the top of the waterfall some fifty yards in front of them. The sound of the body hitting the water was lost in the roar of the falls.

"Did you see that?" Zedaine shouted over his shoulder.

"He'll be lucky to survive the drop," Kildare replied in answer. He swore under his breath. "Get a fire going," he yelled to Zedaine, while sprinting forward. "He'll freeze to death otherwise. Do it now!"

The elder brother shed himself of his pack and ripped off his shirt, tossing it aside. Appearing out of the mist of white water, a body was floating face-down in the current. Ignoring the cold as best he could, Kildare waded quickly into the water and dove out toward the still form. He felt something drag on his left side and cursed himself for not removing his sword. Kildare surfaced only a few feet away from the limp body. Despite the cold, he swam to the listless figure in seconds, with a flurry of powerful strokes. Grabbing the tunic, Kildare roughly flipped the inert form over, only to blink in surprise.

It was a tribeswoman, dressed in a manner he'd never seen.

Recovering his senses, Kildare quickly wrapped his right arm under the woman's neck and managed to sidestroke them both to shore.

Dragging the girl free of the water, Kildare knelt on the ground and planted his ear to her chest. Her skin was freezing to the touch and for a long moment he heard nothing. Despite his harsh words on the rocky outcrop, Kildare did not want the girl to die. A moment later, he sighed with genuine relief at the sound of her faintly beating heart. By some miracle, she'd survived both the jolt of the fall and the icy grasp of the water. The immediate danger now was keeping her from freezing to death.

"Zedaine, get that fire going!" he shouted, turning to see where his brother had gone. He was shivering with cold himself, his hands and feet almost numb.

"Zedaine!" he yelled again.

Out from the line of trees strode four snarling Caniadon, each bearing a magada hunter.

Kildare cast his eyes to the edge of the forest. There was no sign of his brother, anywhere. He *did* notice a pale violet flower growing in a smattering of sunlight to the left of where the magada stood.

"Figures," he muttered bitterly.

Grimly he drew his sword from its scabbard while he could still feel sensation in his fingers. "All right, you bastards," he spat, rage building inside him. "You want a piece of me? Come and get it! Which one of you sons-of-bitches wants to go first?"

The largest of the beasts shot forward in answer.

Chapter 4

Thirteen horses cantered west along a paved stone highway, leaving the stench of the fisherman's wharf in their wake. Five newly appointed watchmen rode underneath the iron portcullis of Dreadlock, the northernmost gate leading into Gallanse. At their head rode the magus, his white cape billowing behind him. To the rear of the formation, a like number of soldiers followed, clothed in chainmail and the scarlet cloaks of the Blood Watch. Between them, riding on a stallion the color of newly fallen snow, was Dragomir. Next to him was his grim-faced general. Cobal's eyes were fixed on the magus as he expertly guided his gray mare in the midst of the company.

A mile from the city's gates they rode, passing by the blue-green waters of the Emerald Bay on their right. Abruptly the sound changed from the sharp staccato of horseshoes on stone to the dull thrum of metal over sunbaked earth. The road veered away from the shoreline, heading further inland and leaving the waters of the bay behind. The highway was lined with laurels whose green foliage rose toward the sky overhead. Interspersed among them were the gnarled trunks of olive trees beginning to flower a pale yellow with the coming of spring. They continued onward for a mile, perhaps two, until the magus raised his hand and slowed the company to brisk walk.

Leaning in toward the prince, Cobal spoke quietly, just above the sound of hooves.

"I have sent word to your father, highness," Cobal said, carefully swatting away a wasp that had flown too close.

The prince gave him a dark look. "That runs counter to what Eliphas ordered," the prince muttered in response, with a furtive look toward the magus.

"*He* does not command here, highness; *you* do," Cobal replied, his tone biting.

Dragomir glanced at his general in mild annoyance. "*He* has convinced both the Baron of Tybir and the Baron of Pallistar to cast their votes in my favor, which is more than his predecessor ever accomplished," the prince said evenly. "Eliphas assures me we can add the azure and gray of Chard to our ranks as well. With those votes, I'll have the majority I need to ascend the throne. Eliphas has done well since Anir's...dismissal."

The reins in Cobal's hands whitened. "Since Anir's *execution*," he spat, struggling to keep his voice down. "This magus has no idea what he's doing. I sat in on those meetings too, highness.

Intimidating Antikas and threatening Baird? Should High Lord Waymon learn that his vassals are plotting with you, it's liable to start a civil war."

"'Ware your tone, commander," Dragomir said, turning his attention back to the road. "Don't pretend to play at politics; it does not suit you. Your job is to keep me safe—that is all."

Cobal glanced around him before guiding his mare closer to the prince. "I cannot protect you when *these* are the men I've been assigned," he said softly, reaching for his waterskin.

"They are of the Blood Watch, are they not?" Dragomir asked evenly.

The general unfastened the top of his container, careful not to spill the contents. He drank deeply, trying to retain hold of his temper. Carefully, he replaced the stopper and let the waterskin fall to his side.

"My men have been replaced," Cobal murmured, "by these…criminals."

Dragomir shrugged his shoulders. "I fail to see your issue, general. One squad is as good as another."

Cobal cursed under his breath. "Are you so naïve, highness?"

"You had best let it lie, commander," Dragomir answered, with a meaningful glance toward Eliphas. "Or you will go the same way as Anir."

"There are more than a thousand men in the Blood Watch, my prince," Cobal continued relentlessly. "How is it that the worst of them ended up here? Now of all times?"

Pulling a handkerchief from his saddlebag, Dragomir wiped at his brow. "Blast it, but it's warm tonight," he muttered.

"Are you listening to me?" Cobal hissed, close to losing his patience.

"Is that not the fabled Captain Sinclair?" Dragomir answered, nodding toward the second man from the front. Absently, he put the dusty handkerchief back in his saddlebag. "It's said he's quite the swordsman, likely to compete for Dagor in The Great Games two years hence. I, for one, am happy he's here to protect me."

"He would cut your throat for a bent copper coin," Cobal said with disgust. "He never should have been given the scarlet cloak, no matter what his skill with the blade."

The foliage had become thicker all around them. Instead of continuing on the road, Eliphas signaled the company to step into the forest. They moved more slowly now, ducking under low-hanging tree limbs.

"Where are we going?" mumbled Dragomir, leaning over the pommel of his saddle.

Cobal, now riding directly behind the prince, glanced at the next man in line behind him. "You see the brute riding at our back?" he asked softly. "That is Barthon. I filed charges against him three months ago. He raped a young woman."

For the first time Dragomir looked concerned. "I thought it was a slave girl from the poor quarter?" Dragomir queried with pursed lips.

"It was a grieving widow who was kneeling at the grave of her husband," Cobal rumbled in disgust.

"That's not what I heard," Dragomir said with a shrug. "One isolated incident should not derail the career of a fine enlisted man."

"It's hardly isolated," Cobal said, his voice like ice. "I have *seen* his exploits in the field. The gods only know how many such atrocities have not been reported. The thought of him wearing the scarlet makes me sick."

"Are you finished?" Dragomir asked, failing to mask his growing irritation.

"Not by half, highness," Cobal continued, his normally taciturn face flush with anger. "Just in front of you rides Vars, the sadist, who tortures his enemies before killing them. Saddled next to him is Broteus, the sodomite. Look around you. Scum, every one of them. These are the men sent to keep you..."

Cobal was cut short as the procession came to a halt inside a small clearing, scarcely large enough to fit them all.

"Highness, general, join me," Eliphas said, dismounting from his brown gelding.

"What are we doing out here?" asked Cobal, absently rubbing the neck of his mare.

"Captain Sinclair," Eliphas continued, ignoring the question, "we should not be long. Keep our mounts ready for us upon our return."

A whipcord lean man sporting a dark beard saluted curtly in response.

"Barthon, Vars," the magus continued, motioning two of the guards forward, "join us."

A large man in his mid-thirties dismounted swiftly and strode forward. Barthon's pockmarked face wore a perpetual scowl. Mimicking his actions was a second man with cold, dark eyes. Sporting a neatly trimmed goatee, Vars looked younger than his thirty-four winters. Both moved well, each displaying the trim build marking those who spent hours practicing with the sword.

Leading his mare toward the magus, Cobal spoke, anger apparent in his words. "I asked you a question, magus. You will answer."

"Come, my prince, general," Eliphas said softly. "Your questions will be answered soon enough."

With that, the magus walked briskly into the thicket.

"After you, general," Barthon said coolly, bowing his head.

Cobal eyed Dragomir, who smiled and climbed off his stallion. "Let's see what he has in store for us."

Cobal sighed and dismounted stiffly. "Stay close to the prince," he ordered the two watchmen quietly.

Barthon's pitted face turned upward with a smile. He and Vars turned and strode into the thicket, Dragomir following closely behind. Cobal loosened his sword in its scabbard and trod warily after his prince.

The five made their way through the undergrowth of the forest as the sun approached the horizon. In front of them was a massive laurel tree, half again as tall as any they had seen. Hanging from one of the bottom branches was a nest buzzing with hundreds of wasps. Eliphas raised his hand, calling for a halt.

"What is it?" Cobal asked, his green eyes searching the surroundings.

"He is here," whispered the emotionless voice of the magus in explanation.

Stepping from behind a thicket of chaparral came a man wearing a conical hat of straw. Cobal's hand dropped immediately to the hilt of his sword. Barthon and Vars swiftly followed suit, flanking the prince defensively.

"What treachery is this?" barked Cobal, staring balefully at the magus.

"There is no treachery here," answered Eliphas coolly.

"Who is this person?" Dragomir asked, taking in the man's muddy tunic and leggings with a dark look.

"May I present Ry'Tung, your highness," Eliphas answered softly. "He's here to help you secure the Gray Throne."

"This…peasant?" Dragomir asked dubiously.

Dressed in the nondescript brown twill of a farmer, the man stood quietly, studying them all with a pair of almond shaped eyes.

"Highness," Cobal said softly. "Look at him. He does not hail from these parts. He is of the Seven Provinces."

Dragomir's visage turned to a scowl. "We came all the way out here for this?" he asked, with the hint of a sneer. "What can this…foreigner… possibly do that my own Blood Watch cannot?" he continued with anger.

"He has his uses, highness," the magus answered simply.

The prince snorted, not bothering to hide his skepticism.

Cobal noted signs of irritation from the magus, for the first time since Anir's death. Eliphas narrowed his gaze at Dragomir and squared his jaw as though clenching his teeth in frustration. The general blinked and the mage's visage returned to its steady calm, all signs of irritation gone.

"Tell me, highness," Eliphas began, his voice steady, "what prevents you from ordering your Watchmen to kill Conidon?"

"The High Lord's Peace," Dragomir answered after a moment's thought.

"What is that?" the magus asked.

It was the general who answered. "If any lord—or man under his command—draws a weapon in aught but self-defense, he forfeits all claim to the throne. It has been so since Luther, First Lord of Gallanse, three centuries past."

"Luther the Betrayer," Dragomir said bitterly under his breath.

"In the absence of the High Lord's Peace, would you order your men to kill Conidon?" the magus asked.

Dragomir shook his head. "Nothing is so simple, magus. The Blood Watch may house the finest blademasters in all of the world, but the soldiers of Conidon's Home Guard are well trained. My squad of twenty could not hope to defeat his thousands."

Eliphas nodded his head thoughtfully. "I agree with you in one regard, highness. Lord Conidon *is* too well-guarded here in his own castle. The same cannot be said for High Lords Dillion and Fallon."

For a long moment there was silence as Dragomir considered those implications. "What is it you are suggesting, magus? Kill both under the very roof of our host?"

Eliphas smiled. "Think of how it would make Conidon look."

The prince paused and shook his head after a moment's consideration. "Even if I gave such an order, my men would be seen. *I* would be guilty of breaking the peace."

"That is the purpose of Ry'Tung's presence," Eliphas said with a smile. "He cannot be connected to you in any way. He will kill Dillion and Fallon. You and your men will be in the clear."

"By the gods," thundered Cobal, turning to the magus, "I've heard enough!" Fury was etched on his face. "You would bring in this assassin and risk war with every city in Shaara?"

"An assassin?" Dragomir asked, turning his eyes once more to the short man standing in front of them.

"Look at him," Cobal hissed, nodding toward Ry'Tung. "Hair of ebony, skin the color of summer wheat, almond shaped eyes." He turned his gaze to Eliphas, not bothering to hide his contempt. "I have knowledge of the Night Tong, the Order of the White Iris, and half a dozen other cults of *Hashin*. What you are suggesting is treason of the highest order. It is entirely without honor!"

Motioning to Barthon and Vars, the general barked a command. "Restrain the magus. If he resists in any way, kill him."

With a steely rasp, both men slid their swords free and strode toward Eliphas.

"Highness," Cobal said, turning back to Dragomir. "I suggest you inform your father of this treachery. Send a report and leave out nothing…"

"I would belay that order, Prince Dragomir," said the calm voice of Eliphas.

Turning back to the magus, they saw Barthon and Vars standing next to him, facing the general.

"Restrain him," Cobal repeated with a frown.

"No," Vars said with a toothy grin. "We don't take orders from you, old man."

Cobal cast his gaze from one to the other and his eyes narrowed. "I wondered why my men were replaced with filth like you. Tell me, magus," he continued glancing at Eliphas. "Did the order even come from Dagor, or did you scour the Watch for vultures like these?"

Barthon snorted with laughter. "I volunteered, general. Your testimony sent me to the stocks for three weeks, and for what? Some scrawny piece of ass?"

Cobal's face flushed with anger. "You forced yourself on a grieving woman, you sick bastard! Damn near killed her in the process."

"Cost me my promotion," grumbled Vars, twirling his sword expertly. "Since I was the sergeant on duty."

"You held her down for him, you twisted cock," sneered Cobal. "You couldn't perform yourself unless she screamed. Isn't that right?"

Drawing his sword, Cobal spoke to Dragomir. "Highness, get out of here. Go back to the clearing. Get on your horse and run. These traitorous pups cannot hope to defeat me in time to catch you."

Barthon smiled with contempt. "You are an old man, well past your prime. I've been looking forward to this."

"Highness, go—now!" Cobal barked, knowing Barthon spoke the truth.

"Stand fast, highness," Eliphas stated, his voice cool. "There is something you should see."

"You said we could kill him," growled Barthon.

"I want to hear this bastard beg for mercy," added Vars hungrily.

"Patience," the magus said in his cool voice.

"Stop this, all of you," Dragomir snapped, his voice steady. "This has gone far enough. No one is killing anyone today."

Drawing a small piece of parchment from inside his robes, the magus looked at the prince. "I have something here, highness. I hoped I wouldn't need it to convince you, but—you leave me little choice."

With a wave of his hand, the parchment floated gently over to the prince, who neatly snatched it from the air.

"I intercepted that message late last night," the magus continued. "It was meant for your father. If you would be so good as to read it, aloud."

Dragomir unrolled the parchment and began to read.

Rexor, Eliphas cannot be trusted. My men replaced—why? Anir is dead, and Dragomir has failed miserably. Please advise. Cobal

"That is your stamp upon this letter, is it not, commander?" Eliphas said with a cold smile.

The silence of the clearing was broken only by the faint buzzing of the wasps working fastidiously in the last hour of the setting sun.

Dragomir's eyes came to rest upon the general. "I'm a miserable failure?" he asked quietly. "In what way, commander?"

Cobal sighed, knowing he had been outmaneuvered by the magus. "In every way, highness," he answered honestly. "Ever since your mother's death, you have let fear rule your heart."

"Do not speak of my mother!" he hissed in sudden vehemence. "She has nothing to do with this. I am not weak, nor am I am failure!" Dragomir raged.

"The magus is using you," Cobal replied, drawing his sword. "The same way your father has used you. The same way everyone in your life has used you since the day you were born. They will cast you aside the moment you stop being useful."

Dragomir's eyes narrowed in hate. "My father needs me. Dagor needs me! I am the heir," he pointed his finger at Cobal. "It is you who have lost your value, general."

Turning to the Watchmen, Dragomir issued a command. "Kill him. Kill the general, and I'll see you promoted to lieutenant, both of you."

Barthon's eyes lit up and Vars gave another toothy grin. Before either man could advance, the magus raised his hand.

"While I appreciate the desire for vengeance, you will stay your wrath a moment longer."

"What the hell for?" Barthon asked, his temper flaring.

Ignoring the question, Eliphas addressed Dragomir directly. "You asked what use Ry'Tung might be? I thought a demonstration might be in order." Looking back to the small man, Eliphas spoke, his voice simple and direct.

"Disarm the general, but do not kill him. I promised the Watchmen their sport."

Cobal's eyes flicked to his prince and then to the assassin. Wasting no time, he rushed forward, hoping to take the assassin by surprise.

The tiny man had not blinked through the entire exchange. His gray eyes turned to Cobal with no emotion. He stood with his arms crossed as the general moved forward.

Cobal had drawn close enough and struck, knowing he still had to face Barthon and Vars. Despite his sixty years, the general thrust his blade forward with a strength and speed honed by years of training.

Faster than any of them would have believed possible, Ry'Tung sidestepped the lunge. One moment he was in line with the blade; the next he wasn't.

Before Cobal could react, the small man kicked out with tremendous force and struck just below his knee. An audible snap could be heard as the general crashed to the ground, screaming in pain. Cobal's leg had been snapped at the shin from the assassin's lightning kick. He rocked back and forth on the ground, holding his shattered leg with both hands.

Dragomir blinked in surprise. The foreigner had scarcely moved. He was standing in nearly the same spot he had occupied all along. His gray eyes had not changed at all. He simply stood there, observing the downed general.

The prince stepped to Cobal, who was struggling to regain his feet. Dragomir wore a look of fury and contempt. Angrily he kicked out at the general's already broken leg, striking it harshly. Cobal screamed in agony, writhing in pain.

"Who is the failure now?" roared the enraged prince.

Dragomir walked in a slow circle around Cobal, speaking softly. "You have failed, general, in both your duty to me, and to Dagor."

"Highness, please…" pleaded Cobal, his voice shattered in agony.

"Did I tell you to speak?" thundered the prince.

Cobal looked up, eyes begging for mercy. Dragomir slammed Cobal's jaw with his fist. "Do not look at me! Keep your disgusting face on the ground like the worm you are!"

Dragomir turned to Barthon and Vars, barking orders. "Remove his armor, cloak, and sword. After that, he is yours."

Dragomir looked to the magus. "You were right," the prince said, glancing at Ry'Tung. "He does have his uses."

"That was executed well, highness," Eliphas stated, smiling at the prince. Turning to the Watchmen, the magus spoke quickly. "You have a quarter turn of the hourglass. Join us when you are done."

Placing his hand around the prince's shoulder, the magus motioned for Ry'Tung to follow him. The three left the clearing just as Barthon smiled and drew a heavy-handled knife.

"Wait," Vars said, looking thoughtfully at the hive of wasps. "Cut me some stakes," he said thoughtfully. From inside his pack, the youthful-looking watchman began to unravel a coil of rope.

"Can't we just cut on him?" the pockmarked man complained.

"We will," Vars answered, smiling. "But let's stake him to the ground first, under that hive. I've got some honey in my pack. I'll smear it all over his skin, so when we leave him to bleed to death, the forest will take its toll, nice and slow."

As Dragomir walked away, he could not block out the distant screams of his fallen general.

Chapter 5

C hameleon stirred at the sound of distant thunder. She could see the storm forming, a storm she had seen before. Dark clouds swirled against the red sky of dawn. Steadily the clouds grew, billowing out of the east until their strength threatened to blot out the light of the rising sun.

Inside her mind's eye she saw herself standing upon a barren shore, looking out at a vast body of water, larger than any she'd ever known. No wind blew here, nothing that would cause so much as a ripple.

Echoing from the skies behind her, Chameleon heard a bestial roar. Turning sharply, she saw a huge, winged serpent, covered from head to toe in ebony scales. The creature was streaking toward the growing darkness, its massive wings beating mightily overhead. Heart hammering in her chest, Chameleon ducked low, praying the creature would pass her by. Fortune was with her; the serpent sped past, taking no notice of the tribeswoman. Instead, the beast continued east, racing toward the ominous horizon. Narrowing her gaze, Chameleon caught a glimpse of something, a shining silver object clenched tightly in the serpent's claws. As she watched the winged monstrosity grow smaller with each passing moment, a second cry sounded from the skies above. This time she saw a white eagle, proud and majestic. Its golden eyes were locked upon the retreating form of the serpent. The eagle sped after it, screaming in defiance. She watched until it, too, disappeared against the rising darkness.

Shifting her gaze away from the water, Chameleon tried to make some sense of it all. *"This isn't real,"* she thought. *"They are visions of my own making."* Closing her eyes, Chameleon fought to regain her focus. *"I must find my center."*

An outside pressure began to build at the edge of her subconscious.

"Another attack," she cursed, trying to shield her mind. Despite her mental prowess, Chameleon found she could not match the power set against her. These intrusions to her psyche held a strength like nothing she had ever known. Already weak from days of travel, Chameleon knew she could not hold back the tide.

Like a floodgate opening, dozens of images filled her mind, images she did not comprehend. A dusky throne wet with blood, the heads of two snakes facing one another, a clear glass bowl filled with lush, red berries, a quartet of faded bronze coins. She fought to maintain tenuous hold upon her sanity as the barrage continued. A white and green banner sporting the head of a wolf, a carved obsidian scepter, a barrel of fetid water, a pale violet flower. One after another, like an avalanche they came.

Slowly—ever so slowly—the visions ground to a halt. Chameleon was left gasping for breath. The pause, however, gave her no solace. The last image, she knew, was still to come.

Lurking at the furthest edge of her subconscious, she saw them. Two figures cloaked in shadow; she could *feel* them watching her. Shapeless at first, they slowly took form. With eyes as black as onyx, feathers the color of midnight, they appeared as two birds of darkness. Long steeped in the legends of her people, Chameleon knew what they were. Sentinels of the netherworld, guardians of the dead, harbingers of doom.

They were the Raven and the Crow.

Their image lasted only moments, fading quickly. Chameleon shuddered. The sight of the two creatures was unnerving. Whispered to be hunters of lost souls, Chameleon could not help but feel she had become their prey.

Something else was watching.

An awareness she'd not sensed before. A new presence, one filled with power. The same power that had overcome her defenses.

"*Awaken*," it pulsed a thought into her mind.

Chameleon sat up with a gasp.

She was in a clearing of tall evergreen trees, the ground blanketed with reddish orange needles that had fallen the previous autumn. Far to her right ran a stream, the sound of its eddies bubbling faintly in her ear. She was wrapped in a woolen blanket, lying next to a fire that had burned down to embers. In the distance, she could hear the faint roar of a waterfall.

Chameleon's eyes grew wide as memory of her recent near-death experience returned.

What had become of the magada? How had she survived the fall? Who had made the fire?

A cool breeze blew off the eastern side of the mountain, caressing her face, though she did not feel its gentle touch above her right eye. Curious, Chameleon ran her fingers gently across her temple. Someone had bandaged the cut.

I need to leave this place, Chameleon thought, scrambling to her feet. The brisk spring air hit her skin and she gasped in shock. She realized a moment too late that she was completely naked under the blanket. Bending over quickly, she tore the blanket off the ground from where it lay crumpled around her ankles. Chameleon pulled the coarse wool over the light brown skin of her chest and shoulders in an effort to cover herself.

"About time you woke up," a voice said from behind her.

Whirling, Chameleon nearly fell in surprise. Standing in front of her was a man, lean and well-muscled. His face was young, perhaps only a year or two older than her own twenty winters. He was absently scratching his neck and wearing nothing but a tiny loincloth that did little to hide his olive-colored skin.

"Careful," he warned, the corners of his mouth curling in disapproval. "I didn't go through all the trouble of saving you just to see you crack your skull open."

"Where are my clothes?" Chameleon demanded, her flushed face twisted in anger.

The man narrowed his brown eyes in irritation. "Did that drop from the falls blind you or something?" With an annoyed gesture he motioned off to Chameleon's left, to the far side of the fire. "Your clothes are drying on the rock behind you."

Brushing dark hair from in front of her eyes, she saw her doeskin leggings and tunic spread neatly on a lichen-covered boulder. Propped up on a small stone near the fire were her worn hide boots. She was surprised to see that they'd been brushed clean. At the sound of movement, Chameleon turned to see the stranger moving toward her.

Shuffling backward, Chameleon wrapped the blanket more tightly around her shoulders, not knowing what to expect.

The man ignored her completely.

He looks like a hawk, she thought, watching him close, *and moves like a hunter. I must be wary.*

He sat down on a flat rock near the fire, where a second set of clothing had been laid out in similar fashion to her own. A sudden thought occurred to Chameleon, and her face flushed with anger.

"Did *you* undress me?" she snapped, accusation dripping from her tongue.

"No," he answered bluntly. "My brother did." He picked his forest-green shirt off the rock and pulled it over a tangle of chestnut hair. "I was busy prying my own clothing off last night so that I wouldn't freeze to death."

Chameleon was at a loss. She didn't know where she was or how she'd gotten here. Worst of all was the strange presence of this man. With his terse manner and distant attitude, she'd taken an instant disliking to him. Chameleon drew breath to speak, but he cut her off with a wave of his hand.

"Look," he began, sliding his legs into dark gray trousers, "as much as I'd love to chat it up this morning, I'm pressed for time. I want to know who you are and what in the name of the gods you're doing way the hell up here in the mountains? After saving your skin, I think you owe me an explanation."

She glared at him. Before she could stop herself, the words came out.

"I don't like you," she hissed.

"I don't give a shit," he fired back.

"Ever the cordial gentleman, aren't you Kil?" came another voice from behind a large boulder off to Chameleon's left. She watched as a second fellow, this one taller and leaner than the first, came strolling up to the fire. She noticed immediately that his hawk-like face was nearly identical to that of his companion. He carried a longbow of yew in one hand and a small sack in the other. "Did you even introduce yourself?" he continued.

"We've lingered here long enough," grunted the first, pulling on his scuffed black boots. "We should've left already."

"You'll have to excuse my brother," the newcomer said, leaning the longbow up against a tree. "He's usually not this bad tempered till the afternoon." Reaching forward, he picked up Chameleon's clothing and handed it to her. "Here, you might be more comfortable talking to us after you get dressed."

Chameleon looked at his outstretched hand as if it were holding a snake. Never taking her eyes from him, Chameleon snatched up her belongings, careful not to let the blanket drop.

"My name's Zedaine," said the taller of the two, his voice friendly. "This sour miscreant," he continued motioning toward the first, "is my brother, Kildare. He's very pleased to meet you."

"Shut up, Zee," Kildare growled, buckling on his sword belt.

Zedaine laughed with genuine humor. "Why don't you stoke the fire, Kil? Perhaps its warmth will lighten your mood."

"So every magada within twenty miles can see exactly where we are?" Kildare answered acidly. "No thanks."

Zedaine shrugged. "Fine. I'll do it." He took the sack in his hand and flung it toward Kildare, where it landed with a thud on his chest. "You can clean the rabbits. I'd like to eat something besides hard tack and dried fruit before we set out today."

Kildare stared daggers at Zedaine. Angrily tearing his knife out of its sheath, he pointed it at his younger brother. "We'll eat first. After that, we're leaving." Without waiting for a response, he emptied the sack and went about his task of skinning two large coney.

Underneath the blanket, Chameleon had been struggling to pull on her clothes. The tunic and leggings were a bit damp, but it was better than being naked in front of the two men. She was not in the habit of trusting strangers, especially out here in the wild. The sooner she got away from them, the better. Neither was paying any particular attention to her. With luck, she could slip away before being missed. Picking up her boots, she struggled to pull them on as quietly as she could.

"You think they'll come today?" Kildare was asking.

"The magada?" Zedaine questioned. "Unlikely. It's not any warmer up here than it was yesterday, and we've kept the smoke to a minimum. I couldn't see it from the falls."

"I'd almost forgotten," Kildare said, shaking his head. "Did you find any?"

"Zedaine flashed a triumphant smile. "*Two* were blooming this morning, if you can believe it. They were right next to each other, where a little patch of sunlight broke though the shade of the trees. I harvested them before checking the traps."

"That makes three then, with the one I found at dusk," Kildare said, eyebrows raised in surprise. "If yours were truly in blossom."

Zedaine opened a small pouch on his belt. "You think you're better than me in the mountains because you got lucky yesterday?" he scoffed. "Take a look."

He pulled out a pair of plants. Both the stem and leaves were dark green in color. The flower itself was a pale violet. "*Viasha*," he said with a smirk, "two of them."

Kildare grunted, but said nothing.

Chameleon was stunned. The sight of the violet flower was like a slap in the face. It was identical to the one she'd seen in her visions only minutes ago.

Abandoning the idea of escape, Chameleon stood and walked quite deliberately toward Zedaine. "Where did you come by that?" she demanded.

Zedaine cocked an eyebrow toward Chameleon, but it was Kildare who spoke.

"I see you've decided to stick around." It was not a question.

"What do you mean?" she asked.

"Don't play with me, girl," he answered. "A moment ago, you were ready to light out of here."

Instead of showing the surprise she felt, Chameleon glared at him icily.

"How far do you think you'd have gotten before we ran you down?"

"Answer my question," she said, in lieu of a response.

"Not until you answer mine," he shot back. "You've had a change of heart because of that flower," he said pointing at the *Viasha*. "Why?"

Chameleon said nothing. She stood, stubbornly facing Kildare.

The elder brother sighed and swore under his breath. "Why do I always have to be the bigger person?" he muttered. "We could sit here all day, you and I," he said, pointing at Chameleon. "You could yell at me with that pretty face and those pouty lips, but it will get us nowhere. You don't trust me; that's understandable. In your position, I'd feel the same way."

He stood up and leaned toward her, his voice quiet. "But if we'd wanted you dead, we could have left you to the magada, or strangled you last night while you slept. I'd just as soon *not* kill someone I went through all that trouble to save, but you need to start talking."

In answer, Chameleon crossed her arms defiantly in front of her.

Zedaine snorted at them both. "We've finally met someone as pig-headed as you," he laughed.

"I'm not..." Kildare protested.

"You might be a great swordsman," Zedaine said, cutting him off. "But you're the absolute *worst* at making people comfortable." Shaking his head, the younger of the two sat down, tucking the *Viasha* back into his pouch.

"Be that as it may," Kildare said sharply to Zedaine. "She *will* answer me." His tone left no room for argument.

Chameleon's mind was racing. Kildare's eyes were hard, unforgiving. *He is formidable*, she thought, considering once again the possibility of flight.

Seeing her tense, Zedaine spoke, his voice thoughtful. "Kildare is right about one thing. We could have let you die yesterday, but neither of us wanted that. I know it isn't easy, but you're going to have to trust us, lass. We may be a rough-looking pair, but we aren't evil."

Chameleon shifted her gaze to Zedaine, peering into his dark eyes. She could sense no lie there, no deceit. Only an honest concern for her well-being. *Remember why you left,* she thought to herself. She needed answers, and it was possible that these men had them.

Chameleon let out a nearly imperceptible sigh. *So be it.*

Standing at her full height, Chameleon placed her right hand over her heart. "I am Chameleon of the Black Pond Drannock, daughter of Mountain's Ford and Golden Sky. I am the First Wanderer of my people." Taking her hand off her chest, she opened it, palm to the sky, in a gesture of friendship.

"Well met," Zedaine said with a smile.

Kildare's face, however, held a look of surprise. "*You* are one of the Drannock?" he questioned.

"You know of my people?" she asked, a bit more harshly than she'd intended. The Ab'dural Valley was hidden far to the south. No one outside of the Drannock knew of its existence…or so it had been believed. "How?" she demanded.

Kildare rubbed the stubble on his chin absently. "I've heard of them," he admitted to Chameleon.

"What have you heard?" she challenged.

Kildare sat back down and resumed his work on their meal. "I've heard they live in the southern parts of these mountains," he answered, skewering the rabbits on a pair of sharp sticks. "It's rumored that they have strange powers, though that is unconfirmed. That's the extent of my knowledge."

"Where did you come by this information?" Chameleon asked.

Kildare's face hardened. "From a tight-lipped sage who has some explaining to do," he growled in reply.

"How come you know about this tribe, and I don't?" Zedaine asked, raking the smoldering coals with a stick.

Kildare grunted loudly. "Because you were busy talking to that blue-eyed serving girl at The Wild Boar the night Blade and I discussed it."

Zedaine smiled in remembrance. "Ah yes, that was Sherri... no, Carri! That was a good night."

Kildare rolled his eyes, placing both spits over the hot coals.

Zedaine turned back to Chameleon. "I fear we are neglecting our guest," he said. "I expect you have questions. I'll do what I can to answer them. Ask away."

Chameleon sat back down, draping the blanket over her shoulders once again. "How is it you came to find me yesterday?" she asked. "All the way up here in the mountains?"

"What's the last thing you remember?" Zedaine asked, extending his hands toward the fire, rubbing them together.

"Going over the falls," she replied. "There was a pack of magada and caniadon chasing after me."

The brothers looked at one another for a moment until Kildare waved his hand toward Zedaine. "You tell her. I'll keep an eye on the food."

Zedaine reached behind himself, grabbing his pack, and placed it on the ground between his legs. Reaching a hand inside one of the pockets, he pulled out a handful of dried biscuits. He handed one to Chameleon, who bit into it ravenously. "I caught sight of you leaping into the water," he began. "We made a beeline for the falls, but by the time we got there, you'd already gone over."

"It was a miracle you survived," mumbled Kildare, biting into a piece of dried fruit he'd pulled from his own pack.

"True," Zedaine affirmed. "I ran into the trees to gather wood for a fire while Kildare jumped in the water to save you."

Chameleon almost choked on her biscuit. "You saved me?" she asked, looking at the elder brother.

"That was before I knew you," he said with an oily smirk. "If we had to do it again, I'd have thrown *him* in," he continued, motioning to his brother.

"Could we try to remain pleasant to one another?" Zedaine intervened, raising his eyebrow.

"Zedaine is better at making fires," Kildare explain with a sigh, "and I'm the stronger swimmer."

"In what world are *you* the stronger swimmer?" Zedaine said, throwing a piece of his biscuit at Kildare.

"In every world," Kildare replied in annoyance. "What difference does it make who did what? Just get on with it."

Rubbing at the stubble on his cheek, Zedaine continued. "Once Kildare pulled you from the water, I got you out of those wet clothes. Between my body heat and the warmth of the fire, we were able to keep you from freezing to death last night. Kil cleaned that scratch over your eye this morning. Once the blood clotted, I covered it up the best I could. It wasn't deep and should heal in a few days."

Chameleon sat quietly a moment in thought. "What of the magada?" she asked finally.

Zedaine paused and glanced at Kildare.

"They followed you," Zedaine said with a sigh, turning the rabbit in front of him. The smell of roasting meat reminded Chameleon of how long it had been since she'd eaten a full meal.

"Here," Kildare said to Chameleon, tossing her what was left of the dried fruit he had been eating. "I can hear your stomach rumbling."

Deftly catching the fruit, Chameleon stared hard at the pair. "So, what happened to the magada?" she persisted, sinking her teeth into the food.

"We had to kill them," Zedaine answered curtly, passing Chameleon his water skin.

Chameleon took it and drank deeply. "All four?" she asked, wiping her mouth and handing the skin back to Zedaine.

"Yes, all four," Kildare answered, lifting his gaze to his brother, "along with their mounts."

Chameleon was stunned. Magada did not go down easily, especially when paired with caniadon. "How?"

Zedaine exhaled, absently chewing his food. "It wasn't easy," he said.

"Easier for some than others," Kildare mumbled under his breath.

Zedaine looked at his brother with something akin to disgust. "We went over this last night, Kil. I did exactly what you said, I started getting the fire ready. How was I supposed to know the magada found a way down?"

"I yelled for you three times," Kildare snapped back.

"It was two times, and I ran over the instant I heard you," Zedaine argued.

"So you say," Kildare replied dubiously.

"I took out the big one, didn't I?" Zedaine questioned sarcastically.

"Took your sweet time about it," Kildare muttered. "I'm lucky to be alive."

Zedaine gave a harsh laugh. "Oh please, I saw you. You were having the time of your life, laying about with your sword left and right! The magada never had a chance."

"That last mount and his rider almost had me," Kildare argued.

"I know—that's why I shot them," Zedaine answered flatly.

Neither spoke for several moments. The only sound that could be heard was the quiet sizzle of roasting meat.

"Anyway," Zedaine said, turning his attention back to Chameleon. "That's the story of how you came to be with us."

Chameleon cast her gaze from one to the other. It was clear they had saved her life, both from the magada and the icy water of the mountain stream. She shuddered in remembrance of the shock of cold she'd felt upon leaping in. Despite her distrust of outsiders, it was clear that these men had risked much to save her—a person they'd never met. She owed these men her life.

"Thank you for saving me," Chameleon said grudgingly.

"You can thank us by explaining why that flower is so important to you," Kildare answered. He turned his spit over, and the aroma of roasted meat inundated Chameleon. She felt her mouth begin to water.

Zedaine ripped off a haunch of the rabbit in front of him and handed it over to Chameleon. "Careful," he said, "it's hot."

Taking it gingerly in her hands, she set it down on a small stone, waiting for it to cool.

"I will tell you how I came to be here," she said, "and why that flower is so important to me."

"Finally," Kildare uttered under his breath.

Chapter 6

A cool wind blew off the Emerald Bay, carrying a last vestige of winter through the bustling docks of Gallanse. The breeze sent a shiver down the back of a leather-faced fishmonger unloading his catch upon the salt-crusted wharf. He shuddered, gesturing with his hands in a sign meant to ward off evil spirits, before turning back to his work.

The wind made its way up the gradual slope of the city, until reaching the sandstone bulwark of the castle's outer wall. There it ascended the central tower above the throne room, where it whipped the blue and white banner of Gallanse into a trembling sail. The cold found its way through an open window, blowing in above a sconce near the Gray Throne. The ivory-colored candle housed within was quite suddenly snuffed out.

Princess Lydia glanced at the candle, distracted by its strange behavior. *Blown out in the still air of the great hall?* she mused to herself. Her eyes followed the smoke as it slowly wound its way through the vast space of the enormous room, until making its escape through the open window. She reluctantly turned her attention once again to the matters of court, wishing that she, too, could leave.

Lydia sat next to her father's throne, listening to the seemingly inexhaustible deliberations of suitors, advisors, pages, and their cohorts. Most sought to gain favor with her father or one of the other powerful lords in attendance. For weeks now she had watched them scheme and plot among one another, all in an effort to become her husband.

No, she reminded herself, *not to become my husband. That ploy is just an excuse—an inconvenience they would say.*

None of them would give her so much as a glance. Each wished to become High Lord of Gallanse; *that* was the real prize. Marriage to the princess was nothing more than a means to an end.

She shifted uncomfortably in her straight-backed chair, knowing the next hour would not pass quickly.

"Stop fidgeting about," clucked the voice of Madora, from behind her. "Be glad you are seated on a goose down cushion rather than standing on the hard stone, like me."

It took the princess some effort to keep from rolling her eyes at her soubrette. "Says the girl who did not return to my quarters until an hour past dawn. Do tell me, Madora, from whose bed did you arrive? Was it the gallant, blue-eyed corporal of the Lion Guard? Or was it the rugged sergeant-at-arms who serves the silver and red?"

"'Twas neither," she sniffed, absently touching her strawberry blonde curls.

"You came from someone's bed," quipped the princess smugly. "I caught a hint of quim upon your arrival."

"Hush, child," her father said, with a disapproving glance. "Your lady-in-waiting has her own assignments, as do you."

She glanced at her father and her smile faded.

High Lord Conidon was weary, but sat alertly upon his throne. The blue mantle of High Lord was draped across his thin shoulders. His health had been waning for weeks. Hours ago, he lay in his bed, an ailing old man not long for this world. It was only this morning that his health had rallied, baffling his medical staff. His color had returned, and his lungs had somehow cleared overnight, returning his breathing to normal. Knowing the succession was nearing its final days, Conidon wasted no time. He called the barons and high lords to council, hoping to sway them to his way of thinking.

"I am aware of my duties, father," Lydia said, reaching out and gripping his forearm with a sad smile. She lowered her voice. "Though I doubt I enjoy them as much as Madora," she finished, with a wink at her friend.

"My lord," said a tall, light-skinned man of perhaps thirty winters. He was flanked on both sides by guards wearing tunics of green and gold emblazoned with the head of a stag. With practiced ease, the man raised his fingers to forehead in the formal greeting of Shaarian nobility. He bowed politely, more deeply than required for one of his station. "It is good to see you looking yourself again."

Conidon smiled and inclined his head a hairsbreadth lower than necessary, repaying the courtesy. "My thanks to you, Lord Byron," he responded.

The baron of Baristal leaned toward Conidon, away from the ears of his guardsmen. "There are whispers on the wind, my lord. Rumors swirl."

"What have you heard?" Conidon asked patiently.

"It has reached my ear that prince Alexander arrived late last night," he continued quietly.

"Indeed," Conidon responded, his face calm.

Pulling at the bottom of his tunic, the baron of Baristal looked quizzically at Conidon. "It is the talk of the Great Hall."

"I see," Conidon said simply.

"Many of the thirteen are on the fence already, my lord," Byron continued, determined to make his point. "The thought of turning the city over to

Alexander… well, he is young, my lord, very young."

"Is there anything else?" Conidon asked, rather pointedly.

Byron straightened the green and gold of his tunic and frowned. "I do hope that you and Lord Dillion know what you're doing," he mumbled skeptically, stepping rather stiffly to rejoin his guards. "Else we'll fall under the shadow of the dragon."

The dark-haired princess watched as Byron bowed again and strode away, followed closely by his men. She smiled inwardly. Lydia had seen her father manipulate these noblemen against each other until most did not know whom to trust. Shaara was a deceit-filled country, even in times of peace. It was a place of political rivalries, where sworn allies changed sides in the blink of an eye to achieve greater power. The princess should have been married weeks ago, but Conidon had kept her suitors at one another's throats. No single lord had been able to claim enough support to make himself the clear successor.

"What did you learn of him?" Conidon asked, turning his head slightly toward his daughter's lady-in-waiting.

"He remains loyal to Dillion, my lord," Madora answered from behind the throne.

"As Kantik expected," rumbled a voice from the other side of the throne.

"Yes," Conidon agreed, nodding thoughtfully. "Let's send word to Kantik. Find out where we stand with Baron Lars."

"There is no need to send General Hollus," interjected Madora softly, looking at the old soldier. "Lars will follow Fallon's command. The Ice Barons will not abandon their liege, no matter how many bribes the red and gold throw at them." She paused, pursing her lips in thought. "Though Fallon himself has yet to commit one way or another."

"Where did you learn that?" Lydia asked carefully, masking her surprise. "Their guards are insanely loyal and remarkably tight-lipped."

One side of Madora's mouth twitched upward as she suppressed a smile. "Lars did not utilize the services of his favorite mistress last night... so I did."

Lydia stifled her laugh by covering her mouth with her hand.

"I might have known," General Hollus said, shaking his head in disapproval. "It seems your talents can unearth any secret, girl. Though everyone knows that women are notoriously garrulous, especially in the company of other women."

"It was Lars who confided in his mistress first," Madora responded archly. "A man spilling his secrets to a woman."

"Enough, both of you," Conidon said dryly. "Hollus, inform Kantik anyway. He needs to be kept up to speed."

"As you command," the general answered, banging his fist to chest in the warrior's salute. As quickly as he could, Hollus limped down the dais, the wooden leg below his right knee clicking softly against the stone.

"There is no need to tease him, Maddy," Lydia said, using her friend's nickname.

"He is wrong, my love," the blonde woman said, shifting in her dress. "It took me all night to get her to talk. You would not believe what I had to do. Men, on the other hand, cannot wait to sing their secrets to me, especially in the throes of passion."

"I'd wager…"

At that moment, Conidon began to cough. Lydia forgot what she was going to say as despair pulled at her heart. Taking a metallic flask from under his robes, Conidon drank deeply of its contents. As quickly as it started, the coughing fit faded away. Recovering, he turned and winked at this daughter.

"I'll shake this malady yet," he said with a wan smile.

Despite his sudden recovery, Lydia knew her father was dying. It was only a matter of weeks, perhaps even days, until that time. She had begged him to stay in bed this morning, to gather his strength. He refused her request, saying he would not lay idle while there was hope for his daughter's future.

Known only to Conidon's inner circle was her father's most desperate wish; a secret that might tear the country apart. He yearned for Lydia to become ruling lady of the city, to become the first High Lady in centuries. Unfortunately, the laws of Shaara were steadfastly set against this. Only a male could inherit and be named as successor. Unless the law was changed, she was doomed to marry one of these lords.

Weeks ago, Conidon had dispatched his diplomats to Northpass, home of Lord Fallon. There, they had managed to draft a new decree, and would be ready to present it before the next Council of Lords, set barely a fortnight from now. If her father could delay a few more days, the suitors would be forced to attend the conference, giving he and his daughter what they needed most: time. Should the decree pass, Lydia would become High Lady of Gallanse and keep the city out of enemy hands.

A short, stocky man of middle years approached the throne, forcing Lydia's wandering mind back to the present. High Lord Waymon sported a neatly trimmed mustache and eyes gleaming with immense vanity. If chosen as High Lord of Gallanse, she knew he would use the fortune entailed upon him by their marriage to do what he did best—lavish himself in riches.

"My Lord Conidon, forgive me, but how long must we wait?" he asked, speaking directly to Lydia's father in his nasal voice, completely ignoring the princess. He cast his gaze about the throne room once more. "Surely Lord Dillion knows of this meeting?"

"Perhaps something more important has come up," suggested Prince Dragomir, stepping from behind Waymon, sarcasm dripping off his tongue. "Or more likely he has simply given up on winning the High Lord's favor. I don't believe Dillion has the stomach for court politics."

Several of the gathered men, vassals to Dragomir's father, laughed at the prince's remark.

Lydia narrowed her gaze. She would rather wed *any* suitor before Dragomir. Dagor's prince was arrogant beyond belief. Worse still, he exuded a cruelty she found frightening. Servants whispered of how his concubines bore new marks and bruises every day, testament to his violent appetites. The castle staff spoke of how the prince lambasted them with profanity-laced tirades, promising violence or worse for any mistake, real or perceived.

A well of anger rose inside her. Before she could stop herself, Lydia spoke, her tone like ice.

"Surely you mean *Lord* Dillion, highness?" she said angrily. "It does not do well to insult your fellow noblemen in their absence. It only makes you look like an ill-bred mongrel."

All talk ground to a halt on the floor of the Great Hall, as Dragomir stared at her in shock. Her words had rendered everyone in the room speechless. Even her father looked surprised.

"How *dare* you speak to me like that?" Dragomir sputtered angrily. Turning to Conidon, he stepped forward, brushing past the stunned Waymon. He pointed his finger at Lydia. "I demand an apology from this insufferable daughter of yours, Conidon, or your line will end in this room tonight!"

A gasp rose from the crowd. Dragomir clasped his fingers upon his sword hilt, ready to draw steel. Falling in behind him were five of his Blood Watch, their eyes fixed on the throne. In his rage, the prince seemed to have forgotten his oath of peace; here he was, insulting Conidon and threatening Lydia in the throne room, the very center of Conidon's power. A score of Home

Guard stepped forward, preparing to defend against such an attack.

Conidon stood slowly from his throne and raised his hand. At seventy-five years of age, his body was painfully thin. His shoulders, once broad and powerful, were now stooped and frail. His wrinkled face was careworn and tired, not only from age, but from fatigue born of over forty years spent governing his city. His voice, however, was still commanding. Slow and steady, it rang out clearly, reaching everyone in the great hall from the ground floor to the upper galleries.

"You would threaten me under my own roof?" he began, voice rattling with age. "Your anger is understandable, highness," he continued, with a chastising look to his daughter, "but you are on the brink of madness. I will say this one time only: stand down, else you will forfeit all claim to the throne."

Dragomir licked his lips nervously and glanced back to his white-robed advisor, who gave him a nearly imperceptible nod. Slowly his hand left the hilt of his sword, his men following suit.

"What of the princess, Conidon?" he snarled. "She has insulted my honor."

"My daughter, I fear, does not always think before she speaks," he replied sternly. "I hope you will forgive her hasty words. They are almost certainly caused by the impetuosity of youth, and her inexperience in these matters."

Conidon turned back to Dragomir, who was looking at Lydia with contempt.

"Her message, though delivered coarsely, does ring with conviction. I know when you spoke of *Lord* Dillion," he said, stressing the title, "you made an error in judgment. Surely, you would not sully your family name by speaking at the expense of a High Lord of Shaara? Such words, uttered in the heat of the moment, can, and should, be forgiven. Wouldn't you agree?"

The pale-skinned prince glared at Conidon, looking unconvinced.

Conidon continued, his voice remaining even. "I see you are skeptical in this matter, Prince Dragomir. Perhaps you need an example of forgiveness first?"

Conidon's smile disappeared, replaced by a look of barely-suppressed fury. When he spoke, his eyes bored into the prince. "I forgive *you* for not addressing *me* as *Lord* Conidon just a moment ago, in *my* throne room, in front of *my* guests, while enjoying *my* hospitality; a crime punishable in Gallanse by flogging in the Great Square."

He narrowed his eyes and dropped his voice, so that only the prince could hear. "I will even forgive your asinine threat to my daughter. However, should you raise so much as a finger against my family, I will have you executed. Not even that whoreson Rexor will be able to save you."

The hall waited, holding its breath while Dragomir weighed Conidon's words.

The thin hand of his advisor rested suddenly upon Dragomir's shoulder. The prince glanced at it, took a breath, and stepped back. "I will think on your words, Lord Conidon. You are, of course, far wiser than most here. I would never wish to insult you or Lord Dillion."

He did not mention his threat to Lydia.

"As to your question," Conidon replied, dismissing Dragomir with a brush of his hand and turning back to Waymon, "I think the rest of you have waited long enough. We shall begin without Lord Dillion."

Lydia exhaled, not realizing that she had been holding her breath through the entire exchange. What was wrong with her? She had just insulted the son of the most powerful and ruthless high lord in the country. She glanced at Dragomir, who had withdrawn with his advisor inside a knot of his sycophants. Narrowing her gaze, she tried to focus on the advisor, but could not see him clearly through the press of people in the Great Hall.

Looking to her father, Lydia felt a sharp pang of guilt. It was barely past midday, and already he looked spent. Lydia's stupidity had forced him into that confrontation.

"Interesting," Madora mused quietly from behind her.

"What?" Lydia asked.

"Dragomir was trying to pick a fight with your father, but he didn't know what to do when *you* insulted him and he lost his temper." Lydia could hear Madora laugh quietly behind her. "You threw him for a loop, princess. Even Dragomir is not stupid enough to threaten Conidon like that. He nearly drew steel, right here in the throne room! Only his counselor's intervention saved him. Whatever he was playing at was thwarted by you."

"Ambassador Macklore, come forward," Conidon said, forcing his weary voice over the crowd as he sank back onto his throne.

From the back of the room, a man in his mid-twenties strode forward. His russet-colored hair was short and impeccably groomed. He was one of the tallest men in the room, standing well over six feet in height. He moved well, with more of a warrior's grace than an ambassador's shuffling step. In his hands he held a polished black scepter, denoting his rank as Ambassador of the Realm. The obsidian rod carried great respect in every city across the Crystalline Sea, serving as a symbol of office.

He had come a week past, hailing from the city of Brisbane to the west. He served as delegate between the two powerful cities. Thus far, he had negotiated an offer of peace and trade with great success. Conidon had asked him to stay and act as mediator between Gallanse and an independent village along the coast.

"My Lord, as always it is good to see you. I hope you are well?" Macklore spoke in a polished but friendly tone, a wide smile on his handsome face.

"Now *that's* someone I'd enjoy learning secrets from," Madora whispered to Lydia.

"Indeed, I am," Conidon replied, with a wan smile. "It is good to see you again, ambassador."

"And you, my lady," he said, shifting his attention to Lydia. "I am sorry we have not had the opportunity to meet sooner. Looking upon you is like viewing the first rose of spring. I see why your father speaks of you so highly."

It was Lydia's turn to be caught off guard. Not a single man in the Great Hall had addressed her directly in the past three weeks. She was taken completely by surprise.

"I…thank you, ambassador. You are too kind," she replied, quickly regaining her composure.

His eyes lingered on her a moment more, before he turned his attention back to Conidon.

"Shall I begin, my lord? I do not usually have the honor of addressing such a numerous and noble audience as that assembled before us today," Macklore said, gesturing to the noblemen behind him.

At his words, Lydia looked to her father. She alone was privy to what he was about to do. Normally, Conidon preferred biding his time, letting his opponents become rash or impatient. More often than not, he could take advantage of any situation, whether political or on the battlefield.

That was no longer the case.

Dragomir had consolidated his power quickly. Under the direction of his new advisor, Dagor's prince was using his influence far more aggressively. Lydia did not need reports from her father's network of spies to know that Dragomir was ready to make his move for the throne. Conidon needed to act, and now, while his strength remained.

Her eyes shifted from the ambassador to her father, as she recalled their exchange of words that morning.

"What if you're wrong?" she'd asked.

"I am not wrong," Conidon countered. "King Medyha is no fool. You think it is coincidence that the ambassador is here? Young he may be, but Macklore is his finest litigator."

"His skill in the courtroom is not in question," she'd argued. "Sadly, that is not essential right now. We need someone powerful; someone we can trust. Do you really believe the ambassador is capable of balancing Dragomir's influence?"

"A month ago I sent a missive to every ruler of the Crystalline Sea," he said quietly. "Queen Zenobia, King Asher, and a dozen others. Only one has responded, and he has sent Macklore. Whether I believe the ambassador is enough is irrelevant. He is what we have been given."

She shifted again in her seat, hoping her father was correct. Like it or not, Macklore was a piece of the game now.

"I was hoping you might humor an old man," Conidon said with a brief smile.

Lydia felt her stomach tighten in fear; once they embarked upon this path, there would be no going back.

"Of course, my lord. It would be an honor," Macklore answered with a bow.

It was time to cast the die.

Chapter 7

hameleon looked thoughtfully at the brothers, wondering where to begin. It was not a thing she shared lightly. Chameleon had scarcely been able to tell her mother. These men, however, held the mysterious flower she'd seen in her visions. Perhaps they could make some sense of it all.

"It was eleven days ago," she began. "I started having visions again, though the cursed ones know why." She noticed looks of confusion on the brothers' faces and decided to explain further. "My second naming day has already passed."

"Visions, you say?" Zedaine asked hesitantly. "Do you mean dreams?"

Chameleon shook her head. "No, dreaming occurs while asleep. Visions come while gathering psychic energy," she explained, feeling like she was speaking to a child.

"Psychic energy," Kildare said thoughtfully. "So…Blade was right, the Drannock do have powers."

"Do your people not have visions?" Chameleon asked. *How did they get their names?* she wondered to herself.

The two brothers looked at one another in bewilderment, shaking their heads. Chameleon decided to explain further.

"Visions occur only once in our lifetime, on our second naming day," she began. "From these we discover our true names. Afterward, we are thought of as adults in Drannock society. My first vision was of a reptile blending in with its surroundings. Thus, I am Chameleon," she explained.

"You're saying that should have been the end of your visions?" Kildare asked. "They're only supposed to happen once in your lifetime?"

Chameleon nodded, relieved that she had gotten her explanation across.

"But you've had another vision," Zedaine reasoned. "That's not supposed to happen, is it?"

"Whatever was in that vision has brought you out of the Drannock lands," Kildare said, scratching his chin thoughtfully.

"Yes," Chameleon said, feeling tired. "I was gathering my energy two weeks ago, and the vision came upon me quite suddenly. I saw…many things…things I don't understand…things I'd never seen before. When I asked my mother what it meant, she grew pale and pleaded that I forget them."

Chameleon reached down and grabbed the rabbit that had been cooling next to her. Blowing on it, she ripped off a piece with her teeth and began chewing mechanically.

"The next day the visions came again, stronger than before," she continued, feeling the warmth of the greasy meat slide down her throat. "It has been the same every day since. Always these images await me in my meditation. They were all I could think of, like a plague upon my mind. When I could stand it no more, I approached the council of elders and asked for their wisdom."

Her eyes narrowed and she clenched her jaw angrily.

"They would not hear me! Willow in the Brush suggested I suffered hallucinations of the *Tugura* root." Chameleon sounded disgusted. "As though I would experiment with such a dangerous toxin."

She paused, taking another bite of her rabbit leg. "There was something about that meeting…" she said, barely loud enough for Zedaine and Kildare to hear.

"What?" prompted Kildare.

Chameleon shook her head. "It's nothing," she replied, turning her thoughts back to the present.

"It's not nothing," Zedaine said. "That meeting with your elders, it's obviously bothering you. Why?"

"I don't know, but…" she trailed off, looking directly at Zedaine. "The elders are the wisest of our people, chosen for their wisdom and bravery. They are steeped in knowledge of all things Drannock; our history, our lore, our future, and our past. Yet none of them, not even the eldest of the council, Lone Wolf, would look me in the eye. Whatever I told them, whatever it meant, I could sense their fear."

Chameleon's face grew more troubled.

"It was my father who finally explained it to me. He spoke of an ancient story among my people, the legend of the thrice-named Drannock. It has been nearly forgotten, for it was written down in a book," her tongue fumbled over the unfamiliar word. "The art of the written word has been nearly lost to us. Only Mountain's Ford can still translate the old symbols."

"Wait," Zedaine interrupted. "The Drannock don't read or write?"

Chameleon shook her head silently.

"Where did the book come from, I wonder?" Kildare mused.

"The book belonged to those who lived *before* the delving," the Drannock said in a reverent whisper, as though speaking of beings of great power. She made a sign in front of herself to ward off evil spirits.

"What was the delving?" Kildare asked.

For the first time, Chameleon looked unsure of herself, and she paused a long moment before answering. "I cannot say for certain. I can only tell you what has been passed down through the years. One tale says we once lived in great cities many generations ago. Somehow our people angered the gods and were driven from our homes. Another legend speaks of our ancestors learning the secrets of the gods, and states that they were punished because of it. A third warns that we disturbed an ancient god's slumber. No matter which you believe, they all come to the same conclusion. Our ancestors were driven mad and nearly perished. We speak of them now as the cursed ones. Only a few survived. My people, the Drannock, are all that's left. This is what I have heard of the delving. It is difficult to understand, even for me."

Kildare let out a breath. "That book you spoke of," he said, "it must be hundreds of years old. What I wouldn't give to get a look at it."

He reached into the fire and pulled his own rabbit off the coals. "I'm sorry, Chameleon, I didn't wish to interrupt. Please continue."

The brown-skinned Drannock nodded and took up her tale once again.

"As chance would have it, my father knew the story of the thrice-named Drannock. He was *selyte* to Summer's Wind in his youth. Mountain's Ford alone still commands the written language among my people. In the book, my father said a woman named Farsight spoke of the story long ago. He told me she could see things that were yet to happen."

"An oracle?" Kildare asked.

"I am unfamiliar with that word," Chameleon answered.

"It's someone who can see into the future," Zedaine replied.

Chameleon nodded slowly. "Yes, that sounds like what my father explained to me. This oracle, Farsight, she spoke of a leader, one yet to come, one who would bring a time of blood and death like nothing we have never known. She foretold of the thrice-named Drannock, who would become First Wanderer of my people."

Chameleon hesitated, looking concerned once more.

"My father was troubled because he knew the time Farsight spoke of had come. Though frightened for my safety, he knew what I must do." Chameleon looked at the rapt faces of the two brothers. "He defied the council and sent me away. He knew I had to find my answers here, outside my people's lands, perhaps where the cursed ones had been when they angered the gods so long ago. Only away from Ab'dural Valley can I solve the mysteries of my visions. That is why I've left the lands to the south. I am the First Wanderer of my people. I am the thrice-named Drannock."

The two brothers said nothing at first, taking in Chameleon's words. Zedaine finally let out a low whistle. "Now that," he said, "is quite a story. Can I ask—what's your third name?"

"It has not yet been revealed to me," Chameleon answered with a shrug. She went back to her rabbit leg, taking several large bites, wiping the grease away with her sleeve.

"I have many questions for you, Chameleon," Kildare said, "but one presses more than the rest. What have you seen in these visions of yours? What has made you risk your life to come all this way? It's obvious you've seen the flower Zedaine is carrying. I don't know if we can help much, but I'm curious to hear of your other visions."

Chameleon closed her eyes and focused on searching through her most recent memories. As they came to her, she spoke them aloud.

"I see a great winged serpent the color of darkness riding upon the winds," she began. "A white eagle against a red sky racing after it..."

"A white eagle?" Kildare interrupted.

Chameleon opened her eyes, surprised at Kildare's question.

"It's got to be coincidence," Zedaine said, shaking his head.

"A white eagle against a red sky?" he said, frowning at his brother. "I don't believe in that kind of coincidence."

Turning back to Chameleon, Kildare asked, "What else can you tell us about this eagle?"

Closing her eyes once again, she did her best to recall the details of the image she'd seen.

"The eagle, it's completely covered in white feathers," she began. "It's much larger than others I've seen. And its eyes...it has fierce, golden eyes."

Kildare rocked back in astonishment, eyes wide and mouth open in shock. Zedaine was just as surprised, and he began cursing under his breath.

Opening her eyes again, Chameleon looked intently at them both. "Do you..." Chameleon began.

"What else," Kildare demanded, cutting off the stunned Drannock. "What else did you see or hear? Anything you can tell us may be important, even the slightest detail."

Chameleon had not expected such an outburst. What did these visions portent? Clearly, they meant something to the brothers.

The Drannock drew a deep breath and calmed herself. Gathering her focus, she began weeding out all distractions. One by one, the sights and sounds of her surroundings melted away. The crackling of the fire, the smell of the rabbits, the breathing of Zedaine and Kildare, the distant roar of the waterfall. All of it disappeared as Chameleon entered a state of meditation.

In a flash, a vision was upon her.

A brown-haired youth she'd not seen before was walking toward her. She sensed he was the one who had overcome her defenses in the past. He wore a smile on his face.

"You have taken your first steps into a dangerous world, Chameleon," he pulsed, using a form of telepathy. *"But it is only the beginning."*

"Who are you?" asked Chameleon.

He shook his head. *"Already the hour is late,"* he responded with some urgency. *"Listen carefully, for there is little time. The birds of darkness must arrive in the city of hope in four days, or all will be lost. The seed of the white eagle is in danger. Warn them! An ancient evil is coming. Awaken, my friend, awaken..."*

"Chameleon!"

The booming of Kildare's voice roused the young woman from her trance.

She blinked several times and shook her head. "Did you hear? Do you know what it means?"

Kildare nodded, looking grimly determined. "Can you walk? If not, I'll carry you, but we must be off, now."

Zedaine had left his half-eaten rabbit on the spit and was already gathering his things. For a man of his size, he moved with *speed*. All his weapons had been collected, and his pack was hanging behind him. He had the look of a hunting cat in his eyes and was clearly ready to leave.

Somehow, Kildare had moved even more quickly than his brother. Already he was looking down the trail that would carry them away. He grabbed the blanket from around Chameleon and stuffed it into his pack.

"*Viasha,* my ass," he was muttering under his breath. "I'll *blind* Blade when I see her."

The Drannock's confusion mounted. "Do you know what the visions mean?" she asked.

"Yes," Kildare answered curtly. "I know why we were sent into these mountains," he said, peering intently at the Drannock. "We were sent to find you, Chameleon. What you have told us is of the utmost importance. I know you have many questions. Given time, we will answer them, but for now we must be on the move."

He pulled a steel knife from his belt and handed it over to Chameleon, who examined it briefly. Her own stone knife had been lost in her plunge over the falls. She had never owned a metal weapon before. Its novelty, however, was short lived, as Kildare spoke quickly to Zedaine.

"Stick to Thorn's trail as much as you have to, but we need to use our shortcuts. We've got to make haste."

Zedaine was shaking his head. "She said we have only four days, Kil," he said, glancing at Chameleon. "There's no way we can make it that quickly, not from here."

"We have to try, damn it!" Kildare hissed. "We can't just stand here and let him die."

Zedaine sighed, with a long look at Chameleon. "She'll slow us down, you know."

"You leave her to me," Kildare answered. "You just get us to Staltshore in one piece."

"We're going to have to skirt any number of magada encampments," Zedaine warned, hefting his longbow.

"I know. There's nothing we can do about it now; just do your best."

Zedaine looked at Chameleon and then back to Kildare. "If we're dragging her into this, she deserves to know."

"I will tell her," Kildare assured his brother grimly. "Now go. Use the standard trail markers and keep your wits about you. We need to get off this mountain quickly, but alive."

Zedaine nodded, and without another word he bolted down the trail.

Kildare turned to Chameleon and spoke. "Today will be a hard day. I want you to try to keep up with me the best you can. If you injure yourself or become exhausted, let me know right away."

Chameleon's gaze narrowed. She had not moved from her spot. "Why should I go with you?" she asked.

"You wanted answers to your questions," Kildare said, kicking dirt over the fire. "Well, here's one. You said the birds of darkness need to get to the city of hope in four days' time. Zedaine and I know what that means. The city of hope is called Gallanse, and it's hundreds of miles away."

"And the birds of darkness?" Chameleon asked skeptically.

Kildare stopped and sighed, turning to her grimly. "Sometimes Zedaine and I go by other names," he said, looking at her with his dark eyes.

His next words made her heart freeze in her chest.

"We're known as the Raven and the Crow."

Chameleon's heart nearly stopped beating. *These two are the birds of darkness?* she thought in disbelief. *Kildare and Zedaine are the Raven and the Crow? They are creatures of legend, evil in every tale!*

Time stopped for Chameleon. All the risks she'd taken, all the hopes she'd had, were now pinned on these two men.

"You can stay here if you want," Kildare said, looking off down the trail. "Or you can stay with us and possibly find the answers you seek. Your choice."

Without another word, Kildare loped off after his brother.

Chameleon hesitated, watching the retreating figure of Kildare. *I am the First Wanderer of my people,* she reminded herself. Narrowing her eyes in determination, she tucked the steel knife securely into her belt. *I will not fail.*

Chameleon followed close behind.

Chapter 8

A hush fell in the Great Hall as High Lord Conidon began to speak. He wasted no time, addressing not only Macklore, but the entirety of the expansive room.

"I was hoping you might enlighten this assemblage with the requests of Inniak," Conidon began, with a broad gesture to those gathered in front of him.

"I understand our neighbors to the south seek aid in response to recent attacks upon their village from the Serpent Marsh. I would like to gain perspective on how each of these suitors might handle the request. After all, one of them will inherit the issue after I'm gone."

Murmurs began among the assembled. No one had expected this.

Macklore did not hesitate. "It would be a pleasure, my lord; I would be honored to speak to all assembled here today. Might I make a suggestion?"

"Of course, ambassador," Conidon replied, with a slight inclination of his head.

"There are many sons of Shaara vying for your daughter's hand in marriage. To hear council from each would keep us up well into the night. Perhaps they might select a few from among themselves to be heard?"

"Clever boy," Madora said from behind the princess. Lydia smiled to herself. Macklore knew there were four main factions here that held sway over the others. He was forcing the lords to pick their representatives, keeping his own hands clean.

Conidon nodded in acquiescence to his request.

"How many should we choose, ambassador?" asked a lord wearing the emblem of a falcon in flight upon his tunic.

"A good question, Milord Thimes," Macklore answered, acknowledging Conidon's vassal. He paused a moment, raising his eyebrow as though a sudden thought had struck him.

"May I make another suggestion, Lord Conidon, if you don't object?" he asked, looking again to the throne.

"As you please," Conidon replied.

A slow smile spread across the ambassador's face as he turned to the princess.

"Highness, since you have a vested interest—both civic and personal—in what happens here today, perhaps you would choose the number of suitors we hear from?"

Lydia did not hide her smile this time; her face lit up like the sun. "It would be an honor, ambassador," she answered smoothly.

"She has no say in this," objected Dragomir, stepping forward from the mass of suitors. "Women have no mind for diplomacy; especially this... *princess* of Gallanse who has forgotten her place once today already. There are laws in Shaara that govern against this very thing, ambassador, as you should well know."

There was a stirring among the occupants of the Great Hall. Dragomir continued forward, sneering at Macklore. "You overstep your bounds for even suggesting such an outrage." He looked at him in disgust. "It makes me wonder what *Lord* Conidon sees in you."

The rumblings of the room grew louder. The position of ambassador inspired the deepest courtesy and respect in every nation. On their words alone, wars had been avoided and thousands of lives saved. It was rare to see one treated with such disrespect in public.

Conidon started to stand, but a raised hand from Macklore stopped him.

A look of confusion crossed the ambassador's face. "It seems odd that *you* of all people are considering yourself versed in the art of diplomacy, Prince Dragomir."

"Careful now, boy," Lydia heard Madora mumble. "There's blood in the water."

"It is my right to question you," Dragomir shot back haughtily. "My title gives me precedence here, ambassador; you've overstepped yourself."

"Prince Dragomir," Macklore continued, unfazed, "that was not my question. I asked why you would hold yourself an authority on the subject of diplomacy. However, in answer to your other statement, while your title gives you precedence over me in most scenarios, I am here at Lord Conidon's request." The ambassador slowly and deliberately walked over to the prince, stopping directly in front of him. "Unless he asks me to step down, I have precedence, not you."

The room went deadly quiet. This had become a battle of wills between the two young men. Hands moved uneasily to dagger-hilts as the tension mounted.

"That is enough, both of you," snapped High Lord Waymon of Vykor. "We are not here to argue semantics all day!" He adjusted his violet mantle and looked directly at the prince. "Dragomir, the ambassador is here at the request of Lord Conidon. Disagree with him all you like, but he has precedence. Now let us move on."

Dragomir looked to the speaker and struck a more neutral tone. "As you say, Lord Waymon, though I would reiterate my point. Women have no place in politics, nor do they have the minds for diplomacy. The ambassador will withdraw his request to the princess."

"Would you do me the courtesy of answering the question I posed to you?" Macklore asked again. "For I find myself at a loss, highness. What exactly *is* diplomacy?"

Dragomir snorted in derision. "What kind of ambassador doesn't know what diplomacy is? Why are we wasting our time with this buffoon?"

Dragomir turned around and began addressing the entire hall. "I believe Gallanse to be a great city, and it should be led by someone equal to the task…"

"You will answer my question," Macklore said quietly, stepping in front of the prince.

Dragomir stopped speaking, eyes blazing with heat. "*What* did you say to me?"

"I said, you will answer my question," replied the ambassador, the intensity in his eyes matching Dragomir's.

The prince looked like he was about to fly into a rage, but his councilor stepped forward, placing a hand on his shoulder to restrain him.

"Let me clarify my question," Macklore said loudly, turning to address every member of the Great Hall. "A moment ago, you brought up the point that the princess does not have the mind for diplomacy. I hope it does not speak ill of me, but

I consider myself well versed on the subject of diplomatic relations. I have been apprenticed to three royal ambassadors in the last eight years and spent countless hours in court hearing different sides pertaining to any number of issues. Then, of course, having *been* a diplomat myself over the last two years, and thus leading many such discussions, I would have thought I was something of an expert in the matter."

Macklore turned back to Dragomir, whose eyes had narrowed in anger.

"Your words here today cause me to wonder if my training was complete."

Macklore stood directly in front of Dragomir now, looming over the prince. He was so close, Dragomir inadvertently leaned away from the ambassador. The steady hand of his advisor halted his retreat.

"After witnessing how you have represented your ideals today," Macklore continued, his eyes carrying past Dragomir to rest on his counselor, "I am curious to know just what your idea of diplomacy is, for it seems it does not match what I was taught at all."

Lydia grew cold as Macklore's gaze shifted to the white-robed figure behind the prince. The ambassador knew where the real power was, and he was challenging it. She could not help but feel a sense of pride in this man from Brisbane. He showed no fear whatsoever.

"He has stones, that one," Madora said with grudging admiration. "Though it may get him killed."

Macklore looked back to Dragomir, eyebrows raised.

"Suddenly so quiet, highness? It makes me wonder if anyone but *you* has the mind for this new kind of diplomacy."

"What are you playing at, ambassador?" asked a bold voice. A tall, gray haired lord sporting a short beard stood from his seat. Fallon, ruler of Northpass, was approaching sixty winters. He was broad in the shoulders and stood tall enough to look Macklore squarely in the eyes. He too wore the mantle of High Lord, his silver in color. A powerful man despite his advanced age, his sky-blue eyes glared at Macklore angrily.

"I'll not see you speak to a nobleman of Shaara like this, especially when he is right!" Fallon continued. "Prince Dragomir may not be the most gracious of guests, but his point is valid. For all of your fancy talk, ambassador, you are wrong."

"How so, my lord?" asked Macklore, turning to look at the ruler of Northpass.

"I have heard that in other lands women are given a voice in politics," Fallon replied. "This, however, is Shaara, not some barbaric village at the edge of the world. We have laws here, and we follow them."

Macklore shook his head ruefully. "It is not my intent to insult anyone here today, milord Fallon; you least of all. However, I respectfully disagree with you. Women in Shaara have their limitations, certainly, but they are not entirely without say. I will, with Lord Conidon's leave, educate this assemblage in diplomacy as I learned it. In doing so, I will also gain the opportunity to instruct you in one of the laws of your fine country."

"I know the laws of my homeland quite well, ambassador," Lord Fallon stated, his anger rising. "By Jora, I helped write them!"

"I humbly suggest that you hear what I have to say," Macklore said mildly. "I mean no disrespect, but you are mistaken."

Fallon looked ready to protest, but another voice cut in.

"Let him be heard," Conidon rasped. "I have known the ambassador for a short time, but I trust he has a point to make. He is here by my invitation, and by damn, this is my home! If he is proven wrong, then I will have him cast from the city and banished upon pain of death. Continue, ambassador, and you had best make your point quickly."

Macklore bowed his head to Conidon briefly and turned back to the assembled lords, pacing with practiced ease in front of them. "Lord Fallon, would you agree with me when I say that diplomacy as you know it is the art of managing negotiations between two or more parties?"

"Yes," he stated flatly.

"My instructors often told me that the most important part of mediating is to negotiate with no feeling of ill will for any party involved. Tact, they called it. Yes, *tact* is key—wouldn't you agree?"

The gruff lord harrumphed in annoyance. "I would, but that is not the point, ambassador, and you well know it. No woman is to…" he began, but Macklore cut him off.

"Humor me for but a moment more, milord, and I will come to that very point you and Prince Dragomir have brought before us," Macklore said, gently holding up his hand. The ambassador began pacing again, now addressing not just Lord Fallon, but the entirety of the Great Hall.

"You affirmed a moment ago that diplomacy is the art of tactful negotiations between differing sides. That is what I was taught, as well. It appears, however, that Prince Dragomir would disagree. According to the example he set here today," Macklore placed his hand over his chest, "everything I learned when it comes to diplomacy is useless."

He reached out, pulling the extinguished ivory candle Lydia had observed earlier from its sconce.

"Useless, like an unlit candle in the dark." He held the ivory candle high overhead for all to see.

"I did no such thing!" hissed Dragomir, his face reddening.

"Yet another example," Macklore continued, pointing again at Dragomir, voice rising in volume, "Interrupting me while I speak to you all. He, who has been center stage all day displaying *his* idea of diplomatic relations."

Macklore took the candle and smashed it to the floor, grinding it into the stone with his heel. "He would have us believe that his way of treating people is the way diplomacy should work. Rudely casting aside others' thoughts and feelings; insulting and grinding their ideas to dust before bothering to hear them out or think them through."

Macklore stepped off the candle he had destroyed and scraped it up off the floor. He then slowly walked to Dragomir, offering the ruined wax and tallow to the open-mouthed prince.

"Tell me, Prince Dragomir, is that the result you are hoping for? Policies and judgments based on one man's avarice? The lives of thousands of people staked to a spoiled child's fancy and subject to his tantrums? One who cannot see beyond his own whims? Is this how you define diplomatic relations? Is this the kind of greatness you would bring to Gallanse?"

Holding up the ruined candle, Macklore continued, his voice rising in strength. "This is what would happen if Gallanse were to be governed by Lord Dragomir's idea of diplomacy."

"You have no right…" bellowed Dragomir, surging away from his advisor.

"I have *every* right!" thundered Macklore, cutting him off. In the blink of an eye, Macklore had transformed from a calm ambassador to the most powerful man in the room. Lydia watched him now, unable to take her eyes away.

"The moment you spoke against the idea of a woman offering her opinion, it *became* my right!" Macklore continued, thundering away at Dragomir. "You think your title gives you precedence here? In the eyes of the law, it gives you nothing!"

Macklore's voice echoed with authority throughout the chamber, and Dragomir shrank under its power.

"An ambassador has many responsibilities throughout the kingdoms. One of those is to know the laws of the land—*any* land—in which one is employed. I have spent hours analyzing the laws of your country. Through this study, I have come to understand them quite well."

Macklore set down the candle and lifted a scroll from his pocket. He turned to Lord Fallon and spoke.

"In this nine hundred and fourth year of the High Council of Shaara,

in the matter of women holding public office; it has been decreed that a

woman may not hold public office or any post that governs or makes laws.

Furthermore, a woman may not own or be the majority holder of any busi-

ness operation. Subjects found doing so will be summarily arrested and

dealt with by the nearest governing body as it sees fit."

Macklore looked up at Lord Fallon and Dragomir, addressing them both. "I simply asked the princess to suggest the number of suitors from whom we should hear. There is nothing written stating that a woman's *opinion* cannot be heard. She has not been asked to weigh in on the discussion. She has not been asked to cast a vote. What I have suggested is not against the law. It is simply against *your* traditions."

Macklore looked at Lord Fallon. "Tell me, my lord. After hearing this, do you still believe the princess cannot be asked a simple question? Is it against the law for her to suggest the number of suitors we might hear from today?"

The whole of the Great Hall watched now, completely enthralled.

Lord Fallon stared hard at the ambassador. "Let me see that," he said, snatching the document from Macklore's hands. He leafed through the pages until reaching the end, where he saw his signature. After a moment, he frowned at the parchment and spoke reluctantly. "It seems I was mistaken."

Looking up, Fallon spoke again. "My Lord Conidon, princess, ambassador. I hope you will forgive my oversight."

"Of course, Lord Fallon," Lydia replied, bowing slightly, a sympathetic smile on her face.

"There is nothing to forgive, my lord," Macklore responded. "I thank you and the Lord Conidon for allowing me the chance to be heard."

Dragomir snorted. "This is outrageous. I will not suffer this fool a moment longer," he hissed, turning to leave.

Macklore brought his gaze once again upon Dragomir, his eyes like ice. "I see how you operate, Prince Dragomir. When things don't go your way, you turn tail and run. Is this what the people of Gallanse can expect from you if you gain the throne? Is this an example of the… *greatness* you claim you would bring to Gallanse? You name me a fool for proving my point, and now wish to run and pout in your quarters?" Macklore gestured to Fallon. "The Lord of Northpass had the courage and humility to admit his mistake. That is a form of greatness we in this hall can appreciate. It speaks volumes of his honor and sense of justice. I see you are not cut from the same cloth as he. I ask everyone assembled here today, is this the leader Gallanse deserves? One who runs at the first sign of trouble?"

Lydia had to stop herself from clapping her hands together.

"Oh my, he *is* formidable," Madora whispered with admiration.

Dragomir froze in his tracks. Leaving now would give Conidon exactly what he wanted, a way to dismiss the prince from Gallanse. Dragomir turned, fixing his eyes on the ambassador. "I am not going anywhere. Now, is there anything else in which you want to instruct us, or can we move on?"

The two men stared at one another, the air between them sizzling with hostility.

"You interrupted me earlier, highness, asking what gave me the right to question you. Since you asked, I will provide the answer." Macklore inadvertently stepped closer to the prince, both of them drawing inexorably toward blows.

"An ambassador shoulders the responsibility of upholding the laws of the land. He must make sure that all parties are represented fairly. From the lowest serf to the mightiest lord, part of my responsibility is to ensure that everyone is given a voice."

Macklore continued forward, now only a fingerbreadth separating him from the prince. "*That* is the heart of an ambassador's work, highness. *That* is what gives me the right to question you. *That* is what empowers me to stand before would-be tyrants and make certain the voice of reason is heard."

With great effort, Macklore turned away from the prince, once again addressing the people in the hall.

"However, Prince Dragomir, I was not discussing my responsibilities when you began your rant. I was discussing your idea of diplomatic relations." He smoothly bent down, picked up the ruined candle, and held it aloft.

"Let's say that all we have learned through the centuries concerning diplomacy is correct. Diplomacy, as I learned it and as Lord Fallon affirmed, is not a useless candle in the dark."

Macklore moved his hand suddenly in front of the candle, screening it from everyone in the room for a split second. When it reappeared, there was a collective gasp from the assemblage. The candle was whole again, burning brightly. Macklore lifted it high overhead. "Diplomacy is what keeps our countries at peace, and the light of hope alive."

Turning back to Dragomir, Macklore concluded his argument.

"Perhaps, highness, you will come to realize that your thoughts about women and diplomacy are wrong. Furthermore, it is my belief that after your outbursts here today, during which you have managed to insult an absent lord as well as our gracious host; threatened his daughter, the princess; interrupted and insulted *me*, an ambassador of the realm; misquoted Shaarian law; cried; whined; and generally made an ass of yourself... Yes, I think your actions here today have proven that the least diplomatic person here— and the greatest *fool*—is the same person you see in the mirror every single day."

Absolute silence descended on the Great Hall.

Dragomir exploded. "You will die for this, you *goddamn bastard!*" he thundered in fury. "I will see your head on a stake, you miserable son-of-a-bitch!" Only his advisor's restraining hand kept the prince from drawing his blade.

"How dare you speak to my guest like that?" Conidon rasped, sitting up on his throne. "I am still Lord of Gallanse, and Macklore is here by my invitation. Further, he speaks the truth. You have been nothing short of a boor since entering my hall today. I would…"

The huge oak doors at the entrance of the Great Hall boomed open without warning, cutting off Conidon's outburst. A young man of no more than eleven winters hastily entered the room, looking shaken and pale. Someone screamed.

He was covered in blood.

He ran toward the throne and threw his arms around Conidon, who stood to meet him.

"Prince Alexander, what has happened?" Conidon asked, rising from his throne and taking the boy in his arms.

"My father has been…murdered!" the lad cried out, bursting into tears. The child buried his head in Conidon's robes.

Pandemonium reigned in the hall as cries of fear, confusion, and outrage reverberated throughout.

Except for two.

Macklore stared at Dragomir's white-robed advisor, who had not moved a muscle at the announcement.

His eyes could not penetrate the shadow of the robes, but he could sense the smile hidden in its depths.

Well played, boy, but the day is still mine.

Chapter 9

"Hold here," Kildare ordered, fixing his eyes on the terrain ahead.

Knees shaking with exhaustion, Chameleon leaned her back against a tree, gratefully sliding to the ground. They had run hard, covering twenty-five grueling miles over the course of the last six hours. She was grateful for the chance to stop. The Drannock had thought herself in good physical condition, having been born and raised in these mountains. However, she discovered quickly that she was no match for the two brothers.

From the outset, Kildare had run ahead, keeping alert for any sign of trouble. Chameleon had tried her best to keep pace. Every time she increased her speed, Kildare would do the same. He was always just at the edge of her vision. To his credit, Kildare never abandoned her. He often stopped long enough to allow her a drink from his waterskin, or to help the tribeswoman negotiate a dangerous part of the trail, always giving Chameleon just enough time to catch her breath. Even with those merciful stops, she'd found it difficult to keep up. The trials of the previous week had leached away her stamina. Thankfully, they traveled mostly downhill; else she was certain Kildare would have left her behind.

In contrast, she rarely saw Zedaine. When she did manage to catch a glimpse of the younger sibling, she could scarcely believe her eyes. He made Kildare look slow. Zedaine raced with consummate ease through the mountains, forging ahead, scouting, and leaving trail makers to let his brother know which way he'd gone.

Throughout the day, they had run past all manner of obstacles, none of which slowed them significantly. Twice they encountered magada who tried to block their path. The first encounter ended almost as quickly as it had begun, with Zedaine and Kildare stringing their bows and shooting at the dozen or so fanged creatures that stood in the way. The humanoids retreated in fear, five of their number left bleeding on the mountain trail.

The second encounter had been more serious. The magada had seen Zedaine from a distance and were waiting in ambush near a shallow stream. Luckily, the lean hunter had caught sight of the creatures in time and reported back to Kildare.

"What is it?" the elder brother had asked. He didn't even sound winded.

"Goddamn scout saw me," Zedaine cursed, clearly frustrated with himself. "Just as I'd marked him, too."

"It was bound to happen," Kildare answered. "We were lucky to make it this far without being spotted. Any chance we can go around?"

Zedaine shook his head. "We have to pass through here and the magada know it. The stream widens out ahead, and it's the only place we can safely cross for miles. We'd have to climb down some steep parts of the mountain otherwise, and we didn't bring any scaling equipment. Besides," he added softly, "they already know we're here."

"How much time will we lose if we try to evade capture?" Kildare asked.

Zedaine shrugged, "You know how they are," he said, nodding his head toward Chameleon. "Ask the Drannock how long they chased her. Five, six hours…longer if they're truly determined," Zedaine shook his head, "Even if we did escape, we'd lose half a day at least...probably more, and we don't have that kind of time."

Kildare looked at the trail ahead, seeing a large group of boulders next to the path. "We have maybe three minutes till they get restless," he said, thoughtfully rubbing at his chin.

"You have an idea?" Zedaine asked.

"Maybe," Kildare replied. "Does their scout know you saw him?" Kildare questioned after a moment.

"I doubt it," Zedaine answered. "Per Thorn's training, I didn't give away that I'd seen him."

"Any chance they saw the two of us?" Kildare asked, gesturing at himself and Chameleon.

"Not likely. You two were far enough behind me," Zedaine replied.

"They're probably carrying spears and shields?" Kildare guessed, raising his eyebrows at his brother.

"Might be a war club or two among them," Zedaine said with a shrug.

"Well," Kildare said grimly, "let's go find out."

Chameleon had watched from a narrow gap between boulders as Zedaine walked to the edge of the stream. Instead of readying himself for the imminent attack, he set down his bow and uncapped his waterskin. Drinking the rest of its contents, the big hunter knelt down at the water's edge and proceeded to fill the waterskin back up. He even started to whistle an off-key tune while waiting. At no time did Zedaine give any indication that he knew over a dozen magada were watching him from the other side of the stream some fifty feet away.

Chameleon could not help but admire his nerve.

At that moment, nearly a score of the wild-haired creatures burst from hiding. Screaming a battle cry at the top of its lungs, the largest drew back his stone-tipped spear, preparing to hurl it at the now gaping human. Behind her, Chameleon heard the thrum of Kildare's bowstring. The steel-headed shaft streaked through the mountain air to punch through the magada's throat with tremendous force, spinning the creature around. Dropping its spear, the creature clawed at the air, helplessly choking on its own blood until it fell with a splash in the water.

The remaining magada hesitated, surprised by how quickly one of their own had fallen. The pause proved long enough for Zedaine to hurl his twin knives at the next closest creatures. He cursed as his first throw flashed past the arm of one beast, scoring only a shallow gash. The second was more true, thudding into the chest of a club-wielding brute, piercing its heart.

Chameleon heard the hum of arrows as Kildare shot as quickly as he could from his vantage point atop one of the boulders. Several more shafts fell among the magada, who scrambled wildly for cover. "Run for your lives!" Zedaine screamed, sounding terrified. Snatching up his bow he sprinted back the way he'd come.

At the sight of their quarry bounding away, the remaining magada brought their shields to the fore and leapt to their feet, racing after him.

Zedaine, stringing an arrow to his bow while running full tilt, whipped past the spot where Kildare and Chameleon were hiding. Sliding off his perch, the elder brother counted a dozen creatures run past before bursting out of concealment. Swinging his blade, Kildare slashed at the neck of the nearest magada, severing its jugular. Bright red blood fountained from the creature's throat before it toppled to the ground, futilely trying to stem the flow.

Halting his swing, Kildare rammed his blade through the back of a second magada, piercing the creature's lungs.

Withdrawing his sword in one swift movement, Kildare let the magada fall.

"I am here, maggot spawn, come to me!"

Several of the closest magada screeched to a halt, turning around at Kildare's challenge, while the rest kept after Zedaine.

Shocked at the savagery of her companion, Chameleon was stunned further when Kildare maniacally charged his remaining foes.

It should have been hopeless, Chameleon knew, but on the narrow mountain trail the superior numbers of the magada did not matter. With

Kildare's charge, the creatures' spears were rendered nearly useless in such close quarters.

Kildare's lightning blade proved to be far more effective.

Chameleon watched as Kildare carved his way through the magada, knocking aside their clumsy attacks with ease while his blade ripped through flesh and bone. One of the creatures managed to bring his weapon in line with Kildare, but the nimble warrior sidestepped the awkward thrust. Kildare, now covered in the blood of his enemies, grimly drove his blade through the magada's chest.

Further along the path, Zedaine re-emerged, his sword covered in gore. Mercilessly, he fell upon the rear flank of the magada, quickly dispatching two more of the creatures.

Caught between hammer and anvil, the last remaining humanoid threw down its weapon and ran for its life.

Kildare had wiped his blade on the closest carcass and looked at Chameleon's stunned face. "Let's go."

Now they had stopped at the edge of a wide gorge with stark cliffs running along either side. Far in the distance, Chameleon could make out a winding river cutting through a verdant plain to the northeast. Nestled upon the coastline was a sprawling city, surrounded by a wall of stone. Beyond that was a vast body of water, larger even than what Chameleon had seen in her visions.

Kildare, noting the Drannock's curiosity, spoke.

"That's Staltshore, capital city of the Rhone," he explained. "It's one of the larger cities situated upon the Crystalline Sea, and a significant trading port."

"Is that where we're headed?" she asked hopefully, still breathless.

"Yes," he answered, untying his half-full waterskin and handing it to Chameleon.

"Here," he commanded, "drink. I don't want you passing out. We still have a few miles to go."

Thankful, Chameleon took the skin from him and drank slowly, letting the cool water pass down her throat in small amounts to keep from vomiting it back up.

"We need to move," Kildare said after she'd drank her fill.

Groaning inwardly, Chameleon tossed the empty skin back to Kildare and took his proffered hand. Wearily, she climbed to her feet.

"You must come from hardy stock," Kildare said, surprising her with the compliment.

"What do you mean?" she asked, still wary of him.

"I mean that I can hardly believe you kept up with me through the mountains after your ordeal yesterday."

"I felt like I was slowing you down," Chameleon replied honestly.

He grunted in answer. "Not by much. Truth be told, you'd be a fine distance runner, with proper training."

Chameleon didn't know what to say. Kildare was a confusing man. Arrogant in the extreme, and remarkably unlikable, he seemed to enjoy being angry. Yet it was he who'd jumped into the water to save her, he who'd kept four magada from killing her, and, as much as he'd tried to hide it, Kildare had planned his stops through the mountains to give Chameleon the rest she'd needed. There was far more to this man than he was letting on. She suspected the same was true of Zedaine.

"I'm ready to go," she said, her thoughts returning to the present.

"Let's walk for a bit," he said, retying the top of the waterskin. "Thrimby's bridge is just around that bend ahead. Zedaine knows to wait for us there."

"I've never seen anything like it," Chameleon said, pointing at the vast body of water in the distance. "It's like a huge lake that never ends."

"That's the Crystalline Sea," Kildare explained. "Named for its clear waters, or so I've been told."

"So much water," she whispered in awe. "Your people must never go thirsty."

"It's all salt water," he answered. "You can't drink a drop."

The corners of her mouth turned in disapproval. He was back to acting like an ass again. "I don't appreciate being made fun of," she said, frost in her voice.

His face twisted in confusion. "What? I wasn't trying to..." he began, but stopped. From around the corner ahead, Zedaine had come into view. He was waving in alarm, beckoning them forward.

"Something's wrong," Kildare said, turning to Chameleon. "Come on!" he yelled, setting off at a dead sprint. Forcing her tired legs forward, Chameleon followed.

"What happened here?" Kildare said, disbelief in his voice.

"Two more are inside," Zedaine answered grimly. "All six were killed."

They stood outside a small tower made of stone. Around the tower was a six-foot-high wooden palisade, its logs bound together with long coils of rope. The bodies of four guards lay on the ground in front of them. The corpses emitted a putrid smell that inundated the immediate area. There were signs of decomposition. It was evident that insects and carrion had been at the bodies for some time.

"How long do you think they've been laying here?" Kildare asked.

Zedaine raised his hands helplessly. "I'm no expert, Kil. Judging from the amount of decay and the smell, I'd say at least four days, maybe more."

"That would have been right after we went through," Kildare stated quietly.

"There's no sign of attack from the outside," Zedaine said. "I checked. The defenses are intact, and the door was locked when I got here. I had to climb over."

"It wasn't magada," Kildare said, looking at the nearest corpse. "These four died from sword wounds," he surmised. "A sharp one, at that; these are clean cuts, too clean for an iron blade. These two," he said, indicating the bodies lying face-down, closest to the tower, "were killed from behind. These others were stabbed in the front."

"Yes," Zedaine agreed. "I saw that too."

Walking over to the tower, the big hunter stood behind it.

"Whoever killed them waited here," he said quietly. "Most likely under cover of night. These four were on guard outside the tower, getting ready to pad down for the night. The killer slipped behind the closest two and cut their throats."

"The last two must have seen him," Kildare continued, pointing at the wounds of the two corpses furthest away. "They at least got a chance to die fighting."

Turning the corpse closest to the tower on its back, Kildare swore aloud. "Damn it, this is Varin," he said in recognition, pointing at the dead man's hands. "His wife bought him those gloves in the market not two weeks ago, from Fergison's shop—you remember?"

Zedaine stepped over to the other body, gently pulling a necklace in the shape of a dolphin from around its neck. "You're right," he confirmed with a sigh. "This is Savean. Varin gave her this jade pendant for their anniversary. They always pulled duty together if they could manage it."

"What about the two in the tower?" Kildare asked.

"Same thing. Both killed from behind with a sharp blade," Zedaine answered.

"Why?" the Drannock asked suddenly.

The brothers turned to Chameleon.

"Why what?" Zedaine asked.

"Why were these people killed?" she questioned. "There's usually a reason, isn't there? What were they guarding up here?"

Kildare swore suddenly, his eyes wide. "Did you check the bridge?" he demanded, looking at Zedaine.

"No," Zedaine answered, frowning. "You don't think..."

Without another word, they both ran toward the far end of the palisade where a second door had been firmly shut. Sliding the latch free, the door swung open.

"Son of a *bitch*," roared Kildare, running out of the doorway. "They cut the bridge! They cut the goddamn bridge! How the hell are we supposed to get across now?" he thundered.

On the west side of the gorge, a rope bridge was attached not ten paces from the palisade walls. The anchors for the east side were sitting nearly two hundred feet across the way. The rope holding the bridge to its anchors on the far side had been cut. The entire bridge hung limply down the cliff on the west side, completely useless.

Zedaine stood staring in disbelief until his eyes caught something out of place. Walking over to the anchor on the left side, he saw an object lodged on top of it.

It was an object he recognized.

"What the hell?" he hissed, anger building inside him.

"What is it?" Kildare asked, stomping over next to his brother.

Embedded in the top of the wooden anchor was a shuriken.

"Blade is going to have a shit-ton of explaining to do," Zedaine was saying angrily, minutes later.

"*If* we can even make it to her," Kildare stormed, still furious with their current predicament.

"You know that assassin followed us up here," Zedaine continued, mottled with rage. "How long since we crossed? Five days? That assassin followed us, killed the guards, and cut the bridge. He left his little token so he could rub our faces in it!"

Zedaine was so angry, he hurled his pack to the ground in frustration.

"We don't know for sure if that's what happened," Kildare replied.

"Oh, come on Kil," Zedaine barked. "That's exactly what happened and you know it! That bastard couldn't follow us into the mountains, so he did the only thing he could do. It's like he knew we needed to get to Staltshore tonight."

"None of this is helping," Kildare said, grabbing hold of his brother's shoulders. "You need to get yourself under control."

"Get off me," Zedaine said, knocking his brother away. "Varin, Savean, these other four guards. Those deaths are on us!"

Kildare narrowed his eyes at his brother, trying to keep his own anger in check. "Their blood is not on *our* hands; it's on those of whoever ordered our deaths."

"I promise you this," Zedaine said, his eyes smoldering, "When I find that assassin, I'm going to *rip his goddamn head off*!"

"There's a time for vengeance," Kildare replied coolly, "but this is not it."

"Don't talk to me about vengeance, Kildare," Zedaine raged, "I'm well-versed in what vengeance looks like to you! Had we just hunted that assassin down like I wanted, these people would still be alive!"

Kildare drew a deep breath before speaking. "And what if we'd stayed to hunt that assassin as you wanted? *Maybe* we'd have prevented this."

Kildare raised his finger and pointed it at Chameleon, who was watching the exchange from the tower entrance. "But she would be dead now, and we wouldn't have gotten her message. I share your anger at the loss of these men and women, Zedaine. They deserved better than this. But standing here yelling about it isn't going to fix anything."

Kildare picked up Zedaine's pack and handed it to him. "You were right about one thing."

Zedaine snapped his pack away from Kildare. "Oh? And what was that?"

"It *is* like the assassin knew we needed to get to Staltshore tonight," Kildare said. "If that's true, then he's deliberately stalling us, and he knew about all this five days ago—maybe earlier. I tried to tell you at the Mirrored Falls, there's more to these events than we know. Surely, you can see that now?"

"All right, so what now?" Zedaine asked, still seething inside. "What's the plan, Kil?"

"We have to get moving," Kildare replied, picking up his own pack. "It's twenty miles to the end of the gorge, and another twenty to get back to Staltshore. We have a task; let's get to it."

"That's forty miles, Kil," Zedaine hissed back. "Even if I were running by myself, I probably wouldn't make it."

"We have to try," Kildare said with determination.

Zedaine pointed to Chameleon. "How far do you think she'll get?" he asked. "She's dead on her feet. Even if you carried her, we'd never arrive in Staltshore by morning. That's our only chance of making it to Gallanse in time. It was a long shot even when we thought the bridge would be intact.

Unless you grow wings in the next few minutes, we're screwed!"

"We can cross here."

The brothers turned and stared at Chameleon.

She gave them a weary look. "I will need time to prepare, to gather my energy, but we can cross here."

"How?" Zedaine asked skeptically.

She pressed her lips together and sighed. "I know you don't understand, but this is one of the powers of my people."

Chameleon motioned for them to follow, and they went back out the eastern door. She peered across the open space of the gorge, her hazel eyes searching the far side.

"There," she said, pointing to a clearing directly across from where they were standing. "I'll move us to that spot."

"That's over two hundred feet away," whispered Kildare. "At least."

"I'll need two hours to prepare myself. We'll be on our way after that."

"Two hours of sitting here?" exclaimed Zedaine incredulously.

"What choice do we have?" asked Kildare.

Zedaine looked skeptical.

Kildare turned to Chameleon, "You can do this, yes?"

The Drannock nodded with determination.

"This is ridic…" Zedaine began.

"How about this, Zee?" Kildare said, his anger rising. "How about you take off and run the forty miles around this giant crack in the earth, and Chameleon and I will leave a message in Staltshore as to where we headed the previous day?"

"But Kil, what if…" Zedaine argued.

"No what-ifs. How many times have you said, 'what if?' It's always 'what if?' with you. By the gods, those two words will be etched on your tombstone!"

"Please," Chameleon said, calmly looking at Zedaine. "What was it you told me at the falls? 'You will just have to trust us.' I ask that you trust me now."

Cursing under his breath and shaking his head, Zedaine threw his hands in the air. "All right, *fine*. You think you can get us across here, be my guest."

Chameleon knelt to the ground and looked up at the brothers. "I need to meditate for two hours, perhaps a bit more. Then we will cross and be on our way. I'll need relative silence, if you can manage."

She hesitated a moment and spoke again, rather hastily. "I'll not fail you. Thank you for your trust."

Zedaine and Kildare strode back toward the tower, Zedaine mumbling under his breath. "I'm angry enough to chuck you halfway across that gorge right now, Kildare! We can write, 'I was stupid and didn't listen to my brother, Zedaine,' on your tombstone."

"Nice," Kildare replied sarcastically. "Let's see what we can do about the bodies. I don't want to leave them lying arou..."

Chameleon closed her eyes. She began to breathe deeply, slowing her heartbeat to a crawl. Over and over until her breath and heartbeat became a slow, steady rhythm, the Drannock entered into a sleep-like trance. Her subconscious thoughts were aware of the gorge until she blocked it from her mind. The trees she sensed nearby vanished one by one into the nothingness of her psyche. The sound of the wind, the light of the sun, the song of a nearby bird, the two brothers... Chameleon blocked them all until she was in the void of her own subconscious self. Her body was the wellspring from which her power came. Her mind was the tool that harnessed that energy and wielded it as she chose. Slowly but steadily, she felt power build inside her.

The lure of power, as always, filled Chameleon with a great sense of completeness. Given time, she could gather her fill.

Her subconscious, though, told her that others waited nearby.

Reluctantly, Chameleon sought to escape the calm she had created. In a rush, the sunlight, wind, trees, birds… it all came back in an instant.

When she opened her eyes, Chameleon saw it was dusk, with full darkness less than an hour away.

Kildare and Zedaine were staring at her, their faces expressionless.

"I am ready," she said simply.

"What must we do?" Zedaine asked.

Walking past them to the lip of the gorge, Chameleon focused on the clearing across the way.

"Careful," Kildare warned, "That's a thousand-foot drop."

"Take each other by the hand," Chameleon said, oblivious to the warning.

Glancing at one another, the two brothers clasped hands.

"You will have to hold one another as tightly as you can," Chameleon continued.

"What the hell…" Zedaine began.

"Just do it!" Kildare said harshly.

They held one another awkwardly, albeit tightly, fearing what noncompliance might bring.

"By the gods, Kil, your stench could fell an ox," Zedaine complained.

"You don't exactly smell like a meadow full of daisies," Kildare retorted.

They both heard a brief popping sound while Zedaine snorted at his brother's rejoinder.

"What is she waiting for?" Zedaine asked after a few moments had passed.

Kildare let go.

"What are you doing?" exclaimed Zedaine.

"Jora's balls!" Kildare said, slightly awed. "She did it!"

They were on the other side of the gorge, looking back at Chameleon, who waved and gave a weary smile.

A moment later, Chameleon disappeared from the lip of the gorge. In an eye blink she was beside them, accompanied by the popping sound they'd heard before. The Drannock staggered and almost fell, but Zedaine steadied her, keeping Chameleon on her feet.

"You see," Chameleon said, voice filled with exhaustion. "We did it."

Kildare and Zedaine just stared at one another in amazement.

"Give me a moment, if you will," the Drannock said. "That takes some effort."

"Sit down, lass," Zedaine said. "We need to get moving soon, but take a few minutes. By the gods, Kil, we'll be there tonight!"

"Yes… and then maybe Blade can explain what in the name of the gods is going on," Kildare replied, eyes focused on the walls of the distant city.

Guardsman Whalen sat atop the battlements of Staltshore, trying to look alert while walking his post. There were few late-night visitors who came to the city's western gate three hours past nightfall. Most traffic came from the east. Still, there was always a chance that some random hunter or merchant would get caught on the mountain road later than expected. This happened every odd night or so; such visitors demanded that someone stand out on the wall and keep watch.

Whalen threw an envious glance at his fellow guardsmen, four in all. They were sitting comfortably inside the guard tower, sheltered from the cool night wind that blew off the sea. They were interested only in their game of knucklebones, which they played every night at this time. The official orders given by the watch commander were to guard the western gate and give nightly reports of anything unusual. The others should have been standing watch with him, but the sergeant-at-arms rarely, if ever, came to check on this post, as it was the furthest from his own place of duty. Instead, he would send a runner who, more often than not, would sit and dice with the other guardsmen. As the new replacement for the guard who'd been attacked a few nights ago, Whalen's job was to watch for travelers on the road; but more importantly, he was tasked to keep an eye out for the sergeant of the guard.

Whalen shivered in the cold, and thought back to why he had joined the forces of Staltshore's guard in the first place.

It was because of a girl.

Three months past, a minor noble from one of the outlying countries had led his retinue through the streets of Staltshore. Whalen's friend Shia had watched as the guards passed by, breathless. Shia was seventeen years old, a blonde-haired, blue-eyed beauty of a woman. Whalen had been smitten with her for years.

One of the noble's guards turned his head slightly and winked at her on his way past.

Time stopped for Whalen as he watched Shia blow the guard a kiss and wink back. She broke into the widest smile he had ever seen.

"Did you see him, Whalen? He winked at me. *At me!*"

Whalen, feeling as though he had been kicked in the stomach, managed to eke out a reply. "Yes, I did see that."

"He was so handsome in that uniform," she continued, gushing. "I could give myself to any man who dressed like that."

Whalen signed up for the army the next day.

Across the battlements, the young guard saw the approach of Tule. A short, heavyset man in his late twenties, Tule was the runner for the sergeant of the guard.

Whalen grimaced inwardly. Tule usually had something unpleasant to share with the him before he continued to the tower.

"Well, well, well, how goes duty tonight, private?" Tule asked, smelling strongly of brandy.

"Thankfully, it's been a quiet night," Whalen replied, his tone neutral.

"Best keep your eyes peeled, rube," Tule said, ignoring Whalen's response. "I hear there might be an uprising of crickets attacking the gate!"

Tule whacked Whalen on the back and gave a hearty laugh before continuing on his way.

"Ah, I almost forgot," he said, turning around. "I have a message for you. Came to headquarters right before I left."

Tule reached into his pocket and drew out a neatly folded piece of paper. "From the commander himself. That can only mean one thing," A cruel smile appeared on Tule's face. "It means they no longer have need of your services!" he said with another laugh.

With that, Tule continued on to the guard tower some twenty paces away. Whalen saw the heavy man ease his considerable weight into an empty chair, and pass his flask to the others.

Whalen often speculated about life's little quirks. Drinking was never allowed on duty, yet Tule and Guardsman Garth, the eldest of the squad, drank almost every night. He shook his head in wonder. It was the same army that allowed Tule, one of the slowest guards on the planet, to become a "runner."

Turning his attention to the letter, Whalen ripped it open and read the contents. He frowned and read them again, wondering if he'd received it by mistake. He was about to take the letter to Garth when three figures materialized out of the darkness. As they approached, he noticed the two taller men supporting the third. Looking closer, he noted the shortest of the three was a woman. Whalen saw her stumble twice in exhaustion, nearly collapsing on the road.

Whalen pocketed the letter and ran to the top of the battlements, just above the entryway.

"Ho the gate!" cried the tallest of the three, stopping short of the portcullis.

"A late time to be traveling this cold night," Whalen answered.

"Or to be standing guard in it," the same man replied with a friendly smile.

Whalen found himself grinning back, warming to the tall stranger. "Is your friend hale? I saw her stumble in the road."

"Just weary after a long day of travel," the tallest answered.

"What brings you to Staltshore this evening? Not planning to invade us, I hope?"

The tall stranger laughed with genuine humor. "We will be gracing your fine city for the night only, and gone tomorrow at first light. Until then, my companions and I would like hot food and a warm bed. Can you recommend an inn?"

"I will indeed," Whalen replied. "Your friend looks worn out. Let me rouse my fellow guardsmen and we can open the gate."

"My thanks, guardsman."

Whalen walked into the guardhouse to inform the others of the travelers. As usual, he received nothing but protests and groans from the elder members of the watch, who were now forced to leave the comfortable confines of the tower.

"Three strangers this late?" Garth asked, flaring his nostrils in irritation.

Garth had to be the laziest guard in Staltshore. He was always the first to complain about work, and always the last to do any of it.

"Probably no-good thieves, looking to make a quick score and head out," Tule grumbled, tucking the brandy into his belt and throwing on his cloak.

"They seemed friendly to me," Whalen said carefully.

"Oh, did they?" Garth mocked, surprised Whalen had dared to say anything. "I don't suppose you could tell a dog from a cat, boy, much less spot a thief at the gate. They don't wear signs, rube."

The other guardsmen stomped down the steps, laughing at the furiously blushing Whalen.

Once they'd reached the bottom, Tule shoved the newest guard aside. "Better let us handle this, boy," he said, nodding toward Garth. "You just keep your mouth shut."

The gate swung open and the five guards moved forward, standing with arms crossed while Whalen held back a few steps.

"Names. Now," barked Garth, looking at the trio with contempt.

The tallest frowned, but spoke, his tone friendly. "Zedaine of Adian."

"Adian is it?" Tule snorted, stepping forward. "Well, boy, you're a long way from home. I hear that Adian is a city of tarts. You some kind of tart, boy?"

Instead of answering the question, Zedaine shook his head slowly and frowned. "I'm in no mood for this. Step aside."

"What the hell you mean, boy?" Tule roared. "We'll say whatever we damn-well please! You trying to tell the guards of Staltshore our business? No down-country simpleton's gonna talk to us like that! I don't think I should let you and your little band of tarts inside our city. Don't much like the look of you. How 'bout you get the *hell* out of here before me and the lads thump your little tart ass back to Adian."

Another of the travelers stepped forward, his eyes blazing.

"Is Staltshore now a closed city? A place where the guards accost innocent travelers for no reason?" he asked harshly. "Or is it only the guards who have faces like a bloated pig and breath that smells like cow shit?"

"You bastard," Tule hissed, drunkenly rushing forward.

Zedaine stepped forward and leveled him with a bone crushing right cross, dropping Tule to the ground, where he twitched once and lay still.

Garth looked down at his friend, stunned at the power of the blow. He made a move for his sword and froze where he stood.

Faster than he would have believed possible, Whalen witnessed the second man's blade appear at Garth's neck.

"If you so much as graze that hilt with a fingernail, I'll slice your throat and spit on your corpse," the man promised.

Whalen knew he needed to do something quickly. Tule and Garth were used to bullying farmers and merchants, not dealing with dangerous men like these. Whalen had not even *seen* the stranger draw his weapon. He knew if he did not act now, blood would be spilled.

Whalen stepped forward, easing past the other stunned guards. He managed to work his way in front of Zedaine.

"Please, forgive my companions. Truly, there is no need for this," he said quietly.

"Whalen, shut up! They attacked a guard," Garth said, his eyes wide.

"Tule charged them," Whalen answered. "Zedaine did what any of us would have done— defended himself."

"What of this jackass with his sword at my throat? Are you saying *he* isn't attacking me?"

"He reacted when *you* tried pulling *your* sword on him. He could cut your throat at any time, and yet has not done so," Whalen answered simply. "These men are tired and clearly in no mood for your grandstanding, Garth. Let them by."

"You are not in charge here, boy."

"I said, let them pass."

Garth glanced at the sword at his throat, reluctant to give in to Whalen.

"You'd best listen to your friend," Kildare said, his voice deathly quiet. "He's the only one of you lot who's shown half a brain this evening."

Garth glared at Kildare, hatred evident in his eyes. "Any trouble they cause will be on your head, Whalen," Garth said finally, unwilling to lose face in front of the other guards.

"So, you do have an inkling of sense," Kildare muttered, lowering his sword and sheathing the weapon. He turned away from the irate Garth, looking to his exhausted companion.

"No one pulls steel on me," Garth sneered angrily, drawing his blade the moment the stranger's back was turned.

Kildare, expecting the cowardly attack, did not hesitate. Whirling around, he shot forward, driving the heal of his palm to the sternum, blasting the air from Garth's lungs. He continued the blow upward, smashing his hand under the guard's chin, and snapping the man's neck back violently. He then speared his elbow under Garth's windpipe, stunning him, and causing the sword to drop to the ground. The guard staggered back a step, gasping for air.

Kildare, however, was not finished. He grabbed the back of his assailant's head with both hands and pulled Garth's face downward. An audible crack could be heard when the guard's face smashed into Kildare's rising knee. The impact shattered his nose, and he fell in a heap next to the unconscious Tule.

Whalen paused for only a moment before laughing nervously. "Are you sure you're not here to invade the city?"

Zedaine clapped the young guard on the back. "I like you, lad. A word of advice: make sure you report this to the watch commander immediately. Otherwise, your sleeping friends will tell a much different story than you when they wake up. They don't strike me as the trustworthy type. You tell Commander Taggard if he has any questions, he can bring it up with Blade tomorrow."

Zedaine and Kildare moved forward, assisting their female friend as the other three guardsmen tried unsuccessfully to wake their comrades.

Whalen's eyes widened when he heard the sage's name. The letter!

"You're friends of the sage?" Whalen asked. "Kildare and Zedaine?"

Zedaine turned abruptly, eyebrows raised. "Did she leave a message for us?"

"The Stag and Hound," Whalen blurted, taking out the letter he'd gotten earlier. "I received the message minutes ago. It said to meet her there."

He handed the letter over to Zedaine.

"It's an inn owned by my uncle. It's located close by, on the western edge of town. They have fair prices, clean lodgings, and…a serving girl there. Shia is her name. Can you…can you tell her that Guard Whalen says hello?"

Zedaine nodded slowly. "Indeed, I will, guardsman. You have a good night."

Whalen smiled and turned back to his duty, walking taller than he ever had before.

Chapter 10

Macklore left the palace after darkness had fallen, the day's many new developments weighing heavily upon his mind. He wore his faded brown cloak, which obscured the blue robes of his office. With the obsidian scepter tucked away under his belt, he looked much like any other hardworking citizen of Gallanse. He fervently hoped he could enter the Golden Cutlass without incident. He had already been through enough today.

The ambassador was angry with himself, cursing his own stupidity. He thought of King Medyha's parting words before the voyage to Gallanse.

"Gather information, make the offer—don't get directly involved. Watch out for Conidon, he will use you if he has to. I need you alive, boy; don't be a hero."

He will use you if he has to. The king's words echoed in his mind. Macklore had gathered information and made the trade offer. He was ready to head back to Brisbane with the trade agreement in hand, his mission complete.

Three things had stopped him.

One had been the High Lord himself. The old man had taken his hand at the palace and requested he stay a week longer.

"I am having a problem involving a small village along the western coast—Inniak, by name. It lies a short, two-day journey from here. I need a good ambassador—more, a good man—to help me, Macklore. I was hoping you might take the job and assist an old gentleman? Think of it as a token of goodwill to seal our trade agreement."

Macklore had agreed to go, in part to assist Conidon, but more because he'd heard troubling news.

The prince of Dagor had become far more influential in recent days. This did not match the information the ambassador had been given. Dragomir was said to be spoiled and vain, subject to unbridled fits of rage. How was he unexpectedly gaining such influence, after weeks of idling his time away? This drastic turn of events was the second reason the ambassador agreed to stay.

After his audience today, Macklore knew the reason for Dragomir's meteoric rise. Macklore could sense the power of magic in the white-robed advisor who had stood behind the prince. The ambassador had seen the markings upon the man's head. He was one of the *Moldranni Sor,* the most powerful and secretive of magic cults, and cause of much chaos in the Crystalline Sea's tumultuous past. He'd believed their order had vanished decades ago.

Not anymore.

The ambassador suspected that soon, very soon, there would be blood. Dillion was simply the first casualty of the succession. Macklore knew there would be more.

The ambassador should have left this morning and gotten out while he could. He'd certainly been given his opportunity. If the demon mages of Shaara had taken an interest in the succession, they were capable of getting what they wanted. Conidon was intelligent, powerful, and held the loyalty of his city; but he could not combat the *Moldranni Sor*—not by himself. The cult had access to resources that the Lord of Gallanse did not.

Then there was the third and most compelling reason he had decided to stay.

Princess Lydia Gaida.

The ambassador had smiled fiercely, feeling a surge of pride, when the princess dared to confront the haughty prince of Dagor in the Great Hall. It took courage to stand in the face of such blatant arrogance; especially in Shaara, where women were thought of as little more than breeding stock.

It was not until he had approached the throne, however, that his breath had been taken away.

Macklore had seen beautiful women many times in his life, but none had devastated him like the princess. Standing no taller than his chin, her black lustrous hair hung down past the creamy white dress that clung to her incredible figure. Her full lips exuded a sensuality Macklore longed to explore. Those dark amber eyes, filled with depth and intelligence—a man could get lost in them if he stared too long.

Macklore's mouth had gone dry while he'd absently exchanged pleasantries with Conidon. The normally quick-thinking ambassador racked his brain, trying to find some way to address this woman. Feeling like a peasant boy at his first pole dance, and unable to take his eyes off the princess, Macklore could not consciously remember what he said to her.

Turning his thoughts to the present, Macklore hit his fist to palm. How could he have been so stupid? He was stuck now, stuck *firmly* in the middle of it. Present Inniak's offer and leave. A simple task, he thought, but not for him. Oh no, he had to be a damn *hero* by insulting a Shaarian prince *and* challenging the white-robed blood mage, all for a princess who scarcely knew he existed. Disgusted with himself, he shook his head. After his display today, he was in it up to his neck.

Grinding his teeth, Macklore forced himself to calm down. Macklore was not about to abandon Conidon to his fate, he reasoned. A fractured Shaara was difficult enough to handle. A Shaara united under the wrong leadership would be a disaster. King Medyha of Brisbane had said as much many times in the past. While the thought of Dragomir sitting on the throne of Gallanse was fearful, it was *nothing* compared to the nightmare that would occur if Rexor were in command.

High Lord Rexor, lord of Dagor and Dragomir's father, was a ruthless warlord, sick with ambition. Worse, he held all his son's psychotic appetites, but he exercised the necessary restraint to keep himself focused on his goal. Dragomir would be no more than his father's puppet ruler, were he to gain the throne of Gallanse. Rexor would have access to more than eighty thousand battle-hardened soldiers. Given another year to consolidate his power, those numbers could swell to three times as many. If that happened, every city on the Crystalline Sea—including Brisbane—would become a target for Rexor's greed.

The ambassador slowed, taking in his surroundings and growing more wary now. He had crossed from the well-lit cobblestone streets of the middle city into the darker paths of the lower. Muggings and thievery were far more common here. He would have to pass through with care.

Off to his right, Macklore spotted a tiny street urchin watching him closely. The child could not have been more than five or six years old. She wore a single piece of threadbare clothing; an oversized gray smock, hanging down to her grubby toes. The little girl had a pale face with dark, sad eyes.

"Do you have a spare coin, sir?" she asked in a tiny voice.

"What are you doing out on the street, little one?" he asked kindly.

She pointed her filthy finger up at a dimly lit window. "My mam is working. I have to wait."

Macklore sighed. Her mother was most certainly a prostitute plying her trade this evening, likely making just enough money to keep from starving.

"My mam says if I can get two chalkoi, I can have some sticky cake," the child said hopefully.

Macklore fished in his money pouch, pulling out four of the bronze coins. Bending down to look her in the eye, he dropped the coins in her small hand. "A girl as big as you should get two pieces."

"Thank you, sir," she replied excitedly, her fist clenched tightly around the coins.

"Now, you'd best get off the street, little one," Macklore said, standing back up and putting away his pouch. "It's not safe out here."

The ambassador had stepped away when he heard the girl speak again.

"Can I play, too?" she asked suddenly.

"What do you mean?" he asked, baffled.

She smiled, her dirty face beaming. "The hiding game. When you stop, your friends all hide. I saw three of them just now."

Macklore froze a moment and then laughed lightly, forcing himself to keep his eyes on the little girl. "You are a bright one, aren't you? What is your name, if you don't mind my asking?"

"Wren," she said, twisting her face into a frown. "My mam said I reminded her of a bird when I was born. I don't think I look like a bird, though," the girl said, daring Macklore to argue.

It took all of Macklore's willpower to keep from running off into the night. Who was following him? He thought back to the day's events. Assassins sent by Dragomir were more than likely, though it could have been anyone, he reasoned. Thinking quickly, he kept his voice light, hoping he would not give the little girl away. "Perhaps she knew a secret about you, Wren; mothers are clever like that. The bird you are named after is known for its wonderful singing. One day, perhaps, you will be a singer of songs."

She smiled shyly, then said, "You think I could?"

He crouched down again, looking her in the eyes. "I think you would be a terrific songbird, Wren," he answered, playfully touching her nose with the tip of his finger.

She smiled, even more brightly than when he'd given her the coins.

Leaning in close, Macklore spoke again, feeling knives at his back. "It was clever of you to notice my friends who are following me. We *are* playing a game, right now."

"I knowed it," Wren said happily.

"Tell me," he said, voice dropping to a conspiratorial whisper, "how far away were my friends, the last time you saw them? If they get too close, I get to try to catch them in this game. Do you think I could catch any yet?"

She glanced up the street furtively and leaned right next to his ear.

"One is really close," she whispered. "The other two are further away. You'll have to wait to go after them, I think."

He winked at her and patted her head. "Thank you for your help, Wren. I would love to have you join us, but I am afraid only four people are allowed to play at a time."

The sad eyes returned, Wren's face looking crestfallen.

"But, my little songbird, I'll make a deal with you," he said quietly. Reaching under his robes, he brought out another coin. "If you hide this right now, and don't let anyone find it, the next time I see you we will play a game of our own."

Wren looked up, her big eyes widening at the sight of the coin.

"That's gold," she whispered reverently.

Macklore needed to move. He had stayed here far too long already, and was risking the child's safety, as well as his own.

"Will I have to give it back?" she asked.

"It is yours to keep," Macklore promised with a smile.

"Thank you, sir," she said, impulsively hugging Macklore.

"Go now, Wren, and hide that coin."

She scampered off into the building, her tiny steps fading away.

Macklore, too, was on the move, thanking the gods for the girl's warning. Walking more briskly than before, he tried to catch a glimpse of whoever was following him. Try as he might, he could not catch sight of his pursuers. Whoever it was had enough skill to remain hidden in the dark city alleyways. The ambassador had no desire to be knifed in the back, and considered full flight, but he did not want to get caught this close to Wren's building, fearing that those who hunted him might discover that she had warned him.

Forcing himself to keep a steady pace, Macklore drew closer to his destination and formulated a plan. A half mile from the Golden Cutlass, the ambassador turned a sharp corner and broke into a sprint, cloak billowing behind him. He had moments only, he knew, and swiftly cut left down a side pathway, crooked and filled with rubbish. Chancing a look back, he saw only the empty street behind him. Skidding to a stop, Macklore ducked quickly into a second dark alley. He waited grimly, back pressed up against a ramshackle building, scarcely daring to breathe while listening for signs of pursuit. A moment later, he heard the light padding of footsteps moving quickly, taking little care at concealment.

The ambassador reached under his belt and brought forth his obsidian scepter. The end of it had been sharpened like a stiletto, and he raised it, ready to strike. He saw a shadowy figure appear at the entrance of the alley, face hidden by a black hood and the dark of the moonless sky. The figure came to a halt, listening intently for any sign of his quarry. Hearing nothing, the pursuant moved slowly down the alley, unaware of the ambassador's presence a few feet away.

Macklore reached out with his left hand, clapping it over the mouth of his pursuer, and held the man up against his own body, the scepter's point at his captive's neck.

"Not a sound, and you might live through this," he hissed.

The pursuer was not about to be taken so easily, though, and Macklore received a sharp elbow to the ribs.

Spinning the figure around, Macklore slammed his attacker's back up against the building, rattling loose one of the boards. The ambassador's powerful hand circled the assailant's neck, scepter raised to strike. The sudden move had wrenched the hood from the pursuer's head, revealing long tussled hair and a familiar face.

"Princess," Macklore gasped in disbelief.

Lydia's terrified eyes looked first at the ambassador, and then at the sharp point of the scepter hovering above her head.

"What in the name of the gods…" he began, but looked back down the empty alley behind them while lowering his weapon. "We don't have time for an explanation. There were two more people following me; do you know them?"

She shrank away from him, still consumed by fear.

He drew a deep breath. "Princess, please, I am sorry I treated you roughly. I thought you were sent to kill me. I need you to listen now. I won't let anyone harm you, but we have two more men following us. Do you know who they are?"

She shook her head and let out a terrified breath. "I thought..." she began.

"I know, highness. I am sorry I scared you," Macklore said, still trying to fathom what she was doing this far from the palace.

"I'm all right, ambassador," she said, still breathing heavily. "You nearly scared me to death," she added with a weak smile.

"We need to get you off the street, highness," he said, searching for signs of his other pursuers. "Come with me. Pull your hood back up," he ordered, tucking his scepter back under his belt. "We need to reach the inn, and quickly."

Practically dragging the princess the final two blocks and into the Golden Cutlass, Macklore walked past the inebriated guests, pausing only to exchange a word with one of the serving wenches.

"My room is ready?" he asked briefly.

"As you requested," she replied.

He slipped her a coin and headed upstairs, the princess of Gallanse in tow.

Chapter 11

L et's settle their tab, and we'll call it a night," the innkeeper told Shia, indicating the last table of patrons. It was three hours till midnight, after a long day of business. Every innkeeper knew that morning came early, and with it, demands for hot breakfast and a warm fire.

"Yes, Sampten," Shia replied, giving him a bright smile.

The innkeeper rubbed the weariness from his eyes as he watched her move briskly about the room, picking up the last of the earthenware to be washed that evening. As she walked past her last occupied table, he heard her exchange words and a laugh with the late-night guests. He patted his ample stomach and marveled at her youth. It did not seem so long ago when he, too, could stay up late into the night chatting with his clientele. Now past fifty winters, Sampten found himself wishing he had been in his own warm bed an hour ago.

He untied the grease-stained apron from around his waist and brushed crumbs from the bar. Sampten walked back to the kitchen and reappeared a moment later, broom in hand. He heard the loud scraping of oak chairs moving across the floor as the last customers filtered out the door.

"I'll get that, Sam," Shia said, taking the broom from him as the door clicked shut.

"You are an angel," he replied with a tired smile.

Starting near the fireplace, Shia began sweeping the ash that had fallen on the worn walnut flooring. "Did you hear from your nephew today?" she asked almost too casually, without looking up from her work.

Sampten knew all too well that Whalen had been in love with Shia for years, but had recently joined the city guard, which left him scant time to himself. Shia had never given the innkeeper's nephew a moment's attention before; indeed, she'd scarcely acknowledged his existence. Now she asked after the boy daily, hoping for any word of him.

"I've not heard anything new, child," he responded with a shake of his head.

The young woman stopped her work and looked at Sampten, her shoulders drooping. "I can't believe how much I miss him," she said, turning with a sigh. "It's so strange, but when he was here... you remember how he would follow me around everywhere? He was like a lost puppy! It used to drive me crazy. He was always underfoot; I couldn't turn around without tripping over him."

Sighing again, she went back to her sweeping. "Now he's gone, and I'd give anything to have him back with us."

Sampten nodded knowingly. He, too, missed the boy.

"Perhaps he will visit..." Sampten began but stopped mid-sentence as the front door swung open.

In walked the largest man the innkeeper had ever seen.

Towering nearly seven feet in height, he must have weighed twenty stones. Covered from head to toe in thick slabs of muscle, the man looked capable of shaking the inn on its very foundation. His hands held a broad-headed spear, its serrated blade measuring at least a foot in length. Hanging around his throat was a necklace, fashioned from the teeth of some creature Sampten did not recognize. A chiton made from bear skin hung down past his knees. Slung across his broad shoulder was a horn, crafted from the shell of a large crustacean.

As the man's eyes adjusted to the light of the room, Sampten noted that his mane of unkempt hair held a sheen the color of sea grass. It hung several inches past his massive shoulders. More unusual was the blue-black tattoo painted across his eyes. It stretched from one side to the other, like some ritualistic mask. His visage held a wild, almost feral look that matched his barbaric garb. The man's mouth formed an expression of open hostility, and his green eyes searched every nook of the room, until falling at last upon the innkeeper.

Sampten felt those eyes radiate power, and fought to suppress a shudder.

Before a word was uttered, a second, far more diminutive man, dressed in clothes of fine quality, pushed his way past the giant. Sampten stood a hand taller than this fellow, who was absolutely dwarfed by his colossal companion. This shorter man had an aura about him that suggested he was very much at ease. Indeed, it was he who strode forward boldly and spoke.

"An ale, my good man," he ordered, his voice surprisingly deep, "and something to eat if you've anything left in the kitchen."

"I'm sorry, sir, but we were just closing for the..." Shia began, but was cut off by the innkeeper.

"It's all right, lass," he said, with a glance at the door and a wan smile. "Be so good as to bring out the last of the lamb shank and warm it up for these lads. The turkey pies, too, along with the buttered carrots; there should be some half dozen left in the pantry."

Shia gave the innkeeper a hard look, but walked to the kitchen to fetch the things he'd requested.

"Are you going to come in, or do you plan to stand skulking at my doorway all night, Blade?" Sampten asked, turning his full attention to the front door.

Silhouetted against the distant stars, a third figure walked into the room. Dressed in robes of silver trimmed in black, the slender woman pulled back her hood, revealing dark hair streaked with white at the temple. The fire revealed a pair of steely blue eyes set neatly on a heart-shaped face. She gave the innkeeper a brief smile at his query.

"I hope you will excuse the late hour, Master Sampten, but I have business tonight, and I've deemed your fine establishment our meeting place."

The portly innkeeper gave a small bow of his head. "I'm pleased to have you as my guest," he answered diplomatically. "My serving girl will be attending you this evening, if that meets with your approval? I've been feeling my years lately and must be abed. Morning comes early when you run an inn, and my bread won't bake itself."

"That will suffice," she replied, seating herself at a long table nestled near the fireplace. "We'll need more table settings, and three rooms, if you have them."

"Of course, milady," Sampten answered, heading to the kitchen.

Blade motioned for her companions to sit near the fire. The taller strode over, leaning his spear against the wall. Her second cohort, however, was not quite ready to see the proprietor leave.

"Since we are having a fine meal of roasted lamb, might I inquire as to the availability of some wine to go along with it?" the diminutive man asked. "Perhaps an aged red is sitting quietly in your cellar? I'd take an Agenhelm vintage if you have one—or, better yet, a burgundy from Shan'dar…"

"Leave off, Rion," the massive figure chastised, his voice rolling like thunder.

"Come now, Taeral," Rion protested. "A nip to take off the chill won't hurt any. In fact, I wouldn't be upset if you were to join me for a glass. It would be a worthwhile experience for you. Besides, a rich wine brings out the full flavor of well-cooked meat."

Taeral crossed his huge forearms and leaned back in his chair, staring at his companion. "The last time you took a 'nip' I got stuck carrying you home," he stated, his voice devoid of humor. "Two miles of you crowing songs of the sea like a harpooned seal was more than I will bear again. Give my ears a rest."

Rion looked ready to protest, but Blade spoke up.

"I highly doubt you are looking to… enhance the taste of the meat, Master Wavecrest. You're more likely to drink to excess and numb your senses entirely."

Rion shook his head and mumbled under his breath. "A sailor comes to port and gets *no* wine, *no* women? What's this world coming to?"

Forgotten during the exchange, Sampten cleared his throat and spoke again. "My serving girl, Shia, can show you to the rooms, milady. It'll be the standard rate of two drachmas a night, and a dozen obols for each meal. A baker's dozen in silver, if you please."

Blade's hand disappeared under her robes and withdrew a solitary coin. Its metallic ring sounded sharply as she flipped it toward Sampten; a glimpse of gold could be seen flashing in the firelight. Before it hit the ground, the innkeeper's deft fingers snapped it out of the air, and the coin disappeared into the depths of his pocket.

"Keep it, for the late hour and the inconvenience to your staff," Blade said, as she pulled the cowl of her hood back over her head. She turned toward the fire, watching the dancing flames while she waited.

Sampten bowed his head again. "Shia will fix up anything you need, just let her know. She is one of the finest serving girls in all of Staltshore." He exited the room and headed back to the kitchen, no doubt to speak with Shia about the particulars of his guests.

Blade smiled inwardly. She had paid the innkeeper over five times what he had asked, in part for the late hour, but more for his discretion. Sampten was exactly the kind of man Blade liked: hardworking, loyal, and respectful. He never overcharged his patrons, cooked famously well, and did not abide bad manners or tomfoolery of any kind in his establishment. He would not even refer to his serving girls as wenches. The term had never sat well with him; they were referred to as serving ladies in the Stag and Hound.

Most importantly, the innkeeper was trustworthy. Blade knew her business this night would remain private. Sampten would say nothing to anyone about who had met here or why, and he would take pains to ensure that his serving girl did the same.

Taeral broke the momentary silence with a question. "Where are your men?" he snorted, sounding none too pleased. "You said they would be here."

"Patience," Blade responded, turning her attention away from the fire. "We'll not recover your people's artifact this night, even if my associates were here now. Your search is only at its beginning. Every journey is made up of small steps; however, each is necessary to accomplish the goal."

"Bah," Taeral huffed.

The trio was distracted by Shia, who re-entered the common room carrying plates and silverware, and wearing her customary smile. "Can I get you something to drink? The mulberry cider is quite good," she suggested.

An impish smirk appeared on Rion's face. "A glass of your finest red wine," he ordered, shooting Blade a sidelong glance.

Blade ignored him and ordered a tisane for herself and a flagon of cider for Taeral, who sat shaking his head in disapproval at Rion. Shia disappeared into the kitchen, but returned quickly, toting their drinks on a wooden tray. "I overheard you ask for a burgundy earlier," she said to Rion, placing a half full goblet in front of him. "This was the last we had."

"Thank you, my dear," he said, beaming at her.

Blade inhaled her hot, tea like drink, taking a sip, smiling to herself.

"My thanks," she murmured in appreciation to the serving girl.

"I'll be back with your food soon," Shia replied, heading back toward the kitchen.

In the meantime, Rion was peering at his wine, swirling it expertly, studying its hue. Satisfied, he inhaled the heady aroma of this vintage, smiling in appreciation.

"By the sons of Kelthane, drink it!" bellowed Taeral, failing to understand Rion's deliberate undertaking.

"You are in a mood tonight," Rion said with a grimace.

"Your little habits are grating on my nerves," Taeral continued, clearly frustrated.

"These things cannot be rushed, my friend," the small man explained patiently. "Throughout life, there are rigors and hardships aplenty. I find it fulfilling to appreciate the finer things in life, when given the opportunity."

Taeral looked unconvinced.

"Of course, you are young, and a… man of action, so to speak," he raised his goblet in salute to his companion. "To your good health."

Taking a sip, Rion let the wine rest in his mouth, its flavors moving slowly across his pallet. He sat back and smiled, quite happy with his choice. It was one of the few decisions he had been satisfied with this past week.

He wondered for the hundredth time how he had gone from tranquil retirement to the middle of this nightmare.

His musing was interrupted when he heard Blade whisper under her breath, "They're here."

The door swung open.

In walked Zedaine, his fierce eyes taking in the room with a glance. Seeing the sage, he stormed over to the table, eyes blazing in fury.

"Did you find any?" the sage asked before Zedaine could speak.

"What?" Zedaine rumbled dangerously. "Is that all you have to say?"

Behind him came Kildare, dragging an exhausted Chameleon. His eyes, too, searched the room, taking in the two strangers until falling on Blade.

His reaction was somewhat different from his brother's.

"How much have you already seen?" Kildare demanded. "How much did you already know?"

"I don't..." she began, her face creased in confusion.

"No! No more cryptic messages," Kildare snarled, "I've had my fill of them today. The blood of the innocent has already been spilled. You will give me straight answers, or so help me, you'll not leave this inn tonight!"

Slowly, Blade stood up and stepped directly in front of the brothers, ice in her veins. "I hired you to do a job, and I've seen no evidence of success.

Instead, you storm into this room and threaten me. For what purpose? What wrong have I done to you?"

Reaching into his pocket, Kildare produced the shuriken they'd discovered at the bridge and dropped it with a loud clang on the table. "Can you explain that?" he hissed.

"You were supposed to be tracking him," Zedaine added, his face like stone. "How is it that the assassin slipped from under your nose?"

"Where did you find this?" she whispered, picking up the weapon.

"Thrimby's bridge," Zedaine answered. "Along with six murdered guards."

Blade closed her eyes and let out a deep sigh. "You believe I had something to do with their deaths," she said gravely, finally understanding. "No wonder you're so angry."

Zedaine's initial wrath began to subside. He suddenly felt foolish; Blade was just as surprised as they had been.

Kildare however, was not done. "The murder of those guards is just the beginning," he continued, unrelenting. "You didn't send us into the mountains for that flower, did you? How long have you known, sage? When were you going to tell us?"

"Tell you what?" Blade said in confusion. "I did send you for the *Viasha*, which you have yet to produce."

"Kildare," Zedaine said, placing a calming hand on his brother's shoulder. "She may be as much in the dark as we are."

"She's the Dragon Sage of Rhone," Kildare snapped. "I find her lack of knowledge hard to believe."

"Let's give her a chance to explain," Zedaine said. "Right now, we need food, rest, and council."

The two brothers locked eyes for a long moment, before Kildare's shoulders relaxed. "Here," he snapped, turning to Blade. He pulled the three *Viasha* out of his pouch. "We found your magic plants. I expect payment in our accounts by tomorrow morning."

"Are these the men for whom we've been waiting?" Taeral asked from across the table. His voice was laced with skepticism, clearly unimpressed. "Two loud-mouthed children who do naught but complain?"

Zedaine glanced to his fiery brother, whose glowering visage had turned to rest on the huge Taeral.

"When I want to hear from a talking baboon, I'll let you know," Kildare spat harshly.

Taeral began to rise from his chair, while Rion grabbed onto his shoulder, unsuccessfully trying to force him back into his seat. "Blade," he warned, hoping the sage would intervene.

But she was not listening. Blade had caught sight of Chameleon.

"You are one of the Drannock," she said in a reverent whisper. The surprise in her voice halted Taeral's budding outrage. She moved past Kildare and stepped toward the slender young woman.

Chameleon looked at Blade, her face expressionless. The sage gently touched Chameleon's cheek, caressing it with her fingertips. Her eyes closed momentarily, and she spoke in a hushed voice, almost too silent to hear. "You are the First Wanderer, the Walker of the Planes. You are Delphician's omen." Her last words were spoken so softly that they were imperceptible to anyone, excepting herself and Chameleon.

"Blade," Kildare said, trying to gain her attention.

"Have the years passed so quickly?" she continued, whispering to herself.

"Blade," Kildare said again, louder this time.

"Mankind is not ready; it cannot have come so soon," she muttered, still focused on her own thoughts.

"Blade!" Kildare nearly shouted.

The sage opened her eyes and looked at the two brothers, her train of thought broken. Blade gathered herself and straightened her robes, absently patting them with her hands. "I am sorry... I'm just surprised to see a tribeswoman of the mountains so far away from her homeland."

Sitting back down, the sage picked up the *Viasha* and placed them in a pouch she wore around her waist. "We have much to discuss this night," she said, sipping her tisane. "I am thankful you both have returned safely."

Shia re-entered the room, balancing a wooden trencher loaded with roasted lamb on one arm. The other curved around a tray with six turkey pies and a steaming bowl of buttered carrots. The aroma of hot food quickly filled the room as she placed it on their table.

Zedaine, in particular, eyed the food hungrily, like a wolf watching his prey. "Nothing like arriving to a hot dinner, aye Kil?" he said, helping Chameleon into the chair next to him. He unbuckled his sword belt and dropped it with a noisy clank to the floor.

Kildare exhaled, slowly releasing his irritation. He unbuckled his weapons and backpack carefully, setting them next to the fire. "It's a far sight better than half-cooked rabbit," he replied, picking up the shuriken and handing it to Blade.

"Come on now, breakfast wasn't so bad," Zedaine answered with a laugh. "Better than the lunch we skipped."

"All you ever think about is food," Kildare grumbled, reaching for a particularly juicy piece of lamb.

"...And women; don't forget about them," Zedaine replied, a smile crossing his face. He tossed a wink to Shia, who gave a tinkling laugh in return.

Taeral, however, was still glaring at Kildare. "I have not forgotten your insult," he menaced, pointing his meaty finger at Kildare.

In one blazing move, Kildare drew his knife from Chameleon's belt and slammed it into the table in front of where Taeral sat. He'd struck with enough force to lodge the blade deep into the oak tabletop. Taeral had moved out of the way just in time to keep his hand from being impaled by the knife. Kildare withdrew his fingers from the hilt slowly, eyes never leaving Taeral.

"You let me know when you're ready," he said icily. "Draw that knife any time you want, and we'll take this little chat outside. After all, *you* are the one who first insulted my brother and me."

Taeral's face grew red, and he was shaking with rage. He reached forward and placed his hand on the hilt, ready to rip the knife free and take up Kildare's challenge.

"Sirs!" Shia scolded loudly. "The innkeeper does not allow violence of any kind in this establishment. If you are going to damage the furniture, I'll have to ask you to leave."

Her pretty face was stamped with determination as she looked from the massive Taeral to the sour Kildare. Seeing the two enormous warriors called to task by the tiny serving girl was too much for Zedaine, who tried unsuccessfully to hide his snickering laugh by drinking from his mug.

The exhausted Chameleon turned to Kildare and frowned. "What did that table ever do to you?"

At the Drannock's unexpected quip, Zedaine lost control, nearly choking on his drink as he guffawed out loud. His laughter was joined a moment later by the equally amused Rion. Even Blade shared a smile at their expense.

Realizing he'd overreacted, Kildare's eyes lost their intensity. He glanced somewhat sheepishly at Shia. "My apologies, girl; you are right to take umbrage. It won't happen again."

"See that it does not," she scolded, hands placed firmly on her hips.

He left the knife in the middle of the table, however, with a last long look toward Taeral.

"Do you ever get along with *anyone* when you first meet them?" Chameleon murmured to Kildare, after the laughter had died down.

"Only naked women wrapped in blankets," he answered wryly.

His response set Zedaine off again. His laughter proved infectious, causing the Drannock to laugh aloud.

Smiling sheepishly, Kildare noted two things of significance.

Taeral continued to glare at him, though he'd shown the wherewithal to sit back in a less threatening pose. More interestingly, Blade stole a look at Chameleon. Something about the Drannock was bothering the usually unshakable sage.

When the laughter subsided, Blade rapped the handle of her fork on the table. "Let's enjoy this repast set before us, and you can tell me what has transpired in the five days since I last saw you. After that, I will answer any questions you have to the best of my ability."

The sage snuck a last furtive glance at Chameleon, and looked up to see Kildare watching her closely. She nodded her head toward the food, raising her eyebrows. "Would you pass me the carrots?" she asked him politely.

Kildare almost came out of his chair. The sage was trying to cover her slip with an idle question, but Kildare knew how to read people. For a fraction of a second, he had witnessed something he had never thought to see in the sage.

Fear.

Chapter 12

Sable reached into the soft velvet of the purse, running his fingers along the gold minas to assure himself they were real. His usual sum was twenty-five silver drachmas, but the mark this time was a special case. Sable had demanded ten gold mina for this night's work. His employer paid almost ten times that amount—without even negotiating—to ensure the hatchet man's success.

Sable gathered his men; ten of the best back-alley bashers in Gallanse, bloodthirsty cutthroats, every one of them.

Sable had gotten word that his mark had left the palace and was holed up inside the Golden Cutlass, a dive of an inn not far from the docks, and located on the seedier side of the lower city. It seemed strange to Sable that a man of means would frequent such a place. No matter; soon the mark would be fish food, a rotting corpse decaying in the harbor.

The hatchet man waited until just past midnight, when the flow of customers slowed to a trickle. The mark had been inside for perhaps half an hour and was more than likely asleep. Sable left six of his men outside surrounding the building, ready to pounce in the unlikely event that the mark would try to escape. Sable and his remaining thugs entered the inn, fingers brushing against the hilts of their knives.

The Golden Cutlass reeked of cheap ale and heady perfume. Several patrons were sitting at the dozen or so scattered tables. One, a sailor by the look of him, had fallen asleep at a corner table, propped up by only his elbows. Another was snoring contentedly on the ground, in a puddle of his own urine. A middle-aged whore who stank of lead and ocher was trying to entice the last conscious patron out of his coins before he, too, was senseless. Sable saw only one serving wench, who merely glanced in their direction and went back to work, hefting a tray of empty mugs before heading to the kitchen.

The innkeeper, a pot-bellied former pirate named Nyhlas, stood at the bar, eyeing Sable warily. He knew of the hatchet man by sight and reputation. He did not bother with meaningless conversation.

"The ambassador?" asked Sable.

"Came in an hour ago," the innkeeper remarked. "Second floor, fifth door on the left. Occupied with some new whore."

Even better, Sable thought, as he reached into his purse. A flash of silver spun across the bar.

The innkeeper pocketed the eagle quickly and went back to his business.

Sable and his men quietly eased up the worn steps until they stood outside the wooden door. He listened for a moment, detecting no sound or movement in the room. Grasping his curved iron dagger tightly, he and his men rushed inside, intent on the kill.

The spartan room held little in the way of comforts. A narrow bed lay on the floor, and a single rickety chair slumped in the corner. A lone candle's flame wavered in the draft on the windowsill, casting long shadows that danced eerily throughout the room. It was a far cry from what Lydia was used to at the palace.

The princess sat at the end of the bed, staring at the ambassador of Brisbane, who glanced at the door every few moments. Upon their arrival, he'd left the room without a glance in her direction. She had been able to make out his voice in the hallway, speaking softly with someone. When he returned, the ambassador sat at the rickety desk with parchment and quill. He'd spent the next quarter hour penning a letter, before exiting the room a second time. He had returned only minutes ago, empty handed. Finally, he pulled the chair up next to the bed, running a hand across his temple and letting out a slow, pent up breath.

"Ambassador, I am sorry…" Lydia began in a strained voice.

"You have nothing to apologize for, highness," Macklore said, interrupting her. "It is your city, and you can go where you please. But why leave the safety of the palace? You are far too important to take this kind of risk. What if you were captured, or killed? The whole country would be in an uproar."

She cast her eyes to the floor, downtrodden. "You think me a foolish girl."

He shook his head with a weary sigh.

"No, highness, which is why I am surprised to see you in such a precarious position." He stood up from the chair and knelt in front of her.

"My king has told me, on many occasions, that Conidon does not raise fools," he said with a tired smile. "Your brother, Ecian, was intelligent, brave, and displayed unparalleled nobility. I was impressed with him greatly when he came to visit Brisbane some years ago."

Lydia looked up in disbelief, "You knew Ecian?" she asked, a tiny catch in her throat.

His smile widened. "I would not say I *knew* him, though I saw him on a handful of occasions. The first was during a proposal of alliance between Brisbane and Gallanse. It was before my apprenticeship to my first royal ambassador. I was lucky enough to sit in as an observer, watching the proceedings firsthand. As I recall, my mentor remarked upon Ecian's excellence in oration, which was one of my larger flaws," he said with a brief chuckle.

"After your words today in the Great Hall, I'd say you have improved greatly," Lydia replied carefully, not wishing to offend him.

His smile faded.

"Thank you, highness, though I doubt many will remember my words with the news of Lord Dillion's death arriving in the same hour."

Lydia felt crushed. Lord Dillion was her father's staunchest supporter. His death would weaken Conidon and his allies considerably. They needed Macklore now, more than ever. "I am sorry to have interrupted, ambassador. You were speaking of Ecian?"

"Ah yes, I was," Macklore said, continuing. "The second time I saw him was at an exhibition of arms put on by the King of Brisbane, in honor of your brother. Ecian volunteered to take part himself, crossing blades with two of the king's soldiers and defeating them both. Then the royal sword master was asked to spar with Ecian. It was a rare display few would forget. Both were unbelievably skilled swordsmen. Ecian lost by a single strike. The king's soldiers still talk about it, so great was the quality of swordsmanship."

Macklore stopped suddenly and smiled broadly. "It was even common gossip among the domestic staff of Brisbane that the king's sons all wanted to be like your brother when they grew older, so great was the impression he made."

Lydia smiled at the tale, a faraway look in her eyes. Her brother had had a quality about him that inspired others. He was a born leader, and should have been the next High Lord of Gallanse.

"What is best remembered by those who watched that day," continued Macklore, "is how Ecian handled his victories—and more importantly, his defeat. Your brother saluted all three of his sparring partners, and embraced the sword master."

"The next day, the king informed Ecian that at that time, an alliance would not be possible. Twelve years ago, Brisbane was just one of many minor port cities on the Crystalline Sea. It had a small military and little economic influence. An alliance with Gallanse would have made Brisbane a target for your city's enemies—Dagor, among others. Ecian knew this better than anyone. He understood his mission was destined to fail, but it planted the seed of friendship in the mind of Brisbane's monarch, as your brother had intended all along."

Macklore stopped, a far-off look in his eye.

"Mostly, I remember what Ecian said just as he was leaving Brisbane. I don't suppose he ever told you, highness?"

Lydia shook her head, unable to speak.

"He turned to the king and queen and their five children, and he asked a question."

"Do you know why we light fires at night? To keep our enemies at bay. The brighter the fire, the longer our foes will remain in the darkness. Gallanse once burned alone in my heart, a solitary flame, a sanctuary from the evils of this world. Now, my friends, the fire of your city is ablaze in me as well. One day, perhaps, Gallanse will burn brightly in your hearts, as Brisbane does in mine."

Macklore paused for a moment, running a hand through his hair. "The way your brother spoke, princess, you knew it was the truth. That is why, when I think of nobility, he is always the first person that comes to mind."

Macklore looked at Lydia intently.

"So, princess, I *know* you are not some foolish girl. I ask again, why did you follow me this night?"

Lydia studied the ambassador's face, and saw concern clearly etched there. *So much like my brother,* she thought. Conidon was right to have put his trust in him.

"I would not have come, ambassador..." she began.

"My friends call me Macklore, highness," he said, smiling gently.

"And mine call me Lydia," she replied in return, as Macklore inclined his head slightly.

"My father is in need of help," she continued. "You showed Dragomir's monstrous side to everyone today. I cannot imagine him as ruler of Gallanse—nor, as my husband," she added with a shudder. "I came to plead with you to stay on as an advisor to my father. I was afraid you would return home on the morrow, and I could not risk the chance that you would take your leave before I could speak with you in person. That is why I sought you out tonight. I had to say this, away from the prying eyes and ears of the castle. We need you, Macklore—not only my father and I, but our entire country."

Macklore sat once again, the old chair creaking in protest.

"I have to stay now, highness...Lydia," he responded, correcting himself abruptly. "What you say is true. Brisbane does not want to see Dragomir on the throne any more than you do. However, there's more to it than that. Dragomir's advisor, the man in the white robes, is one of the *Moldranni Sor*, a powerful group of sorcerers—more powerful than most wizards alive today. They worship the demons of old, using powers fathomed only in nightmares. I'm not sure I can offset that kind of strength alone. There is no doubt in my mind that Lord Dillion was murdered by this man's order, if not by his hand."

A staccato rhythm of tapping could be heard on the floorboards in the center of the room.

Macklore quickly stood and snatched up the burning candle, handing it to Lydia.

"Do exactly what I say, highness," he ordered softly. "Hold the candle out in front of you."

"What is happening?" she asked, frightened at his change in demeanor.

"Those men following me are hired killers, most likely purchased by Dragomir or one of his vassals."

"What are we going to do?" she asked, forcing down her sudden panic.

"I was going to escape outside of the city tonight and return with the rising sun, but we've got to return you to the palace," he answered in a hushed voice.

"You knew they were coming?"

He smiled grimly.

"My father has many sayings, but his favorite is, 'always be prepared.' Please listen, highness, as we are running out of time. Hold the candle out in front of you and close your eyes. Don't open them for any reason, do you understand?"

She nodded, not trusting her voice, fearing it would betray her growing fear.

Macklore drew forth his scepter and whispered something she could not make out under his breath. A steely clang accompanied a brief glow of lavender around the scepter. So sudden was the flash of light, Lydia nearly dropped the candle. In place of the scepter was an obsidian staff, nearly two spans in length. He whirled it adroitly in his hands, looking as deadly as any warrior she had ever seen.

"Now, highness, close your eyes, and be ready to move," he whispered, eyes watching the door.

The princess obeyed his order, closing her eyes and holding the candle aloft, praying her hand would not tremble.

They did not wait long. The door burst open, and five men rushed in, iron blades gleaming in the candlelight. Before they could fully enter the room, Macklore raised his hand and closed his eyes, whispering a word that reverberated with arcane power.

"*Accendo*!"

A loud humming filled the room and collapsed in on itself before exploding with a blinding flash of light that emanated from the candle Lydia held. The attackers cried out in surprise, eyes blinded by the sudden brightness. A heartbeat later, Macklore was among them. Like a wraith, he attacked, his black staff whirling about his body. In the span of seconds, three of the hired killers crashed to the floor. Two died instantly with skulls split in half, while a third crumpled from cracked ribs and a spine crushed to powder from a hammer blow across the back. A fourth had reached out blindly and grabbed hold of Lydia's leg. She screamed in terror and jumped back on impulse, tumbling over the bed.

"Now!" Macklore barked sharply.

The princess opened her eyes to see the ambassador hurl his staff like a spear, impaling the fourth assassin through the chest. The last stumbled out of the room blindly, trying to feel his way to safety.

Macklore strode over, ripping his staff out of the assassin's body, and stalked toward the door. Lydia expelled her breath, surveying the carnage left by the ambassador's ferocious attack, unable to comprehend how he had just defeated four armed assailants. What manner of man was he?

Extinguishing the candle and throwing it aside, she hurried out of the room after him.

Macklore had already caught up to the last assassin, who was lashing out with his curved dagger, blindly trying to defend himself, while at the same time groping for the handrail leading down the stairs. Macklore contemptuously swatted the blade aside, where it fell from the balcony to the floor below with a clatter. He sent a crushing blow to the assassin's stomach, doubling the man over as he gasped for breath. The ambassador whispered again, and with a steely snap, his staff changed back into a scepter.

Macklore hoisted the assassin by the back of the neck and slammed him against the wall with a crash. He then grabbed him by the throat and held his scepter's stiletto blade under the hatchet man's chin.

"I don't care if you live or die," he said icily. "But if you have any prayer of getting out of this breathing, you had better start talking. Who hired you?"

Making choking noises, Sable flailed about, unable to speak.

"You're killing him," Lydia said, reaching forward and grasping Macklore's shoulder. "He cannot speak if he cannot breathe."

Slowly, Macklore lowered the killer to the ground. His hand, however, remained around Sable's neck. "You get one chance," Macklore growled between teeth clenched in anger. "Who hired you?"

"I…will…tell you…everything," Sable choked in response. He carefully reached behind his back to a hidden leather belt, quietly sliding a dirk from the depths of his clothing. "The man who hired me…" he rasped in pain, before swinging the dirk with his remaining strength.

"Look out!" Lydia screamed, seeing the attack.

Macklore's left arm shot downward, blocking the blow. At the same time, the ambassador hammered his obsidian blade up through Sable's jaw, with force enough to drive it into his brain.

Macklore, now enraged, looked disgustedly at Sable's bloody corpse. "Idiot. I would have let you slink away had you simply confirmed what I already know. You were dead the moment you took my contract. Your employer will know true fear by tomorrow; I'll make sure of that."

The ambassador let the hatchet man fall to the floor with a thud. He fished under the dead man's tunic, neatly hefting out a black velvet purse, brimming with silver and gold.

"You… you're robbing him?" Lydia asked in shock.

Saying nothing, Macklore pocketed the purse inside his own blue robes.

"What kind of ambassador are you?" Lydia asked.

"The kind that tries to stay alive," he answered without expression. "We're not out of the woods yet, highness. There will be more outside. Come, we must be cautious. Pull your hood back up. We don't want anyone to recognize you."

The pair descended the staircase, the eyes of the few conscious patrons following their every move.

Macklore walked over and retrieved Sable's curved knife from where it had dropped. Turning around, he walked to the center of the room and came to a halt, the innkeeper and serving wench staring at him fearfully.

"Tell me, Nyhlas, how did they know what room I was in?" Macklore asked evenly.

The innkeeper pointed immediately to the serving wench. "No doubt about it, sir, she talked to them right as they came in."

The serving girl shifted uneasily but said nothing.

Macklore stepped forward, looking at both closely.

"You know how I can tell when you are being honest, innkeeper?" the ambassador said at last.

"No, sir, but I'd guess it's because I'm an honest man, sir. Always have been, my whole life," the innkeeper answered.

"No, Nyhlas. I can tell that you are being honest when you're not speaking at all."

Macklore thrust his hand forward, a good three spans in front of the innkeeper.

"Conicio!"

Nyhlas was flung through the air by some unseen power and smashed with a bone jarring collision into the kitchen wall. The former pirate slumped to the ground with a groan and did not rise.

"How many more, Sadie?" Macklore asked the serving wench, breathing heavily, weariness in his voice.

"I only saw four outside, but there could easily be more," the girl replied briskly, with a glance at Lydia. "What shall we do with the bodies upstairs?"

"Leave the four in the room untouched; we don't have time to deal with the authorities tonight. Get what I need from that idiot on the landing… it's time to send a message."

Sadie raised an eyebrow but said nothing.

"Don't give me that look—just do it," Macklore said sourly. "When you're done, get back to camp and keep out of sight. Let the villagers know I could not present for them today... too much is happening at the palace. I'll return later tonight."

Macklore grimaced before continuing. "Report to...the king. I have to remain here until the succession is over. The *Moldranni Sor* are involved. If I don't stay, Conidon has no defense that can withstand them."

"Medyha isn't going to like that, Macklore," she said flatly. "He specifically told you to keep clear of this."

"Things have changed, Sadie. He didn't know the Brotherhood would be involved; none of us did. If he wants to see me alive again, Brisbane might want to openly pick a side. I think the king owes Conidon that, at least. We have run out of time."

Chapter 13

Over the next hour, Kildare, Zedaine, and Chameleon recounted their tale of recent events, including the search for the *Viasha*, and Chameleon's rescue. The Drannock spoke briefly of her message to Kildare and Zedaine, while the brothers told of their own journey back to Staltshore, including the deaths of the six guards on Thrimby's bridge. All the while, Blade sat motionless and listened intently. By the time they had finished, the lamb, pies, and carrots had been devoured.

"While that was a fascinating story," said Taeral, turning toward Blade without bothering to hide his annoyance, "how does it help me? I was led to believe you were an expert on dragons. That's why Rion brought me to you."

Blade shook her head, speaking carefully to the huge Taeral. "There was something in their tale that has given me information about the dragon. Did you not hear it?"

The huge Taeral slammed his fist on the tabletop, causing the remains of their meal to leap into the air. "I don't understand half of what they said!" he stormed. "I didn't leave my homeland,

and sail across the sea on some rickety ship, to figure it out myself. I want answers!"

Zedaine snorted with laughter. "I'd expect nothing less from a triton."

Taeral's eyes widened in shock as his gaze shifted to Rion uncertainly.

Rion, though, was equally surprised. He pursed his lips to speak, hesitated, and shook his head, frowning at Blade. "I must be slipping. I didn't hear you tell them."

Zedaine laughed again, running his fingers through his tangled brown hair. "Blade didn't tell me anything." He motioned to the tattoo on Taeral's face. "Most people wouldn't know your true origin, but I have seen the *Moktow* many times. I know what you are, though I'm sorry to say, I'm not familiar with your clan."

"He is of the *Rakmar* clan, who reside off the shores of Agenhelm," Kildare said quietly.

"How did you know *that*?" Rion asked, stunned for a second time.

Kildare pointed casually to the wall. "The spear gives him away. Very few tritons possess a spear tipped with a razor shark tooth... a big one, judging by the size of that blade. Only the *Rakmar* hunt them during their coming-of-age ceremony, and the razor shark keeps to the northern waters of the Crystalline Sea. The serrated edges tell me he is a war leader or captain of some kind. Only a leader can shape the spear heads like that."

Kildare paused momentarily and rubbed at his day-old stubble. "I'm more interested in hearing about this dragon."

"What's a triton?" Chameleon wondered aloud.

It was Rion who answered, turning toward the Drannock. "Tritons are aquatic creatures. Human-like in form, with webbed hands and feet. Most are larger than humans, as you can see from our friend here. They live in the depths of the Ariath Ocean, as well as in and around the Crystalline Sea. Very few humans ever see them. Rarer still is someone who has actually spoken to one."

He paused, taking a drink of his wine. "Until tonight, I thought I was the only person in the entire Crystalline Sea to have done so. It appears I am not alone after all. We, at this table, are the lucky few."

"Oh yes, I feel mighty lucky," Kildare said, his tone mocking.

Taeral's eyes were boring a hole into the two brothers, blazing with anger. "How do you know so much about my people?" he demanded, his massive fist clenched tightly in front of him.

Kildare shrugged indifferently and raised a mug of cider to his lips. "We had an active childhood."

"Sometimes I wonder if we're even related," Zedaine said, shooting his brother a look of disgust. "Do you have to goad everyone into a fight?"

"When they're acting like assholes, I do," Kildare belched, setting down his mug.

Zedaine turned to Taeral, who looked ready to reach across the table and choke Kildare. "We spent much of our childhood in Brisbane, another city west of Staltshore. About a dozen years ago, the White Coral tribe, or *Kadonmar*, as they prefer to be called, entered into an agreement with the king of Brisbane. The two races have had an open-trade agreement since. Twice a year, they meet to exchange goods and information with one another. Kildare and I were fortunate enough to attend one of those functions, and there we learned a few things about your race. That's how we know about tritons."

"The *Kadonmar* are trading with surface people?" Taeral asked incredulously.

"This is not a history lesson on life in Brisbane," Kildare interrupted, grating his teeth. "I am still waiting to hear about this dragon."

"He'll tell us when he is ready," Blade chided, sipping her tisane.

"Two minutes ago, he was pounding on the table, demanding to know," Kildare snapped, his voice rising in volume. "Now he's more interested in how we know anything about his race. We're wasting time. You think all these events are connected somehow? Then start making sense! For the third time, Taeral, tell us about this goddamn dragon!"

Blade, treating Kildare to a momentary look of irritation, set down her tisane and spoke once again. "Taeral, please, we've heard the tale of the mountains. It is time, now, for you to tell us your tale of the sea. Please, speak of the events that have brought you here."

The huge man narrowed his eyes at Kildare in obvious anger. Kildare returned his stare with ice. Taeral growled in contempt, content to deal with the human later.

"Six days past, we were attacked," he began. "Our underwater stronghold is located near the... I don't know what you would call it, but we've named it the Lahonton Abyss. It's a giant canyon that sits under the surface of the water. Its depths are shallow enough for sunlight to illuminate during the day, but deep enough for it to be difficult to see from ships passing overhead. It's perfectly positioned so surface people will leave us alone."

He stopped and stared pointedly at Kildare.

"We are among friends, Taeral," Rion reminded him gently.

"Hmmph."

"You're wasting time," Kildare said, resting his elbows on the table while cradling his chin on his thumbs.

"Please, Taeral, continue," Blade interjected tactfully.

The triton shifted uncomfortably in his seat before starting again. "It was sunset. I had just placed my sentries on guard outside the temple of Kelthane when a great shadow blotted out what little light remained. There were four of us swimming near the temple's entrance, but no one had time to react. We turned to see a huge, winged serpent diving toward us. Before we could do anything, attack or defend, it was upon us."

"A winged serpent," Chameleon whispered to Kildare, who nodded knowingly, but held up his hand, warning her to stay silent for now.

Taeral had paused, bowing his head for a moment and obscuring his face. When he looked up, his visage was filled with frustration. "My three guards were slain, torn to pieces by dragon fangs. Its massive, clawed hand knocked me aside against the stronghold wall. One of the pillars fell on me, trapping my leg underneath it. I looked on, helpless, as the dragon ripped apart the roof of Kelthane's temple and stole the sacred idol carved in his likeness."

Taeral's voice had taken on a defeated tone, laced with guilt. "It's our most sacred artifact—and I was assigned to protect it. I watched as the dragon swam to the surface, until I lost consciousness. Our shamaness, a powerful spell caster, prayed to Kelthane, Lord of the Deep. When finished, she sought me out, and touched my temple with her staff."

Taeral paused, a scowl fixed on his face. "I don't know why I was chosen, though I suspect it is because of my acquaintance with Rion. Regardless of the reason, I was transformed from a triton into this," he held up his arms, looking at himself in disgust.

"My people brought me to land, and I located Rion, who owed me a debt," he said, looking at the smaller man. "He has led me here, to Blade, the fabled Dragon Sage of the Crystalline Sea." There was a hint of mocking condensation in his final words.

"It had black scales, didn't it?" Chameleon asked quietly.

"What?" Taeral said, startled by her question.

"The dragon, it had black scales," Chameleon said again.

"It did," Taeral answered, brow furrowing. "How could you know that?"

"I saw a great serpent in my visions," the Drannock replied. "It was carrying something in its claws. Something that glowed silver."

Taeral stood up, surprised. "Where did it go?" he demanded. "You must tell me!"

"I saw it fly into a storm," she answered. "A white eagle was chasing after it."

"What does that mean?" Taeral asked, looking at Blade.

At that moment, Shia appeared from the back room. She had already cleared away their plates and dishes. Only their drinks were left.

"Will there be anything else, milady?" she inquired politely.

"You are wonderful, just as Sampten promised," Blade told the serving girl with a smile. "Give us the room for a bit longer, please, and then we will retire for the night."

"Yes, milady," Shia said, and strolled back to the kitchen.

The sage turned her attention back to her companions.

"We have been given the pieces to this puzzle," she began, taking in everyone at the table. "Taeral has told of the events that led him here. Before tonight, I believed the theft of his city's idol a random, though tragic, event. In light of what Chameleon has told us, I believe the two are connected; I simply do not yet understand how. I suspect, however," she said, looking at Kildare and Zedaine, "that you do. That is why you were so angry when you came in tonight. What do you know?"

Zedaine ran his hands through his thick hair while leaning back in his chair. "It's clear to us that Chameleon, for whatever reason, was meant to be found, but not just by anyone. She had to be found by Kildare and me. Her visions contained a white eagle. That, by itself, could mean almost anything, but it piqued our interest."

"Why?" Rion asked curiously. "It's just an eagle, isn't it?"

"Normally, I'd agree with you," Kildare said. "For Zedaine and me, however, it struck a chord. I asked Chameleon if there were any other specifics about the eagle she could remember. She told us it was a white eagle with golden eyes, flying in a red sky."

"I still don't understand," Rion said, face twisted in confusion.

"That's because the message wasn't meant for you," Zedaine explained. "But to us," he continued, pointing to his brother, "its meaning was obvious."

"The white eagle is the personal seal of Medyha Whitelance, King of Brisbane," Kildare explained.

"Very few people outside that city would know this."

"I've sailed throughout the Crystalline Sea for many years," Rion interrupted. "I've seen hundreds of emblems and banners. Dozens have flown a white eagle."

"The crest of the royal family of Brisbane is a white eagle with golden eyes, on a red background," Zedaine snapped. "How many banners have you seen fitting those specific qualifications?"

Rion pursed his lips but said nothing.

"When you were relating your story to us," Blade said quietly, "you said the seed of the white eagle is in danger."

"We think it's a reference to the king," Zedaine said, looking at his brother. "Who else besides Kil and me, two former citizens of Brisbane who *happen* to be familiar with the royal family, would know that?" He stared a moment at Blade, who nodded thoughtfully.

"No offense, lads, but that's a stretch," Rion said skeptically.

"Normally, I'd agree with you," Kildare replied again. "But the last thing Chameleon said was that the birds of darkness need to arrive in the city of hope in four days' time, or all would be lost."

Blade whistled, sitting back slowly in her chair as the weight of the words hit her.

"I still don't..." Rion began.

"The Raven and the Crow," Blade said thoughtfully. "Those are the code names of Kildare and Zedaine," she explained. "Those names are known only to me and two... maybe three, others."

The sage looked at Chameleon. "How is it that you came by that information?"

"A man came to me in my visions," she answered simply. "He told me."

"What is the city of hope?" Rion asked, still struggling to piece together their logic.

Zedaine flashed a quick look at his brother, who nodded almost imperceptibly in answer.

"It's a name that the king of Brisbane gave to Gallanse, once," Zedaine answered.

"How can you know what name the king of Brisbane gave to a city?" Rion questioned dubiously. "Do you know him?"

"Kildare and I were acquainted with his children a long time ago," Zedaine answered, after a moment's pause. "Quite close with them, really, and privy to all kinds of things those outside the palace wouldn't know. So, to answer your question, we do know him...after a fashion."

"Not as well as we thought," Kildare murmured under his breath, too quietly to be heard by anyone but his brother.

"Regardless," Zedaine continued, "We have to get to Gallanse as soon as possible."

"Why?" asked Rion.

Again, Zedaine looked to Kildare, who expelled a deep breath.

"The current state of politics in the Crystalline Sea is the same as it's always been: keep the Shaarian lords at bay. The only way to do that is to make sure they aren't united. The most powerful cities of Shaara are Gallanse and Dagor. Thankfully, they hate one another. It's in the best interests of the rulers around the Crystalline Sea to keep it that way. They can't afford to see Shaara united."

"Why not?" asked Taeral.

Kildare turned to Blade. "You explain it to him."

"The one great fear among the rulers of the Crystalline Sea is seeing the armies of Shaara come together under one High Lord," she began. "If this happened, a coalition formed by all the other cities in the entirety of the region would be hard-pressed to defeat such an army." She paused, sipping her tisane. "Especially if that army came under the command of High Lord Rexor, the ruler of Dagor."

She turned to Zedaine and Kildare, her eyes thoughtful. "It's the same reason I considered sending you into Shaara before. I received a report three days ago, stating that Rexor's son, Dragomir, is inching toward the throne of Gallanse."

"I still don't see what King Medyha has to do with you lads?" Rion said in confusion.

"Medyha is the most powerful mage on the Crystalline Sea," Blade explained. "In the last fifteen years, Brisbane has become a force to be reckoned with, both economically and politically. He has amassed a standing army powerful enough to stand against Shaara. Even Agenhelm, in all its splendor, cannot say the same. Should the White Eagle fall, so, too, will the peace of the Crystalline Sea."

"And so, it falls on us to get to Gallanse in four days' time—three now—or something is going to happen to the 'seed of the White Eagle,'" Kildare said in frustration. "At least, that is what we've garnered from Chameleon's cryptic message, 'all hope will be lost.'"

"I find it strange that two swords-for-hire, even childhood friends of the royal family, would know all this," Rion interjected. He was staring at the two brothers intently, a puzzled look on his face.

"You think we're lying?" Zedaine asked softly.

Rion raised his hands defensively. "Not at all, lad, I believe you. I'm just amazed at how much you know."

"We work with Blade," Kildare said, with a wave of his hand. "She keeps us informed of what's going on. She sends us into the political arena from time to time."

"I seem to remember hearing about an ambassador named Macklore who worked for Brisbane a few years back," Rion said thoughtfully. "Some business in Gauth, I believe it was. Do you know anything about that?"

Zedaine was taken off-guard by the seemingly simple question. Stalling for time, he reached for his mug and drank the rest of its contents.

"My report says he is in Gallanse now," Blade said quietly, looking intently upon the brothers. "I'd guess you suspected that already?"

Kildare and Zedaine said nothing.

"Perhaps we could get back to business?" Blade said, changing the subject.

"Yes," Taeral growled. "I fail to see how this is connected to me, as you allude."

"I didn't either, until Chameleon reminded me of the serpent from her visions," Kildare said, addressing Taeral. "Why would a Drannock see a vision of a huge flying serpent, unless it was somehow part of this? Tell me, Rion, you've traveled throughout the Crystalline Sea. What lies just west of Gallanse in the Emerald Bay?"

Rion raised his eyebrows and whistled, as Kildare's thought dawned on him. "The Serpent Marsh."

"I see it now," Zedaine said, with a nod of his head. "Where else would the largest of serpents live?"

"Well done," Blade said, congratulating Kildare.

"Whatever was stolen from you, Taeral," Kildare continued, still talking to the triton, "must've been significant to that dragon."

"I agree," the sage said, looking at Taeral. "That's the same conclusion I'd reached earlier. Now we come to the heart of the matter."

She sipped at her tisane again before continuing.

"From the information shared tonight, and from my own knowledge on the subject, I believe the dragon you seek is one that men call Ebonfire. He is a huge black dragon who has long lived in the confines of the Serpent Marsh. He's no mere drake or giant snake. He's a true dragon, one of the more powerful still in the world today. Finding him will not be easy, and defeating him may well be nigh impossible."

She paused, a wrinkle of confusion on her face. "One thing troubles me, however."

"Just one?" Zedaine muttered, causing Kildare to grunt in amusement.

"The race of dragons are the children of the gods, left behind as caretakers of this world. Only in times of great danger would they take a hand in the doings of mortals, and even then, it would be indirect, or a subtle manipulation."

"Looks like one of them decided to act a little more openly," Zedaine said wryly.

Blade shook her head. "Long ago, the dragons swore an oath against such acts. By stealing that idol, Ebonfire has taken an active hand in the world of mortals, and broken that covenant. He would not have done so unless forced."

"I'll be sure to ask him about his motives when I speak with him, Blade," Zedaine said sarcastically.

"Were you dropped on your head as a child?" Kildare said in irritation. "You're missing the point! Something or someone made that dragon act the way he did."

"So?" Zedaine asked.

"So, who can force an immortal dragon to do anything?" Kildare finished quietly.

Zedaine sat in contemplation while his brother's words sank in.

"I don't care why he did it," Taeral hissed, standing suddenly. "I care only that it was done to my people." He reached behind him and grabbed his spear. "Now, I know where to find him."

Rion was shaking his head at the huge triton. "By the gods of the wind and sea, sit down! You can't just go traipsing off into the Serpent Marsh like you were off for a walk on the beach. It's one of the most dangerous places in the world. The inhabitants are deadly, and I am not referring to the species of poisonous snakes that abound there."

"He's right, Taeral," Zedaine said in agreement. "There are plants growing in the marsh that can kill you just by brushing up against them. Not only that, the place is a maze of small ponds and rivulets that appear and disappear with the changing currents."

Taeral reluctantly sat back down.

"The question, now, is what's next?" Kildare asked. "Even if he is an ungrateful oaf, Taeral has a mission that must be seen through."

"I am beginning to *really* dislike you, little man," Taeral threatened, glancing at the knife still embedded in the table. He envisioned himself driving it through Kildare's heart.

"Join the club triton, it's list is long and numerous," Kildare spat back. "I will not, however, leave Macklore to his fate when I might have done something to prevent it from happening. I don't care what holy relic has been stolen."

"No one is suggesting that, Kildare," Blade said shrewdly. "In fact, I have an idea that will help both your causes."

"What is it?" Taeral asked, leaning forward.

"*All* of you must go to Gallanse," the sage said, "together. Kildare's right. If ambassador Macklore, or one of his ilk, is in danger, he or she *must* be saved. You, Taeral, will gain something as well. Gallanse is not far from the Serpent Marsh. There are villages on the outskirts of that swamp whose inhabitants are knowledgeable about how to survive its dangers. Once there, you can purchase supplies, and perhaps even hire a guide from one of those villages who can lead you to Ebonfire."

"That's all well and good, Blade," Kildare said in frustration, "but the problem now is getting to Gallanse in three days. It's over four hundred miles from here."

"I will hire a ship tonight, one headed for Adian," Blade said thoughtfully. "I believe Captain Tross is in port. He claims his is the fastest ship on the Crystalline Sea."

"Even the fastest ship on water couldn't make four hundred miles in three days," Rion said. "Unless it ran with typhoon winds."

"Tross has hired the services of a windmage," Blade replied. "He boasted to me a week ago that he could make it to Shaara in two days' time."

Rion raised his eyebrows but said nothing.

"With full sails and the eastern current, you should arrive in Adian tomorrow night. That will give you the evening to settle your affairs with Judoh. With the right conditions and a little luck, Tross can have you in Gallanse the day after. That will put you there in time to find ambassador Macklore."

"If nothing goes wrong," Rion said, but his words fell on deaf ears.

For the first time all night, Kildare smiled, as the possibility of arriving in Gallanse on time became a reality. The sense of dread that had plagued him since Chameleon first spoke of it dissipated, replaced by hope. He felt a great weight lift from his shoulders.

"I think it is time we were off to bed," Zedaine said, looking at Chameleon, who was barely conscious.

"Be ready to leave a half-turn of the hourglass before dawn," Blade reminded them. "I still have much to do this night, so I will bid you farewell. Kildare, walk with me; I'd like a word with you in private."

He looked at her, puzzled, but nodded in compliance.

The sage gathered her dark robes around her and pulled the hood up over her head. Lying next to the door was a bronze lantern Shia had left for her walk home. Lighting the wick, Blade placed a lamp chimney over the top. She walked quietly out the door, followed closely by Kildare. The rest headed up the stairs to their rooms, Zedaine leading the exhausted Drannock.

Shia was cleaning up the last of the drinks, when Zedaine returned and called to her.

"Your name's Shia, right?" he asked, beckoning her to come to him.

She walked over, a puzzled look on her face. "Yes."

"Your man, Whalen, says hello," Zedaine said softly. "He guided us here tonight and helped us enter Staltshore unharmed."

"You saw Whalen?" she asked, dropping one of the mugs in her excitement.

Zedaine smiled. "Aye, we did. He sends his regards."

Shia's cheeks flushed at the news. Tears came unbidden to her eyes, and she sat down on one of the chairs, covering her mouth with her hand. "Please, excuse me," she said, trying to pull herself together. "It's just been a long time since I've heard from him… two months, now. You'd think he'd come and see me, being in the same city and all, but he never seems to get a chance."

Zedaine bent over and picked up the things she had dropped, placing them on the bar. He walked back to her and gave a slight bow of his head.

"I must be off to bed, lass. You have a good night."

Shia stood abruptly and spoke in a hurried voice. "He's not my man. I mean… he and I, well, we have never…" She did not finish, just leaving the words hanging in the air.

Zedaine paused and looked back, a smile on his face. "I think he *is* yours, lass. You just didn't know it until today." He winked again and climbed the stairs leading to his room.

Shia, now alone, looked around the room, as tears ran down her face. She wore a smile from ear to ear.

Chapter 14

They exited the Golden Cutlass, leaving through the back door as quietly as they could. Sadie had insisted on leaving simultaneously through the front, in hope of creating a diversion. Macklore and Lydia crept along undetected, slowly working their way along the edge of a poorly constructed shop, when a dog inside the building caught their scent and began barking excitedly. Six shadows detached themselves from the walls nearby and raced toward the sound.

Macklore thrust the princess behind him as the assassins approached in a rapidly narrowing half circle, trapping them inside. The ambassador whispered under his breath, and his scepter extended with a metallic clang, transforming itself once again into a long staff. The lavender pulse of light momentarily revealed his cold expression. He swept the black obsidian staff in a wide arc, calling upon his innate magical powers.

"Infligo tergum!"

As Macklore's staff moved, the air rippled with force, and a sound like thunder rolled outward. The six attackers were rocked back, knocked from their feet as an unexpected wave of air surged into them.

The ambassador grabbed Lydia's hand and dashed past the hired killers before they could recover. The two raced up the alleyway, not daring a look back, as the thugs scrambled to their feet and began tearing after them. Macklore led, winding through the back avenues and crooked paths of the lower city. Lydia did not know whether he had a destination in mind, or if he was choosing a course haphazardly, just trying to lose the dogged pursuit. Her legs began to tire, and her breath was coming in short gasps as she struggled to keep up with the ambassador's lengthy strides.

Just as a cramp was forming in her side, Macklore stole down a dark avenue that reeked of raw sewage. They splashed through what Lydia fervently hoped was runoff and came to a halt.

"We've lost them for now," he said, eyes searching everywhere. "Take a moment and catch your breath." He did not even sound winded.

"Did you see where they went?" a man's hushed voice echoed down the avenue.

"Shut up and listen, dolt," came a second speaker. "You'll give away our position with that racket."

"You're not in bloody charge, Sevan," the first voice said harshly. This was followed by a meaty smack and the sound of a body hitting the ground.

"Until Sable gets back, I am," the second speaker answered.

Macklore did not stay to hear the outcome; instead, he quietly stole down the avenue with Lydia in tow. Several large crates had been stacked against the building behind them. They could hear someone snoring inside through the thin wooden wall. The princess slid between the stacks of crates, with Macklore protectively in front of her. A minute passed, then two, while Lydia's breathing returned to normal.

"Have they gone?" she whispered hopefully.

"I doubt it," the ambassador answered. "They'll keep at it for a while. They want to get paid," he growled in disgust.

Lydia rubbed at her left elbow. She had banged it against a corner wall in their haste to escape. With the immediate danger past, she started to feel the pain, and knew it would soon swell.

"Highness, you're injured," Macklore said, noting her movement.

"It's nothing," she replied, forcing herself to stop rubbing at it.

"Let me see," he said, moving closer.

"*Luminos*," he whispered. A faint glow came from the end of his staff, much like the lavender color she'd witnessed when it had transformed back at the inn. Carefully, he brought the light near her elbow, seeing a grimy abrasion and the beginnings of a bruise.

"It doesn't look too bad," he said, upon examination. "Here, hold this," he continued, handing her his staff.

"Really, I'm fine," she stated. "We don't have time…"

"You hush, now," he said with a kind smile. "We can't have you getting an infection, can we? This will only take a moment. Keep my staff low and behind these crates. No reason to announce our presence to every thief in the lower city."

From beneath his robes, he drew a waterskin. Carefully he poured the clean liquid over the wound.

She looked at him, taken aback by this attention. It had been a long time since a man other than her father had treated her with such kindness. Even General Hollus, who was as loyal as they came, did not grant her the concern Macklore was showing now.

"Why are you treating me like this?" she blurted out. It was almost an accusation.

"Like what?" he muttered, not really listening. The ambassador ripped a piece of cloth from the shirt under his robes and carefully began wrapping it around her elbow. "Not much of a bandage, princess, but it'll have to do until I can dress it properly back at the castle."

"You don't even know me," she continued. "Why are you helping me? Why do you care?"

He leaned back from her, a quizzical look on his face. "Because you're a person," he answered evenly. "One I do care about."

"But I'm a woman," she said, as if that should explain everything.

He laughed, a warm sound touched with genuine humor, despite their current predicament. "Yes, Lydia, you are a woman," he agreed. "A beautiful, intelligent, brave woman who is fighting for her city and all of the people who call it home."

For a moment, she was speechless. No one, not even her father, had ever spoken to her like that. For reasons she could not explain, tears came to her eyes.

"You should not say such things to me," she said, drawing back into the shadows, trying to hide her tears.

"Why not?" he countered, his tone light. "They are true, are they not?"

A clattering sound at the end of the avenue interrupted their discussion.

"They're on the move," Macklore said sternly, looking back the way they had come. With a whispered word from the ambassador, the light from the staff went dark. "I will draw them off, highness; you make for the palace. Stay hidden and stay safe. I will join you if I can."

"Wait," she said feebly, not wanting their time together to end.

He reached up, softly caressing her cheek with his fingertips, as the ghost of a smile reappeared. "Go, princess. Don't argue." The gentleness of his touch and concern in his voice startled Lydia. She reached up and took his hand in hers, heart beating wildly in her chest. There in a dark alley of Gallanse, rotting with the rancid smell of human excrement, she found herself complete for the first time in her life.

"You see them?" came a voice from the avenue they had just exited.

"Shhhh, quiet, you nog. Just shut up and listen."

"Go, highness, now," Macklore whispered a final time, and jogged back to the larger avenue, appearing in plain sight of the thugs.

"There he is!" one shouted.

Macklore turned back up the pathway and ran in the opposite direction of the princess, all six killers hot on his heels.

"That's three castles," Nold snorted into his drink, "and tops to me." The huge dockhand with a shaggy brown beard tossed ten copper obols into the middle of the table. They clinked against the other coins, spinning awkwardly, minted as they were in the crescent moon shape of ancient Agenhelm. Quickly, he finished off the contents of his tankard and asked for another.

Nold was one of five men seated at the nefarious Box and Rum gaming house, located at the border of middle and lower city. It was a place where denizens from any quarter of Gallanse could try their luck in a game of chance. Seated to Nold's right was Danimen, deacon of the local church. He was a holy man with a less than holy reputation.

"It's far from over, dock man," the deacon rumbled, mopping sweat from his brow with the sleeve of his cassock. He pushed a triangular silver coin into the middle of the table. "I will see the bet."

Play turned to Strum, a wandering minstrel of perhaps twenty winters. Dressed in bright plum and canary yellow, he rubbed at his thin mustache and measured the odds. "My two-pair is not up to snuff," he said at last, turning his cards over. "Not in the face of the Red Army and a trio of castles. I'll pass and hope for a better turn on the next go-round."

"A wise decision," said Petar, the fourth player at the table. The ink on his fingers revealed him as a scribe to a wealthy merchant of middle city. "One I should think to follow." He turned his five cards facedown and folded his arms in front of him.

"What of you?" asked Nold, somewhat rudely, to the final player. "You got the stones to gamble, old man?" Tellar was a stout merchant in his mid-fifties. He had won two of the last three turns, each time narrowly defeating the vengeful dockhand. As chance would have it, he'd flipped both the red elixir and the white ring on his last turn, and now held three magic cards, stronger than the Red Army, but no match for the castles. Nold, sick of losing to the elder merchant, was trying to bully him from the game.

"I'll see the bet," Tellar answered, pushing in a pair of silver coins, "and raise it an eagle."

Nold grinned and dropped ten more crescent obols into the middle of the table, as the serving girl placed a new tankard in front of him.

"I, too, will play," Danimen said in his deep voice. The deacon drew from his pile a silver drachma.

The stakes of the game had risen considerably and began attracting a crowd of curious onlookers. As the rules dictated, the church deacon took his turn, flipping his second to last card.

A champion, the red archer.

"Gentlemen, I give you the Phoenix Rising," he said with a smile, "tops to me, I suppose." With a fourth red card in front of him, Danimen confidently flipped two more silver drachmas into the pile. "A pair of eagles, if you will."

Tellar had to make change from a gold talon in his money pouch to meet the bet. The now sour-faced Nold followed suit.

The crowd gasped on Tellar's turn. The green wand appeared on his flip; a fourth magic card gave him the Mage, a powerful hand, stronger even than the deacon's Red Army.

Staring at the few remaining coins in front of him, the balding merchant grabbed a half dozen crescent-shaped obols. "Six shields, if you please," he said, dropping them in the middle of the table.

Nold and Danimen saw the bet, and the dockhand flipped his sixth card angrily. Incredibly, it was the blue crown, a fourth castle card.

"Ha! I give you the Iron Crown," he sneered triumphantly. "It bests both your Phoenix Rising and the Mage. I bet six—no, seven eagles!" he shouted, tossing the silver coins into the middle of the table. The big dockhand drained his tankard and called for more.

Tellar once again had to go to his money pouch, while Danimen shook his head sadly but met the wager.

Each player had but a single card remaining. The crowd had swollen in size. Those in front had to whisper the events to onlookers careening their heads from the back. With a quick look to the heavens, and a silent word of prayer, the deacon turned his last card.

It was a champion card; quite aptly, the red priest.

The crowd gasped and shouted in surprise. It took several moments for order to be restored. "Gentlemen, I give you the Crimson Army," Danimen yelled over the din of the common room. His face was covered with a broad smile. "The bet is a talon!"

With a sigh, Tellar dove back into his money pouch and met the stakes, nearly beggaring himself in the process. Nold also had to dig deep, his face flushed with anger, as he took a massive pull from his fresh tankard.

All other activity had stopped, as every eye in the Box and Rum was fixed on the game of Fives and Sevens. "It's your play, Tellar," Danimen crowed with a smile.

"I know full well that it's my turn, deacon," Tellar replied coldly. "It seems I will have to trust in Arianal, the lady of gamblers, tonight, since a witless goat like you is cursed with luck this evening," the merchant replied testily. Reaching for his last card, he turned it over and slapped it down.

The green sigil, the last of the magic cards.

There was an explosion of sound as scores of patrons burst out in disbelief. A fifth magic card gave him the Archmage, a nearly unbeatable hand.

Danimen sat down, his mouth wide open. The deacon stared at the card, pulling at his hair in surprise. Nold's face had gone bright red at the incredible turn of events. He had but a handful of obols remaining, and only a slim margin of victory.

At that moment, Cybol, the finest lady the establishment had to offer, descended the stairs leading from her room on the second floor. She sauntered over to the table, her red lace dress hiding none of her voluptuous curves. Her practiced eye and ocher lashes took in the pile of coins at a glance. "Perhaps one of you would like to see if your luck continues, this night?" she purred with a suggestive smile.

Tellar grinned hungrily, and looked to the nearly bankrupt Nold. "What say you, boy?" he said, his voice like ice. "I've little coin left, but should you win on the last card, I'll spring for you to enjoy the evening with this beautiful lady," he said, inclining his head toward Cybol. "But if I win, you will do the same for me."

He smiled coldly as the dock man stared at him in hatred. "Unless, of course, you don't have the stones for it."

Nold's bearded face changed to purple, mottled with rage. "Done!" he shouted through clenched teeth. Standing from his chair, Nold thrust his hand forward and Tellar shook it.

"May the better man win," Nold growled. Tellar nodded, and the dockhand flipped his card.

The black skull of the raging horde.

Nold had lost.

The huge dockhand stormed into the street, drunk and foul tempered. It had taken him nearly a month to save that money, and now *his* well-earned ride belonged to that old bastard. Cursing his infernal luck, he turned a corner and came across three other men. Two, he recognized as fellow dockworkers, and the other was a stranger he'd not seen before.

"'Hoy there, Nold," the first cried, a little fellow who went by the name of Scar. "By the gods, you've a scowl to match a thunderstorm."

Nold swore bitterly and recounted his tale of loss.

Scar clapped Nold on the back and shook his head in understanding. "Damn shame… that Cybol's a fine ride, all right. Rorst here was hoping to mount her himself," he said, waving at the second dockworker. "Looks like he'll have to wait till tomorrow. As it happens, you are in for a bit of good luck." He nodded toward the silent stranger. "Our new friend here works with a—a maker of spirits, shall we say," he said, smiling back at Nold. "He just happens to have some damn fine fire-whisky in that flask of his. How 'bout a pull for our unlucky friend here, Cirath, what do you say?"

A tall, slender man of perhaps twenty-five winters frowned slightly. "I don't make alcohol by trade. I mix elixirs to cure sickness and brews for all manner of…"

"Yes, yes, you're a crowing *genius*," interrupted Scar. "Jora's balls! Give the man a drink."

With a sigh, Cirath offered up the flask to Nold, who tasted its contents and smiled.

"Damn, but that's fine," he said, offering the flask to the others.

From out of the night, someone turned the corner and ran straight into Nold's chest. Recovering quickly, the slight figure mumbled an apology and began to move past the huge man.

"Just a minute, you," Nold said drunkenly, grabbing at the figure's cloak and ripping away the hood.

A dark haired, beautiful girl emerged, squirming away from Nold's grasp.

"Oh no, you don't," smiled Scar treacherously, clasping hold of the woman's arms and pinning them to her sides.

"I think our luck has changed, boys," Nold said, leering at their captive. The woman elbowed Scar viscously in the sternum, knocking the wind from his lungs, and shook herself loose.

"Grab her," Nold yelled in delight.

Rorst leapt in, tackling the girl to the ground. Still, she fought on, rolling to the left and swinging her tiny fist, striking Rorst in the nose and causing him to loosen his hold as he fell back in pain.

By this time, Nold had lumbered over and snatched the girl off the ground in a bear hug from behind. She snapped her head back, smashing him in the cheek, kicking with all her strength to break free.

Nold spun her around on the ground and backhanded her across the face with a roar. She fell roughly, skidding along the cobblestone street, trying to clear her head from the blow.

"That bitch broke my nose," moaned Rorst, as he wiped at the blood oozing down his face.

Nold strode over to where she lay and kicked her to the ground as she struggled to rise. "Well, lads, looks like we are gonna get our rides tonight, after all."

Motioning to Rorst and Scar, they hoisted the girl up between them and dragged her into the alley nearby.

"We shouldn't be doing this," said Cirath, shocked at the sudden attack.

Nold turned to the slender young man. "You ain't got the stomach for it, boy, then turn your head. Me and the lads are takin' advantage of our luck."

Cirath hesitated a moment, but with a sigh of resignation, followed the others into the alley. The girl's cheek was starting to swell and she had blood dripping down her temple. She looked defiantly at her captors, and opened her mouth to scream.

Nold struck her again across the face. "One word, girlie, and I will snap your neck and ride you while your body cools," Nold said, narrowing his eyes.

The woman sagged to the ground from the powerful blow, her head ringing.

"I go first, and will enjoy every damn second of it," he continued, starting to lower his pants. "Strip those clothes off her."

A steely clang reverberated suddenly in the alleyway behind them, followed by a lavender flash. Silhouetted faintly in the alley's entrance, a man carrying a staff approached.

"Who the hell are *you*?" Nold challenged.

"Death," came the reply.

Nold lurched forward, swinging clumsily at the man's head. The stranger ducked under the blow, hammering his staff up into Nold's ribcage, and rammed him with terrific force into the stone wall, face-first. Nold sprawled to the ground, wheezing in pain.

The big man struggled to rise, bracing himself against the wall. He turned back just in time to see Rorst's head snap backward, struck by a sweeping blow from the man's staff. Scar lunged forward

with his knife, aiming for the stranger's neck. The
staffer swayed under the lunge and reversed the
momentum of his swing, driving the sharpened end
of the staff through the stunned Scar's chest, letting
him fall to the ground. Before Rorst could recover,
the newcomer had circled around behind him and
snapped his neck in one violent motion.

Nold charged forward, anger lending his body
strength. "That ride is *mine*," he bellowed
drunkenly, his cry ringing through the alley. He
felt something explode against his jaw, and he
staggered back, trying to discern what had hit him.
More blows rained down on him, breaking his face
open, causing blood to pour out of his mouth. He
heard a cracking of bone, and his world vanished
in darkness.

Macklore turned back toward the last man in the
alley, his fists dripping with blood. He strode
forward, barely-contained fury in his eyes. The
slender fellow meekly raised his hands, "Please…"

Macklore slammed the man against the wall,
ready to unleash his rage.

"Don't," Lydia said, struggling to rise, "he tried
to stop them."

The ambassador glanced at the princess and
back at the young man, sensing his fear. "I saw a
coward standing there, while this scum was trying

to rape you. How in the *hell* is that trying to stop them?"

"He took no part in the attack on me, and he tried to convince them to leave me alone. He is a good man, with the wrong people, at the wrong time."

Macklore, normally slow to anger, did not want to let him go. He felt Lydia's hand on his arm, and with her touch, the initial rage drained from him. He looked to the still frightened man, and released his hold. "Go, before I change my mind."

Cirath drew a shaky breath, unable to look the ambassador in the eyes. "I am sorry, ma'am. I wish I had done more to help you. Your man here is right about me. I am nothing but a coward."

Without another word, he stumbled away into the darkness.

Macklore and Lydia exchanged a quick look. The ambassador was still flush with anger. Lydia found herself holding her breath, wondering what he would say.

"We are not out of danger yet," he said finally, starting off down the crooked alley. "Come, highness, we need to get you to safety."

She looked back to where the young man had made his exit, wondering what would become of him. Macklore was wrong this time; that young man *had* aided her. He'd given her hope when the others had her helpless. His voice was the one she heard most clearly. With a sigh, she turned and trudged after the ambassador.

Chapter 15

"I'll be dealing with the Triton tomorrow," Kildare grumbled to Blade as they left the inn together. "And I'm not going to be polite about it."

"I trust you will handle it as you see fit," she replied, without turning around.

Their footsteps could be heard echoing on the cobblestone in front of the inn. Blade led Kildare up the street past several two- and three-story structures. This was a relatively affluent area of the city, being located far from the docks. While the buildings here did not provide views of the sea, they remained free from the smell of rotting fish and raw sewage. The soft glow of candlelight could be seen emanating from a handful of buildings, but the majority of windows were dark; most folk had turned in for the evening.

As they walked, Kildare's curiosity grew. There had been only one other instance of her pulling him aside without Zedaine: the very first mission they'd ever done for her. Blade had wanted to make certain her new recruit obeyed orders.

Kildare smiled ruefully at the memory.

He and Zedaine had been forced to improvise from the beginning, as nothing went according to plan. It turned out to be far more dangerous than the sage had expected. After giving Blade an account of the fiasco, she'd invited them to become members of her organization, the Knights of Steel. They had accepted her offer, on the condition that they would be able to freelance for her part time.

Now she was asking to speak to him alone, once again. The last time had been a near disaster. Kildare was curious, and somewhat leery.

She was doing her best not to show it, but Kildare knew Blade was on edge. If he wasn't so concerned about getting to Gallanse, he would have made more of an effort to find out what had unsettled her. Something about Chameleon bothered Blade. Her manner had changed at the sight of the Drannock. What was it she'd said? Kildare cursed himself for not listening more closely.

They turned a corner, heading down an alley a few blocks away from the Stag and Hound. On their approach, Kildare recognized it as the building Blade used as her office. She hung the lantern on a hook next to the back-entrance door and pulled off her hood. Kildare could see Blade's face glowing softly in the candlelight. As always, he noted her strong features and intelligent eyes. While Kildare had never found himself attracted to Blade, he respected her inner strength and fortitude. Looking closely, he noticed something else—something he'd never seen before.

Silent tears streaked down her face.

Kildare blinked in surprise. He had been stunned by her outburst at Dusk Gate five nights ago. That had been the only time he'd ever seen her emotions get the better of her. For the taciturn and stoic sage to show vulnerability like this, something must truly be wrong.

"I had a sister, once," Blade said without preamble, still staring up at the night sky. "Delphician was her name. She was stunning, Raven; if you had seen her, you'd know what I mean. She had honey blonde hair, as soft as the finest silk. Her face was so beautiful that men and women alike would stop and stare as she walked by. The men, in particular, made fools of themselves. Nobles, commoners, it did not matter—all of them would flock to her. Rarely did she pay them heed. Like me, my sister focused on causes rather than people."

Several heartbeats passed and still Blade watched the heavens.

"Delphician was gifted in many ways," she continued softly. "She could run as swiftly as the wind and fight like a warrior born. When she sang, her voice brought maidens to tears. And to watch her dance," she said, smiling despite her tears, "was to see elegance and grace unmatched in this world."

"It wasn't just in her physical prowess that she excelled," Blade said, wiping the tears from her face. "Delphician could heal the sick, even those on the brink of death. She could speak more languages than I can remember, and spin tales master bards would envy. Her knowledge of this planet was unparalleled. No one, not even I, knew more."

Blade dropped her eyes to the ground.

"Delphician's greatest gift was her ability to read the future," she whispered, so quietly that Kildare had to lean forward to hear. "She could predict when storms were coming, or the exact hour of someone's death. She was an oracle—an extremely rare ability for our kind, almost unheard of in those days, even when magic was more prevalent in the world. I fear that the talent of foretelling may be lost. I have searched and never found any others with the ability."

"What happened to her?" Kildare asked, not unkindly.

Blade was quiet for a few moments before sighing deeply. "She fell in love."

"What?" Kildare said, reacting to this unexpected answer. "You're upset about this?"

Blade shook her head without turning around. "No. It was the happiest I'd ever seen her. Even if I could take back all this time I've had to live without her, and have her with me now, I'd not rob her of that happiness. Part of my sorrow stems from knowing it did not last long."

"Sometimes it doesn't work out," Kildare shrugged. "You know how it is."

"She died giving birth to her child," the sage said sadly.

"Are you trying to make me feel like an asshole or something?" he asked, at a loss as to where this conversation was going. "I mean, how was I supposed to know that? Next thing you'll say is that the father stole the child away and dropped it in a hole."

"No," Blade answered, her voice strained with emotion. "The father did not know of the child's birth. He was shattered at Delphician's death, for he, too, had known great joy. He was lost without her... as was I."

"Blade," Kildare said, getting annoyed. "I am not sure I'm following you. Why are you telling me this?"

She turned around and looked at Kildare with an almost terrifying intensity.

"Don't you see, Raven?" she said desperately, her hands shaking. "I'm moving blindly for the first time in years. I have not felt like this since my sister's passing. I only have two of her prophecies left to guide the path of mankind, and I have no idea what course to take. Should I guess wrong…" Blade broke off, looking lost. "If Delphician were still alive today, I might know more! But she's gone, leaving me to do this on my own! I am alone in this, Raven; I have no one to aid me. I am mystified—uncertain of what to do!"

Kildare was shocked. Never before had he seen her like this.

"Look at me, Blade, look at me!" he said, grabbing her shoulders and forcing her to meet his eyes. "I haven't known you that long, but I do know you don't need some prophecy to guide you. You have more knowledge and fortitude than anyone I've ever known. Almost single-handedly, you've managed to keep the peace here in Rhone for twenty-five years. You command the greatest network of agents in the world… hell, you've even corralled me into your web! Calm yourself, and we'll work through this."

Blade inhaled several deep breaths in an effort to steady her nerves.

"That's it, Blade, just breathe," Kildare repeated over and over.

Once her hands stopped shaking, Blade looked at him quizzically.

"Since when are you the comforting kind?" she asked. "You don't even like me."

"That's not true," he answered.

She looked at him, raising her eyebrows.

"That's not... completely true," he said, correcting himself.

"You threatened to kill me two hours ago."

"Zedaine and I threaten to kill each other every other day," he explained with a wave of his hand. "It doesn't mean anything."

He saw her smile sadly in the candlelight. "I remain unconvinced."

Kildare swore to himself. He'd made himself a promise never to get close to his business associates. Doing so had burned him too many times in the past. He was close only with his brother, who'd proven his loyalty a thousand times over—and one other, who awaited his return to Adian. Now he stood in a dark alley with Blade, who had let her guard down, probably for the first time in her life. Kildare wanted to know why.

"Look," he began, taking a deep breath, "you anger me sometimes with your secrets... hell, most of the time I don't understand your motives. Now it looks as though you are going to make me walk the earth with that ungrateful triton... but mostly, I trust you—and I don't trust easily."

He paused and dropped his gaze to the ground. "I never told you this, but when I was at my lowest, you took me into your service. You gave me purpose again, and that is something I never believed would be possible."

He looked back up at her, sincerity in his voice. "For that, I owe you a debt. Maybe you're afraid of the future and what it holds, but no matter what's to come, you won't have to face it by yourself."

Blade bowed her head at Kildare's words. "I am sorry, Raven; I should not have burdened you with this. I have felt very much alone these past several years. I always imagined I would have my kin, my people, with me when the coming events unfolded. I find myself lacking confidence at this critical time."

"It happens," he said simply. "Sometimes it helps to talk to someone… even someone like me."

Blade smiled wryly. "Be careful. You're starting to sound like the Kildare of old," she said softly. "The one before Gauth."

"Watch yourself," he warned. It was not a subject he wished to discuss.

"The world will need him in the coming days," she pressed. "You were a leader then; you could be again."

"Enough," Kildare said dangerously. "The person you're describing died on the marbled halls of a courtroom. Murdered by the cowardice of three men. You already know this."

"You say that," she said reluctantly, "but where are you heading in the morning? On your way to..."

"I said, that's enough," he hissed with finality.

She nodded in understanding. "I am sorry; I will leave it alone. I am happy with whatever help you can offer. We have enough to deal with as it is."

"What's going on?" Kildare asked, his curiosity overcoming his anger. "What's happening that's got you so spooked? If you want my help... well, I'm in the dark here, Blade. You've got to tell me something."

She looked at him and nodded. "It is best if you hear the prophecy for yourself," she told him.

"I'm all ears."

Blade closed her eyes and spoke.

"When the descendants of the Alo-Shen lay before the waygate of the gods, those banished beyond the planes will come again. The Rage King will wage a war upon mankind that will bring about the end of days."

Kildare stared at Blade, his eyebrows bunched in confusion. "Is that all?" he asked sharply. "Well, it doesn't make much sense."

"It will," she said, opening her eyes. "What do you know of the Drannock? Who is she? Where did she come from?"

"Chameleon?" he asked, surprised. "Why are you asking me? You're the expert on Drannock lore. I only know what you've told me."

"I'm hardly an expert," she replied. "I want to hear your thoughts on her."

Kildare shrugged his shoulders. "It's just as we told you. She claims to have come from the southernmost part of the Rhone Mountains. We found her lying unconscious in the water at the Mirrored Falls. For what it's worth, I believe everything she's told us."

Blade looked thoughtful, resting her fingers on her lips. "Tell me," she said slowly. "Are you familiar with how the Mirrored Falls came by its name?"

"I assumed it was because the dark waters below the falls reflect them perfectly, like a mirror," Kildare answered with a shrug. "I really hadn't given it much thought."

"Yes," Blade agreed with a nod. "That is what scholars around the world believe, as well. I have even given a lecture on it."

Pursing her lips, she sat down on a barrel next to the door. "Do you know why Estan went there?"

Kildare snorted. "Estan? He was a power-hungry warmonger. He claimed he was looking for some ancient temple of the gods, or some such nonsense."

"You don't believe that?" Blade questioned.

"Who knows what he was thinking?" Kildare answered in exasperation. "I've always thought he was a greedy treasure-seeker who ended up getting his men killed. Why are we talking about this?"

"Estan was looking for *Kumara,*" Blade explained.

Kildare's face twisted in confusion. "The City of the Gods?" he asked skeptically. "Why would he think it was in the Rhone Mountains?"

"Because the entrance to *Kumara* lies at the Mirrored Falls," she answered.

"What?" he exclaimed in surprise. "How do you know that?"

"Because I have been there, Raven," she explained. "How do you think I knew of the *Viasha*? Why do you think that is the only place in the world that it grows? Those plants are touched by the magic of the gods. Even the magada know it is a holy place."

"I was just there, Blade; I didn't see any city," Kildare protested.

"That is because you do not know where to look," she answered simply. "The Mirrored Falls gets its name from the second set of identical falls *inside the mountain*."

Kildare could not believe his ears. The information she was telling him was priceless. Thousands of people had died through the centuries searching for the lost city of the gods. It was rumored to be filled with treasures beyond imagination—and she was telling him right where it was!

Trying to refocus, Kildare shook his head. "What does this have to do with your sister's prophecy?" he asked.

"I'm getting to that," Blade said. "Tell me, what you know of the Alo-Shen?"

He furrowed his brow in confusion. "You're skipping all over the place, Blade; none of this makes any sense."

"Just answer me," she said.

He let out a frustrated breath and spoke, slightly annoyed. "There's nothing to know. I have heard of the Alo-Shen mentioned in your sister's prophecy, but their culture is ancient history. It disappeared ages ago. What do they have to do with any of this?"

"What have you heard about their downfall?" she asked.

Exhaling sharply in frustration, Kildare raised his arms over his head. "I know what every child has been taught," he began. "One day, the Alo-Shen were the most powerful empire on the continent... and the next, they weren't. Their empire was brought down in a single day, but no one knows how or why."

"Why do you think it fell?" Blade asked.

"I have no idea," Kildare answered, tired of this game. "No one does. It's been hundreds of years and no one has any idea of what happened. Of the few fools who have tried to enter what remains of the Alo-Shen lands, most have never been seen again. The select few who did manage to return all went insane. They babble incessantly for the rest of their lives."

"Well done, Raven," Blade said, nodding, "and quite accurate. You could be a sage yourself."

"No, thanks," he declined flatly.

"The Alo-Shen Empire fell more than seventeen hundred years ago," she stated, "but..." she paused, looking closely at Kildare, "what if some remnant survived?"

"You're talking crazy, Blade," Kildare snorted, fed up with the discussion. "We would have known if anyone lived; it would have been reported centuries ago. There were no survivors—everyone agrees on that. Even those who were out of the country died. There were reports from all over the Crystalline Sea saying the same thing. One account even came from the Seven Provinces! Every person with a drop of Alo-Shen blood went mad and killed themselves, without exception."

"I think scholars have been wrong, all this time," Blade persisted. "You have studied maps of the Alo-Shen empire, have you not?"

"When I was nine years old," he huffed, shaking his head, "I saw one in a museum."

"Humor me for a moment," she requested, her hands folded in front of her.

"I've been humoring you all night," he grumbled.

"Say you were a survivor of the Alo-Shen empire," she continued, ignoring him. "Where could you have gone and been safe?"

"This is ridiculous," he muttered.

"Please, Raven?" she said, nearly pleading.

Kildare thought back to her near-breakdown and let out a deep breath. "All right, I'll play along, but I still think this is a waste of time."

Kildare sat down on a barrel opposite Blade, rubbing absently at his chin. "You realize that I'm using a map I saw once for about ten minutes as a reference? A map that dated back fifteen hundred years."

"Just do your best," Blade told him.

"The choices would be limited," Kildare told her. "To the west are the Frost Claw Mountains.

The creatures that live there are the most ferocious upon the continent. Going there would mean certain death, so that's out. To the north is Tal'Mur. That would place you in the southern part of the Crystalline Sea. No survivors made it that far, or we would have known about them, so that possibility is rot. It's a similar situation to the south, which would have taken any survivors to the coast of the Ariath Ocean. Lower Valasca was in ascendance at the time, and they reported no survivors."

Scratching at the stubble on his chin, Kildare nodded thoughtfully. "Only the east would give *any* chance of safety, but even *that* would be remote, as that would bring them to the deadliest parts of the Rhone Mountains… which, as we well know, are filled with creatures only slightly less dangerous that those to the west. Even the magada avoid those places."

"So you believe, as I do, that the east is the only possibility for survival?" Blade asked, raising her eyebrows.

"That's not what I said," he growled. "I don't believe any of them survived, but I take your meaning. *If* any of the Alo-Shen *had* survived, their presence would have been reported."

"What if their survival through the centuries was not reported?" suggested Blade. "What if they were overlooked?"

"How would that be possible? Any survivors would have to have been shut off from the outside world completely. How could anyone live in complete isolation like that? Surely, someone would have wandered..." he halted, and his eyes widened as realization dawned upon him.

"Yes, Raven, you see it now, don't you?" Blade said grimly. "What if I told you that the ancient word for 'the people' in Alo-Shen is *Drannock?*"

Kildare swore under his breath and looked up at Blade, whose eyes burned red in the candlelight. "That means..."

"That yesterday, a descendant of the Alo-Shen lay before the waygate of *Kumara,* the waygate of the gods. Dephicians's prophecy has come to pass," Blade said quietly. "The war for this world has begun."

Chapter 16

L ydia stumbled into her chambers an hour past midnight, more exhausted than she could ever remember being. In addition to her injured elbow, she had a small cut above her left eye, and her cheek was one huge, swollen bruise. Blood had congealed on the edge of her black cloak. None of these things concerned her. She had eyes only for Macklore.

The ambassador's knuckles were covered in dried blood. He was limping slightly, but otherwise seemed hale, though deathly tired. The terror and flight of the past hour seemed almost surreal to her now, standing as she was in her father's palace, safe inside her own room.

Once they reached the outer walls, Lydia had finally felt that she was of some use. Like many old castles, this one had its share of secret passageways. That was how Lydia had been able to observe Macklore and follow him earlier that night. She led her rescuer through the narrow corridors until they were back in her room, sliding in from behind the mahogany wardrobe.

Lydia looked at the ambassador, her thoughts a jumble. What were his plans? Was he angry with her? Would he be true to his word and stay to help her father? She fought off a sudden panic at the thought of him leaving. She prayed he would not abandon them to their fate. He still looked furious, having said nothing since they'd left the alley near the Box and Rum.

"Ambassador," she began, keeping her voice even. "I want to thank you for your assistance this evening. I understand that I put you in danger, and..." she faltered, "I know you're upset with me..."

"Is that what you think?" he said, interrupting her, his voice hoarse. "You think I'm upset with you?"

"Aren't you?" she breathed nervously. By the gods, what was wrong with her? Never before had a man's opinion of her mattered so much as it did now.

He expelled a huge breath and shook his head.

"Princess, you came to me for help in the middle of the night on the streets of the lower city. Your intentions were noble, but for mercy's sake, that was a dangerous risk to take!"

"I had to know if you would stay on, ambassador; my father and I need you," she said defensively.

The ambassador raised his hand apologetically, "I know, highness, I should have anticipated that," Macklore said, drawing closer. "I cannot and would not abandon Gallanse now… far too much is at stake."

She breathed a quiet sigh of relief. *He is staying,* she thought, and her heart skipped a beat.

His eyes shifted to the floor momentarily before resting on her once again. His handsome face looked strained. "I didn't know I could make so many mistakes in one day," he murmured finally.

Lydia studied him intently and tilted her head in confusion. What was he talking about?

Macklore took a deep breath and plunged forward. "I'm not upset with you, highness. I'm furious with myself."

Lydia's brown eyes widened with surprise. This was the last thing she had expected to hear him say. "Whatever for?" she asked in confusion.

He looked at her bitterly and spoke. "What for? Highness, you came to me for help, and what did I do? I attacked you—almost killed you myself—at our first encounter."

"You didn't know it was me," she protested.

"No, and it was only a stroke of fate that your hood came loose," he continued. "That's when I recognized you. Had you not fought back…" he shook his head angrily. "Within the hour we were beset by assassins in my room and scarcely managed to escape. Then you were attacked on the street by thugs, and we were barely able to outrun their pursuit!"

He paused, his face showing nothing but fury at his next words. "To top it all off, I *left* you alone on the streets of the lower city! *Alone,* and what happened? Four god-forsaken animals beat you into submission! Every bruise you carry, every drop of blood you shed, is because of my stupidity."

He slumped down on the bed, while Lydia held her breath. She had witnessed anger many times in her life, but none like this.

"As if that were not enough," he hissed, "those men—those bastards—tried to...were going to..." he did not even finish the sentence, so great was the look of rage on his face. She half expected him to stand up and rip a hole in the wall with his bare hands.

"I left your side, highness, in the middle of the lower city, with a band of killers on our heels! By the gods, what the hell is wrong with me?" he stormed. "All of these events happened because I didn't think to stay here and talk to your father myself. Had I possessed the foresight to have done so, you never would have been at risk. Never before have I ever done so many idiotic things in my life, and I managed to do them all in one *goddamn night*!"

He shook his head in disgust. "And you think you need me, highness? I'm liable to get you killed."

Lydia looked at him, a well of sympathy rising inside her. She stepped close to him and raised her hand to his cheek. "Highness, don't…" he began. "I never should have gotten close to you like this. It's not right, and we can ill-afford any more mistakes." He looked away, his eyes unreadable.

Lydia paused a moment and considered his words. *"I never should have gotten close to you like this."* What was he saying? What did he mean?

Like the sunrise breaking over the mountains, realization dawned on her. Lydia finally knew why he was so angry with himself.

He was afraid of losing her.

Her heart started beating wildly for the second time that night as she studied his face. This man, this ambassador, cared for her. Not as a prize to be won, but truly cared about her, how she felt, what she thought.

"Look at me," she said.

"Highness…" he protested, still looking away.

"Macklore, look at me," she commanded gently.

She turned his cheek toward her and their eyes met.

"I know you're scared," Lydia whispered to him, her voice husky with emotion. "I, too, know your fear."

"My fear is not for myself," he replied, helplessly trying to brush away the feelings that rose inside him.

"As mine is not for me," she said softly.

A groan escaped his lips as he tried to maintain control of himself. "What if I had been too late? What if I'd guessed wrong about which alley you had taken? You could have been killed! Where would I be then? Gods, woman, what if…"

"Hush, ambassador," she whispered, placing her finger over his lips.

Her touch ripped away what was left of Macklore's self-control. He leaned in and kissed her with an intensity he had never known. Her lips upon his were soft, filled with the heat of passion. A hunger filled him as her lips burned against his. He could feel her tongue intertwined with his, and it fired his blood in a rush of excitement. He moved from her mouth to her neck, kissing it while Lydia moaned in pleasure. His blood was beyond fire now, flowing like molten lava through his veins. He reached up, fingers grasping her ebony hair. It was like fine silk to the touch. He opened his eyes and gazed upon her beauty once again, drinking it in.

A subtle knock came at the door.

The princess ignored it, leaning in to kiss him again.

With a tremendous amount of will power, Macklore pushed himself away from her.

"No, don't…" Lydia said, unwilling to stop.

Macklore continued gently stroking her long hair, his voice filled with regret. "I'd like nothing more than to stay here, highness, and enjoy the pleasure of your company. Unfortunately, our enemies do not sit idly by, and neither can we. I still have much to do this night."

Lydia held his hand and smiled sadly up at him. "Did I not please you?" she said, her voice breaking.

The knock came again, more insistent this time.

The ambassador smiled kindly. "Highness, if I could, I'd carry you away this very night and spend the evening showing you just how much you please me."

Her heart skipped at his words, and yet, Lydia found herself sighing deeply. She should not have indulged in this. She had long known a princess does not marry for love, but instead for politics. Macklore was not one of her suitors, nor was he a noble. He was not even from her country.

"I wish…" she began, and then laughed to herself. "I wish we could do exactly as you said,

Macklore. Ride off together, just the two of us, for as long as we wanted. I have never allowed myself such dreams. A princess cannot live that kind of life."

For a third time the knocking came at the door, accompanied by the worried voice of Madora. "Lydia, I can hear you; I know you're in there. The whole castle's been looking for you."

"Come in," Lydia snapped, like frost on a winter night.

The princess's lady-in-waiting practically barged into the room. "Where have you..." she began, before seeing that Lydia was not alone. "Ambassador," she said, with a quick curtsey, surprised by his presence. "I had no idea you were here."

"We've only just arrived," the princess said a shade too quickly. A touch of red appeared on her cheeks as she realized how it must look to the far more worldly Madora.

"That's a shame," her lady in waiting responded, a playful look in her eye. A slow smile started to spread across her face, but it came to a screeching halt upon seeing the cut on Lydia's brow. "What has happened to you?" she asked, now glowering at the ambassador. "Did he do this?" she demanded, her anger flaring. "I'll have your head!" she threatened in outrage.

Holding his hands up innocently, the ambassador gave a rueful smile. "You know, for a country where the women are supposed to be as docile as lambs, you're awfully opinionated," Macklore said wryly, looking from Madora to the princess. "The both of you."

"I'm fine," Lydia said, quietly rubbing her elbow. "It's just a few bumps and bruises, nothing more. The ambassador saved me, else it would have been much worse."

Madora, however, narrowed her eyes and glanced at the wardrobe against the wall. "You went out again, didn't you? I warned you not to go after him! By Dourn, girl, look what's happened to you!"

"I'm fine," Lydia repeated with finality.

"Hmmph," Madora snorted, letting the matter drop. "Well, while you were out gallivanting across Gallanse, much has happened here at the palace."

"What has occurred?" Lydia asked, standing up and straightening her dress.

"I will tell you in a moment," Madora said, stepping toward the door. Opening it, they heard her speak to someone in the antechamber. "Let the guards know that I've found her—discreetly, mind you, there's no sense in telling the whole castle. Upon your return, bring me honey, a cool cloth, and a clean bandage. Swiftly now; I'll see you soon."

"Yes, milady," came the response from a young girl outside.

Closing the door, Madora pulled up a chair and sat down. "One of Dragomir's cronies met with a well-known hatchet man," she said with a glance at Macklore. "They tried to sneak out, but one of our...servants followed them to the Laughing Horse tavern."

"The Baron of Cimmeron, or more likely his niece, I'm guessing," the ambassador said, rising to his feet.

Madora's eyes widened. "How did you know that?" she asked, narrowing her eyes in suspicion.

"I assumed that after today's events in the throne room, Dragomir would want blood," Macklore explained tiredly. "Specifically, mine. Hiring killers has always been his way. However, he's clever enough to know that he doesn't want it traced back to him. He sends word to his vassal, who then dispatches someone nobody will believe capable of hiring a contract killer. In this case, Lord Brak's niece, Talia. Even if it were traced back to her, they'd claim that she's 'just a woman.' They'd kill her and move on. Gods, I hate the laws of this country."

Both Lydia and Madora stood staring open-mouthed at the ambassador, seeing him in a new light.

"What has become of the hatchet man?" Madora asked carefully.

"He will hatchet no more," Macklore answered simply. "Now, what else of note has happened since I left?"

"You seem awfully well-informed for an ambassador," Madora said, hands dropping to her sides.

"The same could be said for you," Macklore countered. "As a lady-in-waiting, you seem to know a lot about what goes on in the palace and the surrounding countryside." He leaned in close to Madora, looking directly into her pretty blue eyes. "If I were you, I'd stop caressing the hilt of that ivory-handled knife inside your sleeve, and listen carefully. We don't have time for this game."

Madora locked eyes with the ambassador and sniffed dismissively, letting her hands fall loosely to her sides. "I don't know what you're talking about," she responded coolly.

Macklore snorted and spoke again, his voice commanding. "Inform Lord Conidon that Dragomir's new councilor is one of the *Moldranni Sor*. If they want my help, they'd best keep me in the know. I've much to do tonight and little time.

I will return to the palace in the morning to pay my respects to Lord Conidon. I pray he has the wisdom to see me immediately. Now go, I have unfinished business with the princess. Don't concern yourself overmuch… she will be safe with me."

Madora blinked, first at him and then at Lydia.

"I will see you shortly," the princess said, with a glance at Macklore. "We do have unfinished business. Please return within a quarter turn of the hourglass. I'd like you to dress my wounds personally."

Madora dropped her head in obedience and gave the ambassador a withering glare. "As you say, your highness." Turning to the door, she swung it open and exited, quickly pulling it shut behind her with a loud click. They could hear her footfalls on the stone tiles as she carried out her orders.

"You're not just an ambassador, are you?" Lydia asked solemnly.

Macklore sat down on the bed and bade the princess to join him. "In answer to your question," he began, rubbing thoughtfully at his cheeks, "a woman I once knew made the finest bread I've ever tasted. Simply remarkable. No one, including her husband, knew how she did it. One night, a thief broke into her shop and picked the lock of her safe. The woman walked in during the deed and a scuffle ensued. Much to her dismay, she ended up stabbing the thief during the ruckus. He later died of his injuries. Did this make her a warrior? A killer of men? No, she was still a baker who did what needed to be done."

He reached out and took her hand, tenderly pressing it to his lips. "To answer your question, I am an ambassador much of the time. Sometimes circumstances change. When they do, well, I have to improvise."

She looked at him, then, with a kind of wonder in her eyes. "Do you think this feeling we share will last?" she asked wistfully. "We've known each other but a day, yet I feel I've known you far longer."

He shook his head ruefully. "I wish I knew, dear heart," he replied honestly. "I can only tell you that I feel the same way about you. I hope that is enough for now."

She sighed and furrowed her brow. "Many of my servants talk about men just wanting one thing from a woman. Are you like that, Macklore?"

The ambassador shook his head and smiled. "I knew someone once who fell in love with a woman the moment he saw her. He'd proven time and again to be fickle when it came to matters of the heart, so I paid his sentiment little heed. When I scoffed, he told me that unless I experienced it myself, I would never know what it was like. I did not believe him…until now."

He took her hand in his and kissed it again. "I am for you, highness, if such a thing were possible. Events move us forward. The best I can do is help your family keep the throne of Gallanse out of enemy hands. With Lord Dillion's death, it will be far more difficult; no place, it seems, is safe. Do you have a weapon? I would like you to keep something upon your person at all times, even in this room."

"I…yes. I have a knife that my father gave to me last year. I seem to have misplaced it recently, but I will find it."

"Good," he said, standing from the bed. "I know it's not much, but these are dangerous times."

She stood next to him and they looked at one another in silence, neither wanting to part, both knowing the ambassador had to leave.

There were so many things Lydia wanted to say to him, but she knew they had no time. Already, he had tarried too long. She dismissed all the questions she had for Macklore, save one.

"Did your friend find happiness with the woman he fell in love with?" she asked.

Macklore's face darkened. "No. She betrayed him. In fact, he was betrayed by almost everyone he held dear, including me. Nothing has been the same since."

The ambassador wrapped his cloak around his shoulders. "It is time for me to leave, highness. Our time is running out."

"What are your plans?" Lydia asked.

Macklore grunted, a shadow of his anger returning. "It's time for the prince of Dagor to feel terror. He wishes me dead? He'll find I don't go down so easily. I will see you tomorrow, highness. Until then, be safe." Swiftly, he kissed her on the lips and swept out of the room via the hidden passageway behind the wardrobe.

Lydia could not help but feel sadness at his departure.

"I pray you will come back to me, ambassador," she whispered to the chasm of emptiness she now felt inside her heart.

Chapter 17

"Lass, did it ever occur to you that you might be wasting your time?" Phelas asked, struggling to keep exasperation from his voice.

"No," the young woman replied.

The large merchant sighed and shook his head at his wife. "Try and talk some sense into her, Vil; I have to head to the docks."

The middle-aged merchant unhitched a wooden cart from the back of his fruit stand and rolled it carefully into the market square.

"Don't forget, we're out of moss melons," Vil reminded her husband, smoothing her iron gray hair.

"Captain Lazlo is supposed to have a shipment of persimmons," he grunted back. "I know he arrived last evening with the tide. With any luck, he'll have picked up melons as well. They would sell quickly in the midday heat."

He leaned in and gave his wife a peck on the cheek.

"You need to shave," she said with a mock pout. "Your stubble scratches my face."

Phelas leaned in with his chin. "You mean like this?" he teased, rubbing his wife's cheeks and neck with his facial hair.

"Stop it," she shrieked, laughing outrageously.

They may have carried on like that for some time, but Vilma noticed their young guest staring at them from the other side of the fruit stand. Seeing his wife's face, Phelas tilted his head toward the young woman and ceased his antics.

"I'd best be off," he said, kissing his wife's nose playfully. "See if you can't get her to stop scowling at all the customers," he whispered in her ear. "The watch may come by, and I don't want them threatening to run her off again."

"I'll do my best," Vilma replied skeptically.

"Back in an hour," he said, leaving her with a wink and a smile.

Vilma beamed at her husband as he scuttled off to the north of the city and its harbor.

She and Phelas owned and operated the largest and most successful fruit stand in Staltshore's bustling marketplace. The main square was starting to come alive as the reddish glow of dawn crept out from under the horizon.

Vilma carefully eased herself onto a stool next to their guest, giving her arthritic knees a break. Once the customers started rolling in, she would have to be on her feet and ready to sell. Best to take her rest while she could.

She turned to the girl seated next to her. Even in the dim light she could see the shock of cropped blonde hair. It had been spiked on top and dyed a dark hue down the middle, giving the wild-eyed woman a look of untamed savagery. Vilma smoothed her gray smock unconsciously and licked her lips with nervousness.

What problems will she bring today? Vilma thought wryly. The girl's appearance had already caused a commotion when she arrived two days ago. It wasn't just the way she looked; it was, well, *everything*, Vilma mused.

It had been business as usual when the young woman, barely past twenty winters, walked into the market square near their booth. She was tall, lean of build, and moved with predatory grace. Her full lips were pursed with annoyance, set on an attractive—if fierce-looking—face. Stopping ten paces away, the girl scanned the area, until her flinty blue eyes came to rest on Vilma's fruit stand.

"Can I help you, dearie?" she had asked.

Without saying a word, the girl had walked over the cobblestoned ground to stand directly in front of Vilma. Tattooed upon her cheeks were a pair of ebony serpents poised to strike, adding to her already savage-looking features.

"Is there something I can interest you in?" Vilma tried again, picking up a date and offering it to the girl.

The young woman ignored her. She was busy studying the stand as though looking for something in particular.

"Vilma, who is that?" called a voice. It was Jyvan, a rival vendor who sold fruit across the way.

Vilma set the date back on the stand, raising her hands with uncertainty.

"If she's not going to buy anything, she needs to move on," he called testily. Vilma knew he was upset because the girl had ignored Jyvan's stand in favor of hers.

Phelas sidled over from where he'd been unloading pomegranates. "Come on now, Jy," he called back. "She's just looking, what's the harm?"

"I'll not have some tribeswoman dressed like that scaring off my customers," he complained loudly.

Jyvan did have a point. The woman wore hunting leathers crafted from the skin of some unidentifiable animal. They fit the contours of her body tightly across the hips and legs. The top of her tunic had been loosened in the midday heat, revealing more than what Jyvan considered to be an appropriate amount of skin.

Their loud discussion had drawn a small crowd of onlookers. Despite Jyvan's clear disapproval, the woman made no move to cover herself from prying eyes. It was obvious that she was aware of how dissimilar to everyone else around her she looked, and just as obvious that she didn't care.

"Look at her," Jyvan continued sourly. "She's armed to the teeth. The girl's likely to stab one of us to death just by turning around."

Slung across her back was a beautifully made bow of bamboo and a hand-stitched quiver of arrows. Circling her waist was a belt holding a well-used machete and a pair of ivory-hilted throwing knives.

"You'd best be on your way, girl," Phelas said to her quietly. "He's likely to call the city watch."

"I need to stay here," she said crisply, speaking for the first time.

"What did she say?" Jyvan asked loudly. "Is she leaving?"

"Said she needed to stay here," Phelas called back with a shrug.

"That settles it," Jyvan growled. "I'm getting the watch."

Before Jyvan could take a single step, the woman whipped around and threw one of her knives. She did it so quickly that no one had time to react. Vilma heard the result of the throw before she saw it. The knife was embedded to the hilt in one of Jyvan's winter melons. The orange fruit was sitting on the top shelf of his stand, not three inches from his ample stomach.

Jyvan stood in absolute shock. His eyes looked unsteadily from the knife to the girl, but he remained frozen in place.

The woman strode slowly over to Jyvan's stand; dozens of people watched in fascination. Never taking her eyes from him, the girl withdrew her knife and returned it to her belt. Reaching out, she picked up the melon and dropped a single copper coin on the ground at Jyvan's feet.

"I need to stay here," she repeated.

With that, she walked back to the other side of the street, sat down on the ground, and proceeded to eat her melon.

Nearly an hour later, an officer of the city watch came by to investigate. The young woman refused to leave, repeating over and over again, "I must wait here." After a quick word with the officer, Phelas convinced him to let her stay, on condition that he agree to keep her out of trouble.

Vilma smiled inwardly, knowing the real reason her husband had wanted the girl to remain right where she was.

Phelas, ever the shrewd businessman, knew that the girl's presence was attracting a larger volume of customers than usual. Once word had spread, the people of Staltshore had come in droves to catch a glimpse of this mysterious female.

Who was this curious young woman dressed as a huntress? Her weapons alone had brought a small crowd of onlookers. Archers from around the city came to wonder at the design of her bow and arrows. The shafts had been fletched from an assortment of feathers never before seen in Staltshore. The knives she carried were fashioned from the fangs of an Emerald Lancehead, one of the deadliest snakes known to mankind.

She heard a barrage of questions from the curious onlookers. Where was she from? How did she come by such items? What was she doing in the marketplace? What was she waiting for? Her refusal to answer only caused speculation to abound. The conjectures ranged from a secret quest for her homeland to tracking down a blood enemy.

It had been like that for the last two days.

Vilma looked again at the young woman, wondering for the hundredth time what she was doing here.

"You will have to forgive Phelas," she said finally. "He is a good man; he worries about you, is all."

The girl ignored Vilma. Instead of answering, she stared out at the early risers making their way through the stalls of the marketplace.

"What is it you're searching for?" Vilma could not help but ask again.

"I will know it when I see it," she said curtly.

"Well, at least try to smile if you aren't going to tell me," Vilma replied rather shortly. "Buyers don't like being frowned at." As soon as she'd said it, Vilma felt a pang of guilt. While close mouthed, the girl had caused no further issues, and sales had nearly tripled.

Standing up, Vilma flashed the young woman a kind look. "You really should smile more, dearie. You are quite lovely."

The girl ignored her.

By now, several customers were starting to infiltrate the marketplace, and Vilma got to work. She exchanged greetings with many of them, selling all manner of fresh fruit hand over fist.

"What is this?" asked an enormously large man who had ambled over to the stand.

"That's a mango, sir," Vilma replied, her finest business smile in place. "It tastes both sweet and tangy on the lips. They come all the way from the jungles of Lower Valasca. Those arrived just yesterday morning, still smelling as fresh as the tree they grew on. Only three brass chalkoi each.

An obol will get you four of these delicacies. What's your pleasure, sir?"

"We don't have time for this," cut in another voice, filled with annoyance. "We've a ship to catch, Taeral. We are not here to sightsee."

Vilma watched as the huge man tightened his grip on his deadly looking spear and glowered at the newcomer.

"You do not command me," Taeral threatened, loudly enough to cause all conversations nearby to stop. "I have not forgotten your insults from last night!"

The man who had spoken against Taeral smiled grimly and walked forward. "You think to contest me in this? By all means, try."

Vilma could sense how quickly the situation had escalated and held her breath. She glanced at her young companion, hoping she would have the wisdom to stay out of it. The young woman was watching the exchange intently. It was the first sign of excitement Vilma had seen from the girl.

"Is this really necessary?" a small man chimed in, trying to step between the two.

"Leave off, Rion," said a fourth, a tall, rangy fellow. "This was bound to happen. Best to get it over with now before we set sail."

Vilma watched as space around the two opened quickly, with a score of onlookers scrambling out of the way.

Taeral lifted his spear and moved forward, brimming with confidence. His adversary had not bothered to draw his sword. Kildare only backed into the open space of the marketplace and loosened his shoulders. Taeral lunged forward, serrated spearhead leading the way.

Kildare sidestepped it contemptuously.

Taeral did not relent. He continued his assault, wielding his spear like a quarterstaff, its haft and blade whirring through the air.

Vilma kept waiting for it to end with the smaller man impaled or crushed to death. Instead, she watched as Kildare dodged every strike aimed at him. Like a dancer, Kildare was always one step ahead of the darting spear.

Taeral's offensive had gone on for longer than he'd expected, and still the triton had not touched the warrior in front of him. Taeral's face had become flush with frustration, his brow gleaming with sweat. He was starting to tire and had come no closer to victory.

At that moment, Kildare chose to speak.

"Is that really the best you can do?" he said in disgust. "*You* are the finest warrior your people could offer? By the gods, you moved like a pregnant whale. You're an embarrassment to the *Rakmar*."

Taeral went berserk at Kildare's insults. With a roar he took a colossal swing with his spear, trying to slice the arrogant man in half.

Instead of backing away, Kildare stepped forward, seizing the haft in his own hands before Taeral could complete his attack. Using the triton's momentum, Kildare dropped to his back, pulling the huge Taeral forward and off balance. Kildare raised his legs, planting them squarely upon Taeral's broad chest, and flung the enormous man over his head to land with a crash in front of Vilma's stand.

In a flash, Kildare was on his feet, holding Taeral's spear to the triton's throat.

"You will accept my command from here on out, Taeral, or I will finish what was started," Kildare's voice sounded very matter of fact, not caring one way or the other what the triton decided.

Taeral eyed Kildare without fear.

"A battle challenge ends only in death," he said bitterly. "That is the custom of my people. I have been defeated, so you must end it now."

"You're not with your people," Kildare replied bluntly. "You're with me. This wasn't a battle challenge; it was a discussion. You lost. I've agreed to help you for the time being. If you wish to continue this foolishness, by all means, attack me again."

Dropping the spear with a clatter of wood on stone, Kildare squatted down next to Taeral's head. "I have no more time for this stupidity. Either follow me or stay here. I care little which you choose." Kildare strode off, heading north, followed by the rangy hunter and a wide-eyed tribeswoman.

Rion walked over to Taeral and offered him a hand.

"You have to admit," Rion said, straining under Taeral's weight, "the man has a certain style."

"Be quiet," Taeral rumbled.

Picking up his spear, Taeral joined Rion and hurried off after the others. Vilma noted that the massive Taeral was given a wide berth by the market-goers.

"Well, you don't see *that* every day!" Vilma said excitedly, turning back her young guest.

The girl was gone.

"You woke up cheerful this morning," Zedaine said, mocking his brother. They were waiting on a narrow schooner named the *Duquanes*, standing with Chameleon who was trying not to stare in wonder at the rush of new things she was seeing for the first time.

"He had it coming, Zee," responded Kildare quietly. "His arrogance is overwhelming. We don't have time for his idiocy. He's fortunate I didn't lose my temper and impale him on his own spear." He gestured to Chameleon. "At least the Drannock has the sense to stay quiet and not waste precious time."

Zedaine raised an eyebrow at his brother, looking unconvinced.

"Don't look at me like that," Kildare said. "You're not going to make me feel guilty about it. It had to be done; you know that as well as I do. I hastened the process, that's all."

"Yes, I think attacking and humiliating our boon companion is a *great* way to start off our journey together," Zedaine said mildly. "Nothing says 'trust me to lead you, strange triton,' quite like a morning thrust to the heart."

Kildare clenched his teeth and drew breath, ready to protest.

Zedaine merely tilted his head in a *'you know I'm right'* kind of way.

Kildare exhaled slowly and cursed under his breath. "Damn it. Now I have to go molly coddle that idiot." Without another word, he stamped over toward Taeral, who was sulking alone at the other end of the vessel.

Zedaine smiled impishly at Chameleon, his eyes alive with excitement.

"Won't they fight again?" the Drannock asked, watching the volatile Kildare walk away.

"No, Kildare defeated him in combat. Tritons place great stock in physical prowess. Besides, Kil is more than capable of thrashing him again. Taeral challenged Kildare's authority and lost. Now he'll do what he's told, it's the triton way."

Zedaine suddenly laughed, almost maniacally. "I just love tweaking Kil when I get the chance. He *hates* being wrong. He needs to clear the air with Taeral, and he knows it. He just doesn't like being told by me to do it. He'll never admit it, but he and Taeral are very much alike, I think."

Chameleon looked over and saw Kildare speaking with Taeral. She could not hear what was said, but Kildare was motioning with his hands, and the big triton was nodding slowly. "What if Taeral had beaten him? Wouldn't he have died?"

Zedaine snorted. "Kildare hasn't lost a fight in a long time." He leaned in a bit closer to the Drannock. "Don't tell him I said this, but he is damn-near unbeatable. It's not just his speed and skill with that blade. He's smart. Always one step ahead of everyone else. I have yet to meet anyone who could outthink him in a fight. He beats me three times out of four when we spar, and *I'm* nearly unbeatable," he said with a wink. "It's galling as hell."

"What did your brother mean when he said it had to be done?" Chameleon asked. "The fight with Taeral?"

"Cast off lads. We've far to go, and the winds are fair," shouted the captain to his crew.

Rion, who had been talking to the captain, was walking toward the pair and heard Chameleon's question. "He meant that Taeral was going to cause difficulty sooner or later. Best to get it out of the way now, when we are not in danger. Might come a time when he will have to take orders lickety-split. My guess is Kildare will be the one to give them, and he didn't want Taeral questioning him in a moment when it really counted." He looked at Zedaine. "That about the size of it?"

"Indeed, it is," said Zedaine, giving the small man a slightly raised eyebrow. "I have to say, I am curious. How did you end up traveling with a wayward triton? I didn't have time to ask you last night."

Rion waved his hand as though shooing a fly. "It's a long tale I'll not bore you with now. Suffice to say, I owed him a favor, and he is calling it in."

Zedaine noted how easily Rion sidestepped the question and decided to try a different tact.

"What do you make of our vessel?" he asked. "Blade told me this morning you're something of a sailor yourself."

Rion's eyes hardened a moment—so quickly, a less trained eye would have missed it. To Zedaine, however, it spoke volumes.

"The ship seems right enough, certainly built for speed. A good waterline. I'm curious to ask what her hull speed is? The wood is more buoyant than the common stock I've seen. By Kelthane, she has enough sail to…" Rion realized he had rambled on more than he'd intended and caught himself before saying anything else. "It's seems like a worthy vessel," he finished, trying to dismiss the whole discussion with another wave of his hand.

"I guess Blade misspoke at the inn," Zedaine said lazily, no longer looking at Rion. "Or more likely, I misunderstood," he continued, acting casual and turning toward Chameleon. "She said he knows a bit about the sea."

"A bit about the sea?" Rion said incredulously. "She said I know a *bit* about the sea? Fah, I was once captain of the fastest ship on the ocean! Captain Wavecrest of the *Windrunner*, I was," he bragged, proudly thumping his chest. "I could run from Shan'dar to Shaara in less than a week, navigating the shoals of the lost city of Kara. I know every nook and hideout from the coast of Upper Valasca to the southern tip of Cha'kar. I've sailed around the entire continent a dozen times over and always come back alive. Once, I even sailed all the way to the Seven Provinces..."

Rion stopped talking, eyes narrowed at Zedaine in suspicion as he realized the ruse for what it was. "Yes, I am something of a sailor, young man. And I see you are something of a scoundrel, getting me to spout off like some landlubber on his first voyage."

"I just asked a simple question, Rion... or is it Captain Wavecrest? I'm confused." Zedaine said innocently.

"Shhhhh, bloody hell, be quiet," he said, looking around the deck uncomfortably. The small man looked annoyed to no end. "Let's just keep it to Rion, shall we? Captain Wavecrest is long retired and sails no more. I prefer it that way." He took a breath and got himself under control. "As for your question... yes, the vessel is seaworthy, and the good Captain Tross seems to know what he is about. I think..."

"What is she doing?" blurted Chameleon, pointing to the quay. Zedaine and Rion turned to see a young woman sprinting down the length of the dock toward their ship, which had already pulled some ten or twelve feet away from its moorings. Rather than slowing down, the girl lowered her head and increased her pace.

"By the gods, she is going to jump," Zedaine whispered.

Some of the crew had spotted her by now, and several dock workers were shouting in surprise as the girl sped past.

Reaching the end of the quay, she sprang forward, launching herself in a heroic attempt to jump aboard the ship.

She almost made it.

Her feet hit the wooden railing that ran along the edge of the ship. For a second, Zedaine thought the girl's momentum would carry her on-board. She teetered precariously for a long moment.

The weight of her pack made the difference.

It was just enough to pull her off balance. Waving her arms in a desperate attempt to keep steady, she slowly began to topple backward toward the blue waters of the sea.

Acting instinctively, Zedaine reached out and grabbed hold of her belt, yanking the girl forward. Unfortunately, he was a bit overzealous in his efforts. He pulled on her belt so hard that she toppled forward into him, carrying both of them to the deck in a tangle of arms and legs.

Zedaine looked up from where he lay on his back with the intent of saying something witty to break the tension, and stopped. Gasping for air from her mad dash down the dock, the girl turned her eyes upon her savior.

Zedaine was rendered speechless.

He had seen beautiful women before, but none had affected him like this. She was, quite simply, exquisite to behold. Only a few inches separated his face from hers. He took a deep look into those fearless eyes. They were clear and bright, as blue as the waters upon which they sailed. It was more than just her looks that captured his attention. He sensed in her a kindred spirit, unfettered, wild and free. He continued to hold her despite the fact that she was safely on deck.

"What the hell is going on here?" demanded the captain, stomping over. He was a wide-shouldered man wearing gray pants and a brown jerkin. His heavyset face was darkly tanned from standing in the sun for hours at a time. Hanging from his side was a deadly looking cutlass, which he seemed to be on the verge of drawing from its scabbard.

He did not look pleased in the least.

"You bilge rats, get back to work!" he screamed at his crew, removing the black tricorn off his head and waving it at them. "I'm not paying you to gawk at some girl." The sailors scrambled back to their tasks, buzzing about the girl's leap from the dock.

"And you," said the captain, roughly turning to his newest passenger. "What gives you the idea that you can jump aboard and cause chaos upon my ship?"

The girl let go of Zedaine and stood up, matching the captain's stare. "I am here because of him," she said, pointing at Taeral. All eyes turned to the massive triton.

"You know this girl?" Captain Tross demanded, turning to the triton.

Taeral, clearly confused, studied the wild-eyed girl a moment and shook his head. "I've never seen her before."

"I didn't say I *knew* him," she replied, a hint of steel in her tone. "I said I am here *because* of him. I need him… my people need him."

"Does anyone know what she is talking about?" asked Captain Tross in confusion. With a frown, he placed the tricorn back on his head. Every one of them exchanged looks of bewilderment.

"If no one will vouch for the girl…" the Captain began.

"I have a name, captain," she said, cutting him off. "Adecia. I prefer it to *girl*."

"I don't give a whale's tit what you call yourself," the captain said angrily, "no one travels on my ship without paying. Do you have the coin for passage?"

She said nothing. Adecia just stared at him fiercely.

"If that's the case, then you are leaving my ship. Now!" the captain ordered.

"Wait," Chameleon said suddenly. The dark-eyed Drannock stepped forward and looked closely at Adecia's face. "What are those?" she asked, pointing to her cheeks.

Adecia narrowed her eyes, saying nothing. She was already tense, and the captain's words left her unsettled. Her hand rested upon the hilts of her knives, ready to draw them should the need arise.

"They are serpents, are they not?" Chameleon said, with quiet excitement motioning to the tattoos upon her cheeks.

"No one is going to hurt you, Adecia," Zedaine said from behind her.

Adecia slowly released the tension she was feeling. At least someone was acting reasonable.

"They are the *Mok'uu*," she said proudly to the Drannock. "I earned them."

"Twin serpents," Chameleon said quietly to herself. She turned to Kildare, "She is part of this, like Rion and Taeral."

Kildare stepped forward, looking at Adecia intently. He glanced at his brother, who tilted his head and raised an eyebrow. Kildare frowned at Zedaine momentarily and looked back to Chameleon. "You're sure?" he asked skeptically.

The Drannock nodded in affirmation.

Kildare let out a deep sigh. "It seems you are meant to be here, young lady," he said in resignation.

"Unless she pays me two silver drachmas, she isn't staying," Captain Tross stated flatly.

"We need her, captain," Kildare said again, with more insistence in his voice.

The captain whistled, a high-pitched keening that pierced the sea air. Nearly a dozen crewmen walked over, armed with all manner of weaponry. From grappling hooks and cudgels to harpoons and knives, each sailor was armed and ready to fight, many of them looking eager to do so.

"You might be some high-and-mighty on shore, boy," Captain Tross said to Kildare, "but on this ship, I'm the law, and what I say goes. Now, I like you lads well enough. Your employer had the good grace to pay in advance, and that always lightens my mood. But unless the girl hands me the proper fare, she goes over the side. Anyone else who disagrees will find the same treatment waiting for them." He rested his hand upon the hilt of his cutlass to further stress his point. "So, tell me, what's it going to be?"

Several seconds passed by as Kildare took the measure of Captain Tross. With a snort, Kildare reached into one of his pockets and fished out a pair of silver coins. He tossed them over to the captain and the tension faded. "That should suffice to cover her passage to Gallanse, and then some. I'd like to use your quarters to question the girl, if that meets with your approval."

The captain guffawed heartily and shook his head. "You've got some brass balls on you, boy, I'll give you that. On this vessel, no one but me uses my cabin. However, you can use the cargo deck 'neath the ship. 'Tis the only place that'll fit the six of you, and it stands only half full since your beneficiary demanded as much speed as possible. After that, you can bunk two at a time in the first mate's quarters below deck until we land in Adian."

He looked back to his men, who were still hovering nearby. "Don't just stand around, you slack jaws, we've got work to do. I want to make Adian at least an hour before sunset, damn you. Watson, get your skinny arse up that rope and secure the rigging…"

All eyes turned to Adecia as Kildare leaned forward, addressing her directly. "You'd better hope Chameleon is right about you, girl, or you'll be wishing the captain *had* thrown you off the boat." He didn't even sound angry. "Follow me, all of you," he said. Without another word, he headed below deck.

"You should see him when he's upset," Zedaine said with a playful smile.

Rion snickered behind them and followed Kildare.

The cargo hold below deck was much like any other Rion had seen in his many years at sea. Filled with the salty smell of bilge water, it held a number of different crates and barrels, most prominently foodstuffs grown in the fertile lands to the south. Such goods could be sold at any number of ports around the Crystalline Sea, and would make the captain and crew a fair profit as long as no trouble occurred. The cargo had been raised onto beams specially installed on the bottom of the craft to keep the goods dry.

Standing in the bowels of the ship taking in its familiar aroma, Rion could not help but remember his first voyage over thirty years ago. A slight lad of fifteen trying to stay one step ahead of the local bailiff, Rion had snuck aboard the *Fire Opal*, a small trawler departing from the sleepy hamlet of Vyne. It was on board that wreck of a ship he'd first found his true calling.

Rion thought back to old Captain Chane who would become the first of his many mentors.

"The first rule of being a captain is convincing everyone else you're the best man for the job," Chane would say. "If you can't hack it, the crew will know soon enough, and you'll find yourself captain of driftwood!"

He smiled, thinking of how long ago it was that he had been that young man at sea. *Not like now,* he thought to himself, wondering again how he had gotten himself mixed up with this group. He looked at the grim-faced Kildare, interested in assessing the young man. *Let's see what kind of captain you are*, he thought.

Even with only a partial load, the six companions found the cargo area cramped, especially Taeral, whose head just cleared the ceiling. Once they had managed to squeeze together, Kildare looked at Adecia.

"Well, girl, I'd like an explanation as to your motive for that magnificent leap onto the boat," he said.

"My name is Adecia, not *girl,* as I explained to the captain," she replied coldly.

"And I just paid two silver drachmas for your passage, so I expect you to answer me," he fired back. "You said it was because of Taeral. What did you mean?"

She stared at him and her eyes hardened. "You are the leader here?" she asked suddenly. "Why not him?" she continued, pointing to Zedaine.

The younger sibling laughed out loud. "I'm not built to lead, Adecia. All that planning and thinking ahead… it's not for me. Kildare here is the one for that. He excels at it. I'm just along for the ride."

Adecia looked at Zedaine with skepticism, the corners of her mouth turned down. "If you say so," she muttered, casting sullen eyes back to Kildare.

"All right, I will tell you, *Kildare.*" She spat his name out like it was a curse. Leaning back against the hull, her hands never far from her weapons, Adecia began. "I'm from Inniack, a small fishing village south of Gallanse. My people have been under attack these past three weeks. Normally, that would be nothing new for us, as Inniack lies on the edge of the Serpent Marsh."

"You live near the marsh?" Taeral asked in surprise.

"I just said as much, didn't I?" she answered, irritated at the interruption.

"Have you seen...?" he continued, a note of urgency in his voice.

"Taeral, let her talk," Kildare said coldly, cutting the triton off.

Taeral glowered at Kildare. "But she..."

"I know what she said, and I know what you're going to ask," Kildare explained, forcing himself to remain calm. "You will have time. We are many hours from Adian."

Taeral narrowed his gaze and nodded curtly.

"Continue, please," Kildare said, looking back at Adecia.

"Over the last three weeks my village has been attacked by Ettu," she continued. "Are you familiar with them?"

"Reptilian creatures that live in the wetlands," Zedaine answered. "Bigger than most men, they are highly intelligent and quite vicious."

"They have been known to attack outposts in the Emerald Bay from time to time," Taeral's deep voice chimed in. "I've fought them before, and they are formidable."

"I know some have attacked ships at night when they anchor too close to their territories," Rion added.

"If we could continue," Kildare said, trying to keep his temper in check.

Adecia, however, was looking at Chameleon. The Drannock was staring at the woman intently, her eyes unblinking.

"Why are you looking at me like that?" Adecia asked firmly.

Chameleon blinked.

Suddenly a huge reptilian creature stood in the middle of the cargo hold. It was sneering malevolently at Taeral, while baring teeth stained red with blood.

Taeral swore and fell backward, reaching for his spear. At the same time, Adecia shot forward, drawing her knives and slashing at the Ettu's neck and chest. Both of her blows passed harmlessly through the creature, as though it were not there.

"Hold," commanded Kildare, raising his arms.

"Are you crazy?" demanded Rion, who'd dropped into a crouch, knife in hand.

Kildare looked at the creature with a frown. It was covered in olive green scales standing upright on a pair of long, powerful legs. It had an assortment of finlike sails, each several inches long, protruding along its back, while a short tail hung between its legs, swaying slowly back and forth. Its face was a bestial mix of man and serpent, with a long greenish snout underneath two piercing yellow eyes. It stood almost as large as

Taeral. In one hand it held a crude war axe, while the other gripped a wooden shield.

Kildare stepped toward the creature, walking right through it. "That will do, Chameleon," he said, frowning at her.

Each of them turned toward the Drannock in wonder. A moment later, the Ettu flickered and disappeared.

"So that is what they look like," Chameleon said in awe.

"How... what did you do?" asked Adecia, staring at the Drannock, eyes wide with amazement.

Chameleon looked back at Adecia. "I am sorry. I read the image in your mind and cast a reflection of it in front of us. I did not mean to startle everyone, but I had to see it for myself. I do not usually intrude upon people's thoughts like that, but..." pausing, she shook her head. "It will not happen again. I just... I have never seen such a creature before. My curiosity got the better of me."

"Who are you?" Rion asked, not taking his eyes from Chameleon. "What sorcery was that?"

Taeral, too, was looking at Chameleon in horror. "I'll not be party to that kind of witchcraft!" he said, his voice shaking.

"Says the triton transformed by his shamaness," clucked Zedaine with a frown.

"She is a demon of the mind!" Taeral continued angrily. "Who knows what she's capable..."

"Enough!" Kildare thundered suddenly, eyes blazing with fury. He leveled his gaze at all of them, ready to explode. "None of us wants to be here! I can think of a thousand things I'd rather be doing than standing in this hold! But that is not my reality. In my reality, I have to help Taeral recover the idol of his people. In my reality, I have to go save a man I'd just as soon kill and be done with. That is the world I live in."

He pointed to Chameleon. "This woman has risked her life to provide me with information. She did it crossing some of the most dangerous terrain known to man. She was armed with nothing more than a stone knife and her courage."

Kildare paused, letting his words sink in. "Adecia is here on Chameleon's word alone, and that is enough for me. Now, if we could all just shut the hell up for *five goddamn seconds*, we can listen to what she has to say!"

All but Zedaine were taken aback. They had not seen Kildare like this before. It was more than just his anger that subdued them; it was his voice. Filled with power, it rang with authority.

Zedaine leaned in toward the stunned Adecia. "That's why he's the leader," he whispered loudly enough to be heard by them all.

"Now," Kildare looked back upon the huntress, "If you would continue."

Adecia blinked several times, staring intently at Kildare.

"As I was saying," she said finally, "my village has been attacked by Ettu of the Red Claw tribe over the last three weeks. Usually, it's nothing more than a foray of a dozen of their raiders bent on stealing my people for slaves or food. We suffer these occurrences every odd year or so. These recent attacks, however, have been much more than raids. Nearly a hundred of the creatures assaulted the main settlement ten days ago! It's the third major attack we have seen in as many days."

"That's a bit of news," Zedaine said, raising his eyebrow. "The Ettu have gathered in number again. It's been...what, twenty-five years since they last boiled out of the swamps, killing and pillaging up and down the southern coast all the way to Adian."

"Has it been that long?" Rion asked, shaking his head.

"As a matter of fact, it was twenty-five years ago...today," Kildare said, frowning at the thought.

"I wish my tale was complete, but there is more," Adecia said grimly. "The day before I left, we were struck again. This time, it was the Ettu of the Jagged Fang tribe. Nearly fifty of them surprised us as they skulked out of Emerald Bay, killing many of my people. At the same time, the Red Claw attacked us again in force. We were barely able to drive them off."

Zedaine let out a low whistle in understanding. "If the tribes are working together... it's only a matter of time, isn't it?"

"I was able to question a Fang scout that had been mortally wounded in the last foray. He told me," she licked her lips hesitantly, clearly having trouble with what she was about to say, "that the last attacks were *nothing* compared to what was coming. Once I informed the village headman of the creature's words, a request was sent to the High Lord of Gallanse, begging for aid," Adecia continued. "I, however, was compelled to do something else," she paused, looking uncertain for the first time. "I cannot explain what led me to Staltshore but, I *felt* a compulsion to go there."

She looked up at Kildare, confusion on her face. "I left Gallanse four days ago on a ship bound for Staltshore. When I arrived two days past, something compelled me to travel to the marketplace. I waited at the fruit stand until I saw you today, Taeral."

She leaned in close, peering at him intently. "I know what you are. My people need your help.

We need the help of the Tritons. Only your kind can combat the Ettu under the water, where they spend the majority of their lives."

Taeral narrowed his gaze in disbelief. "How does everyone... how do you know I am a triton?"

"I am a huntress of Inniak," she replied. "I walk the Serpent Marsh every day. It's a place where you see many strange sights. Less than a year ago, I was tracking a band of Ettu that had wandered into our territory. I followed them all the way to the borders of their lands, until they disappeared back into the darkness of the Marsh. I waited, making certain they were gone. That was when I saw a sea snake surface in the waters of the bay. It was followed by a young female triton. I watched as she battled the snake. It was something I never thought to see. The snake dove back into the waters, with the triton female in hot pursuit. I recognized the marks around her eyes; they were similar to yours. That's how I knew you for what you were."

"Must have been on her blood quest," Taeral mused quietly. "I am not sure what you think I can do for you," he said to the young huntress. "I am on a mission of my own."

"You said you were a huntress of Inniak," mused Kildare thoughtfully. "How much do you know of the Serpent Marsh?"

Adecia narrowed her eyes and looked at Kildare. "I know the swamplands better than all but my mentor. I have tracked Ettu all the way to their tribal lands undetected. I can identify any number of plants and animals that call those swamplands their home. I earned these," she said, motioning to the snake tattoos upon her cheeks.

"Could you lead us to Ebonfire?" Kildare asked.

Adecia did not say anything for a long moment. She scanned the five faces surrounding her. They all looked serious. "Why would you do such a thing?" she asked. "It's suicide."

"Could you lead us to it if doing so meant that Taeral could help your village?" he pushed.

Taeral did not look pleased. "You cannot make that kind of promise…" he began.

"So quickly, you have forgotten the marketplace," Kildare said mildly, cutting him off. "Where I believe you had your chance at leadership."

Rubbing at his chin, Kildare shook his head in exasperation. "Wouldn't you agree to help if she could guide us to your idol?"

Clever lad, Rion thought to himself, covering his smile.

The triton was not used to this. He was a battle commander and used to being the one in charge. He calmed himself. By gar, the man could fight, and he had a point. "Yes, I would summon help, as best I could, if she agreed to lead us to the dragon."

"What do you say, Adecia?" Kildare said to the huntress. "Taeral's help for yours."

The huntress ran a hand through her spiked hair, lost in thought. "That dragon is going to kill us all," she said at last.

"That's the spirit," Zedaine said with a grim smile.

Chapter 18

The sun rose off the western horizon of Emerald Bay, its faint rays piercing the gloom of Dragomir's chamber. The prince lay upon his mattress, shrouded by the fine lace canopy that hung from atop the bed. Sitting upright, the young heir swatted aside the drapes in annoyance as he rolled to his feet. The dim light of the room revealed Dragomir's disheveled hair, sallow skin, and sunken eyes—clear evidence of a harsh night with little slumber. When he had been able to sleep, his dreams had been troubled, even fearful. One bothered him in particular: he dreamt of the wretched ambassador of Brisbane entering his room, sending a sliver of fear down his spine. Dragomir reached out, cupping his hands full of tepid water from the washbasin. He splashed it on his face, rubbing his eyes as he tried to clear his head of the vile memory.

The Shaarian prince strode over to the balcony, brushing aside the gossamer curtain and stood naked in the yellow glow of the rising sun. His ice blue eyes overlooked the city for the hundredth time, seeing none of it. The chill of the morning air upon his pale skin did not touch him. Even the sounds of the city below waking with the daylight left him unperturbed. His thoughts turned inward as he mulled over the events of the past day.

Dragomir's initial success in the Great Hall the previous afternoon had gone according to plan. The princess's insult had been something of a surprise, but Dragomir had used it to his advantage. Eliphas had warned him that the brash girl might intervene and had prepared his pupil well. Conidon looked and sounded like a shell of a man, barely having the energy to refute Dragomir.

The prince's nostrils flared as he thought of the ambassador, Macklore. All of the painstaking planning he and Eliphas had undergone over the past week had been eradicated by that gods-forsaken ambassador. The bastard had publicly insulted *him*, a prince of Shaara. Worse, Dragomir had been ridiculed and humiliated in the Great Hall in front of every noble in Gallanse. By mid-afternoon, word of his embarrassment had swept through the streets of the city. The prince was seething underneath, and even now, hours later, he bristled at the memory.

A grim smile crossed his face. No, he reminded himself, his embarrassment would merely become a forgotten whisper. The death of Lord Dillion would overshadow all the rest of yesterday's events, even Dragomir's public outburst. The shocking murder of the lord of Janril, the most loyal to Conidon of any noble, was sure to change much in the politics of the succession. The trouble caused by Macklore would be naught but a faint memory.

The prince's smile broadened at his next thought. With any luck, he would receive news of the ambassador's death within the hour.

He thought back to his conversation with Brak, Baron of Cimmeron, the night before.

"I want him dead!" Dragomir had growled to his father's vassal.

"I gathered," Brak had replied dryly. "I will send Talia to our man Krone. It has been some time since I last employed him, but he will see to it."

"No, not Krone," hissed the prince. "I want Sable, he is the best."

"He is costly, your highness," Brak stated, tugging at his ear.

"I don't care. I want the job finished—tonight."

"Your will, highness," his vassal answered.

They were meeting in Brak's private chamber, the doors secured by his Black Guard. A quick word to his page and moments later, an auburn-haired woman of medium height, wearing the black and red of Cimmeron, entered the room. On the right side of her temple was a cherry red birthmark the size of a large man's thumb.

Dragomir could not guess her age, though she moved with the grace of an older woman. Still, her lithe body and youthful face suggested someone not yet past the age of thirty. Talia stepped forward and gave a deep curtsy. "My lord, highness," she said formally, greeting first her uncle and then his guest. "How may I serve?" Her voice was surprisingly deep for a woman.

"You are certain she's up to the task?" Dragomir asked, eyeing the girl warily.

Brak smiled and motioned for Talia to sit. "She knows the paths of the lower city well enough, highness. She will get you your man."

"Good," Dragomir growled, hefting a bag of coins. He dropped them on the table in front of her with a loud clank. "There's enough gold there to hire ten killers," he said to the girl. "Whatever his asking price, double it, do you understand?"

"Of course, highness," she said, bowing her head low. "Who is the mark?"

The prince's eyes narrowed in fury. "That miserable dog, Macklore," he spat in answer.

"The ambassador?" she asked with a frown. "Your forgiveness, Prince Dragomir, but someone of his importance will not be easy to isolate, nor to kill."

"I don't just want him killed," Dragomir continued, his visage twisted in hate. "I want his beating heart on a plate! Is that clear, girl?"

She glanced at her uncle, who gave an almost imperceptible nod. "I will meet with Sable, highness," she conceded quietly. "The contract will be in your hands tonight."

Dragomir's hand slammed down on the carved marble table in front of him. "I want his head as proof," the prince said, still smoldering. "I told that son-of-a-bitch I'd see it rammed on a stake. He may have forgotten that, but I have not."

As good as her word, Talia had delivered Sable's contract two hours later and set the wheels in motion.

That had been last evening.

Now, he was awaiting word from Sable on the completion of the deed. He could envision it, so close he could taste it. With Dillion dead and Fallon soon to follow, there would be little opposition left to stand in his way. Waymon was a coward at heart and could not gather enough support to claim the throne. Conidon was nothing without his golden boy Macklore to help him. Once the ambassador was out of the way, Dragomir could marry the princess, kill her soon thereafter, and be free to run this city and use its armies to unite all of Shaara. He and Rexor both knew that the time was ripe to invade the countries of the Crystalline Sea. Agenhelm was a fading power, and Rhone was simply begging to be overrun. It had few standing armies and acres of rich farmland to supply the thousands of soldiers Shaara would produce.

Behind him, he heard a timid knock at the door, no doubt a servant bringing him his morning fast.

"Fetch me my robe, girl," he commanded with a tilt of his head. A moment passed, and he heard her fumbling around in the dark, searching frantically for his silk attire. The prince was not known for his patience, and the consequences for making him wait were often short and brutal. He turned to see a plump woman of perhaps forty winters brush past the flimsy curtains and present him with his clothing, her head bowed low.

"Your robe, highness," she said, a quiver in her voice.

Dragomir, enjoying the terrifying effect he was having on the servant, snatched it out of her hands and threw it over his shoulders. "And what, pray tell, is Conidon having served up this morning? I hope it is not that same tired meal I was forced to endure yesterday," he said, pushing past her.

Quickly, she followed after him, reaching the breakfast she had left on the table upon entering. She lifted the silver cover off the tray to reveal a meal of perfectly poached eggs upon oven-toasted bread. Next to it lay ham slices baked with an infusion of pepper and sage. In a crystal bowl was a generous portion of green grapes, picked from the castle vineyard minutes ago, still glistening with the morning dew. The girl set down the cover and poured him a cup of hot tea. Though everything looked perfect, she waited anxiously, nearly holding her breath.

The prince picked up his silver fork and made as if he were about to eat. He stopped suddenly, and the servant felt her stomach fill with knots.

"Tell me, woman. Is your chef grotesquely stupid?" Dragomir asked, looking up at her.

"Highness? I don't take your meaning," she stammered, trying not to panic.

"I don't understand why he would put my eggs *on* my toast," he continued as if she hadn't spoken. "Did he think I wanted it on my toast? If I wanted it there, I'd have put it there myself."

"Highness, please, yesterday you... you were upset because you had to put the eggs on yourself," she croaked, eyes bulging in confused fear. "The chef was just trying to..."

Her words ceased as Dragomir upended the tray with a violent sweep of his hand. It landed with a crash on the floor, sending food flying across the room. "That was yesterday, woman," he said contemptuously. "You have ten minutes to get me the breakfast I want, or I will have my guards ram a sword through your chest. Clean up this mess, and get out of my sight."

In a rush, the woman picked up every scrap of food she could find and fled the room in terror, somehow having the presence of mind to bow as she left.

"I need to speak with you, highness," came the voice of the magus, from behind Dragomir a moment later.

The prince whirled in surprise, rising out of his chair, stunned to see Eliphas in the room.

The mage had pulled back the cowl of his hood, revealing his shaved head, covered with a dragon tatoo. His dark eyes were sunk back into his face, and his skin pulled tightly, as if it had been tucked in around the skull. His white robes were disheveled, looking like he'd been up all night laboring in them. Upon his face, Eliphas wore a humorless look.

Dragomir gathered himself, brushing his hands down the front of his silk robe, trying to look unbothered by the surprising intrusion. "What would you like to discuss, magus?"

Eliphas stepped toward the prince and struck him with a backhand across the face. Dragomir's head snapped to the side, the blow staggering him enough that he nearly fell to the ground. The prince struggled back up with a mixed look of shock and rage.

"You…"

The magus dealt him a second blow, this time sending Dragomir sprawling to the floor, wheezing in pain.

"You are not here to speak, boy," the magus hissed, his tone like ice. "Just sit there and listen."

Eliphas sat down at the empty breakfast table, his face once more his usual mask, displaying none of his emotions. "In the past eighteen hours, you have very nearly destroyed all of our progress in the succession. You almost displayed Conidon as weak yesterday, but then you foolishly pressed your luck against an unknown adversary in the ambassador."

Dragomir was wiping blood from his mouth and looked accusingly at the magus. "You told me to force the issue. I thought that is what you wanted me to do, so that's what I did."

"And what happened?" Eliphas asked, his ire rising again. "He was able to insult you, publicly shame you, and he made it so that Conidon was able to save face. He bested you in every way he could have!" The mage stood again, pressing closer to Dragomir, who was still sitting on the floor, his back to the wall.

"I didn't think…" the prince began.

"No, you *never* think!" Eliphas thundered, his hand clenched tightly on his green staff. "You are arrogant to the point of stupidity and have only one emotion: rage! Instead of thinking, you act impulsively on your feelings." He stood, clearly frustrated, and paced the room.

"Surely, with the death of Dillion," Dragomir said, standing back up, his voice hesitant, "I have scored a victory."

The magus looked at Dragomir with absolute malice. "*You* have scored a victory?" he responded, incredulous.

Dragomir shrank back against the wall, speechless in the gaze of such intensity.

"It was *my* assassin who killed Lord Dillion. It was *my* plan to have it done during the middle of the assemblage, when Conidon should have been weakened enough to push you to the throne. It was *me* who brought three of the Barons under your control in the past week. *I* accomplished this, boy, not you."

The white-robed mage turned and pointed out toward the city through the balcony window. "If you want to rule Gallanse, you cannot let your anger cloud your judgment, not when dealing with someone like Conidon. He's as wily as a fox and has held command of this city for over four decades. More importantly, his power and influence have kept his enemies—even your father, the most powerful lord in Shaara—at bay."

The magus turned and began pacing the room once again. "Now that he is allied with the ambassador of Brisbane, things will become more difficult."

Neither spoke, each absorbed in his own thoughts.

"Who is this ambassador? Why is he even here?" asked Dragomir finally, picking up a folded cloth towel from next to the wash basin. He dabbed at the blood trickling from his lip.

The magus stopped, staring out from the balcony's view, a breeze swaying the sheer curtains. "I told you, his name is Macklore, and he is far more than a simple ambassador. He is apprenticed to one of the most powerful wizards on the Crystalline Sea and should not be underestimated. Right now, he is the key to your rise to the Gray Throne."

Eliphas looked back at Dragomir, jaw set firmly. "Might I remind you, highness, that he is the reason you and I are working together. He is the man you have to assist me in killing."

Dragomir stood slowly, the beginnings of a smile upon his face. "Is he really so powerful? So dangerous, even *you* need help in killing him?"

Eliphas seemed genuinely surprised at the prince's words as he turned away from the balcony to address Dragomir. "Did you not see him yesterday in the hall? He is a skilled speaker, a trained Ambassador of the Realm. He did more than simply stand his ground against you; he completely turned the tables! His reputation is one of peace, but he is no mean warrior. He is able enough in the military arts to hold his own against any of your Blood Watch."

Dragomir sauntered forward, confidence in his step as he sensed something in Eliphas that had not been there before.

Uncertainty.

"Why not send Ry'Tung after him?" Dragomir asked, taking advantage of the pause in conversation. "Your assassin should have no trouble with the ambassador, no matter how strong a warrior he is."

The mage shook his head, fighting to keep his own temper in check. He needed this idiotic prince for the time being and forced himself to remain calm. If Eliphas could find a way out of this debacle, he would be rid of Dragomir in a few days. It was unfortunate that the finest warriors in the city were under the command of a fool.

"It is not only his skill at arms that makes him dangerous, highness," snapped Eliphas, unsuccessfully trying to keep frustration out of his voice. "Did you not see what he did with the candle?"

Dragomir faltered. What had he seen? The ambassador had held the ruined candle up and then, somehow, it had been remade in his hands. The prince scoffed at the notion that it was true magic, despite what he'd seen Eliphas do. Sorcery of that kind was rare, almost legendary. It was usually nothing more than back-alley tricks, designed to fool the feeble-minded or lowly peasants. It would take more than such contrived deception to convince the prince.

"He made a candle appear from his sleeve," Dragomir replied, with a dismissive wave of his hand. "Such parlor tricks may dupe simple-minded folk, but they do not work on me."

Eliphas, unable to contain himself further, spoke, his voice shaking with rage. "Have you forgotten what I did to Anir?" he shouted, losing his temper. "You miserable imbecile! That was no parlor trick; he created the candle anew! He is at least as skilled in the magical arts as I. If I could handle him alone, I'd never have bothered with you at all! He is extremely powerful and well trained. You cannot dismiss him as though he were one of your servants. You are simply too stupid to realize it!"

Dragomir, however, sneered back at the magus, thrusting his jaw under Eliphas's nose. "Macklore is dead! I had him killed last night after he left the palace. You, no doubt, were cowering in your room while *I* had this done, magus—me." Dragomir looked with superiority at the mage, glowering. "Maybe I don't always think things through, but I get *results*. I have the will and ambition to get things done, while you waste your time plotting in some dark corner. I did not come to you for help, magus; you came to me!"

Eliphas said nothing. He just stood there, looking down upon the maniacal face of the prince.

"What's the matter, mage? Too shocked to say anything? How is it that I, an 'imbecile' who only acts impulsively, was able to accomplish what you could not?"

The magus had not moved an inch; he just continued staring at Dragomir as the moments passed by. Finally, he spoke, his voice quiet.

"You fool."

A timid knock came from the hallway, breaking the silence. Dragomir flicked his gaze to the door, having forgotten his breakfast during the exchange with the mage. When he looked back, the magus was gone.

"Good riddance," he thought to himself.

"Come in," he bellowed, more loudly than he'd intended.

In walked the serving maid, absolutely terrified, a new tray in her hands.

"Leave it and get out," the prince snapped.

The girl practically ran to the table, set down the tray, and exited the room with a swift bow.

Strangely, Dragomir felt no satisfaction in his victory over the mage. He had expected more of a reaction from the man. The mage should have thanked him, at least. Instead, Dragomir was left with a gnawing emptiness in his gut.

He shook his head, trying to clear himself of doubt. Dillion was dead, and so was the ambassador. He did not need the magus any longer. He was a day or two from the throne—at most. All he had to do was push his advantage. He smiled and regained his former good spirits, all traces of uneasiness dissipating.

He sat down to his breakfast, stomach rumbling. He lifted the silver lid and dropped it suddenly with a metallic clang, his mouth open in horror. He tipped back, falling off the chair with a crash, gagging as the rotten smell of decaying flesh engulfed him.

Lying upon the polished silver tray was Sable's decapitated head. The dead eyes of the hatchet man lolled to one side, his bloated tongue sticking out of his mouth. On top of the skull, driven all the way to the hilt, was the hatchet man's prized knife. Pinned to the head by the curved blade was a crumpled note, smeared with blood. It contained a single word scrawled upon it.

Dragomir

The prince looked frantically around the room, the sound of his heart pounding in his ears. How had Macklore survived? How was he able to deliver the head into Dragomir's room? Horror like he had never known coursed through him.

"Magus!" he shrieked in terror; his eyes drawn again to the macabre scene in front of him.

"*Magus*!"

Chapter 19

Zedaine decided he could get quite used to life on the water.

The rangy warrior stood at the bow of the schooner, looking out over a picturesque view. On all sides, the ship was surrounded by the blue-green waters of the Crystalline Sea. A mile to the south, the rugged greenery of Rhone's coastline moved steadily past, as pounding waves crashed time and again against the rocky shores. Soaring on the winds overhead, an albatross flew past, its soft white wings silhouetted against the backdrop of azure skies.

Every time he sailed, Zedaine experienced the same exuberance he felt now. The sun shining on your face and the wind at your back—this is what it was to be alive!

Captain Tross had left Staltshore's port behind nearly six hours ago, after spending what Kildare called "an eternity" getting out to sea. In truth, the captain and his men knew their business and had put out in a timely fashion.

Kildare just liked to grumble.

Zedaine turned around, watching the crew at work. The *Duquesne's* three largest sails had been raised in the captain's effort to maximize speed.

There were other, smaller sails aloft as well: the jib, the fore, and the gaff. Zedaine chuckled to himself. He could never keep them all straight. All he knew was that the ship had made incredible time. Now, an hour past midday, he guessed they were more than halfway to their destination.

Standing in the middle of the deck was the reason for the ship's incredible speed. A red-haired man in a wide brimmed hat, whom the captain called Kendrik. He was the *Duquesne's* windmage.

Once they'd cleared the shallows of Staltshore's harbor, Kendrick had performed an incantation. With a wave of his hand and the power of his magic, the man had conjured wind out of the calm morning air. Small at first, its strength had grown in time. The ship was now moving at nearly twenty knots an hour!

Zedaine shook his head in wonder.

He watched as one of the crew ascended the mizzenmast adroitly, like a squirrel climbing a tree. The man was casually dangling by one hand, thirty feet above deck, searching the horizon for signs of trouble.

Zedaine was envious. What would it be like to perch atop the ship with nothing but your skill to keep you alive? No cares beyond making it safely to the next port. Yes, he could easily see himself living at sea.

Zedaine sighed, and focused his attention on the main deck, where he spotted Taeral standing on the port side of the ship. He had stowed his spear below, but even without his weapon, the triton looked powerful, towering over everyone else on board. Although he'd been defeated by Kildare earlier that day, Zedaine recognized the skill at arms displayed in that contest. His sweeps and thrusts had been well timed, honed with hours of practice. There was no doubt in Zedaine's mind that he was a warrior to be reckoned with. Taeral would bear watching.

Standing next to him was Rion. A *very* curious addition to the group, he was certainly an old hand at sailing, and no doubt his experience at sea would prove valuable. Zedaine did not know what kind of martial prowess the smaller man might have, but if Zedaine's suspicions about him proved true, he would bear watching as well, albeit for different reasons.

There was no sign of Chameleon, who had retired below deck, still exhausted from her many ordeals over the past twenty-four hours. Zedaine could not believe that a day ago, they had been racing through the mountains, trying to get to Staltshore.

Then there was the huntress, Adecia. She was standing next to Rion and Taeral. The three were deep in discussion, no doubt speaking of the daunting tasks that lay ahead. Zedaine simply did not know what to make of her. She was certainly not a ravishing beauty; he had seen many other women who were more attractive. Yet, she had made an impression upon him, nonetheless. She was striking to behold, not curvaceous like the women to whom he was usually attracted. She was all lean muscle and predatory grace. An image of a lioness entered his mind.

Yes, he thought to himself, *that's what she reminds me of.*

When he had seen her sprinting down the docks of Staltshore, he had been transfixed by her speed and determination. She struck him as a wild spirit, unchained by any rules but those of her own making. Instead of pulling up short, the girl had hurled herself through the air, risking everything to get aboard. And the way she had spoken to the captain, defying him on his own ship! There was no give in the woman. She had even attacked the apparition of the Ettu below deck without hesitation. The emotions he was feeling for this woman were a new sensation for Zedaine. His world was wondrously out of balance. He found himself contemplating, almost in a panic, if he was in love.

"Quit gawking at her, you calf-eyed moon brain," came a voice from right next to Zedaine's ear.

The big hunter nearly jumped out of his skin in surprise. Turning around, he saw his brother smirking at him.

"Gods, man, how about a little warning next time before you decide to scare the hell out of me!" he said, his face flush with embarrassment.

"The ability to sneak up on you is a rarity," Kildare said wryly, "I couldn't waste my opportunity." Leaning up against the rail, his smile faded away. "That reminds me, I need to spar with you before we arrive. I'm accepting the challenge tonight. I want it decided before we leave for Gallanse."

Zedaine pulled at his lip in thought. "Judoh's not going to like it much," he said.

"I don't care if he likes it," Kildare answered harshly. "He agreed to the stipulation. I've decided it will be tonight."

"If that's the way you want it," Zedaine shrugged, knowing he'd never get Kildare to change his mind. "You know he's going to hire the best sword money can buy. Even you are not infallible, Kil. One slip in the sand is all it takes. Remember that time in Tal-Mur?"

Kildare frowned at his brother. "You always have to bring that up, despite the outcome. I guess we'll just have to see what happens tonight."

Zedaine ran his hand through his long hair. "Since we are discussing such pleasant things," he added after a moment, "we'd best swing by and pay Warlan a visit."

"I was thinking along those same lines," Kildare said, rubbing his chin.

"You have to promise not to kill him," Zedaine said, raising an eyebrow. "Not today, anyway."

"Fine," Kildare muttered. "But his time's coming."

Kildare stood in silence, looking at the ship's crew. "Well?" he asked after a few moments.

"Well, what?" Zedaine questioned.

"I want to know what you think."

"About what?" Zedaine asked, a puzzled look on his face.

"About all this!" Kildare said, slightly exasperated, gesturing around him with his hands. "What did you think I was asking about, the weather?"

"About all what? Try to be specific, Kil. I'm not Chameleon; I don't read minds."

Kildare gave him a withering look. "Don't you find all of this... odd?"

"That we're sitting in a boat on our way to save Macklore?" Zedaine replied. "Not particularly odd, no. We've done stranger things. Remember last winter when we had to put down that rebellion in Kath?" he asked with a short laugh. "We reversed the coup with armed snowmen! I thought Baron what's-his-name was going to throttle you when you suggested it. Point is, Kil, this is what we get paid to do. You and I do the dirty work these politicians can't. So, in answer to your question, no, I don't find it stranger than any of our usual assignments. It's just more personal, with Macklore involved."

"Then you're not thinking, little brother. There's more going on here than we know. The whole thing stinks to high heaven."

"What are you talking about?" Zedaine asked mildly.

"For starters, we're traveling with a wanted pirate captain; you know that, don't you?"

"Bah, I like him," Zedaine said with a wave of his hand.

Kildare swore under his breath. "Of course, you do; you like everyone, you milksop," Kildare replied, his anger starting to rise. "That's beside the point. What if he's recognized? If half of what

I've heard about him is true, it means he's stolen from every ruler and fiefdom on the entire sea! And *we* are working with him!"

Zedaine shrugged, tilting his head to the side, and commented, "He hasn't done anything lately."

Kildare looked at Zedaine, bewildered by his brother's apparent stupidity. "Like that's going to matter! Dealing with him implicates us. If you'd *think* for once in your life, you'd see that it could cause trouble before we even get to Gallanse. That's *if* we're lucky enough to run into authorities who actually *have* laws. It's rumored your new pal, *Captain* Wavecrest, stole something from Reubane himself. You remember him, don't you? The self-proclaimed pirate king! What if we run into *that* little nightmare with Rion in tow? You and I aren't exactly in Reubane's good graces. He finds us with Rion, there will be no talking our way out of it. We're all dead!"

Zedaine looked unconcerned. He just smiled at his brother. "You worry too much. Rion has been able to stay hidden for years. No one's going to be looking for him."

His smile broadened at his next thought. "Maybe Reubane's daughters have convinced him to leave us alone; *they* came on to *us*, after all. Reubane just refused to see it that way. What were their names again? Lisle and Gwen! Oh, that

Gwen was something. You remember what she dared you to do?" He laughed, shaking his head in wonder. "How did you two ever manage to get up on that chandelier?"

"Would you get the female species out of your head for two seconds?" Kildare fumed. "As much trouble as it might cause us, Rion is the least of our worries!"

Shaking his head, Kildare looked out to sea, something clearly weighing on his mind. "You don't think it strange that Chameleon gets some random visions she can't explain, and *we* get sent into the Rhone Mountains to miraculously stumble upon her? She then proceeds to tells us things only you and I would understand?"

"Let's just try to get to Adian, and we'll see what happens from there," Zedaine replied calmly, trying to stem his brother's tirade.

Kildare was far from finished. "Let's not forget the wayward triton who just *happened* to wander into Staltshore on exactly the same day we arrived. What was Taeral's minor request? To help him track down a dragon that broke though the defenses of his impregnable underwater city."

"Maybe it's just coincidence?" Zedaine said calmly.

"Coincidence? *Coincidence*!" Kildare hissed. "I suppose it's just *coincidence* that a guide to the

Serpent Marsh showed up out of the clear blue sky to help us out? The perfect person to lead us to Ebonfire *literally* jumped onto our boat out of thin air? And why did she come to Staltshore, in the first place? Because she had a compulsion to go to a marketplace that was hundreds of miles away from her home to sit around waiting for us to show up. Isn't that how all great heroes meet? Over a mango at a fruit stand? Oh, and let's not forget her asking price for our assistance. A pittance, really, compared to everything else we have to accomplish—just blunt an invasion of Ettu spilling out of the Serpent Marsh by the hundreds."

Zedaine pursed his lips together a moment, thinking deeply. "You know," he said slowly, "you might have a point after all."

Kildare looked ready to explode. "I *might* have a…" he stopped, narrowing his eyes as a crooked smile appeared on his brother's face.

"You… gah, you son-of-a-bitch. You just *love* doing that to me, don't you?" Kildare said, realizing his brother had been goading him the entire time.

"It's really not even that difficult when you're all worked up like this," Zedaine said, taking a playful swipe at his brother's shoulder with the back of his hand. "Besides," he said, sounding serious, "that's not what's really bothering you."

"You don't think all that I just told you bothers me?" Kildare asked.

"No, I don't. You see, I *know* you, brother. You might lament about all those strange occurrences you just outlined. Rion's history, the Ettu, all of it. But you and I, we can handle all that. None of that bothers me; that's just business as usual. What concerns me is the same thing that concerns you."

Kildare let out a pent-up breath of frustration. He turned back to face the open waters of the Crystalline Sea. "Enlighten me."

Zedaine leaned back against the prow of the ship, his gaze falling back automatically to Adecia. "You like being in control, just like I do. *We* are the masters of our fate. No one decides for us. But in all of this, someone or something is moving us around like pieces on a chess board, forcing us in directions we don't want to go. That someone was able to get inside Chameleon's psyche, a task I'm guessing wasn't easy to accomplish. Whoever it was managed to send her out into the world. They also got past Adecia's considerable willpower and stubborn sense, convincing the girl to travel from her homeland to Staltshore during an obvious crisis."

Manfully, he forced his eyes away from Adecia and looked again at his brother. "Is that about right?"

"Most of it, yes," Kildare said, eyes still at sea. "What concerns me the most is the fact that they were able to manipulate Blade. *She* sent us into the mountains. I don't know if someone really needed that *Viasha* plant, but it was a convenient way to get us out there. Anyone who has the power to influence Blade so subtly that she wasn't aware of it—that's someone to be reckoned with."

He turned to face his brother. "I don't like dancing to anyone's tune but my own. I want to know who it is. Who is making these things happen, and why?"

They both turned to stare out at the water, saying nothing, lost in their own thoughts. An evil smirk appeared quite suddenly on Kildare's face. "I could tell Adecia about your bet with Lisle. You remember, right? It's been a year now, and I still haven't changed my mind about the outcome. I think she lost to you on purpose. I think she *wanted* you to shave her…"

Zedaine swatted Kildare on the back of the head.

"It's time for our sparring bout."

The darkness of the first mate's chamber was a welcome relief to Chameleon. It almost made the constant pitching motion of the boat tolerable. The Drannock's head was dizzy from the constant up and down movement that commenced shortly after the ship had sailed. Her face had turned a pale green, and Rion had suggested she lay down out of the sun. Chameleon gratefully retired below deck and remained there, trying to keep the contents of her stomach on the inside.

It was a battle she was about to lose.

Seeing an empty bucket among the scattered items on the wooden floor, Chameleon awkwardly rolled out of bed and landed with a thud. Her head swam with nausea at the sudden movement. Just in time, she grabbed the bucket and managed to get her face over it before retching violently. Her eyes watered and her throat turned raw as it burned with bile. All the muscles in Chameleon's body locked up, and she hugged the bucket as if it were a long-lost friend. After what felt like hours of breathless pain and anguish, she coughed hoarsely, thankful to draw air once again. Chameleon wiped her lips clean and fell down next to the bucket, breathing loudly, mouth wide open. She wondered quite seriously if she were about to die.

Chameleon rejected the thought of climbing back into bed almost immediately. It had not helped with her sickness at all, and she could not summon the energy. She just lay on the planking, praying to hit landfall soon.

No wonder my ancestors feared leaving their own lands, she thought to herself. *One day outside the mountains, and I've already had enough. When I get back home, I am telling everyone never to leave! First Wanderer? I'll be the last wanderer... if I live to speak about this!*

Chameleon instantly regretted her thoughts. Mentally drawing herself up, she told herself, *You are Drannock. This rocking is just a different movement than you are used to. Focus your mind. You are well trained. Mother would be disgusted if you gave up so easily.*

Chameleon took a deep breath, and with great effort, rolled into a sitting position against the bunk. Eyeing the bucket and fighting down a new wave of nausea, she closed her eyes and concentrated on her meditation. She pictured the ship rolling at sea, the room in which she sat, and the sounds that came from above deck. One by one, each disappeared in Chameleon's mind as she gathered her mental energy. She could feel her psychic powers build steadily. She was in control. As her body relaxed, Chameleon entered a deep trance, slowly becoming aware of something she'd not sensed before.

Chameleon opened her psychic eyes to a wide plain of tall yellow grass. It was a flat land that stretched in all directions. Looming on the horizon was a massive sun, three times as large as she was used to. The warm light it cast forth was a deep crimson rather than a yellowish white.

To Chameleon, it seemed both immense and surreal. She stared at the glowing orb, transfixed for several moments. She came to her senses when a smattering of pale orange clouds raced overhead, partially blotting out the light of the sun. The clouds cast jagged shadows here and there upon the seemingly endless countryside.

Off to the left, Chameleon saw a single tree growing in the distance. She felt drawn to it. Without conscious thought, she began making her way towards it, the only landmark in sight. Underneath her feet, she could hear the rustle of dried grass. She reached down, running her fingers along the tops of the golden plants in wonder.

Strange, she thought. *Not a single insect.*

As Chameleon approached the tree, she saw it was quite large. Its trunk was thick in circumference, at least as big around as a full-grown oak. It was covered with grayish-hued bark that appeared to be smooth to the touch. Its many branches twisted skyward and housed dark green leaves twice the size of Chameleon's hand. It was nothing like she had ever seen before. She leaned in to examine one of the leaves more closely.

Without warning, the tree began vibrating and swaying like it had come alive! Every leaf on the tree writhed and twisted until it pointed at Chameleon. In the middle of each leaf, a sharp, needle-like appendage appeared, glistening with a sticky white substance.

Chameleon's eyes widened, completely stunned. Where was she? How could this be? She raised her hands in what she hoped was a peaceful gesture and spoke.

"Easy now," she said, fighting down her panic. Normally, she might feel ridiculous talking to a tree, but in this case, it seemed the natural thing to do. The leaves kept her targeted, but seemed content to hold their barbed defenses. The Drannock took a cautious step backward, not wanting to spook the tree any further. Chameleon did not know how, but she *sensed* the tree relax ever so slightly as she moved away from it. Following her instincts, she reached out with her mind.

Unbelievably, she found it held sentient life! It was no mere plant, but rather a living, thinking organism. Chameleon could feel its emotions: primarily fear and confusion.

She found the concentrated awareness of the tree, located deep in the trunk almost two spans above her. It was not a deep-thinking presence she felt, but rather, the basics for survival. Chameleon could not be sure, but it was almost as though she was dealing with the mind of an infant. She decided to try her luck and made an attempt at communication.

"Hello," she pulsed quietly.

Chameleon felt the tree's emotions change from skittish nerves to abject fear at her greeting. Its leaves tensed again, and Chameleon stopped moving.

It was too late.

The tree had gone into fight or flight mode. It was about to shoot thousands of razor-sharp needles at her.

Suddenly, a new presence arrived. It washed over the tree like a wave of tranquility, causing the fear to evaporate like it had never been.

"Be calm, Mycan," the voice pulsed. *"She is not an enemy. I have been waiting for her."*

The tree slowly swayed back into place, its barbed tendrils retracting into the stems. The leaves and branches also relaxed back into their normal shape, until the tree returned to standing upright and still, just as Chameleon had seen upon her arrival.

Stepping from behind the tree came a slender young man, looking much the same age as Chameleon. He was dressed in worn auburn robes bearing smudges of dirt at the elbows and knees. A shabby straw hat with a wide brim topped his head, shading it from the red light of the sun. He removed his headgear, revealing curly brown hair, matted with sweat to his forehead. A pair of piercing blue eyes studied Chameleon. In his hands he held a sturdy gray staff, etched with symbols strangely familiar to the Drannock.

Chameleon recognized him immediately.

This was the man from her visions.

He was the reason Chameleon had become First Wanderer.

"I am sorry about the mishap, Chameleon," the youth said, his tone gentle and friendly. "She is still quite young, and you are the first living creature she has met."

"You… you know me?" Chameleon asked, completely confused at the sudden turn of events. Only a few minutes ago, she had been seasick on a ship with her assorted companions. Now she was in some strange place—a place with a massive red sun and trees that attacked you! Things were happening too quickly for the Drannock, and she felt lost.

The stranger chuckled and motioned for Chameleon to sit. "You look just as I did when I first came to this place. That was only two days ago, and I am still learning about it. I am only slightly less confused about it than you appear to be."

He wiped his brow with his sleeve before continuing. "And yes, Chameleon, I do know you. I have been searching the continent for *years* looking for you: the First Wanderer, the planes walker, Chameleon, the thrice-named Drannock! I am quite excited to finally meet you."

The young man sat down lightly in the shade of the tree and placed his hat back on his head. He lay his staff next to him on the ground and beckoned for Chameleon to join him.

After a moment of hesitation, Chameleon sat cross-legged in the tall grass opposite the man. She glanced dubiously up at the tree that was looming over them, and the stranger smiled again.

"Do not worry, Chameleon; she will not attack. Even now, she is maturing more quickly than I had dared to hope. What do you think of her? She is the first of my creations."

Chameleon did not know what to say. She did not understand anything this man was telling her. "What is this place? How do you know who I am… and who are you?" she blurted out, more forcefully than she'd intended.

The youth's smile lost some of its luster and he sighed. "I suppose I deserve that. I see, now, that I might have handled this better. You are, of course, curious, and I let my excitement get the best of me. Let me see if I can answer some of your questions and ease your mind."

He took his hat off again and began fanning himself. "Blast this heat," he mumbled, "even in the shade it is uncomfortable. First of all, let me introduce myself. My name is Ty. I come from a city on the Crystalline Sea named Brisbane, not far from the same Rhone Mountains you call home, though I live far to the north, and your folk inhabit the southern reaches."

"Brisbane," Chameleon said with surprise. "That is where the Raven and the Crow are from."

Ty raised one of his eyebrows at the mention of the two brothers. "Yes, they are the reason I could finally communicate with you directly. You and your people have formidable defenses around your psyches. Once you made contact with the Raven and the Crow, the mental barriers you had in place dropped."

"What do you mean?"

Ty's voice took on a matter-of-fact tone as he leaned his back up against the tree, seeming oblivious to any danger it might present. "The Drannock have kept to themselves for so long, they have become xenophobic, trusting no one outside their own clans. While I can understand their need for independence, the time will soon come when they must abandon that mindset... just as you have."

"I have not abandoned my people's ways," Chameleon objected. "The Drannock are an honorable and proud people. We do not visit evil upon anyone."

"That's not what I sa—" Ty said, trying to stem Chameleon's wrath.

"We simply like to be left alone! If you are going to insult my people and their ways, I am leaving."

Chameleon stood up angrily and started to walk away, annoyed with Ty and completely out of sorts.

"*And where will you go, Chameleon?*" The Drannock heard Ty's soothing voice inside her head. She stopped cold in her tracks. Whipping her head around, she looked back toward the young man who sat unfazed under the tree, watching her calmly.

"*Yes, we can speak like this if you prefer; for I, like you, am a telepath,*" he continued. "*A well-trained mind like yours should not be unsettled so easily. I will not force you to stay, but I think it would be in your best interest to do so.*"

Chameleon paused, wondering why she'd lost her cool so easily. *Calm yourself*, she chided. *You are acting like a fawn taking its first steps. So what if I am in a strange place with a strange man and a strange tree? At least I am not plunging over a waterfall with magada hot on my heels.*

Chameleon laughed quite suddenly. She could not help it. Her fate simply did not seem to be in her own hands at the moment. The last two days had been the most confusing and terrifying of Chameleon's life. *No wonder you're rattled; you were attacked by a tree! Calm yourself, and listen to what he has to say.*

Chameleon strode back and sat down sheepishly. "I am… sorry. I don't know what has gotten into me lately. Please, continue," she said, determined to listen.

"I didn't mean to offend you, or the Drannock, Chameleon," he said, putting the hat back on his head. "Quite the opposite, in fact," Ty continued respectfully. "I find your people to be all of the things you described. They are kind, hardworking, honest folk with remarkable strength of mind. Even I, a powerful psionicist, had great difficulty getting a message through to you. Without knowing you at all, I was only able to give you glimpses of the visions as I have seen them. Even when I *could* speak, it had to be in riddles, so strong were your defenses. It was only after you met the Raven and the Crow that I was able to speak with you more directly. Tell me, since you met the birds of the dark, do you not feel differently than you did about people outside of your own—strangers?"

Chameleon thought about it, this time leaving her emotions out of the process. She did not feel any differently, did she? In the last two days, she had told her tale to the brothers, traveled with them over the mountains, and trusted them with the knowledge of her mental powers. Chameleon was now accompanying them to distant shores—shores those in her tribe could only dream of. She was on a ship with three other strangers, one of whom was a transformed triton. Chameleon realized it was only a single morning ago that she had argued with herself about whether or not to tell Raven her name. Now, she thought nothing of displaying her powers openly in front of them, as she had done with the apparition of the Ettu warrior.

"I can see by the look on your face that you *have* changed—greatly, in a very short length of time," Ty said, smiling again. "No longer the suspicious Drannock far from home, you have learned what it is to put your trust in others. That is why you were chosen, Chameleon. Of all the Drannock, you were the most receptive to change."

"Who chose me?"

Ty looked up into the branches of the tree ruefully, not meeting her eyes.

"You did," Chameleon said accusingly.

Ty actually blushed and gave an apologetic shrug. "I hope you don't judge me too harshly until you hear me out. It is not as if I had a whole lot of choice in the matter," he muttered under his breath.

"What am I doing here? Where are we?" Chameleon asked, trying to keep her impatience in check.

"Let me answer the latter question first," Ty said, sitting up straight, "as we are getting to the heart of things. This place in which we sit is a magical construct, made by a very powerful and extremely malicious sorcerer named Sigeroa Lotus."

"What kind of a magical construct?" Chameleon asked, baffled. This place could not have been made magically. It was a huge, empty grassland... except for the single odd tree! And who could create a sun? No one had that kind of magical prowess.

"It is a new plane of existence," Ty replied. "Our world exists as just one of many planets in a vast galaxy, far larger than I would have ever imagined. Even now, knowing what I do, I can scarcely fathom its breadth."

Chameleon was frowning again, and Ty stopped. "I am sorry, Chameleon; that is not what you asked. Suffice to say, this new plane will act as a bridge between our world and another."

"Why would this sorcerer have created a new plane?" Chameleon asked. "What's he trying to accomplish?"

"In order to answer your question, Chameleon," Ty said, suddenly looking serious, "we have to look back into the history of our planet. I do not wish to confuse you further, but it is necessary for you to learn our past in order for you to comprehend what is happening now."

Chameleon nodded slowly in understanding and bade Ty continue.

"What I am about to tell you is ancient lore that many people, even the most learned scholars in the world today, do not know," he began. "I only recently learned of it, and though I have found it to be true, I scarcely believe it myself." Ty took his hat back off, fanning himself as he continued.

"More than three millennia ago, a massive war was fought over control of our world. The fighting that ensued was called the Godwar. The beings who waged that furious conflict were creatures of unbelievable power. We know some of them as the deities we worship today. Jora, the war god, was one. Duorn and his mate Chara were two others. The last survivor was Ben-Sur, the god of death. There were four other elder gods. Some that history still remembers, like Korin, the god of knowledge, and Evaine, the mistress of magic. Those latter two, along with the four others, were slain one by one. The four who remained grew desperate in those last days, knowing that their world was about to fall."

"What manner of enemy could wage war upon the gods?" Chameleon asked, awe in her voice.

Ty did not speak right away. Instead, his face hardened, and for a moment—for some reason— he looked remarkably familiar.

"Our world was a peaceful one. The gods, who acted as its caretakers, had created life, including the races that are still here today. Humans, tritons, barbarians, and thousands of other plants and animals. They all lived in relative balance and harmony. One day, the skies darkened as the portal to our world was ripped asunder, and a new type of beings made their way across the heavens. This enemy used the planes to travel from planet to planet, conquering all in their path. Always, they left desolation and destruction in their wake. These beings were like nothing anyone, even the gods, had ever seen. They were demons, a race of creatures so vile, so evil, even the gods were horrified at their arrival. Our peaceful world was under siege."

"For many years, the two forces fought. The immortal gods clashed with the mighty demon horde time and again, their battles crackling with fire and lightning across the horizon. Scores of powerful demon lords fell at the hands of the gods, only to have hundreds more replace them. Humanity, too, fought against the demon armies that scoured the landscape. On land, in the skies, and under the seas, the two sides slew tens of thousands—hundreds of thousands—of the enemy. Even with such staggering losses, the demons came on, their forces innumerable. Slowly, the raging horde of conquerors were exterminating the gods and decimating our world."

Ty paused a moment, taking a drink from his waterskin. He offered it to Chameleon, who declined politely.

"On the final day of battle," he continued, putting the skin aside, "with only four of the elder gods remaining, they did the unthinkable. Led by the all-father, the gods and their immortal children attacked Malafax, the demon king who ruled from deep inside his obsidian palace. Not expecting the sudden attack, he, along with his vanguard, were driven all the way back into the portal from whence they came. While unable to vanquish him completely, Duorn and Jora cast him into the far reaches of the galaxy; such was the power of their rage. Once the demon king had been exiled, the legions of his followers vanished into the void of space, banished along with their black-hearted sovereign."

Ty paused, looking at Chameleon. "In order to ensure the safety of our planet, Duorn and the other gods destroyed the plane that led to and from our world, forever ending the threat of another attack. Exhausted from years of battle, and filled with grief at the loss of their brothers and sisters, the gods left our planet, no longer willing to walk among us. Instead, they watch over us from Elysium, leaving their offspring, the Dargonni, to help guide our actions."

Chameleon sat quietly a moment, letting Ty's words sink in. Finally, she spoke. "This construct, this plane. It has replaced the one the gods destroyed, hasn't it?"

Ty nodded grimly.

"Sigeroa Lotus is trying to bring back the demons, isn't he?" Chameleon continued, knowing already that she was correct.

"Yes."

"Why would he do such a thing?" Chameleon asked.

Ty shook his head. "Who can say what his reason is? I only know that he must be stopped."

"And you need my help to stop him?" Chameleon questioned.

Ty sighed and stood up, beckoning Chameleon to do the same. "You and I are but part of it, Chameleon," he said softly. "I do not have all the answers, but I do know that it starts with us."

"If the gods were barely able to stop these demons, what kind of chance do we stand?" Chameleon asked.

Ty smiled then and took up his staff. "Our enemy is powerful and has many weapons, but he has made a mistake."

He pointed up to the tree. "You see Mycan, here? I made her. She is the first of our weapons that will help us in the coming fight."

"I don't understand. You made a tree?" Chameleon asked, bewildered.

"Take my hand and let me show you. I want to meld your powers with mine for a few moments. I want you to see what we are capable of."

Reluctantly, Chameleon reached out and interlaced her fingers with Ty's. *"Let me pass by your defenses, Chameleon,"* the Drannock heard inside her head. *"I will not try to take over your mind. I simply want access to some of your power. You will have to trust me, as you have trusted the*

Raven and the Crow. In turn, you will have access to my mental powers as the bond flows between us."

Chameleon hesitated a moment, and then lowered her defenses. She was breaking the cardinal rule of mental combat, she knew, but she chose to trust Ty, who had given the Drannock no cause to fear him.

As the two minds melded, Chameleon's eyes widened as she felt his power. *"You hold far more strength than I,"* Chameleon told him.

"Yet, I cannot do this without you," Ty pulsed back.

There was something else. Melded as they were, Chameleon could read some of Ty's thoughts. He had been truthful in everything he'd told the Drannock. From the history of their world's past to the fact that she could trust him, Ty had not tried to deceive her.

Now, Chameleon could see that Ty was planning to create another tree... no, an entire copse of them. Delving into both Chameleon's power and his own, Ty raised their joined hands over his head. Chameleon detected a third source of power coming from the staff in Ty's other hand. In several places around them, tiny gray stems sprouted from the ground. Quickly, they grew into saplings, resembling the fully-grown tree that was already there. The growth did not stop as Ty drew on more power from both himself and Chameleon. The Drannock was growing weary, but she was fascinated, and did break away from the meld.

The trees had reached full height now, looking much like Mycan, yet still Ty did not stop. He painstakingly crafted an awareness into each of them, giving them the ability to think and react much like a human would. He was giving them sentience.

Ty let go of Chameleon's hand, breaking the meld, and sank to his knees, exhausted. Chameleon was weary herself, but nowhere near as tired as Ty.

"Are you alright?" she asked, concerned at Ty's near collapse.

"Yes, Chameleon; thank you for allowing me the meld," Ty replied with a wan smile. "How did we do?"

Chameleon looked up and saw six new fully-grown trees standing silently, towering into the sky. "That was incredible," Chameleon whispered in awe. "But why create them?"

Ty looked up to view their creations. "I made them to fight against the demons, should they come through this plane. As I told you, Sigeroa Lotus made a mistake. He created this plane, but cannot enter it. He holds an incredible amount of magical energy, but no psionic power. That's why you and I can access the plane, and he cannot. You and I, Chameleon, can separate our psyches from our bodies and enter this place. Here, *we* are the gods. We have the ability to create and manipulate the matter of this plane into what we want. I do not have the power to unmake this place, but I *will* make this place into a deathtrap for demon kind."

Though exhausted, Ty sounded deadly serious. Chameleon could not help it. She felt herself warming to this man, just as she had with the Raven and the Crow.

"What would you ask of me, Ty?" she said, saying his name for the first time.

Ty smiled broadly. "I just so happen to have a task. You and I working together every day for the next year would not be nearly powerful enough to get this plane ready for battle. That black-hearted Lotus does not have enough power to attempt to open the portal to the demon world yet, but he will, soon enough. When that happens, the demons will pass though this plane and enter our world, bringing darkness unseen since the Godwars. What we need, Chameleon, are more of us. We need the Drannock, all of them."

Chameleon's eyes widened as she took in Ty's words. She did not believe for a moment that the clans would agree to help. Ty was right about

Chameleon's people. They kept exclusively to themselves. Contact with outsiders was strictly forbidden.

"I'm... not sure they will help you," she said at last. "It is not our way."

Ty once again wore a grimly determined look. "Times are changing, Chameleon. Either the Drannock will change with them, or we will all perish."

"But how..." she began.

"I will do the convincing," he said, interrupting her. "You just get them here. In two days' time, at three hours past the setting of the sun, come back to this place. You will know the way now that you've already travelled the path. Meditate as much as you can; you will need all your power. Together, you and I will go to your Elders and give them a message. I will convince them that the cause is in their best interest. If the demons come again, nowhere on this planet will be safe."

Chameleon nodded slowly. "I will do what I can, Ty, both for my people and yours. Why wait two days? Why not go now?"

"Your elders don't hold council for another two days. They need to be together when you talk to them. You still have your journey with the Raven and the Crow to complete. That, too, is of the utmost importance. They must get to Gallanse in time to save the seed of the White Eagle."

"You mean Macklore?" she asked. "They don't seem to care for him very much. Why is he so important?" asked Chameleon.

A sign of irritation passed over Ty's face. "The problem with oracles and prophecies, Chameleon, is they don't tell you everything. All I know is that Macklore will be important in the coming days. Perhaps his power will counter that of Lotus? I cannot say with any certainty."

Ty unsuccessfully tried to brush the dirt from his robes. "Here, help me up," he said, extending his hand to Chameleon.

The Drannock reached out and pulled the slender man to his feet with a grunt.

"I wish to thank you for your help, young lady," Ty said, reaching out and taking his staff in hand. "Stay close to the Raven and the Crow over the next two days. They are the best men I know."

Chameleon nodded. "How do I... exit this place?"

Ty smiled. "The same way you entered. Find your calm in meditation and follow your psyche back to your physical form."

Chameleon nodded again. "I will see you in two days at the appointed time. Until then, be safe."

Ty watched as Chameleon knelt down and lost herself in meditation. Not a minute had passed until her ethereal form dissipated in front of Ty's eyes.

He sighed.

Ty knew the future could take many paths. He knew the hardships that were coming over the next two days for the Drannock, but he was not allowed to speak of them. Doing so might upset the balance of fate. He had already discovered that lesson the hard way.

You must survive, Chameleon, he thought. *Right now, you are all that stands between the demons and our world's destruction.*

A sudden painful vision flashed in Ty's mind. In it, he saw scores of huge, lizard-like monsters surfacing from the waters of the Crystalline Sea, surrounding Chameleon, who stood alone on the wreckage of a ship.

An instant later, the vision vanished.

Behind Ty, a tall young woman stepped forth.

"Is this a certainty?" Ty pulsed to her.

"Yes."

Chapter 20

The corridors and causeways of the Gray Palace, normally bustling with servants, guards, and other workers, as well as the occasional lord with his attendees, were deserted with the news of Lord Dillion's death. Servants moved more purposefully than usual, unwilling to spend any longer than necessary in the hallways, while rumors swirled of a murderer on the loose. Conidon had cancelled his meetings with the Lords of Shaara, and a day of mourning had been declared. All of the entrances to Lord Dillion's quarters had been sealed off the day before, and would remain so while the investigation continued.

An hour before noon, Macklore found himself summoned by Conidon into the suite of chambers where High Lord Dillion's corpse had been found. The ambassador had been trying to gain an audience with the Lord of Gallanse all morning, but had thus far been unsuccessful. While frustrating, the wait had given him a chance to catch up on some much-needed sleep.

Macklore walked into an opulent room, its walls covered with tapestries depicting the history of House Janril through the years.

Dozens of guards, dressed in both the blue and white of Gallanse and the green and ivory of Janril, filled the room. All wore grim looks on their faces and moved with purpose. Macklore saw High Lord Conidon speaking with two others as he entered the room. The first was the heavily armored General Hollus, wearing the griffon emblem of Gallanse. He stood somewhat awkwardly on his wooden leg and held a stout redwood cane depicting his rank as City Warlord. The other was Lord Dillion's son. Macklore had only seen the boy once: yesterday morning as he'd broken the news of his father's death in the Great Hall. Seeing the ambassador enter, Conidon motioned for him to join the trio.

"Ambassador, thank you for joining us," Conidon wheezed, somewhat short of breath. His lined face looked tired but alert. "I apologize for the delay. I appreciate your coming on such short notice."

Macklore gave Conidon a flawless bow. "I'm here to serve, my Lord, in any way that I can," he replied.

Conidon turned back to the others. "This is Lord Dillion's son, Prince Alexander," Conidon continued, introducing the lad somberly. The boy was short in stature, the top of his head reaching only to the base of Macklore's neck. He was, however, built like a bull, with short, powerful legs and well-formed shoulders. It was obvious that, even as young as he was, Alexander would be an immensely strong man. He wore a green and white tunic in the colors of his house. Emblazoned upon the front was a wolf, the emblem of his city. His intelligent face was boyish, though his eyes were bleary and red.

"I am sorry for your loss, son of Janril," Macklore said softly. "Though I never met your father, his reputation was that of a strong and just ruler. I share in your sorrow. Should you need anything from me, you have but to ask."

The young prince looked at Macklore and answered, sadness in his voice. "Thank you, ambassador."

Macklore glanced about, wondering why the young prince had been left alone. Where were his retainers and counsel? Surely his advisors would not have left him by himself during this difficult time.

"I know I have already told you this, highness," said Conidon, breaking Macklore's reverie, "but—" he stopped as a sudden coughing fit shook his frail body. "We *will* find the truth of your father's death," he finished, taking a deep drink from a flask he drew from inside his tunic.

"Will the killer come to justice?" asked Alexander, his young eyes filling with tears. "Truly?"

Conidon put his arm around the prince's shoulders. "That's why we are here, lad, to find out who is responsible. You have my word as High Lord on it," he gave the boy a brief smile before tucking away the flask under his tunic.

Alexander looked as though he was going to shed tears again, but bravely held them in.

"You should be in bed, my lord," General Hollus rumbled. "Leave this mess to me. There is no reason to involve anyone else." He cast a quick look of contempt toward Macklore.

"Could you let your men know that we are preparing to leave, highness?" Conidon said to Alexander, with a chastising look at his general. "I want them ready to accompany you to my quarters in just a moment."

"Yes, Lord Conidon," Alexander replied. As he walked away, Conidon spoke more softly to Macklore.

"This is the commander of my Home Guard, General Hollus," continued Conidon, turning to the older man. "I don't believe you've been introduced, though you may have seen him at our last gathering in the Great Hall."

Hollus's face looked like it had been carved from solid granite. With a crooked nose which had been broken half a dozen times, and a horseshoe mustache drooping over his lips, he looked every bit the commanding officer. He, too, was short and stocky of build, wearing the blue and white of the Home Guard. He stared hard at Macklore, less than enthusiastic about the ambassador's presence.

Macklore lowered his head in greeting, "It's an honor to meet you formally, general," he said politely. "I have heard of your great success at the Battle of Spike Canyon some nine years past."

Hollus only hmmphed in reply.

"The general is leading the murder investigation," Conidon continued, taking no notice of his general's annoyance with the ambassador.

"Forgive me for speaking bluntly, but we do not need *him,* my lord," Hollus growled to Conidon, jerking his thumb at Macklore. "This is not the pristine marble of the lecture hall or a fancy dinner among nobility. His silver tongue will not help us uncover the truth of what happened to Lord Dillion."

"I would like to hear his council," Conidon replied, frowning at his general. "I have found that the ambassador possesses a keen intellect in many matters; this is no different."

"As you say, my lord," replied Hollus dubiously, his visage leaving little doubt as to his feelings. Turning to Macklore, the general spoke sternly, his face sour.

"The matter is a simple one. High Lord Dillion was murdered while he slept, his throat cut. There are no signs of forced entry, and no one was seen coming or going. It was almost certainly someone on the inside, close to Lord Dillion. His first advisor has been missing since yesterday. We are trying to locate him."

Macklore ground his teeth in frustration. Hollus was in charge of the investigation? The entire room had been contaminated. Dozens of guards had walked through the area, destroying any evidence that may have been left behind. Now he was speculating about their most likely suspect in front of dozens of witnesses. Macklore had believed that Conidon would employ someone more competent. Hollus was a more-than-able field commander; his exploits were well known throughout Shaara. More accustomed to a battlefield than a murder investigation, in this arena, he was out of his element. Any clues—even the smallest piece of evidence—could be key to finding the truth of Dillion's murder. Why had Conidon not called on one more practiced in the field of investigation?

Forcing his face to remain neutral, Macklore replied. "General, I've no doubt that you've done an excellent job gathering facts and evidence. You're right about me; I'm not an expert on killings or the solving of crimes. Yet, I have found through the years that it is often best to see a problem from every possible angle. The way I see the evidence may differ from your view, and I am certain we don't want to leave any avenue unexplored."

The ambassador's words, though well-spoken, only seemed to aggravate the general further.

"Through the years?" he said, unable to keep the disdain from his voice. "Just how many years have you been at your fancy job of *talking*? I've a cloak hanging in my closet that is older than you, sonny, so you can save your 'through the years' speech for someone else."

The passive look nearly evaporated from Macklore's face. What was it about the men in this country? So many were both arrogant and stupid— a dangerous combination. Did the general not comprehend the significance of Lord Dillion's demise? Conidon's most supportive peer was dead, murdered almost certainly at the hand of Dragomir, and this fool did not see it. Macklore almost laughed. Few, it seemed, understood the intricacies of politics. What it would be to have such a simple understanding of the world. The ambassador, however, had not been given that choice. Macklore forced himself to keep a polite tone.

"Of course, general, forgive me. If you would be so kind as to tell me what evidence you've gathered so far, I'll be out of your way all the sooner."

"I will leave you both to it, then," Lord Conidon said, turning to Alexander, who had joined them once again. "Highness, if you would accompany me to my private chambers, I have a few questions to ask of you."

"Yes, Lord Conidon," the lad replied.

"And ambassador," Conidon said, turning back to Macklore. "I will be busy for the remainder of the day. After you've delivered your report to General Hollus, consider yourself excused. Have a safe trip home."

Macklore bowed deeply in an effort to hide his surprise. This was not like Conidon at all. Something unseen was going on here, but he did not understand what. Lydia had made it clear last night that her father needed him. Now he was being dismissed from the city? It did not add up. "Of course, my Lord, Prince Alexander," he answered absently as his thoughts swirled.

Conidon snapped his fingers once and every guard from both cities accompanied him and the prince out of the room.

Macklore looked at the general, who was still glaring at him as the last guard left, and the door snapped shut.

"Shall we begin, general?" Macklore asked, his mind still racing.

"You'll bloody well wait until I'm ready, ambassador," Hollus sneered. "I've been ordered to catch you up, but unlike you, I have real work to do this day. You can just await my pleasure."

Macklore's brow furrowed as he fought to swallow an angry reply; when suddenly, Hollus touched his finger to his lips and glanced around the room, pointing to his ear.

"I don't know why Conidon thinks you need to know anything about Lord Dillion's murder. It's Shaarian business," he mumbled furiously. "We don't need some outlander sticking his nose in it. I'll do my best to spell it out for you in the simplest terms possible. That way, even a court popinjay like yourself will understand," the general sneered.

His actions however, did not match his words. He had pulled a parchment from inside his tunic and quietly limped over to a nearby table equipped with an inkwell and pen. Silently, he motioned for Macklore to follow.

"I don't need some young pup like you telling me my business! For reasons I fail to comprehend, Lord Conidon wants you to be part of this investigation. I, for one, think he is suffering from dementia!"

While deriding Conidon, the general was simultaneously scribbling furiously onto the parchment. He finished, holding it up for Macklore to see.

We believe someone is listening in... with magic.

Everything fell into place for the ambassador. Conidon wasn't being foolish at all; he was being careful. Whoever was listening would hear that the general was in charge of the investigation, that Alexander's advisor was the main suspect, and that Conidon had dismissed the ambassador. In short, everything Conidon wanted them to hear.

"I can only assume he has a reason for wanting my council, commander," Macklore said after a moment's hesitation.

"Ha—he only called you in because he is slipping into his dotage. As though *you* could possibly offer something to him that I couldn't."

Hollus held up the paper again.

Can you counter the spell or neutralize it?

Macklore nodded to the commander. It was no wonder that the High Lord had called him in. He was Conidon's only chance to repel any magical clairvoyance.

From behind one of the tapestries, a door opened, revealing a secret passageway Macklore would never have suspected was there. High Lord Conidon walked in quietly, holding his finger to his lips to remind the ambassador to stay quiet. Macklore's heart skipped a beat.

Behind him came Princess Lydia.

"Then why are you wasting my time, general?" Macklore said, remembering to stay in character. "It's obvious you aren't going to tell me anything about the investigation. If Conidon does not have the decency to meet with me today, after I have spent half the night patiently wiling away my time, I don't see the need for my services any longer. It is well past time I left this miserable city and its people behind!"

"You stand in the heart of the Gray Palace and insult my lord and city? You can get the hell out! Here, let me get the door, you ungrateful bastard!"

Hollus stomped to the door, opened it, and slammed it shut.

Conidon wrote upon the parchment.

Now.

Macklore nodded once, closed his eyes, and focused his will, concentrating on building a soundproof shield.

"Clypeus silentium."

Once he had it, he simply expanded the sphere to include the entirety of the Janril living quarters. He opened his eyes. "We are free to talk."

"I'm suffering from dementia? Slipping into my dotage?" Conidon said, looking at the general skeptically.

"I could've said you were a cantankerous old ass hat, but I wanted you to keep your dignity," Hollus sniffed. The change in him was extraordinary. He looked at Macklore, and poked the younger man with his cane. "I hope you will forgive me, ambassador," he said with a wry grin. "We couldn't be sure who was listening in, and it had to sound authentic. It is widely known that I'm... impatient when it comes to politics. Always have been. Lord Conidon thought it best for me to play on that reputation."

Conidon smiled briefly and shook first Hollus's hand and then Macklore's, secretly passing the latter a tightly rolled parchment no one but the ambassador could detect. "Well done, both of you. I must say, ambassador, you're a handy man to have around."

"Thank you, my lord," Macklore replied, furtively slipping the note into his pocket. "I'm sorry I wasn't quicker on the uptake, general. I must say, I was confused as to why Lord Conidon would put the investigation in the hands of one so..."

"Inept," said a new voice from behind the tapestry. Stepping forward was an older gentleman of perhaps fifty winters, wearing a black tunic trimmed in silver. His head was shaved, though he sported a neatly trimmed mustache the color of snow. Following behind was Madora, dressed in a blue and silver dress open from the neck down to her bodice.

"Is that what you were going to say, ambassador?" the man continued mildly.

"I would like to introduce you to Lord Kantik," Conidon said with a frown. "My oldest friend and advisor."

Macklore bowed deeply, his mind racing. *So, this is the fabled spymaster of Gallanse*, he thought to himself. *I'll have to keep my wits about me.*

"I was going to say inexperienced, Lord Kantik," Macklore replied, in answer to his question.

Kantik smiled in genuine humor. "Ever the diplomat, I see," he said with a laugh, "and clever to boot."

"I don't take your meaning, my lord," Macklore said in confusion.

"Not many would think that a mere woman could be one of my informants," Kantik explained, looking at Madora. "Especially one of my best. However, as an outsider, I should have guessed you might see things differently. I received your message last night. I'm sorry we could not meet with you sooner, but…" he gestured all around the room. "We've been kept busy."

Macklore bowed his head in understanding, wondering how much Kantik knew. He was Conidon's advisor, certainly, but if rumors were to be believed, the man was far more. It was said that no secret in Gallanse could be kept from him for long. Macklore felt his blood turn to ice, knowing he must proceed with caution.

"Before we begin, ambassador, I've a question," Kantik said blithely. "How do you keep so calm in the face of such blatant stupidity, as displayed by the general in his act? Surely, it must have irked you to no end, having an incompetent man allow all those guards to tromp around the crime scene. What's your trick?"

"I think you will find the ambassador is full of surprises," Lydia said, quietly staring at Macklore, her face unreadable.

Macklore looked briefly to Lydia suppressing a smile. "Remaining calm is not easy, Lord Kantik," he answered, turning back to the older man. "But like any number of things, one can train oneself to handle nearly anything with poise, as I am sure you have reason to understand."

"You are like a breath of fresh air, ambassador," Kantik said with a smile. "It is so nice to deal with a professional, and a powerful one to boot."

He suspects something, Macklore thought to himself, hoping Kantik had not guessed at the ambassador's true identity.

"The sound shield will not stay in place forever, and it seems we've much to discuss," Macklore said, smoothly changing the subject. Kantik had not blinked and was watching the ambassador closely. "What do we know of Lord Dillion's murder?"

Kantik motioned for Macklore to follow and led them all into the bedroom. There, lying upon the bed, was the corpse of Lord Dillion. He had been built much like his son, Alexander: short of stature, but powerful. His dark brown hair was speckled with gray and reached to just above his shoulders. A short beard shaved only at the chin gave him a grim appearance. He lay with his hands held together on his chest, as though resting peacefully.

Unfortunately, that's where the serenity ended. His throat had been cut to the bone. Dried blood stained the white cotton bedding under his neck. His once-proud face was deathly pale, and his eyes were open, staring into eternal darkness.

"What do you make of it, ambassador?" asked Kantik quietly.

Such a simple question, and yet Macklore knew its purpose. He had no doubt that Kantik had already come up with a theory of Lord Dillion's murder. His reputation as a finder of truths was well known.

This was more.

Kantik wanted to know just how good the ambassador was at reading the crime scene. He wanted information about Macklore. Who was he? Why had he shown up when he did? All this flashed through Macklore's mind in an instant.

He glanced at Lydia, wondering for the first time if he was being played for a fool. He had seen it before. A woman feasting on a man's sentiment to get what she wanted. Surely, her love was for her father—not some stranger she'd just recently met.

It did not matter, he decided. He was committed to helping the Gaidas keep Dragomir off the throne. Macklore had come to that conclusion last night as he headed back to the Golden Cutlass, and he was not going to waver now.

Macklore first examined the room itself, looking closely at the stone floor, walls, and ceiling. He also peered at the windows overlooking the inner courtyard. Satisfied, the ambassador approached the corpse, hovering over the neck wound, examining it first from directly above. Then he walked around the bed, taking care to survey the body from all sides. He even went so far as to lift the neck slightly, peering underneath it. Next, Macklore examined Lord Dillion's fingers, unclasping his hands and bending over as closely as he could to get a clear look. The ambassador lifted Dillion's lifeless hand to his nose, inhaling deeply. Lydia and Conidon exchanged worried glances but said nothing.

Macklore gazed intently upon the deceased, a frown fixed on his face. Without a word, he climbed onto the bed, straddling the body, and proceeded to pry open the corpse's mouth.

"What are you doing?" Lydia stammered, stunned at Macklore's lack of decorum.

Even Conidon seemed surprised. "Ambassador, I must ask that you get down! Please, this is most unseemly."

"Leave him be," Madora said quietly, looking at Kantik knowingly.

"But this is…" Conidon sputtered.

"If this investigation is too much for you to stomach, then you may wait in the other room," Kantik said with finality.

Conidon, however, was already approaching Macklore angrily. "Dillion was my closest friend and ally, ambassador. I must insist…"

"Lord Conidon," Kantik said, cutting him off, "you put me in charge of this investigation. You promised Prince Alexander justice. That means finding out all we can… in any way possible. Unless you wish to take over the investigation yourself, please leave him be."

"Interesting," Macklore said, ignoring them all. He peered closely at Dillion's mouth, studying the dead man's tongue intently. He moved closer until less than an inch separated his face from Dillion's. Macklore inhaled deeply.

Lydia's face had grown pale.

"What the hell are you doing?" bellowed Conidon, his face reddening.

"I need a knife," Macklore said absently, studying the tongue closely.

"Whatever for?" Lydia asked, her eyes wide.

"For cutting him open," Macklore answered with a frown.

Lydia's mouth fell open in disbelief. "You are *insane*," she said, horrified.

"We do not defile our dead, ambassador!" Conidon shouted, clearly furious.

Kantik frowned at Madora, looking like he'd swallowed something rotten.

"I told you," she cooed with a shake of her head.

"That won't be necessary, ambassador," Kantik said, looking back at Macklore. "Please, if you would be so good as to share your findings *without* cutting open the corpse."

"Well," he said, hopping off the bed and cleaning his hands with a handkerchief he'd pulled from under his robes. "Some interesting things are apparent to me. First, whoever killed him left no evidence behind. Nothing was on the floor or walls, and there was no chance of escape from the window; we are forty feet above the courtyard, and there are six guardsmen in the garden outside. The killer would have been seen by at least one if he'd escaped from there."

"What does that tell us?" asked Conidon, still fuming.

"Whoever it was knew what he, or she, was doing," Macklore surmised. "No clues, no sign of human entry was left behind."

"Except for the dead body," Conidon growled.

"That doesn't give you the right to crawl all over the bed with a dead man," Lydia exclaimed.

"Hush, child," Madora said soothingly. "He had his reasons, I'm sure."

Macklore looked at Lydia. "The other thing that became apparent is the cause of death. It wasn't this wound on his neck."

"Come now, ambassador, there is blood all over the sheets. It is obvious that his throat was cut, and he bled to death," said Conidon, wiping his sleeve across his forehead.

"What leads you to that conclusion, ambassador?" asked Kantik, giving Conidon a hard look.

"Two things," Macklore said, pointing at the wound. "Usually when someone is killed by a slashed throat, a couple of things happen. The victim will reach up to staunch the flow of blood. It's a nearly unavoidable reflex... like blinking when something comes close to your eyes. However, there is no blood whatsoever on Lord Dillion's hands."

"Maybe his arms were being held," Kantik suggested mildly. "Or he was asleep at the time of his death. The absence of blood staining his hands does not prove your theory, though it does lend it some credence."

Macklore motioned to the neck wound again. "That's true, Lord Kantik. That alone doesn't provide the proof we seek. The other odd thing is the blood itself. I noticed there's not enough of it on the bed."

"What are you talking about? There is blood all over the place," Conidon said with a scowl.

"Let him continue without interruption, if you please, Lord Conidon. You can save your comments for after he is finished," chided Kantik.

Macklore nodded grimly to Kantik, thankful for his intervention. "There *is* blood all over the bed and sheets, true; but it's not enough to have killed him. The artery has been cut. That is the main blood vessel in the neck. If his heart had been pumping at the time his neck was cut, we'd observe twice as much blood drenching the sheets. You see here," he continued, pointing to the area near Dillion's wound. "The blood around the cut is darker and more congealed. Had his heart been pumping, the blood would have splashed outward, covering a much greater area of the bed, as well as the front of his tunic. The blood also would have been a brighter shade of red. Because the blood is dark and thick, I'd guess his heart was still when his throat was slashed, and had been for some time."

Conidon and Lydia looked at the ambassador as though seeing him for the first time. Kantik, however, raised his eyebrows. "Is that all, ambassador?"

Macklore shook his head, still looking at the corpse. "I am afraid not. I believe his throat was cut while he was already lying down. There's no sign of struggle. Not a single drop of blood splashed anywhere else in the room. It is contained inside this small area on the bed only. It's as though the blood were sitting in the artery, already unmoving, and spilled out when the vessel was cut."

They all stared silently as Macklore concluded his findings.

"Last, we have the cut itself. Upon close examination, you can see just how fine the edge of the blade must have been. Whatever cut him was an extremely sharp object; there is no tearing of the skin at all. That suggests a blade of exceptional quality, almost certainly made of steel."

"Only royalty could afford such a blade," Kantik reasoned.

"Or a servant who had stolen it from a noble," Macklore said with a shrug of his shoulders. "Out on the streets, such a weapon would be a rarity… but here?" He shook his head. "Any number of such weapons are common with so many nobles gathered. My point is, whoever it was knew what they were doing. The cut was deep and quick, made in a single motion."

"I'm confused," Lydia interjected. "You're saying that his heart was not pumping at the time his throat was cut? What are you suggesting?"

"The ambassador is suggesting that Dillion was already dead," Hollus answered grimly.

"But why would anyone cut his throat, if he was already dead?" Lydia asked with a frown.

"To cover up the killer's true murder method," Madora said, supplying the answer.

"Then how did he die?" Lydia asked, unable to fathom why anyone would go to so much effort to kill Lord Dillion and then hide how it was done.

Macklore motioned to Lord Dillion's fingers. "You see here? There are red stains upon his fingers. Not bloodstains, but stains caused by the juice of some sort of fruit or berry. It has a very distinctive odor, quite sweet. I found the same color and smell on lord Dillion's tongue. I was hoping to cut open his stomach to see if I could find any of the food still in his system to identify it with certainty. However, my thought is that he ingested this fruit, whatever it was, and it was poisonous. I don't recognize the scent offhand, but I'm not an expert in plants or what they smell like."

"I have been trained in the identification of many types of poisons, both rare and common. I have never seen anything like this," Kantik said. He pulled out a vial from inside his cloak. Contained within was a piece of red fruit, looking much like a huge, plump raspberry.

Macklore moved forward and sniffed it, raising one eyebrow questioningly.

"Alexander had helped himself to one of these from his father's serving tray yesterday, but the two quarreled before he ate it, and this was left on the dining table under a napkin," Kantik explained.

"It looks like a raspberry," Lydia said, looking at it closely.

"Yes, and I checked with the kitchen," Madora said grimly. "Yesterday morning, Lord Dillion was served a plate of raspberries and cream an hour before the meeting in the Great Hall. Only a single person was seen entering and leaving the room… a male servant who brought the food."

"Whoever did this was clever," Macklore said, looking at Kantik. "You are right, Madora, this fruit looks much like a raspberry. Most likely, the servant placed several on the plate and waited for Lord Dillion to eat them. When he came back in, ostensibly to remove the tray, he could easily have slipped into the bedroom and sliced Lord Dillion's throat. Especially if no one else was present."

"I have questioned Prince Alexander and Dillion's advisor," Kantik said. "Both said the same thing. Alexander and his father argued about whether or not the prince would accompany him into the Great Hall for your meeting last night, Conidon. Lord Dillion refused him, and Alexander retired to his room upset. A moment later, Dillion sent his advisor to console Alexander, while he excused himself to his bedroom, feeling unwell. The guards were stationed in the hallway outside the main chamber. No one else was inside. The servant reappeared minutes later, retrieved the tray, and left. The advisor came to wake Dillion for the meeting and found him as we did. He immediately sent for me, knowing that I was used to dealing with... this sort of thing. Unfortunately, Alexander stumbled into Dillion's room. In his grief, the prince ran to the Great Hall and informed you and the public."

All four of them were quiet for several heartbeats. "It seems I owe you an apology, ambassador," Conidon said finally. "Your conclusions match those of Lord Kantik."

Macklore inclined his head saying nothing.

"Yes, your deductions were... quite accurate," Kantik said, staring at Macklore a little too hard.

Yes, I am more than I seem, Kantik... or whatever your real name is, Macklore thought to himself.

"My heart goes out to Alexander; his father and I were friends, and he deserves far better. Tell me, Kantik, where does that leave us?" asked Conidon. "We still don't know who killed Dillion. Are we any closer to finding the culprit?"

Kantik pursed his lips and rubbed his chin thoughtfully. "We know that whoever got in here and poisoned Dillion had to have been extremely good at his craft. The best hired killer in the city is Sable, who has gone missing as of last night. I don't believe he would have been capable of getting inside the palace and side-stepping every single one of my agents. Nor is poison his preferred method of killing. We do know that Sable met with Lord Brak's niece, Talia, last night, but then disappeared into the lower city. No one has seen him since." He glanced then at Macklore, who looked back without saying a word.

Kantik looked Macklore directly in the eyes. "Turns out, Sable's head was served to Dragomir this morning for breakfast. A strange turn of events, wouldn't you agree, ambassador?"

"No less than he deserved, I would guess, for attempting to assassinate an innocent," Macklore said coldly.

"My understanding is that Dragomir nearly soiled himself in terror upon seeing those dead eyes staring back at him. I wonder how that bit of magic was achieved…"

"Probably best if it remains a mystery," Macklore stated flatly.

Kantik could not help the slow smile that spread upon his face. "Regardless of Sable and his remains," he continued, growing serious once more, "I have my agents watching every suitor and his entourage like hawks. If one of them had done it, I would know. The only one I cannot account for is that damn magus; he comes and goes like a shadow. Could the murderer be this mysterious mage who has taken up with Dragomir? Could he have come in here himself and done this?"

Macklore shook his head. "I don't think so. Magic leaves a... residue... that others who practice it can sense. No magic has been used in this room recently, except my own. I would have detected it right away."

"Then the only conclusion I can fathom is that the killer came from outside the city and could be anywhere at this moment," Kantik said, clearly frustrated.

"Then, somehow, a man who was undetected by your agents managed to make his way into Dillion's private chambers, deliver food, poison him, retrieve the tray—removing the evidence—and slash Dillion's throat... all without even one of a dozen guards, agents, and servants remembering anything about him?" Lydia asked incredulously.

They all looked at one another as the magnitude of what Lydia said sank in.

"What is to keep him from doing it again?" she asked.

Conidon looked to Kantik and Macklore. "If word gets out that we've got a killer on the loose, I will be deposed quickly. I will not be the High Lord who could not keep his guests safe. Dragomir must be licking his chops at the idea of seeing me fail. What can we do?"

"I think we should try to identify the poison used," Macklore said. "If we can find out where it came from, at least it may give us an idea of who we are dealing with. I don't know many who could have walked right into the heart of the keep and dealt death so easily."

"I agree," Kantik replied, with a nod toward Macklore. "I know of an apothecary in the city who may be able to identify the poison. I have my suspicions as to where it originated from, but I don't want to speculate too much until I have more information. I will have to take it to him myself, Conidon. There is much going on in the palace, but I believe we can gain knowledge of this assassin, and I dare not send anyone else."

"It will be dangerous," Conidon said. "There is already unrest in the streets. My soldiers have had to put down two riots already."

"I will go with you," Macklore volunteered. "I am supposed to be storming out anyhow, done with you all," he said with a grim smile.

Macklore took a deep breath and let it out slowly. He was part of this now, and there was no turning back. It was time to let Conidon see where his loyalties lie. "Before I go, I need to let you know a few things, and I hope you will tell me a few as well."

"Ambassador?" Conidon asked.

"My orders come from Medyha Whitelance himself. When I arrived, he wanted me to take stock of the situation here in Gallanse and report back to him."

"We surmised as much, ambassador," Kantik said with the nod. "King Medyha has always tried to balance his support by avoiding undue attention to himself."

"Yes, well, be that as it may… he told me not to get involved. In fact, that was his direct order to me: to stay out of it." Macklore looked directly at Conidon, letting his words sink in.

"What is it that you are saying, ambassador?" the high lord asked quietly.

"That I am doing what is right for Brisbane in helping you here; that you cannot stand against Dragomir and his magus without me; that I believe serving you here in Gallanse is in Brisbane's best interest. No one could have foreseen one of the *Moldronni Sor* coming and offering his assistance to Dragomir. You need magic to fight that, my lord, powerful magic. I don't know if I can counter this mage, but I am the best chance you have. I will not break my oaths to Brisbane or Medyha, but I am yours to command during this crisis."

"Are you certain of this course, ambassador? My understanding is that the last time Medyha's orders were not heeded exactly, he exiled two members of his staff. Rumor has it that they were close to him. Yet he banished them both, never to return upon pain of death. Neither have been seen or heard from since, causing speculation as to whether or not he simply had them killed."

"I know the risks, my lord, and I am well aware of the precedent that has already been set," he said grimly. "But to allow Gallanse to be overtaken by Dragomir would be a disaster. Not just for Brisbane, but for the entire Crystalline Sea. It would lead to war on a scale as yet unheard of. What I do is for the good of us all. Right now, your city and mine need me here in Gallanse," Macklore said simply.

"And what would you ask of me?" Conidon said.

Macklore smiled grimly. "Tell me your plans. What do you hope to accomplish here? How can I help?"

"Jora's balls! You aren't asking much, are you, boy? Just tell you everything!" Kantik said, eyebrows raised.

Conidon laughed ruefully. "You remind me of my son, ambassador. Once he had decided upon a course of action, he was all in. Very well. Our plan is to stall these suitors and the upcoming marriage for another ten days. Every three years, the High Lords and the council of Barons meet to discuss the laws of our country. This year, I have put forward a proposal that would allow women take a leadership role in politics, including being named as rulers. My wish is to put Lydia on the throne. Her mother would have been the greatest leader this country has ever seen, had she been given the opportunity. Heaven knows, she helped me greatly. Much of my savvy in dealing with others, I learned from her. It is long past time for Shaara to acknowledge that the fairer sex has more to offer than soft flesh and the ability to nurture hearth and home. That is our goal. The meeting takes place in a fortnight… I want to stave off the wolves and survive until then."

"What of Prince Alexander? Where has his advisor gone?" Macklore asked.

Kantik hmmphed. "You don't miss much, do you boy?" He looked at Conidon then, who gave him a nod.

"I arranged to have him smuggled out last night to return to Janril. Alexander's older brother, Bay, needs to know of what has transpired here. Bay will become the new High Lord of Janril.

Alexander, however, needed to stay here. If all else fails, Lydia will marry him."

Macklore felt his heart drop into the pit of his stomach, and he turned to look at Lydia, who cast her eyes downward. "How do you feel about that, princess?" he whispered.

Lydia looked up, her face expressionless. "I will do as my father commands."

"We, of course, hope it does not come to that," continued Kantik. "Alexander is a fine young man, but he is not ready for the responsibility of running a massive city like Gallanse."

"I see the benefit of the choice, though," Macklore said, nodding to himself. "He would be the puppet, and Lydia would be the true ruler. At least until Alexander had proven himself."

"The biggest threat to our plan is Dragomir and his pet magus," Conidon said. "If we can find proof that he ordered Lord Dillion's murder, I can have him arrested and hanged."

"I'm not sure that the Blood Watch will allow that to happen, my lord," Madora said dubiously. "They are incredible in battle. Even Captain Torrance would be hard-pressed to defeat one of them, and he won the silver sword this year. In all of my years of service, I believe only Ecian would have been able to hold his own against one of the Blood Watch."

"Yes, and Dragomir's brought twenty with him," Kantik said with a nod. "Though I've no report of their general. Rumor is that he was recalled a few days ago, but no one saw him leave the city," Kantik mused.

"Nevertheless, we must find out what we can about this murder. I promised Alexander that I would see justice, and by damn, Dillion was a good man! It burns me to see him killed at the hand of Rexor's whelp." The high lord had a fire gleaming in his eyes. While age had robbed him of his vitality and stamina, it had not tempered his feelings.

For the first time Macklore saw it, and he knew instantly that what he was doing was right. Conidon was angry. He has lost his ally, yes—but more than that, he had lost his friend.

"I have my orders," Macklore said, readying himself to leave. "I will visit this apothecary and see what can be discovered. Ah, wait, there is one last thing. The village of Inniak. They have requested your military assistance and have been waiting all day to hear from me. What shall I tell them, my lord?"

Conidon nodded once. "Yes, I had forgotten them entirely. How bad are the attacks?"

"The village was nearly lost, my lord," Hollus said. "I'd send a century, at least."

"Let's make it two. I don't want our border towns overrun by Ettu," Conidon said shortly.

"I will go with the ambassador. I need to show him the entrance to some hidden tunnels leading into and out of the palace," Kantik said. Then he continued, muttering under his breath, "Ones he doesn't know about already, that is." Kantik cleared his throat, and addressed Macklore, "I would recommend using them from now on, ambassador. The less you are seen, the better."

Macklore turned back to Conidon and Lydia, and bowed. "My lord, highness, I will report to you upon my return. Until then, know that the magic I cast upon this room will last only another few minutes; take care what you say after my departure."

The two strode out through the secret passage and disappeared.

"You did not tell him, father," Lydia said quietly, with a glance at Madora.

"No, our tasks are impossible enough without that burden laid on his shoulders," Conidon replied.

"He should know."

"He will, soon enough."

Chapter 21

Two hours before sunset, the *Duquesne* arrived at Adian. With the windmage on board, it had been an incredibly fast voyage. They had sailed over two hundred miles in just ten hours. Rion found himself marveling at the efficiency of Captain Tross and his crew.

Looking out upon the docks, Rion could see the silver and black of the Wolfguard patrolling the outskirts of the city. As the *Duquesne* pulled into harbor, Rion felt the familiar stirring of excitement build in his chest. He fought it down as it threatened to break through the calm persona he had painstakingly built over the last six years.

Since his forced retirement, the former pirate captain had lived a quiet life, out of the limelight and far from trouble. Rion had chosen to settle in a sleepy village near Agenhelm, nestled on the northern coast of the Crystalline Sea. His simple cottage lay at the edge of town near a babbling brook. He had purposely chosen this peaceful backdrop to keep himself removed from the temptation of adventure seeking. His life, he knew, depended on it.

Little good it's done me, he thought to himself wryly. Now he was smack-dab in the middle of an escapade the likes of which he had never known. The most galling thing was the fact that Rion found himself enjoying it! As he watched Captain Tross guide his schooner expertly into the docks, he was envious. After so many years away from the sea, Rion found something magical about returning to port safely.

"All hands, on deck!" the captain bellowed, causing his men to swarm to life. "Let's get this cargo unloaded, boys! The sooner we get paid, the better!"

Rion smiled in approval. The captain knew that getting the shipment ashore and money into the men's pockets was of paramount importance. Whether the men liked you or not, every sea captain knew that silver bought loyalty like nothing else in the world.

Rion saw Chameleon emerge from the first mate's quarters, her face a sickly shade of green. *Not much of a sailor*, he decided with an amused grin.

The Drannock made her way unsteadily toward Rion, holding fast to the side of the ship as she moved. "We are here?" she asked, turning her bloodshot eyes to the former captain.

"You made it, lass," Rion responded gently. "You now look upon Adian, the jewel of the

Rhone, as she's called. Not to worry, you'll have solid ground under you soon enough."

The city was not as large as Staltshore, nor did it look as old. Instead of the aged granite bulwark of the capital city, Adian was surrounded by walls built of chalky gray heartstone, found at the roots of the ancient black hills to the south. This huge barricade of thick stone surrounded every inch of Adian, making it appear more like a massive fortress than a city. Watch towers were spread evenly along the battlements. Tiny figures could be seen from the harbor, soldiers manning those massive ramparts.

Approaching from the stern of the ship, Adecia and Taeral walked over to join them. In Taeral's hand was his ebon wood hafted spear. It had garnered several curious looks from the crew, though no one had approached the triton to ask about its origin. Rion had spoken privately with the captain when they'd come aboard. The last thing any of them needed was the temperamental triton going into a rampage on deck. Captain Tross saw things the exact same way and quietly conveyed the order to his men.

Rion's keen ears caught the last of their conversation as they drew close. "...ave to get the word out first thing tomorrow," Taeral was saying. "It should spread quickly enough if I can make contact with my people. My clan is allied with the Gray Fin here to the south. My hope is that they send scouts and warriors. If we are lucky, Dayun will lead them. She is the finest war leader they have."

Adecia nodded thoughtfully and looked like she was about to speak, when Kildare strode up from below deck.

"Rion, have you been to the Matron?" he asked.

Rion smiled, not bothering to quell his excitement. "Oh, I've been to the Matron, laddie. Tell me, does Vella still run the place?"

Kildare nodded. "She does. I think the entire city would be in mourning if she retired. Losing her would be a tragedy unlike any I could fathom."

Adecia was frowning. "Aren't you and your brother going with us?"

"We'll meet you there," Kildare answered. "We've another errand to see to. It won't take long, but it's necessary. We have an… acquaintance… here in Adian who will know what the current situation is in Gallanse."

"We should come with you," Adecia said firmly.

"No," Kildare answered softly. "It will be unpleasant enough as it is. I have no desire for any of you to get caught up in the politics of Adian. Zedaine and I will go alone. We'll join you at the Matron when we finish." Kildare cast his eyes skyward and said, "If he ever decides to come down from his latest indulgence."

High above, Zedaine was with the lookout, perched in the crow's nest, seeming to be in no hurry to join them on deck. He was holding a length of rope in his hands and listening intently to the barrelman, who was laughing at some quip of Zedaine's.

"Is he always like this?" questioned Adecia, who was peering up at him as well.

"Unfortunately, yes," responded Kildare. "He sees what he likes, and off he goes. For as long as I've known him, this is his way. I wouldn't be surprised if he's forgotten we are here."

"The Crow in the crow's nest?" Rion quipped. "How apropos."

Cupping his hands to his mouth, Kildare called up to his brother. "Zee, come on! We've got other things to do!"

Zedaine looked downward and gave a friendly wave. "Kil, watch this," he called, with a huge grin on his face.

In one smooth motion he dropped, his foot looped through the bottom of the rope. His descent grew faster until, less than a span from the deck, he slowed just enough to step heavily to the wooden planks below.

"Ha ha!" he yelled, looking up at the lookout. "I told you I measured it correctly!"

From above, the barrelman whooped in excitement. "Well done! You come back tomorrow. I'll teach you to fly!"

Zedaine pumped his fist in return. "Until then, my friend, thanks for the lesson. Be lucky!"

"Ayeeee!"

"Show off," Kildare said, with a rueful shake of his head.

"Bah, nothing to it really. Even you could do it," Zedaine said, laughing.

"By Kelthane's beard, that was a sight," bellowed Captain Tross, lumbering up to the six of them. "I never thought to see a big bastard like you scrambling around overhead like a spider monkey," he said, clapping Zedaine on the shoulder. "Though I should have suspected it after watching the two of you spar. Quicker, nimbler men, I've never seen."

"Thank you for getting here so quickly, captain," Zedaine said in answer. "You and your crew are to be commended."

"That's what Blade paid me for," Tross said with a slight bow. "If you'll excuse me, I need to speak with the keeper of the manifest. I'll see you all tomorrow. An hour after sunrise, we put out to sea.

And no more jumping onto my ship," he said sternly, looking at Adecia.

Zedaine stepped beside the girl and winked at the captain. "We'll keep an eye on her."

Adecia tensed automatically at his closeness, but said nothing.

"An hour after sunrise," Kildare said, stepping forward to shake hands with the captain. "We'll see you then."

Captain Tross grunted his affirmation and walked down the gangplank onto the dock.

"We should be off, as well," Kildare said, turning to Rion. "Take the north gate; it's the fastest way to the Matron."

"When you arrive, tell Vella you're with us," Zedaine chimed in. "She likes me well enough, but for some reason she adores Kildare."

"That's because I can sing like a court bard," Kildare replied with a frown. "You, on the other hand, sound like a sick cow. Tell Vella that the challenge of the blades will be tonight—two hours from now, as the sun begins to set. Let her know I'm ready for the trial. Come on, Zee, we're wasting time."

Kildare walked down the gangplank, heading west, but turned as his brother asked him a question.

"I can't talk you out of this?" he asked.

"After finishing up where we are headed, I'm going to be in the mood to fight someone," he said over his shoulder, starting off again.

Zedaine frowned slightly but nodded to himself. He looked back at his companions, who did not understand the exchange. "We should only be an hour, maybe less. There is a large celebration tonight, the Festival of the Mask, meaning the streets will be teeming with people. Keep your wits about you, and Taeral," he said, looking at the triton with eyebrows raised, "try not to kill anyone on the way."

He turned to the docks and left, running to catch up with his brother. Within moments, the two had disappeared, lost in the crowd.

"What's that supposed to mean?" Taeral asked, looking flummoxed.

"He means, hold on to your temper," Rion answered. "You tend to get angry too quickly for comfort."

"I do *not*!" Taeral hissed, nostrils flaring.

The massive triton looked around as three sets of eyes were staring at him in disbelief.

"Come along, all of you," Rion said after a moment. "And stick close to me. I don't want to lose anyone in the city. You all stand out like sore thumbs."

They made their way along the docks, heading north, as dozens of crews loaded and unloaded goods to buy, sell, and trade. The constant noise and ruckus were like music to Rion's ears. He heard sailors and dockworkers laughing, arguing, and cursing at one another in several diverse accents, many he had not heard in years. Gods, how he missed this!

The port itself was packed, with scores of ships filling the harbor. They came in all manner of shapes and sizes, displaying flags from dozens of countries around the Crystalline Sea. Ships from every city in the Rhone were docked next to carracks and cutters from Agenhelm. They saw caravels from Shaara, galleys from Shan'dar, and sloops from far off Valasca. One huge vessel in particular caught their eye.

"That's a war galleon out of Tal'Mur," Rion said, pointing it out to his less-experienced companions. "Fully equipped with catapults and ballista. Good sailors, tough in a fight. Careful around them… they've a temper to match even you, Taeral."

Just then, three swarthy warriors walked out of the war galleon onto the dock. They were stocky fellows, bristling with weapons. Each wore a black surcoat over ring mail armor, along with bronze greaves to shield their legs. On top of their heads rested burnished bronze helms, reinforced with iron rims and flaring outward, giving them a fierce appearance. Without a word, they strode through the crowd, heading east.

As the quartet continued north, the entrance to Adian drew near. To say it was formidable was an understatement.

Over five spans wide at the base and nearly twelve in height, the gateway had space enough for wagons to pass in and out simultaneously, with room to spare. The top of the entryway was arched and held together by the same chiseled heartstone that surrounded the entire city. Thick wooden doors were held ajar by hinges twice the size of Taeral's hand, wrought from iron. They were painted to match the walls and bolted to the stone face of the battlements. Beyond the doors, a several-inch thick iron portcullis was ready to drop into place from an antechamber above the gate. A second set of heavy wooden doors protected the inner entrance, identical to those on the outside. Above, a trebuchet loomed next to a pair of catapults. A full company of Wolfguard watched from the walls, prepared for action at the first hint of trouble. This gate was made to be defended.

In the entryway itself stood a dozen guardsmen, well-armed and armored. They looked alert and frequently stopped to question folk entering the city.

"A moment, sir," said one, stepping in front of Taeral. The guard was a young man of average height and build, sporting a neatly trimmed mustache that matched his sand-colored hair.

"Get out of my way," Taeral snapped, more forcefully than necessary.

The guard, not expecting such a sharp response, tensed and placed his hand on the hilt of his sword. The other members of his squad did the same, as they prepared to defend themselves. Taeral had not backed down an inch. Instead, he leaned forward on his spear, glowering at the guard in his path. The roadway, bustling with people a moment before, emptied quickly, as they sensed the coming conflict.

"Peace, Enriq," came a voice from behind the guard. Striding forward was another man of perhaps thirty winters. He was dressed similarly to the others but carried a greater bearing. His uniform was spotless, boasting a pair of silver stripes along the collar. His bronze helm had been polished to perfection, and even the red plume atop it shone in the sunlight. He removed the burnished headpiece, revealing close cropped brown hair coupled with a well-manicured beard.

"Peace to you as well, stranger," he continued. "The soldiers of Adian mean no disrespect to you or your friends. Our orders are to question anyone suspicious or from out-of-country to discover their business here. You, sir," he said in his brusque manner to Taeral, "certainly stand out from the crowd, even on a day such as this. Tell me, what is your business in Adian?" His voice was stern, yet respectful; he was very much a man going about his work.

Rion stepped forward. "I see the reputation of the Wolfguard is well earned captain: hard- nosed but fair. Don't mind my friend here," he continued, nudging Taeral. "He has been upset since we docked, having lost nearly five drachmas in silver to me in a game of dice earlier today."

The former pirate captain looked at Taeral. "Stop glaring at everyone; as the guardsman said, they are simply doing their job. You will get your chance to win your money back."

Taeral turned his frown to Rion but ceased his threatening posture. The tension on the roadway immediately lessened.

"As to your question," Rion continued, gesturing to Chameleon and Adecia, "we are on our way to Shaara via Captain Tross's merchant vessel, only just arrived in port. The captain bade us find lodgings for the night in your fine city, as he and his men have much to do before nightfall."

The crowd started moving again, as it appeared no trouble would ensue.

"We were hoping to take part in the festival this evening. Is it true that tonight is the Festival of the Mask?"

"It is tonight, friend…" the guard captain paused in expectation.

"Rion, of Shan'dar, guardsman…"

"Reynolds, Captain Reynolds," the guard said with a brief smile. "I thank you for your time. Enjoy your stay in Adian. Tell your big friend there to hold his temper and stay out of trouble. Perhaps he should steer clear of the gambling booths as well."

Rion nodded, "Thank you for your assistance, captain, it was… timely."

"Good evening," the captain replied, moving out of their way.

"What is the Festival of the Mask?" Adecia asked once they were out of earshot.

"Perhaps you will see," Rion said, abruptly looking at Taeral. "That is if we can get to the Matron in one piece, without this big lummox challenging the entire city."

Taeral growled but said nothing.

Zedaine, if anything, had understated how busy the streets of Adian would be. Now deep in the city, Rion led his companions, taking pains to avoid anyone who might recognize the former pirate captain. Except for several curious stares directed toward Taeral, folks left them alone. They might have made better time, but Rion's three companions were unable to keep from gawking at the sights.

For the inexperienced trio, everywhere they looked abounded with all manner of new, exciting things. Food vendors were widespread up and down the avenues, like nothing they had ever seen. Fresh cut corn from Valasca was slowly grilled over open coals. Seasoned with lime and sea salt, its enticing smell filled the air. One stand served dark green beans steamed to perfection, coated with olive oil and sprinkled with peppered cheese. At another, pale green jicama from Teshlan was displayed. Crisp and raw, it tantalized passersby with its aroma. Fruits, too, were prevalent, ranging from swollen red strawberries and lush orange melons, to candied green apples and juicy grapes sold in bunches of different shapes, sizes, and colors.

On the corner of a wide avenue, an ox of a man sliced off portions of roasted boar from a spit. His hearty laugh bellowed outward, as he served a tiny girl who could not have been more than three years of age. Shrimp skewered on sticks were smoked over slow burning hickory chips, a savory orange glaze coating their outer shell. Cheeses, sweetmeats, pastries, and pies were hawked, sold, and consumed up and down the streets of Adian. These delicacies were washed down with all manner of drink; be it rich amber beers tapped from the kegs of numerous brewers, or lighter-colored ales covered in foam. Wines ranging from emerald green to ruby red flowed from bottles and decanters alike.

Not to be outdone, entertainers lined the outdoor amphitheaters and random street corners, showcasing a variety of skills and feats. A troupe of acrobats threw themselves with reckless abandon into the air, turning remarkable flips and twists of incredible skill.

On one corner, a grizzled old man with a thin white beard hanging past his knees told tales of the ancient gods and spirits to a group of wide-eyed children, who gasped in delight. Music emanating from all kinds of instruments could be heard above the raucousness of the crowd. All the while, hats were passed back and forth among the assembled, gleaming with bronze, copper, and silver as performers were awarded for their efforts.

Adecia came to a halt, watching in fascination as a dark-skinned woman dressed in nothing more than a black corset twirled a baton, fire burning brightly on both ends.

"Look at that," she breathed in wonder.

Chameleon and Taeral had stopped as well, and all three were transfixed by the sight of the baton spinning in the woman's hands. To the delight of the crowd, she made it dance across her bare shoulders, back, and waist. Faster and faster the baton whirled, its ends nothing more than a blur of circular light, mesmerizing the huge gathering of onlookers. Sensing the building excitement, the woman stopped. Posing dramatically, she flashed the crowd a dazzling smile, while the baton burned brightly overhead. To the astonishment of all, the fire dancer lowered a fiery end of the baton and placed it directly in her mouth. The whole crowd gasped in amazement, stunned by her daring. She withdrew the burning brand a moment later, unscathed and smiled widely, bowing to the sound of boisterous cheers."

"I wouldn't, if I were you," Rion said harshly, grabbing the collar of a young boy walking past

Adecia. The boy squirmed like a fish trying to escape the hook, but Rion gripped him firmly.

"Give it up, boy, or I'll send you to the Wolfguard," he said, dragging the child closer. "They'll not go as easy on you as I."

The boy, no more than nine or ten years of age, looked defiantly at Rion. "She's got two of 'em, she don't need it."

"What's going on?" Adecia said, distracted by the incredible act she had just seen.

"There's the Wolfguard now," Rion said, glancing behind the boy. "Gua..." he began, raising his voice.

"Wait! Here!" the lad cried. "She can have the stupid thing back," he said, panic written on his grubby face. He offered one of Adecia's throwing knives to the huntress.

Adecia looked down at her belt. One scabbard was empty.

"You little thief," she hissed, eyes narrowing angrily at the urchin, who shrunk under her withering gaze. Angrily, she snatched up her knife and slid it back into place, still looking at the child.

"That's enough, Adecia," Rion scolded. "Part of the blame lies with you. I'd have robbed you, too, distracted as you were. First rule of thievery: don't get caught. Second rule: look for easy marks." He turned his attention back to the urchin.

"These three were easy enough, weren't they, boy?"

The boy nodded his head slightly, not sure how to answer.

"How do you know this?" Taeral asked, still uncertain of what had happened.

Rion smiled briefly, looking at his big companion. "Was a time I did a bit of thieving myself." His eyes went from Taeral to Adecia, then to Chameleon, and he shook his head.

Suddenly, the nature of the situation dawned on him. No wonder Kildare had left him in charge.

Taeral was a triton who had been out of water only a week. Adecia, no matter how gifted a huntress, had not even seen the boy stealing from her. If his understanding of Chameleon was correct, she had never seen a city before, until last night. They might as well have signs around their necks proclaiming their naivete.

None of them were suited for life on the streets. Rion had been reticent about his own past because he was afraid of being recognized. But now, the excitement he had fought down since Taeral knocked on his door filled him. This time, he drank it in, letting it flow over him. His companions *needed* Captain Wavecrest. Too long had Rion repressed his natural tendencies.

"Boy," he said brashly to the urchin, still in his clutches. "What's the fastest path to the Matron?"

The urchin, still fearing arrest, began stammering incoherently.

"Speak up, or by Kelthane's beard, I'll have that tongue of yours on a stick," Rion threatened, iron in his voice.

"Straight ahead and...and to the right," the urchin squealed, suddenly more terrified of Rion than the Wolfguard.

Rion released the boy, who promptly fell to the dirt of the street. Rion dug into his pouch and tossed the child a copper obol. "That's for your help, boy. Don't let me catch you stealing from my people again, or you'll find yourself in a world of pain."

The boy stood up in a rush, trying to backpedal away from Rion. He promptly fell again in his haste to escape. Finally, he scrambled to his feet and scampered off into the crowd.

"As for the rest of you," he said, turning back to his companions, his voice ringing with command. "That's enough skulking through the city. Adecia," he growled at the now confused woman. "Flank my right side. Taeral, to my left. You," he said, pointing at Chameleon. "You get between them and stick close to me. All of you keep your eyes on the crowd and each other. No more wandering off to see the sights, and if we get stopped, I'll do the talking. Understand?"

"Yes," Adecia said automatically.

Rion took the lead, no longer hanging back, trying to avoid being seen. He walked boldly, a cocky jaunt to his step, right down the middle of the main street. That was how the four of them arrived at the stairs leading to the Matron: with Rion Wavecrest leading the way.

The inn itself was a huge four-story structure sprawling on the eastern edge of an open square. It was painted golden yellow, trimmed in white. Pink bougainvillea spilled down the sides of carved wooden planters that hung outside every window. Flags representing countries in and around the Crystalline Sea flew alongside the frosted panes of glass at the top of the stairs, leading into the front entrance. A pair of large stables lay to either side of the main structure, capable of housing some forty horses apiece if needed.

The place was larger and more opulent than Rion remembered.

Lounging at the top of the stairs on a wraparound porch were a handful of women. Like the foods lining the streets, these ladies came in all variety of shapes, sizes, and colors. They were led by none other than Vella Cordulaine, Mistress of the Matron. She stepped onto the landing and looked down with a delighted smile of surprise at her newest arrivals.

"Captain Wavecrest," she said, greeting him like an old friend. "It has been far too long since you last graced our establishment. I heard that you had retired from the excitement of the sea." Her voice held a rich timbre, warm and welcoming.

Rion smiled and gave the tall woman a gracious bow.

"Vella," he replied, walking up the stairs and kissing her hand. "You have not aged a day. I'd say you've become even more beautiful over the years."

There were few that would disagree.

Standing nearly two spans in height, Vella wore a red satin dress that clung to her beautifully proportioned figure. The dress had been fashionably trimmed in black lace and slit to her hips on both sides. When Vella walked, she'd tease a glimpse of her long, shapely legs with every step. The bodice was made of intertwining red and black lace that fit snugly around her ample and magnificent bosom. An enormous diamond pendant dropped from a thick silver necklace around her neck, displaying her rank as First Courtesan of the city. Fingerless black leather gloves stretched past her elbows, with only a single loop fastened around the middle finger on each hand. Matching boots were pulled up to her calves, sounding loudly with each step on the wooden porch. In her hand she held a polished wooden rod with a red and black festival mask on the end. Dark hair cascaded past her neck on one side, while a pair of brilliant brown eyes gazed at Rion from the woman's flawless face.

Her smile widened at his complement, and she crinkled her nose playfully. "You old flatterer. The girls and I have missed your tales; it's wonderful to see you again." She turned her gaze to Rion's companions. "I fear I am being rude. Tell me, who are your friends?" she asked, eyebrows arched in curiosity.

Rion stepped back, motioning to the triton. "This is Taeral, from a city near the coast of Agenhelm. Taeral, this is Mistress Vella, the finest businesswoman on the Crystalline Sea."

The triton nodded politely in greeting but said nothing.

Several of the girls behind Vella could be heard whispering to themselves. One even snickered loudly enough to hear, "he is *big*."

"You are most welcome to the Matron, Master Taeral. Please make yourself at home," Vella said, pursing her lips thoughtfully. "I think some of my girls would be... quite happy... to make your acquaintance."

Silver tinkles of laughter could be heard behind Vella, as quick smiles were hidden by colorful fans.

Unlike Rion, Adecia frowned upon reaching the landing. The huntress was looking at Vella, unsure what to make of her.

"What do we have here?" Vella said, studying Adecia. "A wildflower resting at my very doorstep? My goodness, girl, I could make you into something special. Tell me, captain," she said, eyes never leaving the huntress. "Is she looking for employment?" Vella's eyes positively glowed with excitement.

"My *name* is Adecia, and you can speak to me directly, rather than addressing my companion as if I weren't standing here before you," she responded, steel in her voice.

Vella's eyes widened. "Not a wildflower, I see, but a rose, thorns and all," she said, even more intrigued.

"I'm sorry to disappoint you," Rion interjected, fighting back a smile, "but she, like the rest of us, are just passing through. This is Adecia of Inniak."

"It is a pleasure to meet you, young lady," Vella said, giving Adecia a warm smile. Leaning forward she spoke again, this time more quietly. "Since you will not be staying, I do hope you will let me play a bit. I have just the thing for you to wear for tonight's festivities."

"I…" she glanced uncertainly at Rion, who smiled with encouragement. "We… will see," she finished skeptically, taking in the revealing attire worn by the other ladies of the Matron.

"And who is this?" Vella continued, turning her attention to Chameleon. "She, too, is quite lovely under those trappings. Wherever did you find her?"

"This is Chameleon, who travels with me from the south," Rion answered, giving Vella a long look.

"I see," she said, understanding immediately that Rion wanted to keep Chameleon's origins private. "You are welcome here, Chameleon," she continued, with a slight bow of her head.

"You know Kildare," the Drannock said quietly.

Vella looked startled at her words. "Yes," she breathed, looking sharply at Chameleon. "How did you guess that?"

"You were thinking of him just now," Chameleon explained. "You are worried about him."

Vella looked to Rion, her beautiful features strained in confusion.

"He's our traveling companion," Rion explained, flashing a look toward Chameleon. "Along with his brother, Zedaine. It was they who directed us here, though I'd have come anyway. He wanted me to tell you that the challenge of the blades will be tonight just before sunset."

Vella froze in place. Whispered conversations ceased. To Rion, it seemed all motion and sound from the porch had ground to a complete halt.

"Kildare and Zedaine are here?" one of the younger girls asked aloud, obvious excitement in her voice.

"Hush now, Ildora," Vella said, quietly regaining her composure.

Rion fought down a smile. *So even the matriarch courtesan has a weakness for these lads*, he thought to himself, wondering who they really were.

"I take it you know them?" Rion asked.

"They are part-owners," she said absently, looking to her staff. "Ladies, let's prepare immediately, and get the area in front of the Matron cleared. "Kiera," she said, pulling aside a flame-haired woman. "Take Cleo and one of the wagons. Go to the market. Get more food, ale, wine... more of everything."

"We are already stocked full, Mistress," the girl said, confused.

Vella smiled wickedly. "They showed up upon the eve of The Mask! The whole city must know.

Once word gets out, Duke Artimus will come and we must be ready. What Kildare does will affect everyone in the city... even the duke. Take Bannon and Brettel with you, in case there's trouble."

Kiera bowed her head and walked inside the inn.

Vella motioned to another woman on the porch to join her. As she floated over, Rion noted that she was blonde and buxom and looked hungrily at Taeral.

"Mortisha, go to the runner's guild. Send messages throughout the city. Make sure they get to the palace. Send a direct invitation to Artimus and Judoh. Tell them the challenge of the blades will take place tonight. Bring Wrade with you. Go, now!"

"Yes, Mistress," she said, with a last lingering look at Taeral.

"What's happening Vella?" Rion asked, wondering just what the brothers had gotten mixed up in.

Vella smiled, bringing her mask up over her face. "You and your friends will be in for quite a night, captain."

"What is this challenge of the blades Kildare spoke of?" he queried.

"You will see," she answered evasively.

Vella snapped her fingers, and the fair-haired Ildora came over.

"Show them to their rooms," she ordered gently. "The Stallion for the gentlemen, The White Lily for the ladies."

"Yes, Mistress Vella," Ildora replied with a bow of her head. "Follow me, if you please," she said to the companions.

As the four were whisked off, Vella walked into the back of the main room, away from her staff and guests. Alone, she dropped the pretense of happiness and covered her face with her hands.

I cannot lose him, she thought to herself, *not again.*

Dark Storm Rising

Chapter 22

Cirath set down his instruments as carefully as he could without disturbing their contents. With a practiced ease, he carefully slid back in his chair, making certain not to accidentally nudge the table with his elbow or knee. Too many times, a careless moment had cost the journeyman hours of tedious work. Not only could his mixtures and tonics be ruined, but the cost of their replacements came out of his pocket.

Once he was clear of the worktable, which was covered in various instruments of measure and hand-blown vials that came in every shape, size, and description, Cirath turned toward the back door of his work room. He sidled past the open pantry, inhaling its savory aroma, filled as it was with any manner of spices and herbs. In particular, he smelled the familiar sweetness of lavender, as it warred for dominion with the bitter-smelling leaves of wormwood. Normally, he would stop and secure the pantry before exiting, but not today; too much was on his mind. Instead, he brushed past the pantry, opened the back door, and entered the street behind his master's shop. It was not until he heard the click of the latch behind him that he allowed himself to take a deep breath and tried to relax.

Cirath placed his interlaced hands on top of his head, wondering for the hundredth time that day how everything could have gone wrong so quickly the night before. *It was not my fault*, he kept thinking to himself.

Then who is to blame? His own mind responded.

Cirath had done exactly as he had been asked by Avery, the master apothecary he worked under. Avery had told him, "Go to the docks, and pick up the shipment of lungwort and dark winter barley from Adian. Have your friend Rorst sign it over to you, and make the payment."

"Why did you have to send me?" Cirath lamented quietly, pulling absently at his short brown hair.

Cirath knew why. He had made the mistake of telling Avery that he knew the dockhand Rorst from childhood. The master apothecary assumed that the two had been friends, so he kept sending Cirath to make pick-ups from his old acquaintance. The problem was, Rorst had been a boyhood tormentor of Cirath's. He had taunted and bullied the smaller boy to the point that Cirath had wanted out of the lower quarter of the city badly enough to learn his letters and get off the streets. When he had become apprentice to Avery six years ago,

Cirath thought himself free of Rorst forever. Now, some kind of cruel twist of fate had intervened, and Cirath was repeatedly sent to deal with his childhood tyrant. Cirath wondered bitterly how a master apothecary like Avery could be so obtuse when it came to reading people.

To make matters worse, these jobs should have fallen to the apprentice of the shop, a young lout named Sacher. However, Sacher was barely able to figure out how to use a mortar and pestle; he could not be trusted to purchase the necessary ingredients an apothecary required to ply his trade, so it fell to Cirath.

He dropped his hands to his sides in frustration. *No one helped* me *when I was an apprentice*, Cirath thought to himself. Even though Cirath had passed all the trials Avery had given him and risen to the rank of journeyman, he was still fetching things from the market, the docks, and wherever else Avery deigned it necessary for him to go.

Over the last few months, Cirath had come up with a ploy that made the business transactions with Rorst far easier to deal with. He had taken to brewing an exceptionally potent fire whiskey savored by the dockhand. Once a month, Cirath would "throw it in" as a little bonus payment. This allowed him to be left alone, and the transactions made uneventfully.

Last evening, however, Rorst had invited Cirath to join him and another dockhand for a night out at one of their local haunts. Cirath had tried to politely decline, but Rorst would have none of it.

"Bring along a flask of the good stuff," Rorst had said, throwing his arm around the journeyman's shoulders.

Fearing years of retribution from his childhood bully, Cirath had agreed.

Hours later, the journeyman apothecary watched, stunned, as his two comrades and a third man they'd met beat a young woman into submission and forced her into a narrow alley, threatening to rape her. His feeble protests had fallen on deaf ears. He entered the alley to make sure that her three attackers did not kill her, though he was not sure what he could have done to stop them.

That was when the man with the staff had appeared. Cirath saw him rip into his companions like they were nothing more than lambs before a butcher. He had never seen anyone so deadly in all his life. Cirath watched as the man killed his childhood tormentor with consummate ease. The journeyman was too stunned to move from his place on the wall, where he stood motionless. It was then that the man with the staff had turned his anger upon him, making his fear of Rorst seem like a happy memory in comparison to the terror that coursed through his body. Cirath knew his death was at hand.

By some miracle, his life had been spared by the girl's intervention. The young woman, who had been beaten to the ground and forced to endure her attacker's threats of sexual violence, had saved him. She had shamed him with her courage.

You make me sick, he thought to himself. *You are nothing but a coward. You never stood up to Rorst once in your miserable life. You couldn't even help that girl last night. She ended up saving you! What kind of a man are you?* He angrily kicked at an empty barrel next to the wall, sending it careening to the ground.

"If you bust that barrel, they'll take it outta yer wages," he heard a voice say behind him.

Cirath turned to see the heavyset form of Sacher, the apprentice, standing lazily in the doorway. The young man was slightly taller than Cirath and nearly fifty pounds heavier. The leather apron he was supposed to be wearing hung loosely around the rolls of fat on his neck as the drawstrings had been untied. Though he was three years Cirath's junior, his plain face looked much older than the journeyman's. *Older and duller*, Cirath said to himself, wondering why Avery had ever decided to employ him in the first place.

"You are supposed to be working," Cirath told the apprentice pointedly.

"I don't take orders from you, Pep," Sacher replied with a slight sneer. "'Sides, Avery ain't even here," he said, taking the apron off over his head. "I'm goin' down to the Earl for a pint."

Cirath narrowed his eyes. "We have over a score of orders left to fill today," he said sullenly. "It will take until sunset as it is."

The bigger man walked up to Cirath and shoved the apron into his chest. "What's this 'we' crap? Yur the big-time journeyman, Pep, not me. *You* have orders to fill. *I* ain't gotta do shit."

With that, Sacher turned, saying, "Don't stay up all night. If you get done early, you can come buy me a round." Cirath could hear his mocking laughter as the door closed behind him.

Cirath cursed under his breath, throwing the apron down at the barrel he had kicked. He heard the door open again behind him. "What do you want now?" he demanded, not bothering to turn around.

"How about getting back to work," answered a woman's voice sarcastically.

Cirath pressed his lips together and shook his head helplessly, wondering how much worse his day could get. *Great, now you're yelling at Master Avery's wife*, he thought to himself.

He turned around with an apologetic look on his face. "Sorry, Myla, I thought it was… someone else."

Myla was closer to fifty years of age than forty, but was still a handsome woman. She was of medium height, with a friendly face that looked younger than her years. Her nose was slightly crooked, and she had a small mole on her cheek. Her flaxen hair hung behind her in a simple braid, the long strands slowly turning gray over the years. She stood, hands on her hips, frowning at Cirath. She kept the books for her husband, and excelled when it came to numbers and accounting.

"I saw the apprentice leave a moment ago and wondered if you knew where he was going?" she asked, clearly having already guessed at the answer.

"He won't listen to me, Myla; he doesn't respect me at all," Cirath complained.

"And he never will, until you do something about it!" she responded coldly. "We have had this discussion before, Cirath. Avery won't declare you a master until you show you can handle being in business by yourself. You have all the training and credentials you need. You are better than Avery at making concoctions and identifying plants. You even took and mastered the exam to become a legal advocate last year."

"Every master apothecary has to pass that exam," he said, with a shake of his head. "In case of retribution."

"You did it on your first try, after only six months of study!" she said fiercely. "Avery studied for five years to pass that exam, and it took him three tries to master it. My point, journeyman, is that you are more than ready for a shop of your own. You have the most natural ability of any apothecary in the city. But until you prove you can handle an apprentice, Avery won't bring you before the guild."

Cirath was frustrated. He had heard all this before, and it stung because he knew it to be true. He sighed with deep resignation. He just did not have the courage to stand up to people. He had known it his whole life, and nothing was about to change that fact.

The journeyman walked over to the barrel, picked it up, and rolled it back against the wall. He lifted Sacher's apron off the ground and cleaned it the best he could.

"I'll get back to work," he said, dragging past Myla.

She just shook her head and closed the door.

It was nearly an hour later when Myla entered the workroom again. "A couple of men here to see you. They need a plant identified."

Cirath caught something odd about her tone. He looked at her, eyebrows raised. "What is it?"

She paused a moment before answering. "Something about them... they seem quite serious, Cirath. Nice enough, but... not men I would trifle with."

Just what I need, more intimidating people in my life, he thought with a momentary grimace. "I have too much to do as it is, Myla," he began.

"No, Cirath, you have to talk to these men," she said, cutting him off. "They have already been to apothecary Quann, and he knows more about plants than anyone in Gallanse. Except you. These two don't strike me as the types to take no for an answer."

He leaned back in his chair, a resigned breath escaping him. "Send them in," he said, trying not to sound irritated.

She nodded her head and exited the workroom. A moment later, the door reopened and two men, one short and one tall, entered the room. Absolute shock ran through the journeyman apothecary; Cirath jolted up from his chair, a high-pitched cry emanating from his throat. He smashed his knees into the bottom of the work table, spilling most of its contents onto the floor. With the sudden movement, Cirath lost his balance, toppling backward out of his chair, arms flailing wildly over his head. With a resounding crash, he fell to the floor, his heart in his throat.

The taller of the two men was the staff-bearer who had killed his companions the previous evening.

Myla entered behind the two men after hearing the commotion, frowning at Cirath who was still sprawled on the floor.

"What hap... by Chara, what are you doing?" she asked, a mixture of surprise and alarm in her voice.

"Ah, nothing… nothing," Cirath stammered, still staring at the tall stranger, wondering if he was here to finish what he started last night. "I was just… er, startled is all." He stood up slowly, dusting himself off and trying to hide the trembling of his hands.

"Sorry to have surprised you, journeyman," the shorter of the men said graciously. "I know that you are hard at work, but I understand that you are the most knowledgeable herbalist in the city. I've a problem I was hoping you could help us with."

Cirath gave them a shaky smile. Gods, he could *feel* the man's eyes on him. "I will do my best. What is it that I can do for you…uh, gentlemen?"

"Kantik, Lord Kantik," said the shorter man, extending his hand for Cirath to shake with little enthusiasm. "This is Macklore," he continued, motioning to the taller man. He had not moved, but stood studying the journeyman intently. Cirath thought he saw Macklore's eyes widen infinitesimally with a flicker of recognition.

A panicked thought ran through the apothecary's mind. *He is going to kill me.*

"If you need me, Cirath, I'll be out front," Myla said, retreating back through the door and closing it softly behind her.

"Yes, thank you, Myla," he replied weakly. He wished he could hide his face from the prying eyes of Macklore.

Kantik reached deep inside his breast pocket and pulled out a small, tightly capped jar. He set it down on the worktable without a word. He nodded then to Macklore, who strode over to the small window by the back door and looked outside, searching for anyone who might be following or listening in. He looked back at Kantik, gave a single nod of his head, and walked back to the worktable.

"Cirath," the older man began, "we need to discern everything we can about this plant. We have already been to Master Quann, as Mistress Myla may have told you. I have known him for years and I trust his judgment. He could only tell us that the plant was not something locally grown. I need to know more than that. He sent me to you."

Kantik took the stopper off the jar and, using a pair of wooden tongs, reached inside, pulling out what looked like a huge raspberry, and placed it on the worktable. He looked up at Cirath and spoke. "What can you tell us?"

Cirath stood frozen with fear. Standing in front of him was the man who had so easily killed three men right in front of him. He had been about to kill Cirath! The young apothecary simply could not focus with Macklore standing there, looming over him. Tightness had formed in his chest as his level of anxiety rose beyond anything he had yet experienced. He was having trouble just drawing breath.

As though sensing his terror, Macklore spoke softly, his tone reassuring. "This is the reason we have sought you out, journeyman. We need you to identify this plant. That is why we are here. It is the *only* reason."

As Macklore spoke, the fear drained out of Cirath like sands passing through an hourglass. The apothecary found he was able to breathe again, the tightness in his chest fading away. He let out a huge gasp of air and turned to look at the contents of the jar, giving the plant his undivided attention.

Just identify the berry, and they will leave, he thought to himself.

Despite being acutely aware of Macklore's presence, Cirath found himself looking at the fruit with curiosity as his scholarly side took over. He peered intently at it, then absently gathered up a ruler, and set about measuring the length and width of the fruit. He then placed it on one of his many scales, recording his findings in a faded green journal and, as he often did when chewing on a problem, started speaking to himself unconsciously.

"Master Quann had the right of it... no chance it could grow locally. Not enough water in this region by a large margin. Look how swollen the seed pods are. Have to be almost a jungle, with torrential rain, to get like that. Much larger than the raspberry. That smell, sweetly bitter. Might be poisonous if ingested in a large enough quantity. Very sticky resin from it as well; no doubt about it, this one needs a lot of water. But what land of origin? Shan'dar? Not likely... the soil is not right, too light for a berry this size. To grow this, you would have to have the richest, most fertile soil. The Rhone is too rugged, and still, the issue of water. The Serpent Marsh? No, this needs to see the sun; far too much shade there, and I would have seen it before. So, a more remote region? To the south perhaps? Maybe lower Valasca… possible, I suppose, but not likely, just not enough rain even on the coast. Hmmm, interesting. Homegrown? Maybe, but it would have to be cared for daily by a professional… someone of master quality, no less. That type of training is rare, and still, the issue of the soil. It would have to be rich in the extreme. Big broad leaves to soak up the sun and feed this monster. Again, that suggests a tropical environment. So where is there a remote jungle…"

Cirath leaned back and whistled to himself as an idea struck him. "Now that's a thought…yes, let me look." Cirath left the worktable and crossed the room to a small chest he kept in the corner. He pulled a key from his pocket and unlocked it, removing several books and setting them aside until he found a thick, leather-bound book and began rifling through the pages.

"Where is it, where is it…ah, here it is… hmmm," the journeyman was reading to himself now, seeming oblivious of the other two men in the room.

"Did you find something?" asked Lord Kantik, somewhat put out at being ignored.

"Maybe, just maybe. Give me another moment, if you will, gentlemen. I need to find… yes, here it is," he said, picking up a second book. It was a small green book, rather thin. He walked back to his seat at the worktable, bringing both books with him. Once he sat down, he motioned for Kantik to come closer.

"An interesting plant you've brought me," he said. "Master Quann, I believe, is correct. It did not come from any local place. In fact, I don't think it grows anywhere near the Crystalline Sea. The size of the berry suggests it needs a lot of sunlight and moisture, the kind you might find in a rain forest, or jungle. No such place exists in or around the Crystalline Sea." He paused then and looked up at Kantik. "I'm sorry if I am rambling, but you said you wanted to know everything you could about this plant."

Kantik shook his head. "That is quite all right, lad, for I did say that. So far, you have come to the same conclusion as Quann. Is there anything else you can tell me?"

In the background stood the sizable Macklore, who waited patiently, though he was watching closely and listening with keen interest. Cirath dared think he might get out of this alive.

Cirath motioned to the first book, the larger of the two. They could see its title now; *Litigation* was scrawled upon the top. "The berry itself reminded me of a case that was thrown out of court in the city of Tan'shi nearly fifty years ago.

Tan'shi is located all the way on the other side of the Crystalline Sea. Most of its people are descended from the Seven Provinces across the Ariath Ocean."

"I'm not sure what that has to do with this plant," Kantik said, confused.

"I will tell you, my lord," Cirath said, glancing at Macklore.

"In this particular case, a powerful merchant was found dead in the city of Tan'shi, seemingly of heart failure. Normally, that would have been the end of it, but his wife, quite a powerful woman herself, believed that a jealous rival had poisoned him. She told the magistrate of a fruit her husband had eaten prior to his death, but none of the fruit was left behind to give her claim credence."

"Does it give a description of the fruit?" asked Macklore.

"Uh, ya… yes," Cirath croaked, his mouth suddenly dry. He looked back in the book and read aloud. "Her description was, 'a large, red raspberry-like fruit,' much like this plant you have brought before me."

"Where did you come by that book?" asked Macklore, frowning.

"It is a copy I made… from the original inside the Litigation Guild's library. I…" he hesitated, shrinking under Macklore's withering stare. "I studied some law... my lord."

"You are a litigator?" the tall man asked skeptically.

Cirath shook his head. "An advocate only. I passed the tests earlier this year, but I have not as yet gone before the High Lord or a magistrate," Cirath responded faintly.

"Is there anything else?" asked Kantik, trying to keep Cirath on track. "That's not much to go on."

"Um, yes, actually. This is the most telling part, really," Cirath replied, relieved to be addressing Kantik. "The possibility of poisoning is what jogged my memory of this other recording."

He picked up the second, smaller book. "This was made by a travelling apothecary named Hayos nearly two hundred years ago; he was something of a roving medicine man, or so I gathered from his notes. I found his journal among Master Avery's mentor's things when I first entered his service."

Cirath turned through the pages, which were filled with rough sketches and hand drawn illustrations of many different and exotic plants and herbs. He stopped at one. There, outlined faintly in black and white, was a berry, very similar to the one sitting on the worktable. Underneath the drawing of the plant it read:

Locally known as the Minta berry or death berry, it is found rarely in the wild. The Minta berry grows at the edges of the Jungles of Ximora. It is formed of large, deep red single pods that grow around a seed core held together by tiny overlapping tendrils. The main bush itself has thorns running along the stem and secondary branches. Broad dark green leaves measuring over a foot in length and half a foot wide sprout outward in an irregular pattern, away from the stem. When the fruit is detached from the seed, the core is left behind, leaving the berry hollow, similar to the raspberry that is grown in drier climates. It is much larger than the common raspberry, often 2-3 times the diameter and weighing significantly more. Upon inhalation, the fruit emits a sweet smell. Used mostly in dyes, it is extremely poisonous if eaten, but I suspect carries a sweet taste as well. Rumored to be produced more readily by the assassins' guilds throughout the Seven Provinces.

As Cirath finished reading, he glanced up at the two men.

Macklore shared a long look with Kantik, both seemed troubled.

"How certain are you of your findings, Cirath?" Kantik asked finally.

The young apothecary shrugged. "I am as certain as I can be, my lord. I have never seen this plant before, but I am quite young. Master Quann's experience is far more telling. If he has not encountered it before... well, he has many more years behind him than I. This journal," he said, holding up the small green book, "provides the only possibility I know of. Though written many years ago, the records are quite accurate and were very well kept. The sketch, though rough, is a close match. My professional opinion is that we are looking at a very rare Minta berry."

No one spoke for a long moment.

"You know what this implies, don't you?" Macklore chimed in, finally looking at Kantik.

"Unfortunately, I do…"

Without warning, the backdoor was flung open, crashing against the inner wall with enough force to rattle the windowpane next to it.

"Was goin' on, Pep? Yu havin' a pardy?" thundered a drunken voice.

Standing in the doorway was the apprentice, Sacher.

"What," said Kantik, scowling, "is that?"

"That's…Sacher, the…apprentice," replied Cirath weakly. The journeyman had been so engrossed in his research; he had forgotten about him entirely.

Sacher came staggering into the room, contempt dripping from him. He pointed his meaty finger accusingly at Lord Kantik.

"I'll tell you what I am! I'm Saasher, apprentish apokacary!" he roared, slurring his words badly.

Cirath's heart sank. This was the last thing he needed. Sacher was clearly drunk and had no idea who he was talking to. Cirath had to get him out of the room fast.

"Sacher, why don't you go back to the Earl? I'll come down soon and buy you that drink," Cirath said in the kindest tone he could muster.

"Shuddit, Pep. These two owe me money, an O'mma not leavin' till they pay!" he sneered, drawing even closer to Kantik.

"You had best go, lad, while you still can," Kantik said mildly.

A look of disgust crossed Sacher's face. "Or what choo gonna do, oldie? You gonna sick yur pet ape on me?" he laughed scornfully, sticking his finger in Macklore's face.

"I've had enough of this imbecile already," Macklore said, his eyes like ice.

"No, please, that won't be necessary," said Cirath, fearing that the deadly Macklore might kill Sacher. The apprentice was big and stupid and drunk, but Cirath did not want to see him dead. The journeyman apothecary stepped between

Macklore and Sacher. "Sacher, please, I will take care of my business with these men, then we can…"

"Ged outta my way, Pep," Sacher cried, grabbing the smaller man by the shoulders and shoving him roughly to the floor. Cirath crashed to the ground.

Sacher turned to Macklore. "I said, gib me my money, you sons-a-bitshes…"

Macklore grabbed the apprentice by the back of the neck, and in one violent motion, slammed his head onto the worktable. A loud crack could be heard as the bone in Sacher's nose shattered under such force. The ambassador then heaved the apprentice out the backdoor, to land sprawling like a ragdoll in the cobbled street. Macklore closed the door, as Sacher was left moaning in bewildered agony on the road. The ambassador walked over to Cirath nonchalantly, hand extended.

"Why does he keep calling you Pep?" Macklore asked, waiting over Cirath.

The journeyman eyed the proffered hand like it was a viper. Macklore locked eyes with Cirath as something unsaid passed between them. Cirath steeled himself, reached out, and took Macklore's hand.

"Apothecaries," he said with a moan as he regained his feet, "are sometimes known by other names. At the beginning of his apprenticeship, I told Sacher that in the poorer quarters, we were once referred to as pepperers, because we often use that spice in our concoctions. Sacher thought it a great joke. He has called me 'Pep' ever since."

Macklore furrowed his brow in consternation. "If I had someone in my employ like that, I'd throw them out on the street," he said with a grim smile.

Kantik let out a short laugh. "Indeed, ambassador, you are quite the revelation." Lord Kantik reached out and shook Cirath's hand. "Thank you for your assistance, journeyman. I will see Myla about your payment."

He packed the Minta berry away, safely in the jar. "I may call upon your service again, lad, should the need arise." He exited through the main door with a nod of his head, leaving the apothecary alone with Macklore.

The two looked at one another, a silent question hanging between them.

"How is she?" Cirath asked quietly.

"Recovering," Macklore answered flatly.

Cirath was beginning to get a cold feeling in the pit of his stomach again. He wondered if the man would kill him, now that he had served his purpose.

The ambassador relaxed slightly. "For your help today, I owe you my thanks... but," the tension quickly returned, "do not be surprised if I call on you again as well, journeyman."

Cirath's stomach did a flip as Macklore strode toward the door, preparing to leave. Suddenly, he stopped, his hand on the knob.

"Maybe you *were* in the wrong place, at the wrong time, last night. I'm glad I didn't kill you... Pep."

Macklore turned the knob, opened the door, and was gone.

"By the gods, I hope I never see him again," Cirath whispered, relief flooding through him.

Chapter 23

Consul Warlan read through the message a second time, his wizened eyes squinting with effort. Upon finishing, he dropped the letter to his desk, trying to quell his rising fear. The news was worse than he'd expected.

It was the third message Warlan had received this last week. Nine days ago, he'd had reason to hope. His agent in Gallanse had sent a pigeon; the message had been simple.

Arrived in good order. Everything going to plan. Macklore has made contact
with Lord Conidon. Assessing situation.

Warlan had naturally assumed from this correspondence that things were well in hand, and he figured that the matter would be closed in a few days' time.

It was not to be.

Five days later, a second message arrived, this time laced with more ominous tidings.

Dragomir has stepped up his claim to the throne. Word of a new adviser has

reached us. Macklore has been asked to join Conidon in the palace tomorrow
  night. More to follow.

This was unsettling news. Warlan had immediately dispatched a pigeon to his sovereign: Medyha, King of Brisbane. Earlier that morning, Warlan had received Medyha's reply.

Trust in Macklore. I am quietly mobilizing a force to sail immediately,
  should the need arise. Keep me abreast of the situation. Report anything
  new without hesitation.

Minutes ago, a third message from his agent arrived. This one was far more worrisome, as it had not arrived by pigeon. His agent had used her imbued parchment and quill to send word. Only in dire circumstances would she have done so, and only at the behest of Ambassador Macklore. Taking the message in hand, he read the contents again, wondering what had gone wrong in Gallanse.

To
his
Excellency,

Chaos has come to Gallanse. Lord Dillion, highly
respected ruler of Janril, has been killed. Macklore
insists it was a no accident. Now, it seems the
Moldranni Sor have taken a dangerous interest in
Shaara. Dragomir's adviser is a powerful mage
of that order. We are gathering information, but
nothing is known for certain. He seems to have great
influence in Dragomir's camp. With Dillion's passing,
nothing stands in the way of Dragomir becoming the
new ruler of Gallanse. Macklore felt he had to
support Conidon openly. The alliance has had the
effect he desired, as Dragomir's ascension has been
nixed for the time being. For how long, no one knows.
Despite this alliance, Macklore has demanded I
ask you to pass on a plea directly to the king.

It reads:

Due to the late hour, I can only forward my concerns
onto you, your majesty. No longer can we watch, as
ruin threatens Shaara. Standing idly, waiting for one
side to win, is no longer an option. This nation is
heading for war. I know, despite your orders, my
actions go against your commands. I have forged
a pact with Conidon and his daughter. Delay would
risk losing the city to the madness of High Lord Rexor
and his fanatical son Dragomir. I know this action
goes against your wishes. Choosing Gallanse may
open hostilities with Dagor. I concur, yet we must

enter into an agreement, else the seeds of war will be sewn. Conidon's hold continues to weaken. It is now up to you to intervene. Brisbane is in a position of power that comes but once in a lifetime. You are in command of a powerful army, one that, even now, continues to grow in power. You know that my fealty is to you and our city. I will await your orders. Look for a new message soon. As always, I will do as best I can for Brisbane. It's up to you. I hope you, make the right choice.

Ever your servant, Macklore.

S.

Warlan let the parchment fall back down onto the desk. The possibility of Dragomir ascending the throne was concerning enough. Such a thing would change the power structure in the countries surrounding the Crystalline Sea. The involvement of the *Moldranni Sor* was also alarming. Theirs was an order of blood magic whose sole purpose was to bring about the end of the world. Their order had perished decades past, or so it was believed. Paired with Dragomir, it could only mean ill tidings for the rest of the region. Things must have become desperate for Macklore to defy the king's orders and openly side with Conidon.

What truly caused fear in Warlan was the hidden message Sadie had sent, written in his primary cipher. Macklore needed aid, immediately.

Warlan slammed his open palm on the desk in frustration.

Therein lay the problem. Warlan had nothing to send him. The consul was unprepared for this sudden turn of events. His other agents were spread thin, the closest more than a week away from Gallanse.

Nervously, the consul scratched the diseased skin of his arms, uncertain how to proceed. Flakes of crusted flesh dropped onto his desk like a reptile shedding its scales. Try as he might, the consul could not come up with any idea—save one—to help Macklore. The thought terrified him.

Warlan would have to go to Gallanse himself.

The heavyset man struggled to lift his bulk from the chair, sweat dripping from his brow. Absently, he mopped his forehead with a cotton handkerchief. Turning around, Warlan stepped to the white doors behind his desk that led to a small balcony four stories above the street. Unlatching the brass hook from the frame, Warlan opened the doors and stepped outside, letting the cool air wash over him.

If only he'd listened to me, he thought sullenly, *we wouldn't be in this mess.*

Warlan had no desire to be close to the political hotbed of Gallanse. He had spent his life avoiding dangerous places. It was that very reason that caused him to request this placement in Adian. It was a city in which Medyha was revered as a hero, with no likelihood of rebellion. It was peaceful; the city's last battles well behind it. Furthermore, much of Adian's considerable wealth was spent on defenses; with towering walls and a powerful army, it was the city least likely to be attacked in Rhone. Only Brisbane itself was safer, in the consul's estimation, but Warlan did not wish to be directly under the king's thumb. Adian was one of the main political centers of the Crystalline Sea. He could work with freedom here without putting his life in jeopardy.

"Leave Shaara alone," he'd pleaded to Medyha, "It will right itself; it always does."

The king had disagreed.

Now look at us, he thought in panic. *Dabbling where we don't belong in the middle of a succession! Why did he not listen to me? Now I have to risk my neck for his stupidity!*

No, he thought suddenly, an idea forming in his mind. *There is no need for me to go personally. Medyha has caused this problem—he and that idiot, Macklore. Why should I risk myself for them? He's under orders from the king, it's*

Macklore's responsibility to sort this mess out, not mine. He got himself into it, and now he can get himself out. I will send word immediately.

Warlan left the balcony and strode over to a worktable in the corner of the room. It was a plain table of oak with a mass of papers scattered haphazardly upon it. He swept them aside where they fluttered to the hardwood floor.

His hazel eyes turned toward the doorway leading to the corridor outside, reassuring himself that it was locked and guarded. He held out his hands, parallel to the top of the worktable.

"Praecipio tibi ut veni foras," he whispered, summoning the arcane power imbued in his body. The top of the table glowed faintly as Warlan continued his chant, his voice growing louder. From inside the wood of the desk, a worn parchment appeared. Yellowed with age, it floated in the air nearly a foot above the top of the desk. It had been embedded deep inside the wood itself, placed there magically by the king. Warlan ended his incantation and plucked it from the air.

Out of his pocket the consul drew his handkerchief and wiped away new streaks of sweat from his forehead. Like many of Brisbane's dignitaries, Warlan was imbued with magic. Warlan hated the pain that always accompanied the initial imbuing, but this was a necessary byproduct of receiving capabilities from a magic-born soul. Not being magical himself, he could merely hold the enchantments for a time. Thankfully, he could not abide pain, and held only enough magic for the simplest spells, like the one he had just performed. Glad that he had managed it, he prepared to write Medyha, praying that he could find a way out of this nightmare.

Warlan turned back to his desk and saw two men sitting comfortably on top of it. One was reading the message sent from his agent, while the other was shaking his head in disbelief.

"I find embassy security severely lacking these days," Kildare chided. "You should really speak to someone about it."

"Kildarian! Zedainian!" Warlan exclaimed, shocked to the core.

"We just go by Kildare and Zedaine these days," Kildare said, his tone bored. "Nothing so grand as when we lived in the palace."

"By Jora, how did you... what are you doing here?" The consul sputtered in surprise.

Kildare sat with his hands under his legs, which kicked back and forth and tapped against the desk like a petulant child's. "Got some questions for you, Warlan... and by the looks of that letter, you might want to answer them."

"Nicer than that," Zedaine sniffed offhandedly.

"What do you mean, nicer than that?" Kildare asked, frowning at this brother. "That *was* nice."

"You need to ask him more nicely," Zedaine said absently, eyes still on the letter.

"That's ridiculous, I used my kindest voice and faked genuine concern," Kildare said, glaring at Zedaine. "What more could you ask for? Warlan did betray us, after all."

"Say please," Zedaine suggested, still focused on the letter.

"Did I not say please?"

"You most definitely did not, and a little please goes a long way."

A grimace appeared on Zedaine's face as he read the letter. "Is that really how you spell 'Monarch'?" he asked Kildare, pointing to the word on the page. "Why the 'ch'? We don't say 'mon-ar-*ch*' after all. It doesn't really make sense to have the 'ch.' It should have the k sound."

"I see you two haven't changed at all," Warlan said, recovered from his shock. His brain had started working furiously. *What the hell are they doing here? Now of all times?*

"Still laughing about matters of the utmost importance," the consul continued acidly. "I guess you didn't learn your lesson after the last disaster you caused. Your sentence was too lenient, in my estimation. Death by hanging would have been better than you deserved," he finished haughtily.

"What an awful thing to say," Kildare said, feigning sadness. "You know in what high regard we hold you, consul. I'm just... well, I'm just *hurt* by your words." He crossed his arms, making a show of sulking.

Zedaine, however, smiled. "There you are," he said, with genuine humor. "That's the grumpy Warlan we all know and hate so much. I was wondering where that inner ass was—now, I see it."

"Oh yes, mock me, Zedaine. I should have you both arrested just for being here."

Zedaine looked around in a panicked show of confusion. "Are we... is this Brisbane? Kil, did we go to the wrong city again?"

"I'm fairly certain it's Adian," Kildare replied, looking around uncertainly. "I'm almost positive we weren't banished from Adian: just Brisbane."

"This is the embassy of Brisbane," Warlan barked furiously, "as you well know. It's part of the nation it represents. You are currently on Brisbane's soil and breaking the king's law!"

"He's not my king anymore," Zedaine said.

"We haven't touched any of Medyha's sacred dirt," Kildare responded lightly. "Have we, Zee?"

"Well, let me see," Zedaine said, making a show of pondering the question. "We jumped the walls outside the embassy and climbed up onto the roof of this building. We never did touch the ground; so, no, we aren't on Brisbane's soil. I suppose we might be guilty of trespassing if Medyha wants to claim all the air as his, but that seems a far stretch, even for him."

"There you have it," Kildare said with a shrug. "We're not on Brisbane's soil, we're not trespassing."

Warlan's face was turning red. "That's not how the law works!"

"We are just trying to give you an answer that… let me see, how did he phrase it at our trial for treason?" Zedaine said, turning thoughtfully to his brother.

"'An answer that fully shows the facts evident in the case against the accused.'"

When Kildare spoke, he dropped the ruse of amusement. His eyes smoldered with barely contained rage.

Warlan swallowed in fear.

"Ah, yes, that was it," Zedaine said, turning back to the consul. "Kildare remembers every little detail, you know. Of course, he absolutely *despises* you, even more so than I do, so it's to be expected."

Zedaine leaned forward in a conspiratorial manner and dropped his voice to a loud mock-whisper. "Since *I* loathe you with every fiber of my being, that's saying something."

Sitting back up, Zedaine went back to speaking normally. "Anyway, getting back to the point, we climbed down from the roof of the balcony onto the railing, and from there, jumped onto your desk."

"So spare us your bullshit diatribe," Kildare said, his voice like ice. "Be thankful we didn't just slaughter you outright and be done with it. We have work to do, and you, miraculously, are in a position to help."

"What work do you have?" Warlan said scornfully, trying to keep his voice steady. "For two and a half years you've been exiled, with no one having seen or heard from you... which, incidentally, is fine with me. But the world has moved on since then. While you two shit sacks have wiled away your time, *I* have been working relentlessly to keep Brisbane safe. Suddenly, you show up demanding my help? Give me one good reason why I shouldn't have you two arrested right now!"

"We'll give you three reasons," Zedaine said calmly. "The first is simple. If you move toward that door, Kildare is going to kill you. If you shout for help, then *I'm* going to kill you."

"The third option is your only chance for survival," Kildare said, his tone deadly serious. "I hope you are not so stupid you don't understand that. Of course, if you are, it won't be a total loss. We will have rid the world of your miserable existence."

The consul glanced at the door, knowing full well that these two were capable of carrying out their threat. Seeing the parchment still in Zedaine's hand, he remembered his current dilemma in Gallanse.

Maybe he could use these two.

Despite their lack of decorum and propriety, they were extremely dangerous and highly trained. They had grown up learning the politics of every nation in the known world and were exactly the kind of men who could help Macklore. The question was… would they?

Making a show of caution, Warlan slowly walked over to his desk and sat in the chair behind it, while the brothers swiveled to face him.

"You have two minutes," he said finally.

"I'm so glad you chose option three," Zedaine said with a grin.

"I was hoping for option one," Kildare murmured under his breath, looking disappointed.

"You're wasting your time," Warlan growled.

"First off, Your Royal Excellency," Kildare began evenly, "despite popular opinion, Zedaine and I have not been wiling away our time. But as dear old dad likes to say, that's by the by. You want to know why you should help us? For starters, you need us in Gallanse. Things aren't going well there, are they?"

"'Chaos,' it says," Zedaine chimed in, pointing at the letter and smiling broadly.

"My guess is that you have only… what, one—maybe two—agents there with Macklore?" Kildare continued, ignoring his brother. "By the stunned look on your moronic face, I'd say it's only one. Probably because you're too arrogant to believe anyone is cleverer than you."

"It's more clever," Zedaine said, looking sideways at Kildare. "Cleverer isn't a word."

Kildare frowned and twisted his face in thought. "Are you sure? 'More clever' doesn't really sound right."

"Think about the verb conjugation," Zedaine said. "I'm clever, he's *more* clever, you are the most clever. See what I mean?"

Kildare shook his head. "That can't be right. You're clever, he's cleverer, and I'm the cleverest. That's the way it goes. That has to be right, right?"

Zedaine pressed his lips together and shrugged. "I don't know, now they all sound wrong."

"If you two are quite finished," Warlan spat angrily.

Kildare looked back at Warlan. "Sorry to get sidetracked; where were we? Oh yes, the asinine look on your moronic face tells me that you only have one agent in Gallanse, am I wrong?"

"How many would you have sent?" Warlan snapped, annoyed that Kildare had guessed correctly.

"Gallanse is a viper's pit even in times of peace," Kildare said as though speaking to an infant. "There's open murder in the Gray Palace, and High Lord Conidon is old and sick. I'd have sent every agent under my command because I know something you, apparently, are too stupid to remember. A divided Shaara is a safe Shaara. Why Medyha ever entrusted the safety of Brisbane to a coward like you is beyond my understanding. Now Dragomir has allied with the *Moldranni Sor*. Things have gotten so out of hand that Ambassador Macklore, Mr. 'I do whatever I'm told, no matter what,' had to disobey the king's orders not to get involved."

"He'll probably get a bloody promotion," Zedaine muttered next to him. "To god-status," Kildare agreed. "We're getting off topic here," Warlan said, folding his arms across his chest, not the least bit amused.

"Macklore is the only thing standing between Dragomir and the Gray Throne," Kildare continued. "According to this message, Conidon has lost his strongest ally with the death of High Lord Dillion. Dragomir's Blood Watch is the most deadly group of warriors on the continent. Even someone as powerful as the ambassador will be hard pressed to handle any one of those obstacles. The *Moldranni Sor*, Dragomir, The Crimson Watch, Conidon's failing health," Kildare shook his head. "Add all of them together, and Macklore's in over his head."

Kildare paused, peering intently at Warlan, who sat in his chair looking ill. "That, consul, is why you need us. Otherwise, you'll be forced to go into Gallanse yourself. As I recall, you have the heart of a field mouse."

Warlan's face flushed with anger. "I followed my orders at Gauth! Unlike you two, I am loyal to Brisbane and its king. This predicament in Gallanse is more your fault than mine. You should be there now, assisting Macklore. Instead, you're exiles, scraping away an existence with no purpose."

Kildare looked ready to argue, but a raised hand from Zedaine stopped him. "We've been down this road before, Warlan. You have your horseshit story… and we have the truth. No resolution is ever going to be reached." He looked at his brother sternly. "None of this is helping Mack."

Warlan gave Kildare a triumphant sneer.

"What are you smiling about, consul?" Zedaine said, not bothering to look in his direction. "The ambassador is at risk, and *you* are to blame. If he dies, you'll have no one to pin it on this time. You will bear the responsibility all by yourself. Best of luck hiding from the long arm of King Medyha. He does not forgive, and he does not forget. No, councilor, your only hope of getting through this is Kildare and me."

"And if Macklore does die," Kildare growled quietly, "you needn't worry about Medyha Whitelance." He leaned forward and placed his hand upon the hilt of his sword. "No place on the Crystalline Sea will save you from my wrath; I promise you that."

Two sets of dark brown eyes fell upon Warlan and, despite the room's warmth, a cold shiver of fear ran down his spine. An icy realization formed in his mind. *They could kill me any time they want.*

"What is it that you propose?" he inquired, trying to regain his confidence.

"We already have a fast ship ready to take us to Gallanse," Zedaine said. "With decent winds and no delays, we should make it. If we can find

Macklore, we'll keep him safe and Dragomir off the throne. Who knows? We might even stick around and save the city for fun. So, what's it to be?" he finished.

Warlan studied their faces. They looked identical to the last time he had seen them. Tall, strong, arrogant in the extreme, and they certainly had retained their penchant for mischief. Yet here they were, ready to risk their lives for the ambassador, a man who had testified against them in court over two years ago, condemning them to exile. More, they were risking themselves for a country that had cast them out for doing what they believed was their duty. Maybe, just maybe, they had changed.

"What do you need from me?" he asked, squirming out of his seat.

"How about you jump off the balcony and save us the trouble of killing you?" Kildare said wryly.

"Kil, play nice," Zedaine chided. "What we needed was in this letter," Zedaine said, holding it out to Warlan. "We could have left, information in hand, without disturbing you, but we wanted to say hi for old time's sake. Let you know we haven't forgotten about you."

The consul smiled condescendingly to them both. "You think you've read the whole letter?

Ha! You two are so naive. There's more information here than you realize."

Taking the parchment from Zedaine, Warlan rolled it out on his desk, crowing with delight. "The pair of you have always carried your brains in your scabbards. You've never understood all the machinations of the agency. It's all about carving up the enemy with you two, isn't it? There are more subtle parts of the game than children like you could possibly know."

He rubbed his hands together in excitement.

"Encoded in this letter is the meeting place, should aid arrive. There is also a plea for help and a warning. There are other strategies besides brute force to gain advantage in the game of politics. This is my latest! I invented the code over two years ago…"

"It's the primary cipher, you windbag," Zedaine said, unable to listen to the pompous rant any longer.

"Macklore's secret meeting place is the Crimson Inn," Kildare said, sounding bored.

Warlan sat open mouthed, gaping at them.

"Time to go," Zedaine said, standing up on the desk.

"Wha… how in the *hell* do you know the cipher?" thundered Warlan, his face beet red.

"Can I tell him?" Kildare asked, as he, too, stood up.

"Kil, we asked Taeral to behave; you need to do the same," Zedaine replied.

"No," Warlan cried, grabbing Zedaine by the wrist. "Only my agents and I know that cipher. How did you learn of it?" he demanded.

Zedaine twisted suddenly, reversing the consul's grip until he was holding Warlan's arm painfully behind his back. He shoved the consul to the floor, where Warlan fell in a heap.

The consul turned around, rubbing his arm where Zedaine had taken hold.

"Touch me again, and you be flying off that balcony," Zedaine threatened, white hot fury burning in his eyes.

Warlan sat, momentarily cowed by the look on Zedaine's face.

"*I* have to behave?" Kildare said pointedly. "What was that?"

"That was far less than he deserves from me," Zedaine hissed, still furious.

Zedaine and Kildare hopped from the desk to the floor and walked out onto the balcony.

"Wait," Warlan said, a sudden panic consuming him. "Where are you going? What will you do?"

The brothers glanced at one another, and Kildare nodded briefly to Zedaine.

"It shakes out like this," Zedaine said, his voice calm once again. "Kil and I go to Gallanse, raise holy hell, and save Mack and your agent. Then we leave and return to wiling away our time. That about cover it, brother?" he asked Kildare.

"Unless he still wants to arrest us," Kildare answered sarcastically.

Zedaine laughed, his good humor returning. "Well then, I bid you a fair evening, consul. Come along, Kil. The night is young, and there's a celebration in town tonight, courtesy of Medyha Whitelance and his long-ago heroics. I mean to take full advantage! Huzzah!" He ran along the balcony, leapt to the roof, and was gone.

Kildare made to follow his brother but hesitated as Warlan spoke.

"You know I'll have to report this to King Medyha," he said, with all of the authority he could muster. He was still fuming over their knowledge of his secret cipher. "Just between you and I, Kildarian," he said lowering his voice spitefully, "I have always considered *you* far guiltier than your brother. The great Kildarian, brought to terms by that little whore from Dagor. Aconia, wasn't it?"

Kildare looked at the consul, murder flashing in his eyes. Warlan knew he had pushed too far, but his satisfaction at wounding Kildare lent him the courage to stand firm under that gaze. Kildare suddenly relaxed, regaining control of his anger.

"Since we are sharing little intimacies, and Zedaine is no longer around to protect your precious feelings," Kildare said finally, stepping forward, now just inches from the consul's face. "Let me fill you in on how *I* learned of the piddling little cipher you're so proud of. Its secret was revealed to me in your office, the very room behind you, by your *dutiful* wife."

The consul's eyes grew wide, "You lie!" he hissed.

"When it suits me," Kildare replied dryly. "But not on this occasion; no, the simple truth will suffice. She's quite an attractive woman, the Lady Athea… much younger than you by what, twenty years?"

"What did you do to her, you bastard?" Warlan said, a cold fear permeating his body.

Kildare smiled cruelly and answered with feigned innocence. "I? Why I did something you could not. A year ago, you met with the consul from Agenhelm, Wil, I believe was his name. You remember him, don't you? The two of you were discussing the possibility of expanding trade with the horsemen on the Plains of Knorr."

"How did you… I won't listen to this…" Warlan said, turning away.

"Oh, but you *will* hear me, you despicable filth," Kildare said, roughly grabbing the consul by the tunic and forcing the obese man to look him in the eye. "Since you thought it seemly to bring up my past, I shall return the favor."

Kildare's next words were slow venom, dripping with malice. "That little angel you lie down with every night; I seduced her while you sat in the next room."

"Please, stop…" Warlan said, his voice strangled with pain.

"You should have heard her, Warlan," Kildare continued savagely. "My lips tasted the sweetness of her flesh, inside and out. Can you picture my tongue bathing her naked breasts in the moonlight? My hands exploring every inch of her body? She pleaded with me to love her, while you stood next door."

Warlan had started to sob, but Kildare would not relent.

"So, I spread your darling Athea right there on your desk and gave her what you could not: extreme satisfaction, over, and over, and over again. Somewhere between the wanton pleasures of the flesh and wordless moans that lovers share, she whispered your little secret into my ear, as she climaxed a seventh time. Even after I was spent, she begged me for more, wishing her husband was more like me, the *treacherous* Kildare."

He released Warlan, who had gone limp in his hands. The consul was weeping openly now as the enormity of Kildare's words sank in.

"Women make fools of us all," Kildare said, standing again.

"You bastard," Warlan said hoarsely, looking up at Kildare, still wracked with sobs. "You miserable traitor. I will have you beaten from this city, you swine."

"I doubt it," Kildare replied skeptically. "That would mean you'd have to travel to Gallanse in my stead, and we both know you'd wet yourself in fear. You ran like a little bitch in Gauth; you'd do the same in Gallanse. It takes a man for that kind of work. Not some pissant like you."

"Medyha will hear of your deceit. I will have you hanged for this!" Warlan hissed, climbing back up to his feet and rushing Kildare in a sudden rage.

Kildare stepped forward and kicked the consul, smashing his foot into Warlan's face, sending him sprawling back into his office with a crash.

"While we are on the subject of *His Royal Majesty*," Kildare said, looking at Warlan as he lay groaning in pain. "Make sure you include in your report that it was Zedaine and I who volunteered to rescue his *favorite*. Should we find success, it will have been by *my* hand that the precious Macklore was saved.   As for you, you lick-spittle, backstabbing, scum of the earth, did you really think there would be no consequences for raking me over the coals? Your wife's indiscretion is the least of what I have planned for you. Pray you don't see me again, Warlan, or I'll do what my instincts have begged me to for years: rip the beating heart from your chest and shove it down your throat."

"You are a monster," Warlan said, horror in his eyes.

"No," Kildare replied coldly. "I am justice--real justice. Not that cow shit you mete out in your courts of law. Out here, *I'm* the law. Now run along while I go save your pitiful nation… and do say hello to Athea for me," Kildare mocked.

Kildare ran along the railing, vaulted the roof, and disappeared into the night.

Chapter 24

Now an hour past sunset, Macklore was able to re-enter the Gray Palace unseen. Lord Kantik had shown him an ancient entrance through the cellar of a barrel maker's shop located in mid-city. It led through a tunnel, all the way to the main structure of the palace, entering the kitchen just below the scullery. From there, it was a surprisingly short walk to the Great Hall and the very center of power in Gallanse. For Kantik to have shown it so quickly to Macklore spoke volumes as to how much danger they were in.

Chancing a glance from behind a cabinet that swung on nearly invisible hinges, Macklore saw that the storage room was empty. He crept out of the secret entrance, no longer dressed in the trappings of an ambassador of Brisbane. He was now wearing the simple gray robes of a common servant. With any luck, he could move throughout the palace with relative ease. He needed to speak with Lydia as quickly as possible.

Luck, he thought grimly to himself. *That has been in short order lately*. His mind drifted back to his conversation with Sadie before he had left the confines of the Crimson Inn.

"Will he understand the message?" Macklore had asked.

"He'd better; he is the one who came up with the cipher," Sadie replied dryly. "I'm more concerned with what he's going to do with the information."

"He'd best think of something," Macklore said with quiet frustration. "As diplomatic consul, he has his uses. He negotiates trade and maintains peace well enough. But under extreme pressure…" the ambassador shook his head. "I saw him at Gauth. He was the first to turn tail and run when the attack became imminent."

Sadie looked at Macklore with interest. It was the only time she had heard him speak openly about the events of two years ago. She and every agent that worked for Brisbane had been kept in the dark about what had transpired there. Publicly, they all knew only what had been reported after the trial. Two of the king's representatives had defied Medyha's orders and taken some kind of active role in the battle. Warlan and Macklore had given evidence at the trial, and the accused had been exiled for treason. The guarded nature of the case made it difficult to figure out the identity of the two exiles, but she knew that they had been close to Macklore. To hear him speak of it now surprised her and piqued her interest.

"What we need is someone else, someone who can help us—someone worthy of our trust. Even if the assistance provided is nothing more than staying here at the inn," Sadie said, staring at the ambassador. Seeing no response from him, she tried another tactic. "Let me go with you to the palace; I am worthless sitting here..."

"No," Macklore said flatly. "I need you where I can find you. You are the only person I trust in this whole godforsaken country. Here, I can get a message to you. More importantly, if aid does come, it will find us here. Besides, I need you to look after our... friend... downstairs," he said, nodding toward the doorway.

He was speaking of an injured man whom the folk from Inniak had stumbled upon on the outskirts of the city three days past. He was feverish and incoherent, bearing many wounds. Macklore had taken one look at him and immediately sent for a healer. For reasons Macklore had not shared, he believed the man could prove valuable.

"Surely, someone from the palace can watch him," Sadie argued, "I am wasted here, and you have no one watching your back. You are far too valuable to risk in the politics of Shaara."

Macklore looked back at her and raised an eyebrow. Carefully, he drew forth a tiny parchment, no bigger than a fingers breadth. "Do you know what this is?" he asked, holding up the paper in front of her. "It's a message, warning me that I should trust no one! It was given to me in the palace by High Lord Conidon yesterday."

Macklore sighed bitterly and shook his head. "If he cannot trust his own people... who is there? Who can we trust? Lydia? Perhaps, but she cannot leave the palace; it would raise all kinds of suspicions. Conidon could order hundreds of guards to keep me safe, any number of whom could be a killer waiting to get close to me. No, Sadie, we are alone."

"Lord Kantik..." Sadie began.

"Is the last person I believe in," Macklore said, cutting her off. "He is Conidon's spymaster and knows far too much for my liking as it is. If he were to guess my true identity... I'm sorry, but you have to stay here, and I need to get to the palace. Risky or not, I know my duty," he glanced again at the parchment before putting it away. "As well as my task," he muttered.

Sadie was burning to know what else was on the paper, but he had refused to show her.

Macklore sat in a poorly constructed wicker chair, looking more tired than Sadie had ever seen him. "That is not even close to the worst of it," he said wearily. "There is a much bigger problem.

The clues we learned from that apothecary suggest that Lord Dillion was almost certainly murdered by an assassin from the Seven Provinces. They train those killers from childhood in guilds holed up tighter than most castles. That means a deadly assassin employed by either Dragomir or that Magus is still on the loose. He will strike again, and I don't know where. I have to ascertain his next target, or this country is going to go up in flames. We lost too much at Gauth. What we need…" he stopped then, shaking his head. "What we need is Kildare and Zedaine," he said quietly.

Sadie looked at the ambassador, stunned. *So that's* the identity of the king's representatives, she thought to herself, eyes widening. *By Jora, we all thought the exiled were agents. They were not agents at all. They were…*

"They'd be here now, you know," he said, interrupting her thoughts. "Had I spoken for them at the trial." He kept his back turned from her, shoulders slumped.

Sadie had been instructed by Warlan never to ask about Gauth. She had wondered why, initially believing it was because something had gone terribly wrong and the king wanted it covered up. Now she was beginning to understand that Warlan did not want any questions being asked because of his involvement in the debacle. She was burning with curiosity, knowing that if Macklore did not talk now, she was likely never to hear him speak of it again. "What happened in Khell?" she asked breathlessly.

For a long moment, she thought he had not heard her.

"I abandoned them; that's what happened," he said with disgust, rising out of his chair and walking toward the window. "They put themselves on the line for Brisbane, for the king— for *me*. They showed the kind of sacrifice and honor that legends are born of. And what was my response? How did I show my support of their heroic efforts?"

Macklore had turned around and was looking at Sadie now, anger etched on his handsome face. "I testified *against* them. And for doing what? Hmmm? I'll tell you what I sold them out for. The *exact* same thing I am doing here in Gallanse. They got involved in political ordeals that they had been explicitly told not to get entangled in, just as I have."

He tilted his head skyward, staring blankly at the ceiling. "For three days, all went as planned. Sydow's consul, along with Rexor's eldest nephew, Hendrick, had agreed to all of Gauth's demands to lay down arms. It was to be Warlan's crowning achievement in peace, as Gauth and

Sydow had been at war for decades. On the fourth day, we were told that Hendrick had taken ill and could not leave his room. Also, the consul from Sydow had been called away early that morning for some kind of emergency involving his son. Therefore, the peace treaty could not be signed. No one thought much of it, except Kildare. He found it strange that on the day of signing, they both had conveniently been unable to appear. None of us bothered to listen to him," Macklore paused as he remembered the day two years past.

"On the fifth day, an invading army came," he continued bitterly. "Gauth was betrayed by Shaara's puppet kingdom, Sydow, as twenty-thousand soldiers were seen not an hour's march from the capital of Khell, breaking the agreement of the treaty. At the head of the army was the king of Sydow, his treacherous consul at his side.

Hendrick also emerged from the encampment and demanded we all leave, or every last one of us would be killed as the army razed Khell to the ground. Every advisor and counselor spoke out against Hendrick, pleading with him to reconsider. When it came down to it, Gauth was left on its own. Not one of the other countries was willing to stand up to the most powerful army in the region and risk retribution. Not when Gauth's army was a three-day march away, withdrawn as an offering of peace that had been suggested by the treacherous Hendrick.

Led by Counselor Warlan, every ruler from the Crystalline Sea withdrew, knowing Gauth was doomed. I left as well, hiding behind the king's orders."

He stopped, a grim smile on his face. "All but two. Kildare and Zedaine refused to leave. They were forced into going to Gauth in the first place, along as observers only. It was their first diplomatic mission without the king. They had one standing order. Go to Gauth, say nothing, and learn from Warlan and me." He laughed bitterly.

"As though either of them had ever listened to royal orders a day in their lives," he mused, shaking his head. "I don't know why the king sent them at all.

"Regardless, they would not desert Khell, no matter how many times I ordered them to leave. Zedaine told me that if they abandoned the city, who would stand up to tyrants in this world? Both of them were so damn noble, they did not see that this battle could have started a war between Brisbane and Shaara, and drawn in every nation on the Crystalline Sea. It was only later that I realized they were right. They acted with the greatest of courage and fortitude, even with the odds so badly stacked against them.

"The next day, a battle ensued; Kildare at the head of whatever warriors could be scraped together. Zedaine appeared out of nowhere, leading a suicidal charge on cavalry from Knorr that somehow arrived in the nick of time. And they held! Outnumbered ten to one, Kildare's strategy and Zedaine's execution carried the day. Four days later, they pushed the invading force all the way back to Sydow! There, Kildare single handedly slew Hendrick, and Zedaine forced Sydow's king to sign Gauth's peace treaty: a treaty that has been kept to this day."

He turned again to Sadie, a pained expression on his face. "And what was their reward for such bravery? Exile."

Macklore paused for a moment, shaking his head. "For stopping an invasion and defeating that tyrant, Rexor—for it was surely his plan—they were cast out with nothing. Not an article of clothing was allowed them, not a single coin. Warlan had always disliked them, thinking them nothing more than spoiled and insolent children. His complete failure to negotiate a peace after years of trying was humiliating enough. But to have Kildare and Zedaine do it in less than a week was more than his pride could bear. So great was his rage at losing the peace treaty to a pair of 'spoiled children,' he made it his business to punish them. It was at his request that a trial took place. Warlan bent the truth into a labyrinth of lies, all to salvage his wounded pride. He twisted the law as masterfully as Kildare wields a sword. Warlan made it look as though Kildare and Zedaine were to *blame* for the attack."

Sadie listened as Macklore closed his eyes and rubbed his forehead, knowing the worst was to come.

"That was from someone who had disliked them for years. Warlan is a snake; I am not. They should have been able to trust in me. What did I do in their hour of need? I betrayed them," he said, in a voice steeped in sorrow. "I was angry with them both for disobeying my command! I took my anger out on them and threw them to the wolves. I refuted nothing Warlan said. I told King Medyha that they refused to obey his orders, never suspecting they would be exiled."

Sadie took a half step toward Macklore and stopped. She did not know what to do or say. "Why are you telling me this?" she asked carefully.

"Should I fail here, Sadie—or worse—someone needs to know the truth." Macklore gathered up his obsidian scepter and made to leave. "I have wronged them both most grievously, and it has haunted me these past years. They should have been revered as heroes. Instead, they were banished from everything they had ever known and loved. All because of my stupidity and pride."

"Wait, I…" Sadie said, reaching out and stopping him from leaving. "You are scaring me. You mean to come back, do you not?"

He stopped and gave her a desperate look. "You should have seen their faces, Sadie. Kildare, I fear, will never forgive me. His last words to me were, 'How could I ever have wanted to be like you?'" Macklore's face burned with shame. "You will tell them for me, won't you? Tell them I'm sorry. Tell them I was wrong."

Macklore had left then, heading to the Gray Palace, leaving Sadie behind.

Even now, years later, the feeling of betrayal clung to him. *This is my penance*, Macklore thought to himself, as he forced his focus back to the present. He continued to walk through the hallways of the Gray Palace. *I left them to rot, and now I am alone.* He laughed bitterly to himself. *Yes, I could use Kildare's cunning and Zedaine's daring in this viper's pit.* Setting his dark thoughts aside, Macklore concentrated on moving unobtrusively, like a servant set on a task. Careful to avoid the guards walking the corridors, Macklore continued on his way to see the princess.

It had been a long and difficult day for the princess of Gallanse. She was just returning from a banquet held in honor of Lord Dillion. The three remaining high lords had spoken well of their deceased peer. High Lord Waymon talked of Dillion's craftiness in politics and commerce, drawing smiles and laughter from many of the other lords in attendance. High Lord Fallon had spoken somberly of his strength of character and ability to see into the heart of matters. When it was Conidon's turn he spoke simply, fighting back powerful emotions.

"Today, each of us has lost something different at the passing of High Lord Dillion," he began gravely. "The city of Janril has lost a leader who guided her through difficult times with steady calm, a bulwark of strength and safety for thousands of citizens. Others of us have lost a comrade in arms, who fought wisely in defense of his city and this nation."

At his statement, several of the older lords murmured or nodded in agreement. "Any number of us who fought alongside Lord Dillion well remember his strength at arms, and lo to any who fell under his blade; for he was mighty indeed!" A brief cheer erupted as many of his former comrades raised a glass skyward in respect for Dillion. Once the noise died down, Conidon continued.

His hand came to rest lightly upon Prince Alexander's shoulder, who sat with tears in his eyes, staring up at Conidon. "One of us here has lost a father. A father who loved and cared for you. A father who left this world far too soon. And while he is no longer with us in life, his spirit and teachings live on through you, and your brothers and sisters, Prince Alexander. I see his strength in you now, highness. Even in the depths of sorrow and loss, you will endure, for you are very much your father's son. You will make him proud."

Alexander smiled bravely and placed his youthful hand upon Conidon's frail one.

Conidon's gaze took in the entire banquet hall, voice echoing with icy command. "Finally, moving on to what I have lost: my closest friend and ally, a trusted companion and fellow lord, who was like a brother to me. I have lost a man who was kind and brave, and who helped me prevent battle and war a dozen times over. I have lost him…"

Conidon stopped, momentarily overcome with emotion. "And I lost him," he said at last, fury burning in his eyes, "to a cold-blooded killer, employed by one of you." He fixed his steely gaze on Dragomir, who glared back with hatred. "And when I find the proof I need, those responsible will be held to account. Mark my words, all of you. There will be a reckoning!" Conidon finished, visibly shaking with rage, struggling to keep his emotions in check.

Dragomir's lips curled in a sneer, and he began clapping slowly for several moments, the sound reverberating through the room. All eyes turned to him. "What a… moving speech, Lord Conidon. I know I'll sleep far better tonight knowing that you and your men are looking for the killer. I hope he doesn't strike again anytime soon. I'd hate to see a second death under the blanket of your protection."

It was all Lydia could do not to attack Dragomir herself.

At the meal's conclusion, Lord Dillion's body had been placed in an intricate casket and loaded on a covered wagon for transport back to Janril. Eight of Dillion's guardsmen had left with the wagon, leaving only a dozen to stay and defend Prince Alexander.

Lydia felt a twinge of panic in her chest as she nodded to the guards at the doorway leading into her chambers. Even with thousands of soldiers in her home city, Lydia felt vulnerable. Her father, she knew, was in a precarious situation. Any more loss of life would show that Conidon could not defend his own home. Dragomir would press tomorrow for a vote from the suitors, and there was no clear way to stop him. Killing him would only make matters worse, for to do so would allow Rexor to unite any opposition against Gallanse and take the city by force. Gallanse could not stand against a united Shaara, despite its powerful army. This was a game of politics, and for the first time in her memory, Conidon did not have the upper hand.

Her father had retired to his room soon after the banquet. After a long day of plotting with Kantik and making his public appearance, what little energy he had been able to muster had drained from him. Lydia knew it would not be long until he succumbed to age and sickness. She fought to keep tears from her eyes. She wished suddenly that Macklore was here. When she was with him, the troubles of the world seemed to melt away. Pushing open her door, Lydia passed through her antechambers into her bedroom, and stopped.

Macklore was sitting on her bed.

"Ambassador," she breathed, taken aback by his presence.

He rose before her, a half smile on his face.

"Highness, I'm sorry to intrude so unexpectedly, but…" he approached her, hesitated, and stopped awkwardly. "I…" he chuckled to himself, visibly relaxing. "I wanted to see you," he finished sheepishly, grinning.

She crossed the few paces between them, enveloping him in an embrace. She buried her face in his chest, taking in his smell, his touch, his entire being. She could not help it; in his arms, she was home.

"I missed you," he said gently, still holding her tightly.

"I am so glad you are here," she replied, finally loosening her hold, but not letting go.

"I could not stay away, highness. I have been thinking of you all day," he sighed and let go of her reluctantly. He did not know why he was torturing himself like this. Macklore knew he did not have time for matters of the heart. Besides, she was already set to marry someone else. He fought down the surge of joy he felt upon seeing her and focused on his duty. "I am happy to see you, princess. Unfortunately, other matters of more importance beckon. These matters require your assistance."

Lydia looked at him with uncertainty. Only last night, he had told her that he wished to whisk her away to spend the rest of their days together. She had immediately regretted allowing him to leave the previous evening, and was not going to let the duties of her city impede her again. With the dangers of the succession looming, she might not get another chance to be alone with this man.

Her heart hammered in her chest, so loudly that she wondered how Macklore could not hear it. She had never known feelings like this. Her spirits had been low all day. Only upon seeing the ambassador had they soared, both that afternoon and now. She had felt incomplete without him. With the closeness of their embrace, and his reluctance to break it, she knew the ambassador felt the same way.

She was in love with him, and he with her.

"No," she said, taking a step back and locking her door.

"What are you doing?" he asked, eyes widening.

Lydia walked back over to him, feeling the blood racing through her veins. "I may never again have the opportunity to be alone with you, Macklore. My city's needs can wait until after mine have been met."

She reached up and unclasped the brooch holding her cloak in place. It crumpled to the floor around her ankles in a heap.

Macklore looked upon her beauty and was transfixed. His resolve crumbled.

Lydia stepped forward and kissed him, unable to contain her rising passion any longer. She felt him hesitate a moment and then give in to his own yearning. Her breathing had intensified, and their kiss became more heated as Lydia pushed her body up against his. Her tiny hands grasped the servant's robes and tore them from his body. The shock of his warm skin so suddenly pressed against her made Lydia even hungrier for her needs to be fulfilled. The dull ache growing from between her thighs caused the princess to groan with desire.

Macklore was standing naked now, but for the loincloth he had worn underneath the robes. She felt his fingers deftly undo the buttons down the back of her dress, and it fell to the ground alongside her cloak. Her hands moved slowly down his lean, muscled arms, past his trim waistline, until she hooked her thumbs into the loincloth and slipped the last of his clothing to the floor.

His lips drank in Lydia's with a hunger that equaled her own. His lips were soft and filled with heat, heightening her arousal.

She drew back looking deeply into his eyes and saw a hunger there that mirrored her own.

Fingers trembling, Lydia reached up and stroked his handsome face. "I love you, Macklore," she said in a throaty whisper.

"And I, you, Lydia," he replied. "Now and forever."

He dipped his head and kissed her again, rekindling her passion.

"You love me?" she whispered in his ear, her heart bursting with joy.

"Yes."

"Take me to bed," she said, voice husky with desire, "and show me."

Dark Storm Rising

Chapter 25

The Great Square outside the Matron was teeming with people. News of the impending duel had raced through the city streets like wildfire, and men and women alike were streaming in from all over the city to witness the bout. Every balcony overlooking the square was full. Every window with a view had eyes eagerly peering out of it. Any accessible rooftops were crawling with spectators aching to catch a glimpse of the action. Perched upon the holy statue of Chara clung a dozen or more inhabitants hoping to watch the duel. In the middle of it all, dozens of the Wolfguard were clearing an area in front of the Matron where the battle would take place.

Just as Vella had predicted, the city was bursting with excitement.

At the Matron, food and drink were being sold at a frantic pace as customers awaited the coming fight. The common room was packed to the rafters with people abuzz with energy.

Zedaine was seated comfortably on the third floor of the Matron, a tankard of golden ale in hand. He watched the doorway carefully and offered a warm smile and friendly word to any of the ladies of the matron who walked past. Upon their return,

Kildare had asked his brother to keep watch and let him know when his opponent arrived. He had then locked himself in his own private room with Vella to prepare.

Zedaine was surprised to see Chameleon walk down the aisle and sit across from him. The Drannock had finally been able to procure newer, cleaner attire. She had washed the dirt and grime of the journey from her body, and gone were her tattered doeskin tunic and leggings. She was dressed in a gray blouse of cotton, open at the neck. Dark pants and polished black boots adorned her feet. She no longer dressed as an outlandish stranger. Zedaine could tell that the Drannock was less than comfortable in the unfamiliar clothing, but she was clearly also glad to no longer be viewed as a curiosity.

"I assumed you'd be resting in your room, Chameleon," Zedaine said, putting down his tankard after a long pull. "I know you didn't exactly love travel on the high seas today."

Chameleon, looking a bit wide eyed, stared back at Zedaine, taking in all of the people in the common room below them. "I never imagined there were this many people in the entire world," the Drannock said in awe. "There are so many thoughts and emotions here; I cannot keep track of them all."

Zedaine laughed quietly. "I must say, I never thought about it. However, I am unable to read minds. I barely know what I'm thinking myself half the time. I suppose it would be a shock to have so many thoughts and feelings present. There are over seventy-five thousand people in this city. I bet nearly ten thousand are milling about in the Great Square getting ready for the duel. No wonder you are overwhelmed, with so many folk nearby. You have come a long way from home, Chameleon, in a very short time."

Zedaine scanned the doorway again, wondering how long they would have to wait. Seeing nothing new, he looked back at the Drannock. "You must have many questions for us. I have to apologize. Since our breakfast in the mountains, I haven't been able to hear any of them. I know that when we left the Mirrored Falls we promised to answer if we could. We have some time now, Chameleon: ask away."

Chameleon looked at Zedaine carefully, a puzzled look on her face. "I have many questions. The farther we get from the Ab'dural Valley, my homeland, the more I have." A picture of Ty flashed in her mind. "I met someone while on the ship…" she began.

Just then, a huge shout went up from the common room as Morticia, the girl Vella had sent to the runner's guild, returned. "The duke is on his way!" she shouted. "He comes within the hour. With him are Judoh and his champion!"

A huge roar went up from the crowd, and Chameleon felt an almost overwhelming surge of emotion from them. The feelings of the gathered masses ranged from excitement and nervous energy to fear, loathing, and hope. The picture in her mind of Ty vanished under such a mental assault, and it was all Chameleon could do to suppress the onslaught of feelings. She gasped in pain while retracting her mental awareness to include only herself and Zedaine.

"Are you alright?" Zedaine asked, looking at the Drannock, concern in his eyes.

"Yes, I'm… I'm fine," Chameleon said, feeling the pain in her head lessen. "What is this duel? The people here… it is all they are thinking of. I heard Kildare mention it on the ship. Mistress Vella spoke of it as well."

Zedaine said nothing at first, just staring at his tankard. Finally, he sighed, took another drink, and wiped his mouth. "The duel is my fault, really," he began, glancing again at the doorway. "There's a merchant here in Adian, Judoh by name. He is the richest man in the city. I doubt even the duke has access to more money. He owns many of the businesses in Adian, in part or in full. Forges, cobblers, food traders; you name it, and chances are he owns some percentage. Bastard has his greedy mitts in everyone's business. Except for one: Vella's."

Zedaine raised his hands and gestured to the inn surrounding them. "The Matron has been in Adian for years. There are other adult establishments of course, but Vella has turned the business of the flesh into something of an art form. She sells more than just physical pleasure here. She attracts the finest clientele in the city, and they spend silver and gold to take part in all aspects of the Matron. These include the finest foods, wines, use of the property's facilities, hot tubs, massages. In short, any pleasure you want is sold here, at the Matron."

"What does this have to do with you and Kildare?" Chameleon asked.

Zedaine smiled at the Drannock and continued. "Once business picked up for Vella a few years ago, she started making a great deal of money, enough to rival Judoh in wealth. Once he saw how successful the Matron had become, Judoh become obsessed with investing here as a part-owner. Vella wasn't interested. This place is her home, and home also to many of the ladies under her employ. The harder Judoh tried to buy the Matron, the more she resisted him. After months of failure, and a standoff that ended in his humiliation, he tried to get Duke Artimus to step in and close the inn as a place of ill repute." Zedaine chuckled, a crooked smile on his face. "Vella is no fool. She knew the duke was a widower, his wife having passed away three years prior. She invited Artimus to come in and sample the wares."

Zedaine laughed again and finished his drink. "He has been a regular customer ever since!"

Chameleon was fascinated by the story, but confused. "What do you mean, she sells pleasures of the flesh?" she asked carefully. "Do you mean," her voice dropped to a whisper, "bringing the rain?"

Zedaine smiled from ear to ear. "I've never heard of it referred to in that manner, Chameleon," he confessed, laughing. "But yes, I suppose that's one way of putting it."

"Bringing the rain has provided all... this?" Chameleon asked, somewhat incredulous, looking around the inn.

"Indeed, it has," Zedaine answered, laughing harder.

"Forgive me for saying this, but that's a lot of rain," Chameleon said, her eyes wide.

Zedaine roared.

"Did this Judoh get what he wanted?" the Drannock asked when his laughter subsided.

"No," Zedaine answered, taking up the story again. "When Duke Artimus failed him, Judoh tried something more direct. He tried to have Vella killed on her way back from the marketplace. He hired a gang of ruffians to murder her on an out-of-the-way side street."

Chameleon blinked in surprise. "He tried to kill her for money?" Such a thought was insane to the Drannock, whose entire society depended on working together for survival.

Zedaine frowned and looked again at the doorway, pursing his lips. "Murder for money is a frequent occurrence here in so-called civilized lands," he answered with a sigh. "Thank the gods, it is still a rarity in Adian."

Zedaine quickly regained his wry humor. "Nonetheless, the greedy bastard went through with his plan." A faint smile crossed Zedaine's lips. "Sadly for him, he picked the wrong day to try to have Vella killed. I don't know how he made his fortune, but luck surely had nothing to do with it."

Chameleon narrowed her eyes in confusion. "Why—what happened?"

"Judoh sent his thugs on a day when Vella had only two guards with her," Zedaine answered, fighting to keep the smile from his face.

"Judoh figured she would be an easy target with so little protection. She usually had at least four men with her any time she ventured into the streets, back in those days. As luck would have it, the two guards she brought with her were new; she'd hired them that very day."

Zedaine gave up, allowing a crooked smile to cross his face. "Those two guards were Kildare and me."

Zedaine started chuckling at the irony of the situation. "There we were, new in town, trying to leave our past behind us. We were just looking for a fresh start in a new city. On the first day of our job, someone tried to kill us! I swear, that brother of mine has a knack for trouble."

"Anyway, Vella was attacked in the street," he continued. "As I'm sure you can imagine, Kildare was his usual, sunshiny self, spoiling for action. As it turned out, the attackers were almost incompetent. They didn't even come close to touching Vella, much less killing her. Since she was the only person we'd found in weeks of looking who was willing to offer us employment, neither of us wanted her harmed. Kildare and I left most of the attackers unconscious, with nothing more than dented skulls and bruises. We may have broken a bone or two; I don't really remember since I was concentrating on keeping Kildare from doing more permanent damage. Anyway, I managed to keep one upright long enough, and we got him to tell us everything we needed to hear. I think Kildare threatening to drop hot coals down his pants did the trick," Zedaine said, shaking his head ruefully. "You *reeeeally* don't want to get on his bad side. Anyhow, Vella brought charges against Judoh the next day, and the case went to Duke Artimus.

"Of course, Judoh insisted that Vella had ordered us to attack his men, claiming that she would do so because they were financial rivals. Unfortunately, the fight had taken place near sundown on a quiet side street, so there were no witnesses other than Vella and her two unknown guards. The eight attackers whom we spared changed their story dramatically, telling the duke that they'd been viciously assaulted for no reason."

He stopped a moment and shook his head helplessly. "That was our reward for showing them mercy."

Zedaine sighed and continued. "Judoh pressed charges against Vella for ordering an attack on his men. As much as Artimus likes Vella, he had to follow the laws of Adian and could not simply take her side. A public trial was set for the next day."

"What happened?" Chameleon asked.

Zedaine scratched his head absently and dropped his chin, looking slightly guilty. "Well, I just *happened* to have read up on the history of Adian, considering the number of trials I had been involved in at the time. I had been intrigued by an interesting custom that had gone unused for over a hundred years called *Corporale Duellum*, or quite simply, Trial by Combat."

Zedaine shifted in his seat, trying not to smile. "I convinced Vella to talk to Artimus. He, being a man of action, loved the idea. Both sides would fight it out, and the winner would be proven innocent. Since it was my idea, I insisted that I champion Vella. Judoh, in turn, bought the top swordsman in the city to champion him."

"And?" Chameleon demanded, now caught up in the tale.

Zedaine, smiling impishly, leaned back in his chair. "I won."

Chameleon found herself chuckling at Zedaine. He was so... *entertaining* to be around. Nothing seemed to keep him down. He made the best of every situation.

"Judoh lost the case and had to pay a fine of one thousand gold minas to Vella, an enormous sum. So delighted was she with the outcome, Vella gave all of it to Kil and me," Zedaine continued. "At Kildare's suggestion, we happily invested it in this beautiful establishment, thus accomplishing all three of our goals: protecting Vella, angering Judoh, and capitalizing on something Kildare and I take very seriously."

Chameleon waited, but Zedaine just sat there grinning like a fool.

"What do you take so seriously?" the Drannock asked.

Zedaine stared at Chameleon in mock bewilderment. "Bringing the rains."

Chameleon burst out laughing along with the irascible Zedaine, who started cackling like a maniac. How did he manage to take such a tense situation and turn it into levity?

After their laughter subsided, Chameleon spoke again. "Why the duel tonight? I thought you already won?"

Zedaine sighed deeply, looking again at the entrance of the Matron. "We all thought it was decided. A year went by, and Judoh went back to the duke. He argued that he had not been prepared for a legal precedent that hadn't been utilized in a hundred years, and he demanded a second chance. Artimus wouldn't allow it. Judoh had been allowed to purchase the finest swordsman in the city and lost. That should have been the end of it."

"That's when things started to get nasty," Zedaine said, his face turning sour. "Judoh waited until Kil and I were out of town. That's when he called in the debt owed him by Duke Artimus. A sum of over twenty thousand in gold, borrowed by the duke to invest in several new ships he'd commissioned to comprise his new naval force."

Zedaine paused, looking back toward the common room door again.

"What happened?" Chameleon asked.

"Duke Artimus didn't have the money," he muttered. "Judoh knew he didn't have it. That's why he threatened to call in the debt."

"Then why try to collect it?" the Drannock asked.

"It was never about getting the money back," Zedaine said, shaking his head. "Judoh wanted the Matron, and he was going to get it no matter what. He blackmailed the duke into giving him a second trial. The greedy little weasel couldn't stand losing to Vella, especially after his aforementioned humiliation, so he went after Artimus where it would hurt the most. Artimus could not afford to lose that kind of capital. It would have meant halting construction on his ships, and he would have been unable to pay the Wolfguard their monthly wages. It would have bankrupted the entire city, and Judoh knew it. Half the businesses in Adian would have been ruined. All because of the avarice of one man! Artimus cares for his people and was stuck between financial hardship and his friendship with Vella. She knew what Judoh was up to and agreed to the second duel, saving Artimus from having to publicly bow down to a merchant. However, she only agreed on the condition that she get to choose the day on which the duel would take place. Vella brilliantly stalled for time, hoping that Kil and I would return."

Zedaine glanced back at the door and then focused again on Chameleon. "Then the crafty little bugger upped the ante. Judoh countered with a condition of his own. If Vella could pick the day, he argued, then she would have to wager her entire fortune on it—including the inn, which is what the greedy little bastard wanted in the first place."

Zedaine shook his head, looking unhappy. "That's when Kil and I returned. Kildare went to speak with Vella alone in her room. I don't know what he told her, but it didn't take long. Afterwards, to everyone's surprise, Vella agreed to the terms with a single caveat."

Zedaine smirked, with a look of triumph.

"Judoh had to agree that if he lost, the controlling interest in all of his businesses would go to Vella."

"He agreed to that?" Chameleon asked.

"Not at first, he didn't, but..." he shook his head. "Kildare told him that since he was forcing the issue, he would either agree to the terms or..." Zedaine paused, smiling in pure joy.

"Or what?" Chameleon demanded.

"Or Kildare would butcher him on the spot and spend the rest of his days on the run from the law. He said that to him, killing Judoh would be worth it. Judoh signed the papers immediately."

Chameleon looked at Zedaine, wondering if he was joking.

"Would he truly have killed him?" she asked finally.

"I was in the room when Kildare issued the terms," Zedaine said, leaning back in his chair. "There is no doubt in my mind that had Judoh bowed out, he would be dead now. Pissing off Kildare is the worst possible thing you can do. Even I'm wary of him."

"Once Judoh signed the contract, he went out to buy the finest sword for hire on the continent. None of us were surprised, as his entire business empire is resting on this little wager."

Zedaine stopped, and Chameleon sensed a sliver of fear pass over him. "When word got out that Kildare was to be Vella's champion, Judoh made another change to the original deal. He demanded the fight be to the death."

Zedaine sighed. "Kildare really knows how to get under people's skin. He can be downright vicious when he wants to be. Judoh didn't like it too much."

"Anyhow," Zedaine said, looking wistfully at his empty tankard, "that's why we will have the second duel, and why so many people have come to watch. The wellbeing of the entire city is riding on the outcome."

Chameleon felt Zedaine's fear pass as he pointed to a lean, powerful looking fellow in his late thirties walking up the stairs, heading toward them.

"Ah, speaking of Judoh's former champion, Wrade here was once captain of the Wolfguard and the best swordsman in the city. He was cast out by Judoh when he lost to me in the first duel. Vella heard about it and offered him a position here as captain of her own personal guard. Now all of Vella's employees are trained by the city's finest blade."

Wrade stopped at the table and gave Zedaine a hearty smile, coupled with a clap on the back. "Always good to see you lads back in town, Zedaine. Did you come for the Mask?" Wrade was a plain-faced fellow with close-cropped brown hair just turning gray. Two of his front teeth were missing, and it gave his voice a slight lisp.

Zedaine shook his head and gave him a smile. "Just passing through. It's blind luck that we're here for the festival. I have to say, I am looking forward to it. How's the training going?"

Wrade smiled broadly. "It is a shame you are leaving so soon, or I'd show you, boy," he answered with a hearty laugh. "I think if we fought again, you'd be working for me."

Zedaine laughed with genuine humor. "Come on, now. Last time we sparred, I had to use my off hand, and you barely held your own. Perhaps I should use no hands to give you a sporting chance!"

"Insolent pup," Wrade barked, in feigned astonishment. "In my day, youth treated their elders with respect."

Wrade pulled up a chair and sat down, looking more serious. "How is he?" he asked, throwing a nod toward Kildare's room.

"You know Kil," Zedaine replied. "Brooding."

Wrade pursed his lips and leaned in. "Word is, Judoh has hired himself a true blade master, one of the semi-finalists of the Great Games at Agenhelm two summers ago. Abrum by name."

Zedaine's eyes widened slightly, and Chameleon felt a pulse of uncertainty run through her companion's mind.

"I remember him," Zedaine said quietly. "Abrum Galtir from Bismark. Murderously quick on the riposte and very patient. He barely lost in

Agenhelm to the Blood Watch's sword master, as I recall. He was at least as good with the blade as I am, and that was two years ago. I wager he's even better now."

"Aye, well, he's a damn sight better than me; I can tell you that," Wrade said. "I'm not ashamed to admit it. A week past he got in a quarrel with a trio of mercenaries out of Tal-Mur, veterans of the civil war from two years ago. Abrum disarmed them all like they were farm children sparring with pitchforks. It was a sight to see."

Standing back up, Wrade pressed his lips together and nodded to Zedaine. "I need to get back to work since the entire bloomin' city has decided to show up on our doorstep, but I thought you should know. Pass it along to your brother."

The noise of the common room quieted, and all three shifted their eyes to see an immensely obese man walk in. He was huffing and red in the face from the effort of climbing the stairs. Rolls of fat could be seen under the blue robes he wore. With him came a robust older gentleman in his forties, wearing a red and green surcoat in a costly design. His face sported a goatee in the shape of a trident, trimmed neatly and matching his dirty blonde hair.

"That's Judoh and Artimus," Zedaine said quietly to Chameleon.

Walking in behind them strode a deadly-looking swordsman, arms folded across his chest.

"That's Abrum," Wrade said quietly. "I hope Kildare is on top of his game. With a blade in his hand, that man is damn-near invincible."

Chapter 26

"**D**id our contact come through?" Eliphas asked the assassin quietly.

Ry'Tung nodded sharply, flashing a steel dagger from under his black silk clothing, its hilt encrusted with dark blue sapphires. Etched upon the blade in beautiful script was a name, though the assassin could not make out what it said in the faint light conjured by the magus.

"We strike tonight. You need to be in position," Eliphas said tersely. He should not have been so short with Ry'Tung, for the assassin had been his only useful tool thus far. His frustration, however, had been mounting. The magus should have been clear of this place yesterday, but now was forced to alter his plans because of Dragomir's incompetence and the skills of the accursed ambassador of Brisbane.

Both men were seated in the shadows of a small alcove located in a vacant guard tower at the southern end of the palace. This was the least patrolled part of the battlements, and both occupants had ways of keeping their whereabouts hidden.

"Go to the courtyard in the west wing of the guest quarters and await my command. I will send our associate to you when all is ready. You must not be seen by anyone."

Ry'Tung's eyes narrowed with scorn at the very presumption that he would be detected. He tucked the dagger away and left without a sound.

Eliphas could almost hear the assassin's thoughts. *Worry about yourself, magus; I do not fail.*

Rexor's agent in the palace had finally contacted him, and the magus had been stunned by the agent's identity. Sudden help from within Conidon's inner circle was unexpected. The timing could not have been better for Eliphas. The traitor had delivered the knife and given the magus the ambassador's current position. Eliphas had suspected that the ambassador's departure from the city had been a ruse, and now knew that his suppositions were in fact certainties. He chose to trust the contact for the time being.

By tomorrow, reasoned Eliphas, *Dragomir will be on the throne, Macklore will be dead, and I will be free to leave this place.* The magus had been uneasy all day, wondering why his master had not contacted him after receiving his report. The *Damakhan* was not a forgiving man, and things had already gone awry.

Eliphas started toward the palace. He needed to assuage Dragomir's earlier fears, which were brought on by the prince's own stupidity. He had been so terrified by the delivery of Sable's severed head at breakfast that the idiot boy had shut himself in his room for most of the day. He had finally appeared at the dinner for Lord Dillion. The magus might have found the whole situation humorous if he were free of Dragomir. As things were, Eliphas had to get to the prince quickly and include him in his plan. The magus knew that the Blood Watch would be critical to his success, and so he was stuck with Dagor's prince... for now.

He had not gone more than a span when Eliphas crumpled to the ground, a shooting pain erupting behind his eyes. It was beyond excruciating, like nothing he had ever felt. White hot agony seared his brain like a fiery brand had exploded inside his skull. For what felt like hours, the unspeakable torment continued without respite.

Just as quickly as it had struck, the pain vanished. Eliphas was lying on the ground weeping in relief, scarcely able to draw breath. His fingers had dug into his scalp in a futile effort to suppress the throbbing agony. His hands were wet with blood that streamed from his ears, nose, and eyes. It took him several moments to remember where he was and what he was doing.

As he lay there gathering his senses, he noticed something floating above him. At first, he believed it to be a hallucination brought on by the mental trauma he had just experienced. It was a pale light that glowed blue. Slowly it took shape; it was a youthful face, with a shaved head covered in many tattoos. The magus knew he was not seeing things. A great terror welled up inside him.

It was the demon mage of Shaara, Sigeroa Lotus, his master.

The wispy visage was an ethereal projection cast by Sigeroa. Only the most powerful mages could even attempt to communicate like this, and then only within a few miles. Sigeroa was in Dagor, hundreds of miles away. To cast such an enchantment took skill of nearly godlike ability. Even lying prostrate beneath the projection, anguishing in pain, Eliphas marveled at his master's power.

"*Macklore should be dead by now, apprentice,*" his sepulchral voice said softly. Eliphas's fear grew. His master was not pleased.

"Yes, *Damakhan,*" Eliphas answered weakly, using Sigeroa's title.

"*Why has this not come to pass?*" Sigeroa continued.

"Dragomir is a fool, *Damakhan,*" Eliphas said, struggling to his feet.

The pain shot through Eliphas's head again, knocking him back to the stone floor. This time it lasted only a moment, but Eliphas understood the message. *He does not want to hear pitiful excuses*, thought the magus angrily.

"I failed you, *Damakhan*," the black-robed magus said, struggling to rise again.

"*I warned you that the ambassador was clever, apprentice*," Sigeroa's voice said, as though chastising a petulant child. "*Find him... hunt him down. I gave you the finest assassin in the Seven Provinces to aid you. Utilize the ninja and the Blood Watch. Isolate Brisbane's ambassador and finish him. Raise that fool Dragomir to the throne, and you will taste immortality.*"

"Yes, master; I know what to do."

"*We need Gallanse to aid us in the coming war. Its army is vast and powerful and will benefit us greatly in the days to come.*"

"It shall be done, *Damakhan*."

"*I have another task for you this night, apprentice*," Sigeroa continued. "*Two men are coming to aid the ambassador of Brisbane. My agent tells me that they are travelling by ship, and will arrive tomorrow morning. Our enemies are no fools, and I fear that they have guessed my intentions. These two men must not reach Gallanse. Do not take them lightly, apprentice, for they are every bit as dangerous as Macklore. If they join him there, I fear you will not be able to overcome them all.*"

"What would you have me do, master?" Eliphas asked, unsure of this new challenge.

The ghostly vision smiled cruelly. "*There is a savage storm at sea tonight, off the northern coast of Shaara. Focus your powers to manifest it further, and use it to destroy their ship in Adian. Even if they survive, they will never be able to arrive in time.*"

"Who are they?"

Eliphas could sense his master's burgeoning hatred, even over this distance. "*Allies of my old nemesis, the Battlemage,*" Sigeroa sneered. "*We must crush them all, apprentice. The ambassador is the most powerful and will be the first to fall. Then we can rid ourselves of the rest. Kill Macklore, apprentice, and your reward shall be beyond your wildest dreams. Fail me, and...*"

The pain returned a third time, causing Eliphas's knees to buckle to the ground once more.

"*...death will seem like a sweet blessing compared with what I will do to your soul.*"

Lydia glowed with pleasure. She was lying in the crumpled sheets of her bed, staring into Macklore's brown eyes, and stroking his face. There were hundreds of things she should be doing other than spending time with this man, but she could not gather herself out of bed to do a single one of them. The only thought prevalent in her mind was childish in the extreme, but she could not stop thinking it.

By the gods, he is gorgeous.

Macklore sat up, giving her an easy smile, and kissed her lightly on the lips. "I fear I have lingered with you too long, highness, but..." he shook his head ruefully, "I would not trade it for anything in the world."

Lydia sighed, knowing that the world waited outside her room. "I suppose you have to leave me?" she said wistfully, a sad smile on her face.

Macklore was pulling on his clothing and shaking his head. "I came to you tonight, highness, to ask you what you think our enemies will do next."

He sat down on her bed, gazing at her intently. "You are a valuable asset that no one has the sense to utilize. It dawned on me, as I kept trying to guess what would happen next, that I should have been asking you. You know the politics of this country better than anyone here, save your father. So, I ask you, what do you think our enemies' next move will be?"

A rush of emotion for this man flooded through Lydia. How could he see what no other male in Shaara did? Only her father and brother had ever treated her with respect. Yet here was Macklore, treating her as an equal. No, as a superior! He was asking for her help! She had to fight back an onslaught of tears.

He must love me, she thought, trying to maintain her composure.

Calm down and think, woman, she said to herself. *This is no time for hysterics. What would hurt father the most?*

"The issue is not Dragomir," she said thoughtfully. "It's that Magus. Father had things well in hand until he made his appearance." Lydia stood up, still unclothed, and began pacing the room.

"Let's consider what the magus needs to do, assuming he still wants Dragomir on the Gray Throne," she said, picking up her clothing. "He has already eliminated father's staunchest ally, so that leaves two other high lords in attendance."

"Which of the remaining lords is most likely to support Conidon?" Macklore asked, trying not to gape at Lydia as she dressed.

"Only Lord Fallon and Lord Waymon have enough influence to make a difference," Lydia said thoughtfully, interrupting his musings. "The Baron of Cimmeron might sway one or two minor nobles, but he lacks the political backing to carry the vote. Dillion had three supporters, but my guess is that they will wait and see who gains the upper hand. Their loyalty was to Lord Dillion, not my father."

"Which of the two remaining high lords has the most to gain if Dragomir ascends the throne?" Macklore asked.

Lydia absently chewed on her lower lip as she thought it through. "Waymon's love is money," she said at last. "It always has been. His avarice is legendary. Every day he is here costs father a small fortune. He is somewhat… reticent when it comes to the martial side of things. He is shrewd, yes, and ambitious as any politician, up to a point."

"What about Lord Fallon?" Macklore questioned.

"As you saw yesterday, Fallon is a warrior who brooks no nonsense," Lydia said. "He hates playing politics and does it only out of necessity. He has never loved father, but neither has he ever been an enemy. His city of Northpass has excellent warriors, but too few to contest Rexor openly. Northpass borders the Great Shaarian Range, far from any powerful allies. It is also the closest of all the cities to Dagor, so Fallon has wisely maintained a decent relationship with Rexor."

She sat on the bed, motioning for Macklore to join her. Macklore eased next to her and kissed her lightly on the cheek. "I'm having trouble deciding if you are more beautiful with your clothing on or off," he said with a smile.

She laughed richly and kissed him back. "I thought we were working?" she answered.

"Yes, yes, ever the slave driver," he playfully replied. "So, my enchantress, which is it then?" he continued, turning serious. "Think like your enemy. What would you do to raise Dragomir to the throne?"

She thought again of the two high lords. *Think like your enemy. If I were the magus, which would it be? Whose alliance with Conidon would I fear more?*

"Lord Fallon will be the target," she said quietly. "Waymon's loyalty can be bought or reined in by force. Lord Fallon cannot be cowed and is unlikely to be swayed by money. If Fallon were to enter into alliance with father, it would cause far more difficulty for the magus."

"You are certain?" Macklore asked.

"Yes."

"Then that is where we must go," the ambassador said, rising and taking out his scepter.

"Wait, I… I cannot just go see him," Lydia stammered, mouth suddenly dry.

"Why not?" Macklore asked, a frown upon his face.

"Because… I'm a woman. No one listens to women in Shaara, ambassador," she answered unsteadily.

"Princess, this is your home. Your father is ill, and Lord Fallon must be warned," Macklore said firmly. "If you ever want this country to change, you need to start convincing the high lords that you are worthy of it. They need to learn to value you, highness; otherwise, you'll never get the respect you want. Show Lord Fallon what you can do. He has voting rights at the meeting you wish to attend in two weeks' time; what better way to show your worth than by saving his life?"

Lydia stared at the ambassador. How could he have cut to the bone of the matter so quickly? *Because he is not a nobleman of Shaara*, she thought sadly. *I wish that he was.*

"I am not sure he will see me," she said shakily.

Macklore rose and stood over her, determination in his eyes. "We will *make* him see you. You are a princess of royal blood. Your father is sick with age and grief. Duty calls you, daughter of Shaara. You will see it done or risk losing Gallanse to a psychotic madman."

Lydia hesitated a moment. What was it about this man that inspired her so? Something about Macklore made her believe in herself. She knew he would support her, no matter what obstacles arose in her path.

"Come, ambassador, we've much to do this night," she said, rising off the bed and walking boldly toward the entrance of her chambers.

"Yes, your highness," Macklore replied, following along behind her.

They walked through the main corridors of the palace without delay. Everywhere, there were soldiers. Most of them wore the white and blue of Gallanse. Each paused and gave a salute as Lydia walked past. As they drew close to the guest quarters, there were fewer of the Home Guard in the hallways; instead, they saw many other soldiers dressed in different colored emblems and designs displaying their various allegiances. They passed by all unmolested, until they came to the crimson and white of Dagor.

"Hold on," said a watchman, a hungry look upon his face. He was young, possessing no more than

Macklore's twenty-five years. Like all of the Crimson Watch, he was dressed in burnished steel chainmail, gleaming with polish. He was tall, standing over two spans in height, and powerful, his arms corded with muscle.

Lydia felt tiny in his presence but was greatly fortified by the ambassador, who was once again posing as a simple servant behind her.

"What is this?" she asked, confused. "I am Princess Lydia. This is my father's castle. Stand aside, watchman, or I will have words with Prince Dragomir concerning your lack of respect."

Instead of moving back to the entryway, the watchman stepped further into the main corridor, now completely blocking her path. "My… sincerest apologies," he said patronizingly. "My orders come from Lord Dragomir himself. Any passerby must be questioned as to who they are and where they are going."

The watchman, clearly holding Lydia in contempt, leaned against the wall, feigning boredom. "Unless you tell me where you're off to, you may not pass. Otherwise, I'd be in direct violation of my orders… highness."

Lydia's uncertainty was growing. A common guardsman was questioning her authority in her own home. All the frustrations she had known for years threatened to overcome her resolve. She heard a light step behind her and knew that Macklore had drawn close. She could feel his presence, and her fears melted away.

"Lord Dragomir is here as a guest of my father," she snapped back, uncowed. "He does not rule inside these walls. High Lord Conidon does! I say again, watchman, stand aside."

"All you have is one pathetic-looking servant," the guard replied scornfully, dropping any pretense of respect. "I don't take orders from females, no matter their station." He stepped uncomfortably close to her, reaching out to caress her face. "There is something I like to do with girls like you…" he began lecherously.

Lydia slapped his hand away, and the guard looked at her incredulously. "So the mouse has fangs!" he hissed, hand dropping to the hilt of his knife. "You will pay for that!"

"Draw steel in my presence, and you break the peace agreed upon by my father and every ruling lord in the city," she warned, not backing down. She narrowed her eyes, sensing his growing rage, "And I promise you, watchman, if you bear that weapon, I will see you swing from the gallows."

Forgetting himself in his anger, the watchman half drew his knife, murder flashing in his eyes. Lydia heard Macklore whisper behind her.

"Cruciatus eum!"

The watchman dropped suddenly to one knee as though felled by a blow, groaning in pain; his knife dropped loudly to the floor. Lydia glanced behind her, and Macklore spoke softly into her ear. "The Blood Watch only respect power, highness, and this scum is the worst I've seen. Make him squirm."

The ambassador was right. All of Shaara was run by whoever commanded the most power, real or perceived. She knew this quite well, but she had never been given the opportunity to exercise it before, since she was of the underprivileged gender. She looked down at the young guardsman, who was now struggling for breath. Lydia reached down and picked up the knife. She placed its tip under the watchman's chin, firmly enough to draw blood. The guard's head tilted up until he was staring balefully into her eyes.

"You tell Lord Dragomir that Conidon rules the Gray Palace, not him," Lydia said icily. "In his absence, I am the law here. Do you understand me?"

The guard was unable to speak but managed a rough nod, followed by another agonizing groan.

"Think yourself lucky I don't kill you," she continued, still holding the knife to his throat. "Were I you, I'd not cross my path again," Lydia said, shoving him roughly into the wall and continuing on her way, knife still in hand. Macklore followed and released his spell from the guardsman, who collapsed to the ground, gasping for air.

"That was dangerous, highness," Macklore said, chancing a look back. "If the magus is nearby, he will sense that I am close."

"It was a risk we had to take," the princess replied, slightly out of breath. She could not believe what she had just done. Her arms felt weak, and her hands had begun to tremble uncontrollably. "What is happening to me?" she whispered fearfully.

"It is the adrenaline, highness," Macklore answered reassuringly. "It will pass."

"I have never done anything like that," she said, looking up at him in wonder. "Thank the gods you were with me."

They continued down the corridor for the next few minutes without speaking. As they neared Lord Fallon's quarters, they slowed, cautiously observing Fallon's guards snap to attention and come forward. Lydia had regained her composure, and her hands had finally stopped shaking. "So, this is what it's like having a pet wizard," Lydia quipped to Macklore, fighting the sudden urge to giggle.

"That is not funny, love," he answered.

Eliphas held his hand up suddenly, and all movement stopped in Dragomir's room.

"He is nearby," he said softly.

"Who?" Dragomir asked, looking around.

"The ambassador. He did not leave Gallanse, just as you said," the magus replied, looking toward a figure cloaked in shadows. "It seems we are to trust you."

Eliphas motioned to Dragomir and the nineteen watchmen in his room. "Quickly, to the hallway."

Once they arrived, the group saw the lone guardsman struggling to lift himself off the floor. "Orman, what has transpired here?" Dragomir demanded, as two other watchmen helped him to his feet.

"It was that…bitch of a princess," he choked out, massaging his throat.

"Tell me everything that happened," Eliphas ordered.

As the watchman spoke, Eliphas's eyes gleamed, his plan forming. When the watchman finished, he spun to face the turncoat. "Go to my assassin, now! He is in the courtyard beneath Lord

Fallon's quarters. Tell him we act in a quarter turn of the hourglass. Go."

The traitor hurried off without a word.

"Are you ready to ascend the throne, Dragomir?" the magus asked.

"It is long past time, magus," the white-haired prince replied.

Chapter 27

Standing in the middle of the packed room, Vella and Judoh stood facing one another while the duke stood to the side, presiding as legal witness. Kildare and Zedaine flanked Vella. The obese merchant Judoh was sweating profusely under his heavy robes; he wiped his brow with an expensive silk handkerchief. Standing behind him was the swordsman Abrum, tall and supremely confident. He glanced at Kildare and Zedaine, dismissing them both, in obvious contempt.

"Can I get you gentlemen something?" inquired Vella courteously. "I have a mulled brandy newly arrived from Shan'dar, your grace. I believe you will find it to your liking."

Artimus smiled and inclined his head. "That would be wonderful, Vella, thank you for the offer."

"For you, merchant?" she asked, looking calmly at Judoh.

"I can barely stomach the confines of this cesspit," Judoh answered, his voice thick like curdled milk. "I wouldn't drink the swill that passes for wine here even if I were dying of thirst."

"Yet you've sought to invest in the Matron for years," Vella answered archly. "An interesting way of showing your disdain."

She leaned in close to the merchant and lowered her voice to a whisper. "Are you certain you still wish to go through with this? There is no reason for it. We can walk away from this and enjoy the night's entertainment."

Judoh laughed, a cold sound, out of place in the warmth of the inn. "What's the matter, Vella? Afraid of losing this unsanitary whorehouse of yours? After my victory, I plan to burn this eyesore to the ground."

An angry murmur rippled through the hundreds of guests in the common room. Vella was highly regarded in Adian, one of the city's most respected citizens. The Matron itself was more than a place of business; it was part of the city's history. The idea of its destruction did not sit well with anyone.

Duke Artimus raised his hands for quiet. He frowned at the merchant as Ildora brought him a snifter of brandy. "I wouldn't get too far ahead of yourself, Judoh," he said, his tone commanding. "Your man here still needs to win the duel, and the Matron will not burn while I am ruler of Adian."

Vella glanced at Kildare, who had moved next to her.

"I suppose I could keep it and charge rent," Judoh continued, as if reconsidering his words. "After all, even sluts need a place to live."

Like a bolt of lightning, Kildare shot forward and grabbed the merchant by his robes. With strength no one expected, he tossed the three-hundred-pound man against the wall with shattering force. The air whooshed out of Judoh's lungs and he crumpled to the ground, wheezing in pain.

"Consider that your warning, merchant," Kildare said quietly, eyes blazing. "You'll keep a civil tongue in this establishment, or I'll cut it out."

Abrum was staring hard at Kildare as he returned to stand by Vella. The speed of the attack had taken everyone in the common room by surprise, including the master swordsman.

"Help him up," Artimus said with a nod to his guards.

"Please," Zedaine cut in, moving forward, "allow me."

Bending down, Zedaine leaned over the merchant, grabbing a fistful of Judoh's robes in both hands. "Don't think any of us are so blind that we don't see what you're doing," his whispered in the merchant's ear while hoisting him to his feet. "You stand to lose a fortune if you continue with this folly. Stand down while you still can."

Seeing the exchange, Abrum stepped forward, his hand firmly resting on the hilt of his sword. "Let him go," he said quietly.

"Of course," Zedaine said with an easy smile, smoothing out the merchant's robes.

Seeing the big swordsman at his side, Judoh regained his aura of contempt.

"How *dare* you touch me?" Judoh snarled at Zedaine, face red with anger. "And you!" he stormed at Kildare. "I'll have you strung up for attacking me like that."

Kildare smiled viciously. "You can try, merchant."

"This is getting us nowhere," Vella said, stepping forward with a look toward Kildare. She turned and raised an eyebrow at the duke. "Your Grace?"

"Yes," he agreed, taking a final drink from his snifter. "It's time to put an end to this."

Motioning Ildora forward, he handed her the empty container. He snapped his fingers, and the captain of the Wolfguard brought him a tightly bound scroll. Untying the string, the duke unrolled the parchment on the counter and glanced at Vella. "Ink?" he asked.

Vella nodded to another of her girls, who brought forward a small bottle filled with dark liquid and an exorbitant quill dyed white and gold.

"I need you both to sign here," the Duke said, looking at Judoh and Vella.

The proprietress of the Matron stepped forward and elegantly signed her name.

"What made you take this contract?" Zedaine whispered to Abrum as they waited.

Abrum glanced at Zedaine and gave him a humorless smile. "I've my reasons, boy."

"They need to sign as well," Vella said, motioning to Kildare and Zedaine.

"What for?" Judoh sneered. "My agreement is with you, Vella, not these two louts."

"We're part-owners," Kildare said, stepping forward. "You wouldn't want us to wriggle out of the agreement because of some technicality, would you?"

Judoh looked at the duke, who shrugged.

The merchant snorted. "Fine, sign it, if you can manage to spell your name correctly."

Kildare wrote his name and handed the quill to his brother.

"You're fast, boy," Abrum said quietly to Kildare. "But that won't be enough."

Kildare pressed his lips together but said nothing.

Zedaine finished his signature and placed the quill back in the inkwell. "I think that should do it," he said, respectfully bowing his head to the duke.

Vella looked to Artimus and nodded. Without a glance at Judoh, the beautiful proprietress of the inn proceeded out the front door and into the Great Square.

"Wait," Judoh barked at the retreating Vella. "Where are you…"

"Vella is done speaking with you," Kildare said coldly, cutting the merchant off. "From this day forth, you will deal only with me; so listen closely, for I'll say this but once. If you *ever* insult Vella in my presence again, I will gut you where you stand, to *hell* with the consequences."

Kildare looked to Duke Artimus. "I'm done talking to this filth. Whenever you're ready."

Kildare directed his gaze to Abrum and nodded toward the doorway. "I will be with you presently, Galtir. I need to fetch my sword."

Abrum smiled. "I admire courage, boy," he said calmly. "You have good manners for a country bumpkin. I promise to kill you quickly."

He exited the room, leaving Kildare staring after him murderously.

Kildare and Abrum stepped through the gathered crowd and entered the rough circle in which the duel would take place. Nearly sixty feet in diameter, the circle was guarded by one hundred of the Wolfguard, with another two hundred on hand to keep the peace. As the combatants entered the circle, they heard the roar of thousands of people anxious for the coming fight. The sun hovered on the horizon to the west, hanging like a red orb in the sky.

Upon arrival, both combatants went through a series of warm-up exercises, readying themselves for battle. Their preparations went on long enough that sweat gleamed on their naked torsos. This was to be a match to the death, so armor had been prohibited. The duelists were both lean, powerful men, with not a hint of fat on either body. Scars could be seen upon both, evidence of past bouts.

Kildare kept his focus on his routine, not bothering to look at his opponent. Quickly, he ran through the information that he and Zedaine had been able to recall about his opponent.

Abrum Galtir, right-handed, from Bismark. Favors the saber over the longsword. Ridiculously fast on the riposte but has a tendency to overextend when excited. Outstanding physical condition and extremely patient. Barely lost to Pataar,

Champion of Dagor, in the Great Games. Has not lost a duel since.

Nor have I, Kildare thought bitterly, anger building in him. *I only lose when facing arrogant swine like that whoreson Warlan.*

He had to stop himself before his temper got the better of him.

Calm down, man. What's done is done. He had his day; you will get yours. Focus on the coming battle. Rage plays no part in a contest such as this. Steady yourself. You are evenly matched in height and strength, but not in talent. He will think himself far superior until after the first pass.

Kildare smiled grimly. *I cannot wait to see that look on your face, Galtir. You'll be wondering who I am after that. Not some bumpkin from the hills, as you now believe. That's when the duel will begin in earnest. Then we'll see what you're made of.*

Kildare's eyes scanned the ground, looking for any loose dirt or debris that would make footing precarious. At the insistence of Vella, the ground had been raked smooth to rid it of any such flaws. Vella, at least, had done all she could for him. He glanced at her and gave a brief nod. She looked calm on the outside, but he knew her stomach was in knots.

"They're saying he cannot be beaten," she'd fretted a half hour ago in the private room they shared.

"All men can be beaten," Kildare had answered, "you leave it to me."

"He's not some common soldier from the garrison," she'd snapped. "He's the deadliest swordsman on the continent! Abrum's been specializing in duels for years. He almost won the Great Games. I've heard he's even better now! How did I ever let you talk me into this?"

"It will take more than Abrum Galtir to take me down," he'd chided.

"You arrogant, idiot boy!" she'd said, her frustration boiling over. "You still don't understand. You can't beat him! No one can."

He'd looked at her for a long moment. "Is that what you think?" he'd asked quietly.

"There is still time," she'd replied in desperation. "I can talk to Artimus! We can get him to delay..."

"No!" Kildare had snapped with finality. "This ends tonight, one way or the other."

He had leaned in and kissed her softly. "I will not allow that swine to bother you ever again. He tries to murder you in cold blood and thinks he can get away with it? This is your city, your place of *business. I will not let him threaten you or the Matron ever again."*

She'd broken down into tears, pulling him roughly to her. "You dear, stupid child. I can afford to lose the Matron," she'd wept. "I cannot lose..."

A knock had come at the door, interrupting them.

"I'm sorry for the intrusion," Zedaine had said, sticking his head around the corner. "But the duke has arrived."

"We'll be right down," Kildare had said, placing himself between Vella and the door as she wiped away her tears.

"It's time," he had said, stepping toward the corridor.

"It's time!" thundered the Duke, striding forward, raising his hands for silence.

Slowly the cacophony of the masses died down and he spoke, his voice carrying throughout the square.

"As these two sides have found cause to dispute one another, I invoke *Corporale Duellum* to ascertain who is in the right. The issue will now be decided by one-on-one combat. No interference with either party will be tolerated."

Artimus let his words ring through the square to ensure that everyone understood his meaning. Not a soul stirred, and the duke continued.

"Both factions have decided upon their champions. The victorious side will receive the controlling interest in the businesses of the other, including deeds to property, as well as any and all goods and enterprises currently owned."

Artimus looked to the two duelists. "Gentlemen, this fight is to the death. May the gods favor you! Draw your swords and begin!"

The duke backed out of the circle and stood upon the front steps of the Matron next to Vella, who watched in complete stillness.

Kildare ripped out his blade, but the steely rasp was lost as a great shout went up from the crowd. He felt no fear at all—only a burning rage he could scarcely control. A single thought echoed through his mind.

Let's see if you can dance with the ice warrior. Where I go, death follows.

Chameleon was transfixed by the battle before her. It had started quickly, with Abrum attacking in a blistering barrage. Kildare had defended every lightning strike, keeping in perfect balance. Abrum ceased his assault, looking stunned after failing to penetrate Kildare's guard. Kildare gave him a smile that never reached his eyes.

"Surprised?" Kildare asked.

"Who are you?" Abrum questioned, narrowing his gaze.

"Let's see if you can figure it out, bumpkin," Kildare mocked, and launched into an attack of his own.

Abrum was not surprised at the speed of Kildare's blade; he'd seen the man move in the common room. What concerned Abrum was the skill of his opponent's attacks and counters. The swordsman from Bismark was forced to use every bit of his own quickness and vast experience to fend them off. A mark of blood appeared on Abrum's upper shoulder as Kildare's sword struck flesh.

"First blood is mine," Kildare said, goading the swordsman. "An interesting technique you're using. What's it called? The papier-mâché defense?"

Abrum snarled and rushed forward, his blade darting back and forth. The ring of steel on steel echoed throughout the square as both men fought like mad for survival.

Chameleon could scarcely see the swords moving. "They appear to be evenly matched," Rion said in awe, appearing from out of nowhere beside Chameleon.

"Aye, they do," rumbled Taeral.

"No," said Zedaine's voice from behind. "They most certainly are not. He was doomed from the outset."

"Which?" Chameleon asked, glancing at Zedaine.

"Watch," was all he said in reply.

The contest had increased in intensity, becoming more furious as the minutes passed by. Abrum had nearly scored a hit on Kildare, who was now breathing heavily, barely able to fend off the attacks. He was clearly winded from the length and intensity of the battle.

"I almost had you," Abrum taunted. "You're better than expected, boy, but you lack stamina. There's only one possible outcome here."

Kildare ignored him, taking advantage of the lull to try and catch his breath.

"Where's your smart mouth now, peasant?" Abrum continued, attempting to goad Kildare into a foolish charge. "Too tired to speak?"

Kildare, however, waited patiently.

"Ready for more?" Abrum said with a smile. "I so admire bravery, bumpkin. Let's see what you're made of."

On they fought, both in perfect balance with one another. Despite Kildare's weariness, he managed to fend off Abrum's blade time and time again. Most in the crowd did not understand just how great the skill on display was, though they were mesmerized by the speed and power of the combatants. Only Zedaine could truly follow what was happening, for only he possessed the same level of ability. Early on, the crowd had been cheering loudly, but now they were deathly silent, as if holding their collective breath as they awaited the outcome of the incredible contest. Back and forth the two men fought, neither able to gain an advantage.

Over a quarter hour had passed, and both men were drenched in sweat. While Abrum was breathing heavily, Kildare was laboring with exhaustion. Seeing his advantage, the swordsman from Bismark pressed the attack, forcing Kildare backward under the whirring blade of his opponent.

Chameleon's heart leapt to her mouth, and the crowd gasped as Kildare slipped in the sand and stumbled off balance. His sword tip dropped to the ground out of its defensive position, leaving him vulnerable. Abrum dove forward, anxious for the kill, thrusting the point of his blade toward Kildare's unprotected neck.

"Now," hissed Zedaine suddenly.

Instead of trying to regain his footing, Kildare continued downward, ducking neatly under Abrum's thrust.

His ploy had worked.

All signs of weariness gone, Kildare placed his weight on his front foot and swung his off hand in a tightly balled fist, striking hard against Abrum's stomach. The unexpected blow knocked the wind from Abrum and threw him off balance. Abrum, realizing in panic that Kildare's exhaustion had been a ruse, desperately tried to raise his blade in defense, but it was too late.

In his thirst for the kill, Abrum had overextended and could not get his sword back in time. Kildare rose up from underneath Abrum's blade, sweeping it aside, and violently slammed the hilt of his own weapon into Abrum's face. Galtir, bleeding now from his mouth and nose, staggered backward, stunned, shaking his head in an effort to clear his senses.

Giving his opponent no time to recover, Kildare swung his sword downward, slicing into Abrum's forearm and causing his opponent's blade to fall to the ground. The champion of Bismark gasped in pain. Kildare kicked out with his foot, driving it into Abrum's stomach and sent the man flying into the dirt. As Abrum scrambled to his knees, Kildare set the point of his sword to his throat.

"If you value your life, do not move," he spat hoarsely.

The crowd cheered wildly, thrilled at the outcome. Kildare raised his hand, asking for silence. "Let Judoh come forth and see what he has wrought!" he bellowed, his face angry.

Judoh was shoved into the middle of the circle, protesting loudly. "It's not over! Neither of the men is dead. This breaks our wager…."

"Give it a rest, Judoh," Zedaine boomed, striding forward angrily. "Kil and I have seen enough laws bent to last us a lifetime. You've lost. There is no need for anyone to die here today."

"Your Grace, surely you see that the agreement has not been met," Judoh whined desperately, looking to Duke Artimus. "My champion lives and will continue to fight."

"He lives only by my whim, Judoh," Kildare said acidly, never taking his eyes from Abrum. "As do you. You have lost and forfeited the controlling interest of your businesses. Now get out of my sight, or more blood will flow tonight, and it will not be that of your champion."

"My wager is not with you two sods," Judoh argued, unwilling to admit defeat. "It's with Vella, and overseen by His Grace."

"It *is* with us," Zedaine replied. "Why do you think we insisted on signing the agreement? Kil and I, as part-owners, have our own say in the wager. You were given three addenda to the original agreement, and Vella was given only two. Now it is our turn."

"That is not what we agreed upon!" Judoh shouted.

"Next time, read what you're signing," Zedaine said with an oily smirk. "It's all right there."

Zedaine turned to the duke. "Your Grace, how would you feel if this duel were not to the death? If one side conceded, would that satisfy the laws of Adian?"

Artimus smiled broadly, seeing how neatly the affair had played out. "Indeed, it would, Master Zedaine. Tell me, is one of the champions ready to yield?"

All eyes turned to Abrum, who was still on his knees, Kildare's sword at his throat.

"You fought well," Abrum said grudgingly. "I have only seen the like one other time… at the finals of the Great Games."

Kildare's face remained impassive. "What's it to be, Galtir?" he asked.

Abrum looked thoughtfully at Kildare and spoke again, lowering his voice so that only Kildare could hear him. "Before I answer, tell me something. Who are you? Truly?"

"Who do you think I am?" Kildare asked, just as quietly.

"The Ice Warrior."

Kildare said nothing. He just stared at Abrum, waiting.

Abrum relaxed. "I've always wondered how I would fare against you," he said softly. "It seems I have more training to do."

He looked up at Judoh and spoke again, loud enough for them all to hear. "I fought my hardest, merchant. I am sorry, but I could not defeat this man."

Judoh looked like he was going to burst. "No! I order you to fight on. I own you! I *own* you!"

Abrum glowered at Judoh and pushed away Kildare's blade, rising to his feet with a grimace. "No man *owns* me, Judoh. You hired me because I am a swordsman, one of the finest in the land. When I take a contract, I fight to the best of my ability. That's what I did here today. I fought and lost to the best damn swordsman I've ever seen."

Abrum strode over angrily to the merchant, who was now cowering in fear.

"Let me make this clear so there is no misunderstanding. You are scum. This man," he pointed to Kildare, blood running freely down his arm, "my opponent, who has no reason to care what happens to me, has shown more honor in one night than I've seen from you in weeks."

Abrum defiantly turned his head to Duke Artimus. "I yield, Your Grace. The victory belongs to the Matron."

A thunderous cheer went up in the Great Square as pandemonium reigned upon the streets.

Dark Storm Rising

Chapter 28

"It is late to be calling, highness," Lord Fallon said gruffly in his rumbling voice.

"I do apologize for the hour, my lord, but it could not wait," Lydia said with a deep bow. "This matter needs your immediate attention, or I would not have come to you like this. Is there a place in which we can speak privately?"

Fallon frowned but waved her in. "Your servant can wait here with my Panthers, highness," Fallon said, referring to his guards. "If you would follow me," he continued, walking across the black and white marbled tiles and heading toward his personal chambers.

"If I may be so bold, my lord," she said quickly, causing Fallon to stop and turn around. "I would have my servant accompany us. It pays to be cautious during these precarious times in which we live; I am rarely left alone these days."

Fallon snorted derisively and continued into his chambers. "If you were any bolder, you'd be Lord Conidon himself! If your servant must come with us, highness, then so be it; but he will enter my chambers unarmed. As you said, these are dangerous times."

One of the guardsmen, a grizzled Panther veteran with hair graying at the temples, motioned to one of his men, who quickly searched them both for weapons. Lydia handed over the knife she had taken from Dragomir's guard, glad to be rid of it. When searching Macklore, they found nothing; not even the obsidian scepter Lydia could have sworn was with him. Once satisfied, the guard motioned them forward.

Lydia and Macklore walked past the dozen or so guardsmen occupying the common area, the ambassador remembering to keep his head bowed in a posture of subservience.

These quarters, like those of Lord Dillion, had been decorated and furnished to suit the tastes of High Lord Fallon. Only one tapestry hung on the walls, depicting a panther looking out over mountains. The sun was either rising or setting, depending on what you chose to see. It was a famous saying of Fallon's bloodline, House Rashaad.

Sunrise or sunset, the panther stands ready.

Entering Fallon's private chamber, Macklore closed and bolted the door. When he turned around, he saw a flickering candle lying on a small table to his right. A large bed lay opposite the table against the wall, much the same as it had in Lord Dillion's private room. The rest of the space was cast in shadows, as the tiny flame was the room's only illumination. Even the moonlight outside was obscured by cloud cover. High Lord Fallon was walking across the room toward the open window.

"I think I can live without the cold draft this evening," Fallon said, closing the window tightly. "I am not as young as I used to be. Please, sit down at the table... I'll be with you in a moment."

Lydia hesitated and pulled out a chair closest to Fallon, while Macklore was seated to her right. The ambassador kept his hood over his head and leaned back, keeping his face in the shadows.

"Now," Fallon said, seating himself in the third and last chair. "What brings you here at his hour?" he asked frankly.

Always straight to business, Lydia mused to herself.

"I hope you will forgive the late hour, my lord," she began, trying to keep the nerves from her voice. "We—that is, I," she said with a glance at Macklore, "am concerned for your safety."

Fallon said nothing for a moment, staring at the princess without expression. "You're concerned for my safety?" he said at last, sounding confused.

"Yes, my lord," Lydia replied, her voice more steady. "Were I Dragomir, I would greatly fear an alliance between our two cities. Dagor is powerful, but unless united with at least one of the major cities of Shaara, Dagor's power can be offset."

"I am not allied with your father, highness," Fallon said, shaking his head with a frown.

"Nor are you allied with Rexor," she countered quickly. "You are renowned for your loyalty to your city and your good sense. The proximity of Northpass to Dagor is cause for concern. In truth, he should be trying to take Northpass under his control, but he cannot. For all his power and the size of his army, High Lord Rexor cannot take Northpass, nor can he coerce a single one of your vassals to ally with him. That is because of you, Lord Fallon. Should something happen to you…" she hesitated, leaving him to come to the same conclusion she had.

"If something were to happen to me, my son would continue on the same path," Fallon interjected.

"Your son is not ready to rule, my lord," Lydia said skeptically.

"He has his uncle to guide him," Fallon stated, struggling to remain calm. "What's this about, highness? Surely you could have discussed this with me tomorrow?"

Lydia glanced to Macklore, her resolve weakening. The ambassador nodded once in reassurance, as if to say, *you have to do this yourself.*

Lydia took a deep breath and plunged forward. "I believe there will be an attempt on your life—tonight. That is why I have come to you at this late hour."

Lord Fallon's eyes grew wide and he sat up slowly. "What makes you believe that?" he asked dubiously.

She steeled herself and spoke. She told him of the strong possibility of an assassin working for Dragomir and his magus. She spoke of the poisoning of Lord Dillion, and the true manner of his death. Lastly, she explained how advantageous it would be for Dragomir to neutralize his greatest remaining threat. When she finished, Lord Fallon looked at her in surprise.

"Do you expect me to believe all that?" he asked. "I saw Dillion's corpse myself. His throat had been cut."

"It is the truth, my lord," she said simply. "I'd not have come to you otherwise. I fear there will be an attempt on you this evening."

Lord Fallon scratched absently at his white beard, thinking over what he had been told. "Where did you come by all of this information, highness? It seems a bit far-fetched that Lord Dragomir and this... magus could have obtained the services of an assassin all the way from the Seven Provinces. Where is your proof? How do you know all of this?"

"She knows it all because I told her," Macklore said quietly, pushing back his hood and leaning forward.

"Jora's balls!" Fallon swore in surprise, eyes widening. "I'd heard you'd left the city, ambassador."

"I stand with High Lord Conidon and his daughter," Macklore said evenly. "Everything Her Highness said is true. She has risked much to bring you this information. I hope you have the wisdom to believe her and act on what she says. Dragomir has already killed Lord Dillion, my lord; that is a certainty. And make no mistake about it: *you* are the next greatest threat. I, for one, will not stand by to see good men like yourself fall victim to his ambitions, no matter what your politics are."

Lord Fallon looked from Macklore to Lydia, unblinking. "You are certain of this?" he asked finally.

"I am," Lydia answered.

Lord Fallon relaxed suddenly and let out a snort. "By Jora, you remind me of your mother," he said, looking at Lydia. "The High Lady Aralia spoke her mind far too often for the comfort of most of the high lords. She was intelligent, fiercely independent, and quite beautiful... much like yourself, highness."

"I...I see, my lord," Lydia said, confused and unsure of how to take his meaning.

"I am sorry, princess; I meant it as a compliment," Fallon said wryly. "I am not much of a speaker when it comes to addressing women, it seems. I always liked Aralia. She was a distant cousin of mine. I was greatly saddened to hear of her passing years ago. You very much take after her."

"Thank you, my lord, for telling me. I had no idea that mother was related to you."

"All right," he said, sighing and then looking up at Lydia. "So, there will be an attempt on me tonight? Tell me, what do you suggest we do?"

The candlelight flickered, but none of them noticed because outside the door, raised voices could be heard yelling at one another.

"What the hell is going on out there?" Fallon demanded, standing up and looking at the door.

In an instant, Macklore was up, obsidian scepter in his fist. "Both of you, stay here. I will find out what is amiss."

"Nonsense, I will go," Fallon said, irritated. "These are my quarters; you are under my protection."

"My lord, you and the princess are far more valuable than I," the ambassador replied. "Stay here; I will return in a moment."

Macklore opened the door, allowing torchlight to spill in momentarily, and then closed it quickly behind him. Had he looked back, he would have seen Fallon, Lydia... and the open window.

"I am telling you one of my men overheard a plot to kill Lord Fallon tonight!" Dragomir shouted to the captain of the Panthers.

Flanking the prince were several of the Blood Watch, looking warily at the twenty members of Fallon's personal guard. A like number of the Gallanse Home Guard stood behind Dragomir and his men. No one had bared steel, but the tension in the room was rising.

"Who did your watchman hear this from?" demanded the lieutenant of Fallon's forces.

"I would rather not say," Dragomir replied, shifting his eyes to the Home Guard. "Until I know that Lord Fallon is safe."

"You can't just go running around making baseless accusations, Prince Dragomir," snapped a voice from behind them. Lord Kantik stormed past the stunned Home Guard and marched up to Dragomir, ignoring his dreaded Blood Watch.

"You are going to have to explain what in the *hell* you are doing in this part of the castle at this time of night!" Kantik raged louder than before. "This is Gallanse, Prince Dragomir, not Dagor! There has been enough death in the Gray Palace already—and speculation as to who is behind it— without this cock and bull story. Gather your men and leave—now!"

"Who are you to give me orders?" Dragomir answered haughtily.

"My name is Lord Kantik, chief steward of Gallanse," he spat acidly. "I am the one with the power at the moment, Prince Dragomir. There are two score of the Home Guard in the corridor, awaiting my instructions. Unless you remove yourself, those orders will be to arrest you and chain you in the dungeon."

Dragomir looked around, seeming to realize for the first time that he was outnumbered. Still, he hesitated. "I am not leaving until I see that High Lord Fallon is safe," Dragomir said finally.

"What makes you think that he is in danger?" Kantik asked.

"Watchman Orman, here," he said, motioning to his young guard, "was standing his post just outside my quarters not fifteen minutes ago," Dragomir said, looking at Kantik. "He overheard two people speaking quietly. Much of what they said was hushed and impossible to understand. But the words he overheard clearly were, 'Must kill Fallon tonight.' Orman looked into the hallway to see who had spoken." The white-haired prince stopped, his blue eyes boring into Kantik.

"And who did he claim to see?" Kantik asked impatiently.

"I asked him myself several times, steward, just to make sure there was no mistake," Dragomir said, looking now to his guard. "The lighting was dim and they were trying to keep to the shadows, and yet he was certain of who it was."

He paused a moment, casting his gaze on the captain of the Panthers.

"There were two people in the hallway," he continued. "One was the ambassador of Brisbane."

Fallon's guards began to whisper angrily to one another while Kantik narrowed his eyes. "By all reports, Lord Dragomir, the ambassador has left Gallanse. Your man is wrong."

"Nonetheless, that is who he saw," Dragomir said unflinchingly.

"And who was the other person he claims to have seen in the hallway?" Kantik demanded.

"Princess Lydia."

In the stunned silence that followed his words, one could have heard a pin drop on the stone floor.

"What kind of a sick joke is this?" Kantik asked angrily. "You are accusing one of the royal family..." he could not even continue his thought, so enraged had he become. "Guards, arrest this man," thundered Kantik furiously, pointing at Dragomir.

"Protect me," Dragomir said shrilly to his men, while stepping behind them. Every member of the Blood Watch clapped a hand to his sword hilt, prepared to defend his liege.

"You would threaten steel in the castle?" raged Kantik. "You will not wriggle your way out of this, Lord Dragomir. Your men will not save you."

Kantik motioned to the Home Guard, who were pouring into the room, surrounding the Crimson Watch and their lord. "Prepare to attack," Kantik ordered.

"Prepare to defend," Dragomir replied, hand on his own blade.

"Wait," shouted a new voice.

All eyes turned to see Macklore standing in front of the entrance to Lord Fallon's private quarters.

"This has gone far enough," the ambassador said, his voice carrying throughout the room.

"Ambassador Macklore," Kantik said, clearly surprised to see him. "What are you doing here?"

"I told you that my man spoke the truth, steward," Dragomir panted, slightly out of breath.

"Only about the princess and me being here, Prince Dragomir," Macklore said evenly. "Not about our purpose. Nor has your guard given an accurate account of what occurred in the hallway in front of your quarters."

Fallon's guard captain, however, strode forward, followed by his men. "I need to see Lord Fallon—now!" he hissed, ready to plow over the ambassador.

"Of course, captain," Macklore said, sliding over and opening the door. "I assure you, he is fine."

The captain brushed past Macklore, opened the door, and peered in. "My Lord Fallon..." he began, walking into the room.

Then the captain was falling back through the doorway, a dagger jutting from his throat, his lifeblood pumping from his severed jugular.

"What the..." hissed the stunned Macklore, reaching out to catch the captain in his arms.

"Captain!" exclaimed one of the guards, rushing forward.

"*Princess!*" Macklore bellowed in panic. Letting the lifeless captain fall, he stormed back into the bedroom.

"*Accendo!*" He bellowed, lighting the room with his magic.

The first thing the ambassador saw was the assassin leaping out the window, escaping to the grounds bellow.

Then he took in the rest.

All was in ruins.

Macklore had left the room less than a minute ago, and yet everything had changed. Lord Fallon lay on the ground near the table in a puddle of his own blood. His throat had been savagely cut open all the way to the spine. There were several stab wounds to his upper chest and stomach. He bled profusely from each.

The High Lord of Northpass lay on the ground unmoving.

In the corner, groaning, was Lydia. Her clothing was coated in blood. Macklore quickly ran to her side while Dragomir and several of Fallon's guards entered the room.

"Are you hurt?" Macklore demanded, his eyes blazing.

"No," she said gasping for breath, "the blood…not…mine."

"Treacherous woman," barked Dragomir from the doorway. "You have killed Lord Fallon!"

"Hold your tongue," Macklore shot back, wanting to strike out at something, anything. "She did not kill anyone."

"Hold your own, ambassador," Dragomir continued, unrelenting. "She was the only one in the room with Lord Fallon. How else can you explain it?"

"I saw an assassin fleeing the room through the open window upon entering," Macklore said, standing and helping Lydia to her feet.

"I saw no such thing, ambassador, and I entered right behind you," Dragomir replied. "Look at her! She is covered in blood! How can you explain that?"

Macklore looked at Lydia. "What happened?"

"After you left," she began, still having trouble drawing breath. "I heard Lord Fallon. It sounded like he was choking on something. I turned and… his blood splattered all over me. Someone had cut his throat, just as they did Lord Dillion's," her voice was shaking with fear.

Kantik had entered the room, a somber expression on his face.

"I… wanted to scream for help, but… I was kicked in the stomach so hard, I could not… speak," Lydia continued, still laboring for breath. "It was dark in the room. I could not see who else was in here. Strong arms dragged me over to Lord Fallon and…" she could barely breathe, so great was the panic in her voice.

"He placed a knife in my hands and forced me to stab Fallon in the chest over and over again!" She was nearly hysterical now, recounting the horrendous ordeal she had just been through.

"Then the door opened, and the assassin shoved me to the ground and threw the knife at whoever came through."

She looked back up at Macklore, fear once again filling her. "I thought it was you in the doorway," she whispered. "I thought it was you…" she wept as the ambassador took her in his arms, holding her tightly.

"I do not believe a word of it!" Dragomir hissed, walking toward Lydia. "She is a deceit-filled whore who wiled her way in here and murdered Lord Fallon! The ambassador was her accomplice! My watchman heard them both plotting in the hallway on the way here! How else would I have known exactly where to find them?"

Dragomir turned to Kantik, who had said nothing; he just stared at Lydia.

"Surely, Lord Kantik, you do not believe…" Lydia said, trying to get herself under control. Her eyes were pleading as she looked at her father's oldest friend.

"Highness, I'm sorry," Kantik said quietly, "but…" he held forth a steel dagger. The blade had been wiped clean of blood, but spots could still be seen on the sapphire-encrusted hilt. On the blade in beautiful script was etched a name.

Lydia Gaida.

"Can you explain this?" Kantik said.

Lydia peered closely at the dagger. "That is mine," she said. "But where… what are you doing with it?"

"This is the dagger I pulled from the captain's neck, highness," Kantik replied. "And I believe this is the weapon that killed Lord Fallon."

Both sides stared at one another, saying nothing. "Arrest them," Kantik said finally to the captain of the Home Guard. "Arrest them both, on the charge of murdering High Lord Fallon."

"No!" Macklore hissed, as three of the Home Guard moved forward. "We are innocent."

"You are going to hang, ambassador," Dragomir said. "And I'm going to piss on your grave."

"This is a mistake," Macklore continued, looking at Kantik. "He set this up! Surely, you do not believe…"

"Just come along quietly, ambassador," Kantik said. "You will stand trial for your crimes. You will get to say your piece then."

Macklore looked at Kantik, stunned. This could not be happening. Quickly, he turned to Lydia and saw that she was just as devastated.

He knew that he could escape now if he had to, but it would mean leaving her behind. *You are no good to her locked up,* he reasoned. *But will she ever trust you again?*

That thought alone almost stayed his hand. *That is a risk you have to take, fool! You cannot prove her innocence while locked in a cell.*

He turned to Lydia, having come to his decision and hating himself for it. "Forgive me, highness," he whispered to her.

She looked up into his brown eyes, her own eyes widening. "No, please Macklore, don't leave me now," she whimpered, understanding his intent.

He closed his eyes, steeling himself against the pain of losing her. "I'm sorry, highness, but I have to do this. I will come for you." Macklore stepped back out of reach just as the guards closed on him.

"*Accendio!*"

A flash of light exploded where Macklore stood, momentarily blinding everyone in the room. "Don't let him get away!" Dragomir screamed. The three guards had run forward, reaching out blindly. When able to see again, they held only the princess in their hands.

There was no sign of the ambassador.

"Find him," snarled Kantik. "He could not have gotten far."

Dragomir walked up to Lydia and backhanded her across the face. "Looks like your hero left you to hang alone, bitch."

Lydia, however, did not hear him. Hurting far more than the pain from the blow was the despair that filled her.

Macklore had left her to die.

Epilogue

"We may have a problem," Kildare said quietly.

The two brothers stood in Kildare's private chambers by themselves. The elder sibling had pulled Zedaine aside in the confusion after the duel.

"Don't we always?" Zedaine drawled, taking a bite of a cruller he had stolen from the kitchen.

"Will you be serious?" Kildare scolded, shaking his head. "Abrum suspects."

"What? That you're the Ice Warrior?" Zedaine asked, not in the least bit surprised. "What did you think would happen? Very few outside the Blood Watch could hold their own against Abrum Galtir. You just beat him. Word is bound to get out."

Kildare slid out a chair from under his desk, the sound of the legs scraping noisily across the wooden floor.

"People talk about the Ice Warrior all the time," he replied, sitting down. "It's passed off as nonsense most of the time. That won't be the case with Abrum. If *he* speaks, others *will* listen."

Zedaine stopped chewing his cruller, mulling over Kildare's words. "You still want me to make the offer?"

"Yes," Kildare answered, nodding in affirmation. "But add his discretion as a caveat. If our information on him is good, I think he will keep his word."

"If not?"

Kildare turned his head to the side and gave his brother a simple shrug of his shoulders. "Let's hope it doesn't come to that. If he walks away, word will get out. They will trace it back to the Great Games and that will lead to me."

"I'm not too worried about it," Zedaine claimed with bravado, taking another bite of the cruller. "Sometimes I wish everyone knew."

"That's because you're not thinking," Kildare fumed.

"At least we wouldn't have to hide from it," Zedaine retorted. "I'm not afraid of the consequences."

"I'm not worried about us," Kildare explained, his voice exasperated. "I'm more concerned about those we care about. Vella, Adecia, the pirate king's daughters—all of them would be implicated because they helped us over the last two years at one time or another. If the rulers of enough countries find out who we really are…they will make the lives of those closest to us miserable."

Zedaine sat staring at Kildare and let out a deep breath. "Alright then, I'll go talk to Abrum. What are you going to do?"

Kildare narrowed his eyes dangerously. "I'm going to interrogate Judoh," he said, his voice smoldering with anger. "He's not going to hide the truth from me. I'll get him to talk, one way or another."

Zedaine actually laughed. "By the gods you are in a foul mood. We've won! You've beaten Abrum and we are free of Judoh. Hell, we are richer than we ever dreamed."

"I don't feel like much of a winner," Kildare growled.

Zedaine sighed. "Alright then. Go interrogate Judoh. Try not to kill him."

The younger sibling turned and exited the room swiftly.

Kildare put his elbow on the top of the desk in front of him and rubbed at his temple with his fingers. Leaning back, he opened the narrow drawer and peered down at the three objects inside. One was a black ivory knife, awarded to the winner of the sword competition held at the Great Games every five years. The second was a letter, written by the King of Brisbane, exiling he and Zedaine from their home city. Moreover, it named them traitors to every country on the Crystalline Sea.

The last was a parchment, proof of their service to Blade, referring to them as, 'The Raven and the Crow,' members of her secret force known as the Knights of Steel.

"I'm sick of dancing to other people's tune," he whispered, slamming the drawer shut in a sudden outburst.

Standing, he adjusted the sword at his hip, walked to the door, and shut it behind him.

He had an interrogation to do.

Here ends book 1 in the chronicles of the Raven and the Crow. The story continues in book 2: The Raven and the Crow: The Gray Throne.

Made in the USA
Columbia, SC
21 August 2023